Praise for

Still My Forever

"Sawyer has done it again with *Still My Forever*. From the first page until the last, I devoured this story!"
—KATHLEEN Y'BARBO, *Publishers Weekly* bestselling author of *The Black Midnight* and *Dog Days of Summer*

"*Still My Forever* is a lyrical, heartfelt story of redemption, restoration, and a God who takes all the scattered motifs and melodies of our lives and turns them into a beautiful symphony. Kim Vogel Sawyer beautifully captures the soul of a musician in Gil, and the utterly charming Ava is his perfect match. Their sweet romance; the close-knit Mennonite community of Falke, Kansas; and a cast of memorable supporting characters combine to make *Still My Forever* one of this year's absolute must-reads!"
—AMANDA WEN, Christy Award–nominated author of *Roots of Wood and Stone* and *The Songs That Could Have Been*

"I always love getting my hands on a Kim Vogel Sawyer book, and *Still My Forever* didn't disappoint. When composer Gilbert Baty returns to Falke, Kansas, he has to face not only his failure in New York but also the woman he loved and left behind. Ava Flaming is still single, but she refuses to let her feelings for Gil get to her. After Gil becomes the local band director and has an opportunity to finish the song of a lifetime—written for the woman he loves—her heart soon follows God's call. The details of a love story created through music gives this wonderful Mennonite story a strong sense of faith and romance. I'm still humming."
—LENORA WORTH, author of *The X-Mas Club*

Still My Forever

Books by Kim Vogel Sawyer

Still My Forever

A Novel

Kim Vogel Sawyer

WATERBROOK

Still My Forever

All Scripture quotations are taken from the King James Version.

This is a work of historical fiction based closely on real people
and real events. Details that cannot be historically verified are
purely products of the author's imagination.

Copyright © 2022 by Kim Vogel Sawyer

All rights reserved.

Published in the United States by WaterBrook, an imprint of
Random House, a division of Penguin Random House LLC.

WATERBROOK® and its deer colophon are registered trademarks
of Penguin Random House LLC.

Grateful acknowledgment is made to Bradley Dean Vogel and Kristian
Libel for permission to reprint lyrics from "Whither Thou Goest," music
by Bradley Dean Vogel, lyrics by Kristian Libel. Used by permission of
Bradley Dean Vogel and Kristian Libel.

LIBRARY OF CONGRESS CATALOGING-IN-PUBLICATION DATA
Names: Sawyer, Kim Vogel, author.
Title: Still my forever : a novel / Kim Vogel Sawyer.
Description: First edition. | Colorado Springs : WaterBrook, [2022]
Identifiers: LCCN 2022003498 | ISBN 9780593194362 (paperback ;
acid-free paper) | ISBN 9780593194379 (ebook)
Subjects: LCGFT: Novels.
Classification: LCC PS3619.A97 S75 2022 |
DDC 813/.6—dc23/eng/20220127
LC record available at https://lccn.loc.gov/2022003498

Printed in the United States of America on acid-free paper

waterbrookmultnomah.com

1st Printing

First Edition

Book design by Virginia Norey

For Alana—

You seemed to grow up in the blink of an eye, and now you're off, pursuing your dreams! God has wonderful plans for you, dear granddaughter, and Gramma is praying for you every step of the way.

The LORD is my strength and my shield; my heart trusted in him, and I am helped: therefore my heart greatly rejoiceth; and with my song will I praise him.

—Psalm 28:7

Still My Forever

Chapter One

Falke, Kansas (a Mennonite community)
1905
Ava Flaming

"IS THAT THE TRAIN I HEAR?"

Ava gave a start and turned from placing Papa's freshly starched and folded shirts in the bureau drawer. Mama lay with her eyes closed, but her fine brows were arched in query. Ava pushed the drawer shut with her hip and hurried to the side of the bed.

"Jo, it is." She smoothed her mother's once thick, dark hair, now more gray than brown, away from Mama's cheek and grimaced. Mama's pallor was nearly as white as the pillowcase cradling her head. Why hadn't she listened yesterday when both Ava and Papa told her the gardening would be too much for her? Oh, how *stoakoppijch* Mama could be. But then, Ava was often accused of stubbornness, too. She knew from which parent the characteristic was passed.

Mama opened one eye and pinned Ava with a narrow glare. "I wish your Foda had given more thought to the wisdom of building a house so close to the rail lines. The trains rattle the windows. I often worry our little house will shake itself from the foundation."

Ava smiled to herself. The rail lines had been laid three years after Papa set their stone foundation. But of course Mama knew this. Once when she chided Papa about their close proximity to the silver tracks, Papa asked her how he was to know the railroad would choose to run lines behind their house. Mama pointed at him and said with eyes alight, "Ah, my husband, I used to believe you know everything. Now? I am not so sure." And they'd all laughed. Ava missed the days when Mama teased and laughed.

She sat on the edge of the mattress and gently patted her mother's vein-lined hand. "When Falke's post office was right here in our house, our close location to the railroad line was fortuitous. You thought so yourself. Besides, our house is built solid. Not even last year's tornado shifted it from its foundation, and a tornado is much more powerful than a passing train. Do you really worry about such things?"

A sigh eased from between Mama's chapped lips. "If you are *ne Mutta*, you worry. It goes with the title. You'll find out someday when you have children."

Ava looked aside. She wished Mama wouldn't say such things. Of course, Mama wanted to see her only daughter married and raising children of her own. Maybe even more now that Ava's brothers were gone. Who else would give her and Papa *Grootkjinja* to spoil? But Ava was twenty-one already. The unlikelihood of marriage became greater with each passing year. Maybe she should stop stubbornly refusing her one persistent prospect. She inwardly cringed. Nä. Even for a home and children of her own, she couldn't marry someone she didn't love, no matter how much Joseph claimed to love her.

"As often as it stops here in Falke, we should have our own depot." Mama rolled to her side. "Please close the window. I don't wish to hear the squeal as it leaves town."

Ava started to argue. The raised window allowed the sweet

spring breeze to waft in. Despite her often gloomy thoughts concerning her single state and Mama's poor health, she always found a measure of joy in the glorious scents of new life burgeoning. Might the freshness have the power to revive Mama's spirits, too? But Ava hadn't won yesterday's argument about who should plant the vegetable garden. She'd only further weary Mama by arguing today.

Ava crossed to the window, settled it in its sash, then stood with her fingertips on the sill. She gazed at the black locomotive's dust-smudged nose seeming to poke out from behind the family's barn. The engine's vibration gently rattled the house, sending shivers from her fingers up her arm.

If she wanted to argue, she could rebuff Mama's claim about the need for a depot in little Falke. The community founded by Mennonite immigrants in 1873 and named for the abundance of peregrine falcons preying on the plains' mice and rabbits was hardly a pindot on the newest Kansas map. Trains wouldn't stop—or slow down—except to take on water from the tank or retrieve the dangling mailbag Papa placed weekly on its hook. Now and then someone who'd purchased a ticket to McPherson or Newton but only wanted to come as far as Falke would hop off the train when it took a watering break. But it was such a rare occurrence, she knew not to look for—

Suddenly, a tall, broad-shouldered man moved from behind the barn and into her line of vision. She released a self-deprecating chuckle. Of course someone would disembark at Falke the same day Mama declared the town needed a depot.

She squinted against the bright midday sun and examined the visitor. He wore a dust-smeared gray suit and a bowler hat tipped rakishly forward on his head. The brim of the felt hat threw a shadow across his face, hiding his features from view. A plump brown leather bag dangled from one hand, and in the other he carried a black case shaped like a violin. With long, sure strides he moved toward town.

A traveling salesman, perhaps? Salesmen seldom bothered knocking on the doors of Falke's residents. The people of this little town were too frugal to squander their hard-earned money on frivolities. But if he intended to sell musical instruments, he might find some success. Love for music, Papa often proclaimed, was born in every Mennonite child. Ava had never doubted him. When the community members gathered for worship on Sundays, surely their hymn singing rivaled angel choirs. She had learned to sing in harmony with her brothers even before she was old enough to attend school. If this man was selling instruments, he had chosen the right place to peddle his wares.

She glanced at the music case, and a distant memory carried a tune, both sweet and mournful, from the recesses of her mind. As if the fierce Kansas wind transported her, she was swept backward in time to 1901, New Year's Day. In her mind's eye, she saw Gil with his violin under his chin, his tapered fingers expertly drawing the bow over the strings while his velvety brown eyes fixed on hers and a tender smile curved his full pink lips. *Her song,* he'd called the tune he'd written, his way of expressing to her what words could not.

The remembered notes and his adoring expression flooded her with mingled longing and regret. Determined not to revisit the source of the tune, she started to turn from the window. But at that same moment, the man stopped and raised his face to the sun. The slice of shade slipped away. Recognition burst through her with as much force as a lightning bolt.

Ava stumbled backward a step and pressed her quivering hand to her lips. A single word rasped from her throat. "Gil."

Gilbert Baty

"WELL, AS I live and breathe, Gil Baty just passed my window."

Gil came to a halt. Four years had passed since he moved from small and sleepy Falke to big and bustling New York City. He'd encountered more people, heard more voices, than a man could possibly count in that amount of time. Didn't matter. Even without looking, he knew who'd uttered the statement—Bernard Flaming, the town's postman and, more importantly, Ava's Foda.

He stifled a groan. Not even home for five minutes, and one of the people he'd specifically prayed to avoid—the man who'd regularly taken him fishing when he was a gangly twelve-year-old—had already spotted him. In Falke, word spread faster than whitewash on a barn. He hadn't expected to dodge the Flaming family forever. But God couldn't give him a day, maybe two, before they knew he was back? Should he move on? Pretend he hadn't heard? Yes, he'd ignore it and—

"Gil! You there, Gil!"

He couldn't ignore that. Pulling in a breath of fortification, Gil turned around and strode directly to the gray-haired, barrel-chested man waiting outside the post office door. He placed his suitcase on the planked boardwalk and stuck out his hand. "Hello, sir. It's good to see you again." Such a lie.

Bernard took hold of Gil's hand and pulled him into a breath-stealing embrace. "Welcome back, my boy. Are you visiting or have you come home to stay?"

Gil wriggled loose. "Well, sir, I—"

"Look here, it's Gil Baty! Gil is in town!" The shout came from behind Gil and saved him from stuttering through a reply. Which was just as well, because he had no idea how to answer Bernard's question. Within minutes, it seemed every shop owner and customer in town abandoned their business dealings. Townsfolk surrounded Gil, all talking and laughing and clapping him on the back.

"It's too bad we don't have a band to give you a rousing welcome-home tune, Gil," the town banker said.

The barber nudged the banker on the shoulder. "Now, John, we do have a band. But we didn't get enough notice to round up our instruments." He aimed a mock scowl at Gil. "Why didn't you send word, Gil? We've been working on a rousing rendition of 'When the Saints Go Marching In.' It would have made a fine welcome-home tune for our town's most success-ful young person."

Gil swallowed a knot of mortification. If these people knew how unsuccessful he was, they wouldn't be overjoyed to see him. He didn't deserve their congratulations, and he should tell them so. But weariness from the days of travel and heart-ache from the years of rejection prevented the words from forming. He shrugged and forced a grin. "I'm sorry, Mr. Rem-pel. Next time I'll give everyone plenty of notice."

The man slung his thick arm around Gil's shoulders and squeezed. "Ach, boy, you don't owe me an apology. We are all just so happy to see you home."

Others echoed the barber's statement, then several tossed questions at Gil about big-city life, his musical pursuits, and his future plans. Gil's head spun. He shouldn't have come back here. Even though he'd lost his roommate and couldn't afford the rent for his apartment in New York City on his own, he should have tried harder to find another roommate. He should have temporarily taken a room at the YMCA. He should have—

He shook his head, dispelling the should-haves. It was too late for them now. He was back in the town of his childhood, the place he hoped to lick his wounds, rediscover his peace, and perhaps finally compose a musical piece that would bring accolades rather than yawns from the elite of New York's music community. He held up both hands, and to his relief, the barrage of questions ceased.

"Fellows, I appreciate your kind welcomes. You've made me feel right at home again." His half-hearted comments earned smiles and nods. "But it's a long train ride from New York to Falke, and to be completely honest with all of you, I'm too tuckered to talk."

Laughter rolled, and with farewells and promises to catch up after he'd rested, all the townsfolk except Bernard ambled away. Gil reached for his bag, but Bernard got hold of it first.

The man beamed at Gil. "Let me tote this to your uncle's place for you. Now that I get a good look at you, you're pale and seem as weak as a day-old kitten." He winked. "Did the train ride have such an effect, or did life in the big city wear you out?"

Suddenly a comment whispered through his mind. *"Did you hear that hayseed sawing away at his fiddle? He said he wrote the song himself. I could barely hold back my laughter. What a joke."* The criticism, made by a fellow violinist auditioning for a spot in a Broadway orchestra, stung so much in remembrance, Gil winced. He had no intention of honestly answering Bernard's question. "Thank you, Mr. Flaming, but—"

"Mr. Flaming?" Bernard's voice boomed out on a note of disapproval. "I think we know each other too well to be so formal. You're still the same boy who banged in and out of my house, begging for cookies or the chance to drop a line in the creek, aren't you?"

Somewhere inside him, that boy still existed. Didn't he? Gil gave a meek nod.

"Well, then, I'm still Onkel Bernard to you."

Warmth flooded Gil. So many things had changed since he packed his bags and chased his dreams to New York. Having this one thing stay the same meant more than he could understand. "Thank you, Onkel Bernard."

The man snorted under his breath. "No need for that. Now come." He started toward the south edge of town where Gil's uncle, aunt, and cousins lived, and Gil fell into step beside him. "I don't recall finding a recent a letter to Hosea and Dorcas in the mailbag from you." Bernard peeked at Gil from the corners of his eyes. "Do they know you are coming?"

Gil hadn't written to his only remaining family for close to a year. Why bother? He had little to report, and they rarely wrote back except for the occasional penny postcard. The townspeople had welcomed him to Falke, but how would Onkel Hosea and Taunte Dorcas react to his appearance? He turned a sheepish grimace on his old friend, his feet slowing to a halt. "No. No, they don't."

Bernard stopped and pinched his chin, his brow crinkling. "Well, then, we should make things as easy on them as possible. Dorcas probably already has her evening meal planned out. So here's what we'll do. We'll let you get settled in at your uncle's house"—

Strange how Bernard didn't say *your* house, considering Gil had lived there from the time he was eleven years old. Maybe it wasn't his house anymore. Maybe it never really had been.

—"and then you'll come for supper at my table at seven."

Gil jolted. "Oh, no, sir. That . . . that's kind, but it's an inconvenience for your wife."

Bernard gently pushed Gil's leg with the suitcase, sending him into motion. "It'll be a pleasure, not an inconvenience. Trust me. Ava won't mind a bit."

Gil stopped again and gawked at Bernard. "Ava? Ava cooks for you?"

Bernard released a deep sigh. "Jo. Your Taunte Maria is too weary by day's end to prepare meals. So Ava sees to it."

"So she still . . . she still . . ." Gil couldn't make himself finish the question. He really didn't want to hear the answer.

Bernard's lips quivered into a sad grin. "Yes, Maria still suffers, and our dear Ava still lives with us." Then a real smile broke across his round face. "But Ava is a fine cook. So fine, in fact, the owner of the café orders all her pastries and cakes from Ava. She's even asked Ava to take over the whole restaurant. Imagine our little Ava a businesswoman. Ach, such a wonder! Jo, she's a very good cook. You won't regret sitting at our table."

Bernard was wrong. Gil already regretted it. How could he face Ava? The fact that she still lived at home meant he'd most certainly ruined her life.

Chapter Two

Ava

"OH, PAPA, WHY?" AVA DIDN'T EVEN TRY TO HIDE her dismay at the announcement that her father had invited Gil Baty to supper.

Papa scowled and clicked his tongue on his teeth. "What else would you have me do? His aunt wasn't prepared for his arrival, and you know how high-strung she is. An extra person at her table when she already feeds that whole brood of children would equal a catastrophe to her." He picked up the latest issue of the *Bundesbote-Kalender*, the Mennonite newspaper printed in Newton, from the corner of the dry sink and headed for the parlor. "And why aren't you pleased? Think how long it's been since we enjoyed the pleasure of Gil's company at our table. Why, time was when you begged to invite him over for an evening meal."

That time ended the day Gil boarded the train for New York, choosing the big city over a life in little Falke with her. Ava hurried after her father.

Papa settled into the wing chair closest to the front window, propped one ankle on the opposite knee, and snapped the paper open. "And you don't need to worry." His voice emerged from behind the shielding sheets of newsprint. "I assured him you had become a very good cook."

Ava clapped her hands to her cheeks. "Oh, Papa!"

The paper dropped to Papa's lap. His expression changed from chagrined to puzzled. "'Oh, Papa,' what? It's the truth, isn't it? As I recall, the first time he ate with us, you turned the catfish he and I had caught that morning into chunks of charcoal."

As she recalled, she'd been barely thirteen and already fully smitten with Gil Baty.

Papa chuckled. "Gil ate it anyway, and I'm sure he suffered a bellyache afterward. But there's no concern about him getting a bellyache tonight, because you haven't burned a supper for at least three years."

Ava's arms drooped limply at her sides. "Oh, Papa . . ." She shook her head.

Papa laid the paper aside and frowned again. "Can you say nothing besides 'Oh, Papa'? What has gotten into you? I thought you would be happy to see Gil, considering how friendly the two of you were before he moved away."

Ava sank into the second wing chair, the one she always thought of as Mama's even though Mama spent more evenings in her bedroom than in the parlor. "You're right. We *were* friendly. Do you remember *how* friendly?"

A blush filled Papa's full cheeks, the color visible even behind his thick graying beard.

"Can you not understand how awkward it will be for me to sit at the table with Gil after . . . after he . . ."

Papa harrumphed and lifted the newspaper again. "*Wota unjane Brigj.*"

Ava pinched the top edge of the newspaper and bent it downward to peer into her father's faded blue eyes. "It isn't water under the bridge for me, Papa. I still . . ." She gulped.

Papa's left eyebrow rose high. "You still like him?"

She nodded, not trusting her voice to remain steady.

A grin instantly brightened his countenance. "Good. Then it will be like old times with the two of you chatting and teasing. We haven't enjoyed such a lively meal since his last visit to our table." He returned his attention to the newspaper.

Ava huffed. How could Papa be so obtuse? Despite the passage of time, she hadn't forgotten how much she'd adored Gil. Nor had she forgotten how much he'd seemed to adore her. When he'd asked for her hand in marriage, she had given a joyful yes and leaped into his arms. But immediately after sealing their commitment with a kiss, he'd spoken of taking her far away. Distraught, she told him she couldn't leave Falke—not with Mama so weak. Gil had pleaded, then reasoned, and finally proclaimed he understood. Assuming it meant he'd stay in Falke, she'd nestled against his chest, already envisioning the wonderful life they would have together. But then, to her shock and heartbreak, he'd said he wouldn't expect her to go with him.

Her chest ached anew, proving she hadn't healed from his choosing New York over her. She bolted upright and charged for her bedroom, intending to bury her face in her pillow and allow herself a rare outburst of tears. But she came to a stop in the hallway. If Gil was coming for supper, should she reconsider the menu? The planned boiled butter beans with onion and ham were fine for a family meal. A guest at the table demanded something more elegant. Even if the guest was the former beau who'd jilted her and run off to enjoy a glamorous life in the big city?

She balled her hands into fists and plunked them on her hips, her chin held high. Nä. He could eat beans. And she just might burn them on purpose.

* * *

"AVA?" PAPA HELD out his plate, his smile bright. "Another serving, please. The beans are exceptional this evening. You must have added a secret ingredient. Or maybe they taste better served on Mutta's wedding china, hmm?" He winked.

Ava's cheeks burned hotter than the remaining chunks of coal in the cookstove. Did he have to mention the use of their special-occasion dishes? Or comment that she'd gone to extra lengths to make the beans more company-worthy? She'd only added a jar of home-canned stewed tomatoes and doubled the amounts of chopped ham and vinegar—nothing so notable. Gil didn't need to know this meal was different from any other supper in the Flaming home. She poured a dipperful of beans from the soup tureen onto Papa's plate, wishing she could empty it over his head instead.

Papa set the dish in front of him and picked up his fork. "Thank you, my Leefste."

Leefste, hmm? He wouldn't call her his dearest if he knew what she was thinking. She laid the serving dipper aside. "You're welcome, Papa." She gave him a look she hoped communicated a warning. "And I'm sure it is Mama's dishes that make the difference."

Papa laughed and jabbed his fork into the steaming beans.

Gil swished his napkin over his lips and returned the square of linen to his lap. He glanced in her direction but didn't meet her eyes. The same way he'd avoided eye contact since he'd knocked on their door almost an hour ago. "Your Foda is right. The food is delicious, A-Ava."

He'd finally spoken her name, but did he have to stutter? Was it painful for him to say it? Or maybe the stutter was only in her ears, because hearing her name spoken in his deep, baritone voice stabbed like a knife.

He cleared his throat. "Thank you for your kind invitation."

She hadn't offered the invitation, but since he'd seemingly given her the thank-you, courtesy dictated a reply. "You're welcome. Have you had enough?" She sneaked a look at his plate and realized it still held nearly the entire portion she'd served him. Almost as much as remained on her plate. She hadn't been able to swallow, so wrapped in unease at his presence after their long separation. Why wasn't he eating? Maybe the beans weren't as flavorful as Papa claimed.

"Yes, I . . ." He lowered his head.

Lamplight glistened on the sheen of oil in his dark brown hair. He'd always used Macassar oil to tame his unruly waves. When he arrived, she'd noticed the ruddiness in his cheeks from a recent shave, and during their entire time at the table, the spicy essence of his cologne carried over the savory aroma rising from the tureen. His neatly combed hair and smooth face juxtaposed his wrinkled, dust-smeared suit. Odd that he'd taken the time to shave and put Macassar oil in his hair but still wore the travel suit she'd seen when he crossed the yard nearly three hours ago.

He straightened and sighed, a half smile quivering on the corners of his lips. "I think I'm too tired to eat. I slept very little on the train."

Papa swallowed, clinked his fork on his empty plate, and leaned back. "When Maria and I arrived at Castle Garden in 1872 and rode the train to Newton, we spent almost three weeks in the railcar. I don't think we slept much either, but our Rupert was a small baby then and did a lot of crying." Sadness momentarily pinched Papa's brow, but he ran his hand over his face and cleared the expression. He tipped his head in curi-. osity. "How long did it take you to travel from New York to Kansas?"

"Three days," Gil said. He looked directly at Papa when

speaking to him, and envy smote Ava. She'd never before been jealous of her father. The feeling rankled.

Papa shook his head, wonder blooming on his face. "Ach, so fast the trains go now. What a blessing."

"How long do you intend to stay?" Ava blurted the question, her voice louder and higher pitched than she'd intended.

Gil shot her a startled look, briefly meeting her eyes. "Do you mean here this evening or in town?"

Suddenly she wasn't sure which she'd meant. She shrugged, and a giggle masked as a soft cough found its way from her throat. She chose the least rude option. "In . . . in town."

Gil looked aside. "I'm not entirely sure. I found myself between prospects"—

Ava stared at his stern profile, puzzled. What did he mean?

—"and thought it a good excuse to visit. It's very noisy in New York City, so it's hard to concentrate there. I missed the peacefulness of this little town."

She swallowed a knot of sorrow. He missed the town. But had he not missed her at all?

He kept his face angled to the side, as if intrigued by something outside the window. "I'd like to compose while I'm here. I suppose I'll stay until . . . until I finish a new composition. But there's really no way to know how long that will take."

Papa reached out and squeezed Gil's shoulder. "However long you stay, we'll enjoy your company. It's good to have you home again, my boy."

Gil turned and smiled at Papa. A genuine, heartfelt smile that sent Ava's pulse into wild flutters. Such a strong response, and he'd only been looking at Papa. If he graced her with his smile, she might turn into a puddle. And what humiliation she would suffer.

She rose. "There are apple tarts for dessert." She'd held back a few from the batch she baked for the town's café. "Papa will want coffee with his sweet. What about you, G—" His name got stuck and refused to emerge.

Gil's smile faded. He sent his gaze somewhere beyond her and shook his head. "None for me, thank you."

No tart or no coffee? She should clarify, but clarifying required engaging him in further conversation. She quickly stacked their plates and hurried to the kitchen.

Gil

GIL STARED AT the swinging door that separated the kitchen from the dining room, guilt resting heavily on his shoulders. He should have refused Bernard's invitation. Obviously his presence was inconvenient. Ava hadn't taken a single bite of her supper. Tension hung between them like a storm cloud in the room, making it impossible for him to enjoy the first decent home-cooked meal he'd been served since he left Falke four years ago.

Why was she still with her parents? He'd been certain by now she would be married, maybe with a baby or two. He'd wanted that for her. She deserved it. When he'd asked her to marry him and come to New York, she said leaving Falke would break her heart. So he'd granted her freedom. Why hadn't she seized it?

Bernard cleared his throat. "I apologize if Ava seems distant."

Gil zipped his attention to the older man's face, which reflected both regret and worry.

"I should have given some thought to having a guest this evening. I was so happy to see you, I acted impulsively." Bernard propped his elbows on the edge of the table. "Maria had one of her bad days. That is why she didn't join us for supper. When Maria has a bad day, Ava also has a bad day, because she worries over her mother."

Gil nodded slowly. Maybe he wasn't to blame, then, for Ava's reticence. Or for her continued presence in her parents' home. "If she bakes for the café and has responsibility for Taunte Maria's care, she probably doesn't have time for . . . other activities then, either."

A wry chuckle rumbled. "What Ava does with her time is Ava's choice. She isn't tied to her mother's apron strings."

Such a perplexing statement. What to make of it?

"But what of your time while you're here in Falke?" Bernard looped one arm over the back of his chair and fixed Gil with a speculative look. "Will you work every day on a new composition?"

Given how empty of creativity he'd been of late, he could spend every hour of every day composing and still accomplish nothing more than a simple ditty. He shrugged. "Probably not. I assured Onkel Hosea and Taunte Dorcas I would find a way to earn my keep so I'm not a burden on them." They hadn't been as overjoyed as the townsfolk to see Gil. He didn't resent them for their reaction, though. They had enough responsibility with his seven cousins all living at home. Even Joseph was still there, and he was old enough to have his own family by now.

A sigh heaved from Gil's lungs. "To tell you the truth, Onkel Bernard, I'm battling a dry spell. I hope being in Falke will help me recover my love of music. New York . . ." He swallowed hard. "Well, the big city can rob a man of his dreams."

Bernard gave Gil's shoulder a fatherly squeeze. "You're wise to recognize when you need a change of scenery. I will pray that coming back here to your friends and family will open a wellspring of songs."

Gil had been praying for a wellspring for years, and God had withheld the flow. Would God listen better to Bernard's prayers? Gil could only hope so.

"And"—Bernard snapped his fingers, winking—"I might know a way to fill yourself again with music."

The man appeared so impish, Gil couldn't help grinning. "What is it?"

He pointed at Gil. "You could take my place as director of our local band."

For as long as Gil could remember, men from the community had come together and played in a band. Mostly, they played for the joy of making music together. Music offered a pleasant diversion from hard work. But they also performed at community gatherings, to celebrate national holidays or the end of a successful harvest, and sometimes they played in church as a special feature. But to his knowledge, Bernard had never participated in the band. "Why isn't Mr. Goertz directing the band?"

"He passed away a little over a year ago now."

Gil's jaw dropped. A pain stabbed through the center of his chest. "He . . . he's dead?"

Bernard's eyes widened. "You didn't know?"

Gil shook his head.

"I'm sorry, boy. I thought your Onkel and Taunte would have told you."

He wished they had. Sorrow smote him. Mr. Goertz had been the first to acknowledge Gil's special interest in music. He'd given him private lessons free of charge on the violin, always encouraging him to utilize the gift God had bestowed on him. No one had believed in Gil's ability as much as Ephraim Goertz had. Remorse rose above sorrow. He'd never truly thanked the man for his influence on Gil's life. But—a hint of relief crept in—at least Mr. Goertz would never know how badly Gil had failed.

"After he died, the band was quiet for a while. Then the men came to me. I don't play an instrument, but I do sing and read music well, so they asked me to take his place." Bernard puckered his lips. "I'm not a very good leader, though. The band would never be so unkind as to send me away, but they probably would rather have someone who knows what he's doing. Someone like you."

Step into Mr. Goertz's shoes? Gil laughed softly and shook his head. "I don't know, Onkel Bernard. Those men probably still see me as a little boy. They might not want me taking charge."

"What?" Bernard sent Gil an astounded look. "You saw how they welcomed you today. They're all proud of you, Gil. They would be honored to have our New York City musician lead them."

Gil scratched his cheek. He needed to find at least a part-time job to pay for food and save up for a return train ticket to New York City. "I don't suppose the band pays its director a salary . . ."

Ava entered the room. She balanced a tray holding a pot of coffee, mugs, and saucers of flaky-looking tarts. The scent of cinnamon came in with her, and Gil's mouth watered. He'd declined dessert, but now he hoped one of those tarts was for him.

Bernard gestured to Ava as she set the tray on the table. "Ava has been making treats for the men to enjoy during our mid-practice break. So if you take the position, you'll get to enjoy a bit of her company and the delight of her baked goods twice a week. It's the only payment we can offer. Will it be enough?"

Chapter Three

Gil

GIL LOOKED AT AVA AS SHE GAWKED AT BERNARD. Gil gave a gentle, "Ahem," and she abruptly faced him. A smile tugged at his lips. Why had he so steadfastly avoided her tawny brown eyes? Maybe because he'd feared the effect. Gazing at her had always stirred a melody to life inside him, as if she possessed the notes to the song of his soul. Four years away hadn't changed it. She still mesmerized him. Spending time with her might do him much good, but would it cause her harm? He couldn't knowingly cause her distress.

He said, "Would—"

"Ava?" The thready call carried from the hallway.

Ava glanced over her shoulder. "Coming, Mama." She gave Gil a look that seemed to reflect both remorse and relief—an odd combination. "Mama was sleeping while we had our supper. I'm sure she's ready to eat a little something now. Excuse me, please."

Bernard pushed upright. "No, daughter, you stay and visit with Gil. I'll see to Maria." He splashed coffee into a mug, hooked it on his finger, and grabbed one of the dessert plates. He grinned at Gil. "This is for her. I'll have one myself later." He disappeared around the corner, leaving Gil and Ava alone.

For several seconds they stared at each other, Gil seated and Ava standing beside the table. Then she gave a little jerk, as if someone pinched her, and she snatched up a saucer that held one of the tarts. She rounded the table and placed the dessert in front of him. "These are better when they're fresh, but at least the hob in the stove kept them warm. You said you didn't want coffee, but have you changed your mind?" She reached for the pot.

Gil shook his head. "No coffee, thank you. I never learned to like it."

A teasing glint brightened her eyes. "Some German you are, refusing good stout coffee."

The comment reminded him so much of the girl he'd known, he laughed. "In New York they drink tea, and I don't like it any better."

Instantly the glint faded. She sank into her chair and picked up a mug. But she didn't pour herself any coffee. "Are you happy there . . . in New York?"

He didn't want to talk about New York. If he told her the full truth, he'd have to admit he'd left Falke for no good reason. The Ava he remembered wouldn't be unkind enough to say *I told you so,* but the realization could hurt her. After all, she was the most important part of the life he'd left behind. He wouldn't compound her pain by confessing his pursuits had been fruitless. He forked up a bit of the tart, chewed, and swallowed. "I'm happy enough."

She nodded, seemingly satisfied with his short answer. "Did I hear Papa ask you to direct the men's band?"

Gil broke loose another bit of the tart. "Yes. He asked."

A tiny *humph* escaped her throat. "Papa means well, but he doesn't always think things through. Please don't let him pressure you into something you don't wish to do. I'm sure that directing Falke's little band would be terribly dull compared to the opportunities you've enjoyed in New York."

He'd never admit how few opportunities had opened for him in New York. He took a big bite and chewed slowly, savoring the flavors of apple, cinnamon, and nutmeg. He swallowed, then pointed at the tart with his fork. "If this is the reward for directing the men, then I think it would be worth it."

Her genuine smile gave a sweeter reward. "Practice hasn't changed much since you lived in Falke." She poured coffee into her mug. "They still meet on Tuesday and Thursday evenings in the room above the bank. The time has changed a bit, though, since Papa took over. He preferred starting at six-thirty and ending by eight. But if you wanted to revert to Mr. Goertz's schedule of seven to eight-thirty, I doubt the men would mind. I've been providing cookies or gingerbread or some other sweet, as Papa said, midway through the practice."

Gil put a sizable bite in his mouth and spoke around it. "Has the band grown since your father took it over?"

Ava took a sip of her coffee. "I don't believe so. Why?"

He scooped up the last bit of tart. "Because treats like this would entice anyone to pick up a horn and start playing. Ava, the tart is wonderful. Your father was right—you have become a very good cook."

He expected her to blush, perhaps stammer an embarrassed yet grateful thank-you. But she turned her face away from him and sucked in her lower lip. What had he said to upset her? He put down his fork and pushed the saucer aside. "I'm sorry."

She jerked her attention to him. "For what? You paid me a very kind compliment."

"That's what I intended to do." He chose his words carefully. At one time he would have said anything to Ava without worry of offending. During their growing-up years, he'd been at ease with her, certain she could read the true meaning behind any statement no matter how much he bungled its delivery. But that had been the girl. She was now a woman and something of a stranger. A stranger who still held the ability to play the strings of his heart like a harp. Disconcerting. "But it seemed to bother you instead of please you. Did I say something wrong?"

A sad smile toyed on her lips. "No, you didn't. I was thinking of Mama. She often tells me I've become a good cook, then laments that I've become so by necessity since she is so useless." She waved her hand, as if scrubbing the air. "Not that I view her as useless. Oh, my, not at all. But it's how she sees herself because her heart is so weak."

The fever that swept through Falke when they were children had left a permanent impact. Gil's parents, both of Ava's brothers, and many others in the community succumbed to the illness. Maria Flaming survived, but her life was forever changed. "I'm sorry she feels that way. It must be difficult for her to want to do things yet her health holds her back."

Strange how well he understood—although his circumstance was so different. He longed to write musical pieces good enough to be performed in Carnegie Hall or other prestigious venues. Yet no matter how hard he tried, the notes never came out on paper the way he heard them in his head. He was weak as a composer. Taunte Maria might never gain strength in her heart. Would he eventually gain the skills needed to become a renowned musician?

Ava sighed. "She often quotes Proverbs 24:10, 'If thou faint in the day of adversity, thy strength is small.' She won't stop trying to do the things she used to do, even if physical activity wears her out."

Gil pondered the verse. Had he made his escape back home to Falke because he lacked the strength to keep trying? Was his failure in New York the result of weakness in the face of adversity? Gil hung his head. "Your mother's determination puts me to shame. I hope I will be more like her someday— determined despite obstacles."

Ava examined him, her lips sucked in as if holding back a comment. She lifted her coffee cup and took a sip. "I also heard you ask Papa about payment."

The change in topic disappointed him. He'd hoped for something . . . more.

"The band won't pay you anything to lead them—"

"Except the promise of a special baked treat," he said, hoping to earn a smile.

A small one briefly fluttered on her face. "Except a baked treat." She put down her cup. "But if you need to earn a wage, I might have an idea."

He sat forward. "What is it?"

She ran her finger around the rim of the mug, her eyes following its path. "Mr. Goertz gave music lessons to children in town. With his death, the lessons stopped. Parents might hire you, instead, to teach their children." She glanced up, then focused on the cup again. "That is, if you intend to stay in Falke long enough for it to be worthwhile to them."

Gil guarded his expression. If Ava was still able to read him as well as she'd done when they were nearly inseparable, he might offend her. She'd offered it with a sincere desire to help, and he would accept it as such even though the idea nettled him. He'd been invited to teach music at a small private school on Staten Island. He hadn't rejected the offer, but neither had he accepted it. He'd planned to pray about it while he was in Falke, but deep down he hoped he wouldn't be led to take it.

Teaching was a far cry from composing musical scores and conducting professional musicians. But even if he did decide to take the position, he wouldn't need to return to New York until late August.

He asked, "Do you suppose parents would see three months of time a sufficient investment?"

Her finger picked up speed on the cup's rim. "So you plan to stay the whole summer?" She sucked in her lips again.

He really hadn't made any set plans when he bought his ticket to Kansas, but a few shaky ones now formed in his mind. "I suppose I do." He stared at the part in her light brown hair, wishing she'd look at him. "Will that"—he searched for the right word—"bother you?"

Her finger stilled. She didn't lift her head, but her eyes met his. Her lips parted, and she must have been holding her breath because she released a little puff of air. "Why should it?"

He gave a slow shrug. "Because of . . . memories. Of us." He gathered his courage. "I'll be honest. Sitting here in your dining room, talking across the table like we used to, takes me back to good days. Remembering makes me both happy and a little sad. I wondered if you felt the same."

She turned her face in the direction of the hallway, as if ascertaining no one was eavesdropping. "Those days were a long time ago, Gil." She spoke so softly, he had to strain to hear her. "I remember them with fondness and . . . and . . ." She shifted in her chair and faced him. "You and I were different people then, so revisiting that time really isn't beneficial, is it? In answer to your question, it will not be bothersome to me for you to spend the summer in Falke. I hope you'll build new memories to carry with you when you return to New York." She rose. "I should check on Mama. I'll have Papa come out and bid you farewell."

"Ava, I—"

"Have a pleasant evening, Gil." Her shoulders stiff, she departed.

Ava

AVA HURRIED UP the hallway to Mama and Papa's room, then leaned against the door, her pulse scampering. Such a fib she'd just told. Not bothersome to have Gil in Falke for the entire summer? Oh, it was bothersome. More than bothersome—it was terrifying. How could she see him, talk to him, and not remember what used to be? Not wonder what might have been? Not wish for what could never be?

She'd have to tell Papa her days of preparing treats for the band were done. Why should she continue if her father was no longer involved in the band? After all, she'd only brought them, as Papa had put it, to atone for his clumsy attempts at leadership. But Gil was a professional musician. If he took the position, her presence at the practices would only inspire speculation about her and Gil. People in this little town hadn't forgotten how Gil courted her, asked for her hand, and then abandoned her for an exciting life in New York.

For months after his departure, she'd sensed their pity. But they'd finally moved on, accepting that Ava's place was with her mama and papa. If she spent even a little bit of time with Gil, they'd wonder if the old spark had reignited. Then, when he left at the end of the summer, she'd have to endure the pitying looks and muttered "The poor girl . . ." all over again. No. She couldn't—she wouldn't!—put herself through it a second time.

She gave the door several brisk taps with her knuckles, turned the crystal knob, then poked her head inside the room.

"Papa? Gil is leaving now. Would you like to tell him good-bye?"

"Indeed I would." Papa rose from the chair near the bed and moved through the doorway with an eager stride. He handed Ava the saucer and fork on his way past.

Only crumbs remained on the flowered china plate. Had Mama eaten the tart? She should ask Mama if Papa had actually consumed it, but first she needed to tell Papa she wouldn't make treats for the band while Gil was in charge.

She trailed him up the hallway. "Papa? I—"

Gil stepped out of the dining room. Papa bustled to him. "So you are leaving us, hmm?"

Ava cringed at his question. Odd how such a simple query, stated in such a cheery tone, created such a mighty ache in the center of her heart.

"Yes, sir." Gil put out his hand and Papa grasped it. "Thank you for inviting me to supper. I enjoyed my time with you. And, Ava, thank you for suggesting I give music lessons to children in town. I will give the idea much thought." He sent a quick, weak smile in Ava's direction. After the warmth of his full attention only minutes ago, the half-hearted regard stung. "Onkel Bernard, concerning the band . . . if the men will have me, and you're sure you don't mind stepping aside, I'd enjoy directing them. Thank you for asking."

Papa held Gil's hand in both of his and beamed. "You're welcome, my boy, and do not worry. The men will be even happier than I to have a real director leading them again."

Ava interjected, "Papa, since you won't be involved anymore, I don't think I'll—"

"In fact," Papa went on, "with you in charge, I might be tempted to try playing an instrument myself. Especially if you decide to offer music lessons while you're in town. Am I too old to learn? Both Anton and Rupert played the trumpet, you know." As it always did when he spoke of his deceased sons, Papa's voice caught. "Do you think I could, perhaps, play in their honor?"

To Ava's surprise, Gil leaned forward and embraced Papa. It was a masculine embrace—only one arm slung around Papa's shoulders while continuing to hold his hand—but she recognized the deep emotion behind the gesture. His empathetic response to Papa's request brought the prick of grateful tears.

"Jo, Onkel Bernard. I would be happy to teach you."

The pair separated, and Papa gave Gil several pats on the shoulder, his eyes glistening. Then he turned to Ava with a sheepish look. "Forgive me. I interrupted you a moment ago. What were you going to say?"

Gil's kindness in the face of Papa's grief still warming her, she said without thinking, "I wondered if Gil had a preference about what treat I should bake for his first practice as leader of the Falke men's band."

Chapter Four

Joseph Baty

SOMEONE WAS COMING. AND HE WAS WHISTLING. Had to a be a *he*. Whistling was considered an inappropriate pastime for a lady. The *he* was most likely his cousin, finally back from supper with Ava and her parents.

Joseph moved to a window and lifted the curtain aside. A tall figure topped by a bowler hat approached, a bounce in his step. As he'd suspected, Gil was the whistler. If he was whistling, he was happy. If he was happy, he'd had a good time at the Flamings'. And if he'd had a good time at the Flamings', Joseph knew the reason why.

Ava.

Dropping the curtain into place, he growled under his breath. Why did Gil have to come back, anyway?

The door squeaked open and Gil stepped inside. He spotted Joseph, and his tune abruptly stopped. "Joseph. Good evening. I didn't expect to see you out here."

Joseph raised one eyebrow. "Why not? It's where I live."

"Oh?" Gil took off his hat and moved fully into the small building, then stood on the tattered rag rug in the middle of the dirt floor. "When Taunte Dorcas said I'd need to stay in the old summer kitchen, she didn't mention it was your room now."

Of course she didn't. Neither she nor Pa had ever considered that he'd like to be asked about sharing his room, his clothes—his parents—with an orphaned cousin. Especially a cousin who excelled at everything, making Joseph feel inept in comparison. Joseph shrugged. "Well, it is. I took it a year ago, when the twins outgrew their cradles. Once Pa moved Menno and Simon into the boys' room, there wasn't enough space for me anymore."

A soft chuckle rumbled from Gil's throat. "I imagine not. It was plenty crowded when it was just you, Earl, Herman, and me in there."

The boys' room in the house hadn't felt overly crowded to Joseph until Gil moved in. Strange, too, considering how close the two of them had been before Gil's parents died. Living under the same roof had changed things in lots of ways. None of them for the good.

"Jo, well, your bed's ready if you're tired." Joseph gestured to the cot Ma told him to set up for his cousin's use. To his chagrin, guilt needled him. The cot's frame was rickety, with a hay-stuffed mattress that smelled like the cellar where Pa kept it for sleeping when it was too hot in his upstairs room. But it was the only extra bed available unless Joseph gave up half his bed, the way he'd done when Gil first joined their family. Should he offer to trade beds with Gil? *Do unto others,* Pa often preached. Joseph wouldn't want to sleep on that stinky, lumpy cot, so he probably shouldn't expect Gil to. But Ma must have thought it was good enough for Gil or she wouldn't have had Joseph bring it to the summer kitchen. He pushed aside the uncomfortable feeling.

Gil crossed to the cot and sat on it. He leaned against the brick-framed *meagrope* Pa still used every fall to render the lard after butchering their hogs. "I appreciate you sharing your room with me again. I know it isn't convenient."

Having Gil underfoot had never been convenient, but what was Joseph to do? Gil was family. As Pa had told Ma, family takes care of family even if one more mouth to feed is a burden. Joseph flopped onto his rope bed and propped himself against the wall. He pulled up one knee, looped his arm around it, and examined a hangnail on his thumb. "It's all right." He glanced at Gil. "It won't be for long, jo?"

"Only for the summer."

The whole summer? Joseph thudded his foot to the floor. "But what about New York? What about your music? Can you be away from there for so long?"

"It's kind of you to be concerned about me, but"—

Joseph was more concerned about himself. With Gil in town, would Ava take to ignoring Joseph again?

—"New York will keep. It won't even notice I'm not there."

Was there a hint of bitterness in Gil's tone?

Gil shifted on the cot, making it squeak. "But you might not see much of me, either. Onkel Bernard asked me to direct the men's band while I'm in town."

Joseph always called Ava's father *Oomkje* Flaming—a more formal title. Hearing Gil's familiarity with the man, still in place after a four-year separation, rankled.

"I plan to look for a job," Gil continued, "so I should stay busy while I'm here. I won't be in your way."

Joseph stifled a snort. Gil would be in Joseph's way by being in town. By being where Ava would see him and talk to him. But maybe a job would keep Gil too busy to spend time with Ava. Joseph could hope. He'd lost so much to Gil when they were boys—deprived of his position as oldest child in the household, relegated from pitcher to catcher on the high school baseball team, and earning the title of salutatorian instead of valedictorian when they graduated. When they were boys, he'd fallen for Ava Flaming the same way Gil had, but Gil had won her favor. He'd thought for sure he'd be able to steal her heart after Gil went away. He'd become her friend, maybe even her confidant, but he'd yet to become her beau. If Gil tried to take up with her again, Joseph might—

"It's late." Gil yawned, then sent a lazy smile at Joseph. "We should probably go to sleep and not talk all night the way we did when we were boys."

Joseph gave a little start. He'd forgotten about their sleepovers in Gil's barn loft that never seemed to involve sleep. But that was before Gil's parents died. Before Gil moved into Joseph's house. Before resentment ruined the closeness he'd felt toward this cousin who was only five months older than he. For a moment, nostalgia tried to take hold, but then he envisioned Gil at Ava's dining room table, smiling, laughing, winning her heart again . . .

He stood and stomped to the bureau at the foot of his bed. He yanked open the middle drawer and rummaged through it. "You're right. Tomorrow's Saturday—lots of extra chores." He pulled out a sleep shirt and bumped the drawer closed with his knee. "There's not a set of drawers for you to use while you're here. I hope you won't mind keeping your things in your suitcase. I put it under the cot after I set it up."

"I don't mind." Gil knelt and slid the case from its hiding spot and unbuckled it. "Thank you for finding a good place to keep it."

Did he have to be so polite? But then, Gil had always been polite. Polite. Respectful. Obedient. Cooperative. Joseph silently listed Gil's attributes, inwardly seething. This cousin of his was almost perfect. For reasons Joseph couldn't explain, he wanted Gil to be different now. A big-city bigwig. Self-important. Unlikable. His appreciation for such a ridiculously insignificant act made Joseph feel guilty for having jammed the suitcase out of sight.

Gil pulled out a neatly folded sleep shirt. "Ava suggested I give music lessons to children to earn some money."

Instantly the guilt fled and irritation rose in its stead. What was Ava doing, giving Gil ideas that would keep him in town?

Gil sat on his heels and angled a curious look at Joseph. "What do you think? Would people in town hire me?"

Joseph wadded his striped sleep shirt in his hands. "I don't know. Where would you do the lessons? Mr. Goertz gave lessons at his house." There wasn't any place on Joseph's family's homestead for Gil to set up class. Every room in the house already served a necessary function. But if the lessons were Ava's idea, would she offer her parlor as a location for them?

Gil rose, draped his sleep shirt on the cot, and removed his suit jacket. "I don't know yet. Maybe in the children's homes. That would probably be convenient for the families." A faraway look entered Gil's eyes. "I remember the music room at Mr. Goertz's house. Wood paneling on all the walls, with floor-to-ceiling bookshelves and so many oil lamps shining from their brass brackets there was light in every corner. No shadowy gloom even on cloudy days. Such a . . . a happy place. I'm not sure why, but everything I played seemed to sound better in that room than anywhere else." He frowned and jerked his focus back to Joseph. "What happened to Mr. Goertz's piano and all the books and sheet music from his shelves?"

Joseph shrugged. "I guess they were all lost in the fire."

Gil's hands stilled on his shirt buttons. "Fire? What fire?"

"His house burned down about a month after he died. A

freak lightning strike, everybody said." Joseph tossed his clothes aside and pulled the sleep shirt over his head. "Didn't you know?"

Gil huffed, and he glared at Joseph. "How could I have known? I didn't even know he'd died until Onkel Bernard explained why he was leading the men's band. Why didn't you or Taunte Dorcas write and tell me Mr. Goertz passed away? You knew how much the man meant to me. As much time as I spent with him, you had to know."

Well, well, well. Maybe Gil wasn't so perfect after all. He'd thrown a little temper tantrum. Joseph wanted to be glad about his cousin's disgruntled outburst, but somehow sadness—and more guilt—attacked instead. He drew on defensiveness and tamped down the emotions. "You'd been gone for so long already, never coming back after you left, how could we know if you even remembered him anymore?"

Gil hung his head and stood in silence. Joseph waited a few minutes, but when Gil didn't say anything, he gathered up his discarded clothes and shoved them into a basket near his bureau. As he turned toward the bed, Gil released a heavy sigh.

"You're right. I didn't come back. And I did stop writing to you."

"You were busy," Joseph said. He meant to say it sarcastically, but it came out kindly. As if making an excuse. He pulled his covers back and eased into bed. "About giving lessons to children in town, how much good could you really do in only a few months? And people might not like the idea of you coming into their homes. Especially after you've been away from Falke for such a long time. Folks knew Mr. Goertz, but they don't really know you, do they?"

Gil nodded. "You're right. I should give the idea more thought before I talk to anyone else about it."

He sounded so defeated, Joseph came close to saying he was sorry. But sorry for what? Sorry for wanting to court Ava? Sorry for not welcoming Gil with open arms the way folks in town had the minute he stepped off the train? Sorry for wishing he didn't have to share his family and his private space . . . again . . . with Gil? All of his feelings were honest. He didn't need to be sorry for them. Did he?

Gil headed for the door. "I'm going to visit the outhouse. I'll turn out the lamp when I get back."

"Sounds fine." Joseph rolled over and faced the wall. "Good night."

"Good night. *Schlop die gesunt.*"

The familiar nighttime wish to sleep well, bestowed on them by Gil's ma when Joseph spent nights at Gil's place when the two of them were very young, raised a wave of good memories. Joseph closed his eyes and shut them out.

Ava

AT THE CLOSE of the Sunday morning service, half the congregation surged to the pew where Gil sat with his uncle, aunt, and cousins. Inwardly, Ava strained to join them, but outwardly she remained seated next to Mama. She would not give in to the pull she'd experienced since he entered the building over an hour ago. Before she, Mama, and Papa got into the carriage for the drive to the white-painted clapboard chapel built on a gentle rise a mile north of town, she'd given herself a stern lecture about keeping her distance from Gil. The gossip mill would spin out of control if she rushed over to him in front of half the town. But how she yearned to be part of the throng officially welcoming him back to Falke.

Mama took hold of Ava's arm. "Escort me to the Batys' pew,

please. I didn't have the chance to greet Gil the other evening since I was too weary to come to the table."

Ava hated to deny her mother the chance to talk to Gil. He'd been an important part of their lives for many years, and her parents had missed him almost as much as Ava had when he went away. But how to take her without making it seem Ava wanted to see Gil, too? "Maybe Papa can escort you. Where is he?" She glanced around.

"He went to pull the carriage closer to the porch for me. He'll worry he's blocking others from leaving, so we need to hurry if I'm to speak to Gil."

Ava sighed. "Very well." As she crossed the floor with Mama's hand tucked into the bend of her elbow, she prayed people would see the truth of what was taking place and not presume that going to Gil was her idea. They reached the edge of the circle, and Ava said, "Excuse us, please."

People politely shifted, and Mama worked her way toward Gil while Ava stepped aside. Trusting one of their friends to lend Mama a steadying hand if she needed it, Ava sat at the end of a pew on the opposite side of the aisle and blew out a little breath of relief. She'd escaped being in close proximity to Gil. For now. Someone touched her shoulder. Expecting Papa, she turned. "Mama wanted to say hello to—"

Joseph Baty was sitting behind her. He bounced a snide grin in the direction of the crowd. "How come you aren't over there with everyone else, fawning over our returning hero?"

Ava was familiar with Joseph's scornful attitude toward his cousin. She'd always thought it a shame, given their close ages and growing up under the same roof. Shouldn't they be more like brothers? Her own brothers, Anton and Rupert, were almost five years apart in age but the best of friends. She sometimes wondered if that's why God chose to take them Home at the same time, so neither had to suffer life without the other. She turned sideways in the seat and forced a glib tone. "I wanted others to have a chance to talk to him."

"Ah." Joseph nodded, his expression smug. "So you got enough of him when he came to dinner the other night?"

Ava only wished that were true. There was no good answer for his question, so she remained silent.

Joseph stacked his forearms on the back of her pew, bringing his face close to hers. "He talked about giving music lessons to children in town while he's here."

If Gil had mentioned it to Joseph, he must have taken her idea to heart. The thought made her smile.

"I hope he doesn't do it, though."

Her smile faded. "Why not?"

Joseph angled his gaze in Gil's direction, and the muscles in his jaw knotted. "All he cares about is himself. And you can't depend on him."

Ava gave him a mild frown, unsettled by the resentment emanating from him. "I realize his return to Falke was unexpected, but he does have plans for when he intends to go back to New York. I'm sure he'll tell the families the lessons are short-term."

Joseph abruptly faced Ava. "Are you defending him?"

She blinked several times, searching herself. Her statement had been in support of Gil. Why had she given it? Maybe because she'd always defended Gil against Joseph's petty bursts of jealousy when they were children. But Joseph had no reason to envy Gil. Not anymore.

"I suppose I am." She touched his sleeve. "We always found him trustworthy before he left for New York. Do you think time there has changed his ethics?" As much as Gil's presence tormented her, it would be worse if the Gil she'd known was now dishonest or self-centered.

"The point is," Joseph said, his blue eyes narrowing, "I don't think it would be wise to let the children depend on him since he won't be here for long. Do you understand what I mean?"

She jerked her fingers from his arm. Oh, now she understood. He wasn't talking about the town's children at all. She drew a breath and lifted her chin. "Joseph, what Gil and I had, we *had*. You needn't worry about me taking up with him again."

Relief flooded his features. He leaned toward her slightly. "Then—"

She stood. "If you'll excuse me, I need to see if Papa is getting impatient for Mama and me to leave." She hurried off before he had a chance to say anything else.

Chapter Five

Gil

GIL GLANCED OUT THE WINDOW. HIS AUNT AND uncle had herded their children out the door several minutes ago. There they all were, waiting in Onkel Hosea's wagon, no doubt wishing he would hurry. But people kept coming up and talking to him. How could he walk away without seeming ungrateful for their kind attention?

Maria Flaming stood near, beaming at him as if everything he said was brilliant. The pride glowing in her upturned face didn't dim, even when he had to confess that he'd never played with the New York Philharmonic, although he had heard them in concert. Twice. The man who asked the question about the famous orchestra turned to go, and he bumped Maria with his elbow. She teetered.

Gil reached out his hand, and she grabbed hold. The panic in her expression pierced him. She wasn't an old woman yet—probably ten or so years older than Taunte Dorcas, who was in her early forties. But her weakened heart made her as unsteady as someone twice that age. He whispered, "Do you need to sit down?"

"I need to rest. At home."

He curved his arm around her waist and addressed the

41

group. "Folks, I've enjoyed chatting with all of you and appreciate your warm welcomes. I plan to be in Falke for the summer months, so we'll have other opportunities to visit. Reverend Ediger would probably like to close the chapel, and I'm sure your stomachs are all growling."

Good-natured laughter rolled through the room, and the crowd slowly milled out the propped-open double doors and into the churchyard.

"Thank you, Gil." Tears winked in Maria's eyes, making her pale hazel irises deepen in color. "You always were a considerate young man. I'm glad the big city hasn't robbed you of your gentlemanly ways."

No. The big city had only stolen his hopes and dreams. Would he be able to stay in Falke for months without confessing how few auditions he'd won? Without everyone discovering how poorly his compositions had been received? Again, he pondered the wisdom of coming back here. But he couldn't change it now.

He forced a smile and patted her hand. "Let's get you to your wagon. I imagine Onkel Bernard is wondering what's kept you." He guided her up the aisle, tempering his stride to match her short one.

"As is your family about you."

Gil surmised Bernard was waiting more patiently than Taunte Dorcas. Just as always, his aunt had set the table for the noon meal and put a roasting pan of pork, potatoes, carrots, and onions in the oven before they left for church. By now the food was probably thoroughly cooked and ready to eat. His aunt and uncle would be upset if the meal was burned. But they would eat it anyway. Good stewards didn't waste food.

Maria's fingers bit into his arm, silently communicating her dependence on him. He slowed their pace, and her warm smile thanked him. "Bernard tells me you'll be taking over directing the band while you're in town."

Gil nodded. Several of the men had already told him how happy they were to have him as their leader, and their confidence both pleased and worried him. How he loved music. How he loved conducting musicians. Bringing melodies to a crescendo or dropping them into a tender pianissimo breathed life to tiny dots on a sheet of paper. He never felt more fulfilled than when he held a baton in his hand. But these men had been led by the best—Mr. Goertz. Would he pale in comparison? Would they end up ridiculing him the way the elite of New York had? "Yes, ma'am. I intend to try."

She shook her finger at him. "Now, Gil, don't belittle yourself. You have a God-given gift. He'll embolden you to use it."

Her words sounded so much like something Mr. Goertz would have said, Gil could almost hear the old man's voice in his head. Impulsively he leaned down and placed a kiss on her cheek. "Thank you, Taunte Maria. Your confidence in me means a lot."

She patted his arm. "There are many people in this town who have confidence in you. Remember that."

They exited the building. The Flaming carriage waited near the porch. Ava was settled in the center of the second seat under the full shade of the carriage's bonnet. Bernard hopped down from the driver's seat and clattered up the church steps, his hand already reaching for his wife. She moved away from Gil and took hold of her husband's arm.

"Take me home, *mien Maun.* My energy is spent."

"Jo, *mien Frü.* We can go."

Gil trailed them down the steps, smiling to himself. It had always tickled him when the couple referred to each other as husband and wife, as if they relished the titles. He'd always imagined him and Ava using the terms affectionately. But he shouldn't reflect on that dream now. It was as lost as his hopes of conducting his own compositions in the ornate auditorium of Carnegie Hall.

He reached the bottom of the steps, waved farewell to the Flamings, then darted around the side of the building. To his relief, his uncle's wagon was still there. He clambered into the back with his cousins and sat. "I'm sorry for making you wait."

Onkel Hosea brought the reins down on the horses' rumps, and the wagon lurched forward. He sent a quick grin over his shoulder at Gil. "You didn't *make* us wait. We chose to wait."

"I appreciate it." Gil raised his voice above the wagon's squeaks and pops. "I didn't expect so many people to remember me. And, Taunte Dorcas, you won't need to set a place at the supper table for me on Tuesday or Thursday of this week. I received invitations for meals on the nights of band practice."

Joseph's eyes narrowed, his frame tensing. "Who invited you?"

"The Pletts for Tuesday and the Rempels for Thursday."

Joseph seemed to wilt. He nodded. "Ah. Good."

Adelheid, the elder of the only two girls in the family, giggled. "You might want to eat a sandwich before you go to the Pletts. *Mumkje* Plett is a terrible cook. She burns everything."

"Don't be unkind," Taunte Dorcas said. "Maybe her food gets burned because her family delays gathering at the table. Ruined dinners aren't always the cook's fault."

Gil suspected his aunt's scolding wasn't meant for Adelheid. One of the twins—whether Menno or Simon, Gil couldn't be sure since the towheaded boys looked exactly the same to him—pushed away from Adelheid and tottered across the rocking wagon bed. He flopped into Gil's lap. Gil hummed and manipulated the giggling toddler's hand into directing the tune, grateful for the distraction. He needed to try harder not to upset his aunt while he was in town. Maybe he could avoid it completely by finding a different place to stay.

GIL STOOD BESIDE the oak podium, fidgeted with his tie, and silently counted. Thirty-three men crowded into the upstairs room of the Farmer's Bank. They sat behind the music stands Gil and Bernard had brought from the storage closet, and all stared at him expectantly. He looked at them, suddenly uncertain how to proceed.

The banker, Mr. Siemens, held his polished brass baritone upright on his knee and bounced it. "Gil? Are you going to open us in prayer?"

Gil blinked. "P-prayer? At a band practice?" He'd come prepared to use his baton, but he hadn't considered being asked to pray in front of everyone.

Mr. Siemens laid his baritone across his lap and linked his hands on top of it. "We generally start with prayer."

Gil sent a frantic look at Bernard, who stood at the wall of windows. When Gil had confessed how nervous he was, the kindly man agreed to stay even though he hadn't yet begun the trumpet lessons. Now he strode forward and joined Gil at the podium. "I'll pray, if you'd like."

Gil nearly sagged with relief. "Thank you, Onkel Bernard."

While Bernard dedicated their evening to God's glory, Gil silently begged God to help him do a good job so the men wouldn't regret asking him to step into the director's place.

"Amen," Bernard said.

Gil echoed the *amen* in his head, then took a deep breath. "Bernard said you intend to play 'When the Saints Go Marching In' at the July Fourth parade, so we'll work on that tonight.

But I'd like to start with 'Come, Thou Fount.'" The slower-paced song would help steady his racing pulse.

Everyone brought their instruments into position. Gil held up his baton. At the first downstroke, the opening note blared out. Gil took them straight through the piece without stopping, listening with a critical ear to the blends and volume. He experimented a bit with the tempo to see whether they would match the beat of his baton. To his delight, the bass drum player, a farmer whose name he couldn't recall, stayed perfectly with him, and the others all followed his lead. He had them hold the final note longer than the written four counts, then gave a decisive swish of the baton's tip.

The players all silenced their instruments, with the exception of Mr. Willems, whose tuba rumbled a full measure after everyone else stopped.

The barber, Mr. Rempel, waved his hand in Mr. Willems's direction. "Give Roald a solo, Gil, and he won't try to make his own."

The tuba player's cheeks blazed red, and everyone laughed, including Gil. He'd always liked the jovial bachelor who lived next door to the Flamings.

The man peeked at Gil from around the horn's bell, his expression sheepish. "I am sorry for that extra-long note. I have a hard time seeing you from behind this thing."

Gil crossed to Roald and helped him angle his chair so he would have a clear view of Gil directing. Then Gil resumed his position at the front of the room and went through the piece of music bar by bar. He verbally instructed the men where to increase or decrease the volume and where to watch for changes in tempo. He asked the brass instruments to always play more softly when they served as an echo for the woodwinds, and he reminded the woodwinds to look for the curved lines joining notes. "When you see a slur, please play legato, gentlemen— play through smoothly and without taking a breath in between notes." Then he tapped the podium and said, "All right. Once more, from the top."

As he led, his nervousness melted. His hands moved instinctively, creating in reality what he heard in his head. A smile pulled up the corners of his lips even though he'd been told by one of the most respected conductors in New York that a good leader maintains a sober countenance at all times. "You want the musicians led by the baton, not by your expression," the man had said in a monotone, his face impassive. But Gil couldn't help himself. Whatever emotion the music stirred always found its way to his face. And this tune was so lovely, so soul-stirring, what else could he do but beam?

Roald ended with the others this time, and Gil dropped the baton onto the podium and clapped. Someone joined in, startling him. At the back of the room, Ava stood next to a rolling cart with a towel draped over its top. She applauded even more enthusiastically than he did. When had she arrived? He hadn't even noticed. Joy now exploded through him. She'd seen what he could do, and she applauded it. He let his smile bounce from Ava to Bernard before returning it to the band members.

"Excellent, men, excellent. And I see Miss Flaming is here, which means it is break time. We'll resume after you've partaken of whatever treat she's furnished this evening."

The men laid their instruments on or beside their chairs and ambled to the cart. Ava lifted the towel, revealing a large tray of cookies and a stack of cloth napkins. She folded the towel, placed it under the cart, then hurried across the floor to Gil, wonder shining in her eyes.

"The song sounded wonderful. So much better than when Papa led the band." A flush brightened her face. "But please don't tell him I said so."

Gil grinned. "I won't repeat it, but thank you. I was very nervous before we started. But once I started directing, I . . ." He closed his eyes, reliving the glorious moments of bringing the notes to life. "I felt right at home."

"As well you should."

He opened his eyes and found her smiling at him. Something glowing in her irises made him pull in a breath and hold it, although he couldn't explain his reaction.

"I'm no expert, but I am impressed with what I saw and heard. Mostly, I'm awed by what I saw in you." She glanced aside, then met his gaze again. The rosiness in her cheeks increased. "The baton . . . it belongs in your hand."

Gil's breath eased out. He picked up the slender, silver-tipped ebony rod and ran his finger up and down its length. "Mr. Goertz gave this to me when I graduated from the Falke school, remember?"

She nodded.

"He told me I was a fine musician but I could only play one instrument at a time unless I utilized this." He drew a circle in the air with the baton's tip, the way a story wizard practiced with a magic wand.

Her eyes seemed to follow the baton's movement, then she looked at him again. "I've come to every practice since Papa started directing the men's band. For a full year I've come. I've heard the men at practice, and I've heard them in performances. But, Gil, tonight was the first time since Mr. Goertz passed away that I heard the music."

As much as he appreciated her praise, she was giving him

too much credit. "The men are good music readers, Ava. I didn't teach them that."

"Yes, they can read the notes. They can even play the notes. But with you leading them, they played the *music*." She placed her hand on his sleeve, shortening the gap between them. "I heard the music's heartbeat, Gil. I heard its soul."

Chapter Six

Ava

HE STARED AT HER WITH HIS MOUTH SLIGHTLY ajar, as if he'd never seen her before. Embarrassment struck with force. She'd said too much. And what was she doing, touching his arm? She wasn't Gil's sweetheart anymore. She couldn't even call him a friend after so much time apart. Yet she was addressing him as intimately as one would a beau.

Ava yanked her hand free and took a backward step. "I only wanted to say you're doing very well as director." She tucked a stray strand of hair behind her ear. "If you want some of the cookies, you'd better hurry."

He shook his head slowly. "No, thank you. I'm not hungry."

"Very well. Suit yourself." She started toward the group of band members, who gathered around the cart and chatted with one another.

"Ava, wait."

The urgency in his tone stopped her.

"What you said a moment ago . . ." He spoke in a husky whisper, as intimate as her hand on his arm had been. She should hurry away before the men finished their snack and noticed the two of them huddled together, but something held her in place. "I came back to Falke because I didn't think I belonged in New York. I didn't think I had what it took to be a real conductor. I came back here to figure out what I'm supposed to do with this love for music that refuses to leave me. And you . . . you just gave me the confirmation I've been praying for."

She tilted her head. "I did?"

"Yes. I came here to explore my heart and decide what I was meant to do." His words came out in a rush, as if some inner baton had picked up its tempo. "But if you heard what I hear in the music, then I'm doing something right."

If her impulsive yet sincere words had given him some sort of confirmation, would he return to New York right away? His departure would make things easier on her heart. Having him in town, physically near yet emotionally so far from the relationship they'd once shared, was excruciating. She needed him to go, for her peace of mind. But she didn't ask the question. Because deep down she feared the answer.

The men had finished their snack. They were picking up their instruments and settling into their chairs again. Relieved to have a reason to escape, Ava skirted around them and gathered up all the discarded napkins. She piled them on the crumb-laden tray, listening as Gil announced the title of the next piece of music they would practice. He apologized to Mr. Willems about the song not having a tuba solo, and she descended the stairs with the men's laughter ringing in her ears.

As had become her routine during the months that Papa directed the band, she went to the barn and deposited the soiled napkins in the laundry tub before entering the house through the connecting door. Their home, with its attached barn, marked their family as one of Falke's first residents. The newest arrivals from Russia all built their houses and barns together, as they'd done in Russia where blizzards might otherwise keep a farmer from safely seeing to his livestock. While

Kansas winters were rarely as severe as those her parents described in the "old land," Ava appreciated the convenience of avoiding rain or snow or—more often than not—gusting winds when she saw to their few animals.

Lamplight glowed at the far end of the hallway, inviting Ava to follow it the way a moth was drawn to a flame. She stepped into the parlor and found Mama in her chair. She was already dressed for bed, but she was busily putting knitting needles to work. The puddle of woven yarn in her lap proved she'd been industrious while Ava was away.

Mama looked up and smiled. "Ah, here you are. I've been waiting for you. How was the practice going?" She transferred the needles and partially completed project to the basket beside her chair.

Ava hid a smile. Mama had never asked about the practices when Papa directed. But Mama liked Gil so much. Of course she was curious about his first time leading the men. Ava sat in Papa's chair. "Very well, I think. The men seemed quite responsive to Gil's leadership, and he looked at ease in front of them." The expression on Gil's face—a blend of concentration and exultation—as he guided the men with intricate movements of the baton filled her mind's eye. "In fact, Mama, he looked happier than I've ever seen him. And when the men played, I . . ."

She hadn't been shy about telling Gil what she'd heard. But she'd also been so caught up in the moment, she hadn't given herself time to think before speaking. Should she tell Mama how the music had reached her?

"When the men played, you . . . what?"

Ava met her mother's attentive gaze. Their role reversal, with Ava as caregiver and Mama as receiver, made it awkward for her to open up and share her thoughts. Yet the emotions rolling through her needed a release. Restlessness drove her to perch on the very edge of the seat and lean toward Mama. "I heard the music behind the notes. I told Gil it was as if I could hear the very heart and soul of the melody. Does that make sense?"

Mama's face lit with a youthful smile. "Of course it does. Anyone can learn to recognize and play notes. But there's a vast difference between playing the notes and playing the music. Your brothers had that gift." For a moment, her expression clouded, then became dreamy. "They inherited it from my father. He was a gifted musician, could make a violin sing so mournful or sweet, his listeners were moved to tears. He even played for Alexander the Second by invitation at the palace. The monarch was quite taken with your grandfather."

Ava had never met her grandfather, who died shortly after Mama and Papa left Russia for America, but she remembered being enthralled when Anton or Rupert played their shared trumpet. She made noise with the instrument when they allowed her to touch it, but not once had she managed to produce anything anyone would classify as music. Perhaps the gift had skipped her. The thought made her sad.

"Mr. Goertz coaxed music from the band," Ava said, "and Gil must have learned it from him."

Mama shook her head. "Nä, *Leefste,* Mr. Goertz surely recognized the ability in Gil, but he didn't teach it to him. Skills are taught. Giftedness is bestowed by the Maker."

A chill wiggled its way down Ava's spine. "Mama, I've been so angry at Gil for going away. I felt as if he chose music over me. But if his ability is a gift from the One who crafted him, to not utilize it would be blasphemous." Her thoughts bounced as erratically in her mind as a tumbleweed tossed by the wind. "Which means that going to New York was right for him, no matter how hard it was."

"Doing God's will is rarely the easy thing, but it's always the best thing."

Ava briefly considered asking why God chose difficult pathways for His followers, but it seemed unkind considering the road Mama now walked daily. So she forced a smile and little nod.

"I know his leaving was hard for you." Mama cupped her hand over Ava's. "It was hard for him, too, going without you. I've prayed that you would set aside your anger."

Ava hung her head. "I think I stayed angry to cover up how much I hurt. And no matter how much seeing him do what he's meant to do inspired me, it's still not easy to know he's in town but he's not . . . not . . ."

Mama squeezed Ava's hand. "Not your beau?"

Staring at Mama's slender, vein-lined hand, Ava nodded.

"Do you think he could be again?"

Not unless he gave up seeking a career in music. And he wouldn't do so. Or, perhaps more accurately, he *shouldn't* do so. Not if he was utilizing a God-planted gift. Ava's heart panged. She stood and moved away from the pair of chairs to the opposite side of the parlor, then she turned and faced her mother. "No." Her chest felt so tight, taking a breath hurt. She shook her head hard. "No."

"Why not?"

Ava released a disbelieving huff. "Because his life is in New York. My life is here."

"What *is* your life, Ava?"

Mama's pensive query made Ava squirm. She turned her gaze aside and contemplated her life. It was a busy one. She filled the hours by seeing to her parents' house, animals, and garden, providing baked goods to Dirks Café, and attending church and community events. Her days were full, yet her heart felt so empty. Perhaps taking over the café would bring her fulfillment. Miss Dirks was becoming more insistent each time Ava made a delivery. Ava enjoyed cooking and baking. She'd probably do quite well. But if she took over the business, she might as well put up a sign proclaiming her intention to remain a spinster.

The longing for her own home and family twined through her. Maybe she should set aside her stubbornness and accept Joseph Baty's attentions. Joseph's family and his livelihood were right here in Falke. She could still see to her parents' needs if she lived nearby. Marrying Joseph seemed the best way to build the life she wanted. But how could she marry Joseph when her heart still pined for another man?

Ava slowly returned and crouched in front of her mother. "My life is . . . stuck at a fork in a road, and I don't know which way to turn."

Tenderness glowed in Mama's soft hazel eyes. She gave Ava's cheek a gentle caress.

Ava gathered her courage. "Mama, you said you've prayed for me to release my anger at Gil."

"I have."

She placed her hands on Mama's knees. "Will you pray something else for me?"

"Of course."

Ava drew a fortifying breath. "Will you pray that the affection I've harbored for Gil will leave me? Falke is a small town. I won't be able to avoid him, and seeing him picks loose the scab from my old wound. If my love for him leaves, I'll be healed of the hurt. Then I'll be able to choose my road."

Mama gazed into Ava's face for several seconds, her expression unreadable. Then she stroked Ava's hair, the touch light and tender. "Ava, my daily prayer is for God to reveal His perfect plan for your life and help you walk in it." Her hand slipped to Ava's cheek and lingered there. "I will pray, but you must pray, too. You must listen for and heed His voice. Will you do so?"

Former prayers—for her brothers to survive the illness, for Mama to fully recover, for Gil to stay in Falke with her—flitted through Ava's mind. In each situation, God had done the opposite of what she asked. She had little confidence that any prayer she sent heavenward would find a compassionate ear, but she wouldn't devastate her mother by saying so. Not only had Mama passed down a gift for music, but she'd also passed her faith to her children. Ava didn't dare confess she struggled with knowing whether God really cared.

She smiled, allowing Mama to read the wordless reply however she chose. She pushed to her feet with a sigh. "Papa should be home soon. Do you want to wait for him here, perhaps knit a little more, or would you rather go to bed?"

"I'll wait, but I'm finished knitting for the evening." Mama released a rueful chuckle. "Maybe I should knit. I may never finish this lap blanket at the rate I'm going. But I'm getting sleepy, and I'd rather end the evening with some Bible reading."

Ava knew where Mama kept her beloved Book—on the stand beside her bed. "Would you like me to fetch it for you?"

"Please."

Ava headed for the hallway, but a commotion outside brought her up short. She hurried to the window and pulled the lace curtain aside. The sun had gone down and shadows shrouded the yard, but she made out the shapes of two men running toward the house.

"What is happening, Ava?"

Mama's worried tone drew Ava from the window. "I'm not

sure, but I think that's Papa and Gil out there." She went to the door and opened it wide. Lamplight flowed outward, giving her a clear view. Papa, followed closely by Gil, ran past the porch. Ava darted to the railing and leaned out. "Papa, what's wrong?"

Papa rushed through the barn's side door without answering, but Gil paused and looked back at her. "Your father's getting his carriage. The seat will be softer than a wagon bed." Anguish twisted his face. "Roald Willems had an accident, and it's all my fault. He needs a doctor, so we're driving him to Aiken."

Chapter Seven

Gil

GIL PEERED FROM AROUND THE EDGE OF THE CAR-riage bonnet at the night sky. Thanks to the thick cloud cover, the entire expanse was black as pitch, matching the landscape. Had he really thought the prairie peaceful? Tonight, with the stars extinguished and Roald's soft moans a constant accompaniment to the horse's *clop-clop* on the road, the surroundings were eerie. Or was his guilt coloring his impression? He put his face in his hands and stifled a moan. How could he have been so clumsy?

Roald had stayed behind after band practice and helped Gil and Bernard put the music stands away, sweep the floor, and lower all the window blinds. What a good time they'd had, teasing and joking with so much ease and familiarity that Gil felt as if he'd never been away from Falke. They were still laughing as they headed down the staircase, Roald going first with his tuba, then Gil, and finally Bernard. Suddenly, Gil realized he'd left his baton on the director's stand. He didn't want to risk losing such a precious gift, so he turned to retrieve it. The next events replayed behind his closed lids.

He bumped the bell of Roald's tuba. The instrument lurched forward. The man jerked, his hands scrambling for a hold. Then his heel slid off the edge of the step. The tuba went flying, and Roald tumbled after it. Clangs and thuds filled Gil's memory, along with the image of Roald, white-faced and moaning, lying on top of his battered tuba at the bottom of the stairs.

A gentle nudge on his elbow blessedly rescued him from his inner reflections. "There's the doctor's house," Bernard said. "He always leaves a light burning on his porch. I'll pull as close as I can to the house. Go knock on the door while I hitch the horse to the post in his yard. Dr. Graves will help us carry Roald inside." Bernard's face contorted into a horrible grimace. "I hope we didn't do any harm when we put him in the carriage."

Gil hadn't even thought about that possibility. His pulse pounded in his ears, and a whimper seemed to come from his heart. *Please, Lord* . . . He braced his hand on the edge of the carriage and leaped out before it came to a stop. His feet met the ground with a jolt that momentarily shocked him, but he stumbled around the carriage and up to the small porch at the corner of the two-story house. He twisted the key in the brass doorbell, nearly dancing in place on his tingling soles.

A mustached man wearing a nightshirt and cap opened the door. "Is there an emergency?"

Gil pointed to Bernard's carriage. "Yes, sir. A man fell down a flight of stairs. We don't know how badly he's hurt."

"I'll get my stretcher." He closed the door.

Gil raced back to Bernard, who was leaning into the carriage's back seat. "The doc's bringing a stretcher." He reached in and touched Roald's shoulder. "Hold on, Mr. Willems. The doctor's coming."

Roald's eyes rolled, the way Gil had seen a frightened horse respond to a coming storm. "Jo, I heard you, boy. I will be glad for him to see me. I only wish one thing."

Gil leaned closer to the man. "What is it?"

"That we had brought my tuba, too. It probably needs fixing up as much as I do."

That he could joke at such a time should have encouraged Gil, but the comment stung his heart. Was the tuba beyond repair? If so, he'd replace it. He didn't know how, but he made the silent vow to himself.

The doctor, now fully dressed, came across the yard. He carried an oil lantern in one hand and an odd canvas-looking contraption under his arm. He leaned the stretcher against the carriage, pushed between Bernard and Gil, and hooked the lantern on a nail inside the carriage's bonnet. "So you decided to go down some stairs faster than you should, hmm?"

Bernard grabbed Gil's elbow and escorted him several feet away from the carriage. "I want you to stop blaming yourself." He slid his arm around Gil's shoulders. "It was an accident. Accidents happen. We cannot go back and change it, so now we need to use our heads. If he's badly hurt, he'll worry about his responsibilities. So let's plan how we can best assist him if need be. Thinking of ways to help is better than finding fault, don't you agree?"

Gil nodded his agreement, but inwardly he wondered if he'd be able to set aside his self-recrimination. After all, it hadn't been Onkel Bernard who'd started the chain of events that led to Roald's fall.

The doctor strode over to them, his expression grim. "Gentlemen, I'll need your help getting him into the house. His right leg is broken. I want to splint it before we try to move him to avoid further damage."

A chill broke over Gil's frame. "How bad is it, Doctor?"

"He has a displaced fracture. I hope to set it without surgery, but I'll have to wait until I have him inside to know for sure. With surgery or without, he won't be going home for a few days." The doctor headed for the carriage, and Gil and Bernard followed. "When he does go home, he'll be bedbound for a while."

Surgery. Bedbound. Gil's mind reeled.

"Once we move him inside, you fellows should go on home. There's nothing more you can do for him tonight."

Bernard cleared his throat. "I am not one to argue with an educated man, but there is something more we can do. We can pray."

The doctor sent a quick nod over his shoulder. "Indeed, sir. And I will do so, as well."

ON THEIR RETURN to Falke, Gil didn't speak. Nor did Bernard. Gil presumed Bernard was praying, and he didn't want to interrupt. Gil tried to pray, but words wouldn't form. Worry and guilt stole his ability to string words into sensible sentences. By the time Bernard drove his carriage into his barn, the hour was nearly midnight. Time to sleep. But Gil needed Bernard's opinion.

Instead of getting out of the carriage, he turned sideways in the seat. "Onkel Bernard, Mr. Willems lives alone, doesn't he?"

Bernard wrapped the reins around the brake handle, then leaned back with a weary sigh. "Jo, he does. This time of being bedbound will be hard for him. But people in the community will help him. That's what we do when a neighbor needs a hand. We lend one."

Gil didn't doubt the town would offer to help, but they had other responsibilities. Other than directing the men's band, Gil had none. "I want to lend him both my hands. I want to stay with him while he recovers. I can do his chores, too." He remembered his commitment to replace Roald's tuba, and he cringed. "I had hoped to find a paying job while I was in town—maybe helping with harvest or working at the mill—but I think taking care of Mr. Willems is more important."

Bernard placed his hand on Gil's shoulder. "Let me ask you a question, Gil. Are you doing this because you want to appease your guilt?"

Gil examined his motives. He felt responsible for Mr. Willems's fall, but his desire to help came from concern for the man. "No, sir. He's alone. He'll need help. I don't have a family or other duties taking up my time. It seems to make good sense that I help him."

A tired smile tipped up the corners of Bernard's lips. "Your uncle and aunt won't be upset about you staying with Roald?"

"I doubt it." Gil reflected on Joseph's reaction to sharing the summer kitchen. "I think I'm mostly in the way there. I was already considering finding different accommodations."

"Well, then, it seems the Lord has made you available for our friend Roald."

Had God given Gil the idea of finding a different place to live because He knew Roald would take a tumble down the stairs?

"Maybe you could take over Roald's job while his leg heals, too."

Gil set aside his contemplation for later. "Where does he work?"

"He works for the post office, so I guess you could say he works for me. He delivers mail to people living outside the city of Falke. There are four routes, and he takes a different route each day, Monday through Thursday. And Friday he goes fishing." Bernard chuckled. "Or so he always told me. If he's laid up, he won't be able to drive the routes. Do you think you could do it?"

It had been years since Gil rode a horse or drove a wagon, but he was confident he could do it. The hard part would be finding all the houses. He wasn't familiar with the area anymore. "Does he have maps to follow?"

"Maps?" Bernard scratched his cheek. "Well, I suppose I could draw you some maps." His shoulders slumped. "But not until tomorrow. It's too late to think about that now." He climbed down from the carriage and moved to the horse. The mare nosed his neck as he released it from its riggings. "Come into the house with me. It's too late for you to go to your uncle's place." Bernard led the horse to a stall. "You can sleep in the boys' room."

Gil hopped down from the carriage but didn't head for the door connecting the house and the barn. If he went inside, he wouldn't be able to sleep a wink knowing that Ava's room was across the hall. Especially since she wouldn't know he was there. What if she came out in the morning in her sleeping clothes? He'd be mortified. And so would she. "If it's all right with you, I'd rather stay out here in the barn."

Bernard came out of the stall, swishing his palms together. "You won't be comfortable in the barn."

"There's fresh hay, and I can cover up with one of the horse blankets." Fond memories tugged at him. "Joseph and I spent lots of nights in our barn before my parents died. I'll be fine."

"Well . . ." Bernard sighed. "Ach, boy, I am too tired to argue with you. You sleep in the hay like Little Boy Blue. In the morning, I will come get you for breakfast and draw a map for Wednesday's route."

"Thank you, Onkel Bernard." But as Gil raked hay into a

pile for his mattress, he hoped he would awaken before anyone came to fetch him for breakfast. He needed to retrieve his suitcase and belongings from the summer kitchen, talk to his uncle and aunt about moving into Mr. Willems's house, and find out who could repair the damaged tuba.

Joseph

JOSEPH RUBBED THE sleep from his eyes and sat up. He tossed aside his covers and stood, his gaze drifting to Gil's cot. Gil's empty cot. Joseph squinted through the scant early morning light, confusion muddling his thoughts. Was Gil up already? He crossed to the cot and examined it. Gil's nightshirt lay folded on the pillow, just as he'd placed it yesterday morning. Gil hadn't come back last night.

Something must have happened to him after the band's practice. Their property was only a half-mile distance from the edge of town, but even a half-mile walk at night across the prairie could be dangerous. Had he stepped in a gopher hole and broken an ankle? Perhaps encountered a rattlesnake or a prowling mountain lion? Ranchers had nearly wiped out the large cats, but there were still some sightings. Worry propelled him across the floor. He scrambled into his clothes. He needed to alert Ma and Pa. They should search for Gil right away.

As Joseph snapped his suspenders into place, the summer kitchen door opened and Gil stepped in. Joseph's worry switched to anger. He balled his fists on his hips. "Where have you been?"

Gil crossed to his cot. Bits of hay decorated his dark brown hair and stuck to his clothes. Two little pieces of hay drifted to the floor as Gil sat on the edge of the squeaky cot. "There was an accident after band practice. Onkel Bernard and I took Roald Willems to Aiken to the doctor. We didn't get back until late, and I didn't want to disturb you, so I slept in the Flamings' barn."

Joseph relaxed his fists. He didn't much like the idea of Gil staying at the Flamings' place, so close to Ava, but the hay peppering his clothes confirmed he'd been in the barn, not in the house. "What happened to Mr. Willems?"

"He broke his leg." Gil looked down.

There was more to the story, but Gil apparently wasn't going to share it. Joseph huffed. "You could have sent a messenger so I wouldn't have been worried when I woke up and you weren't here."

Gil raised his face. Remorse pinched his features. "I'm sorry. When the accident happened, all the other men had already gone. There wasn't anyone there to send."

He'd obviously gone for Mr. Flaming's carriage. Couldn't he have asked Ava to send someone? But it was hard to think clearly when things were happening fast. Joseph leaned against the bureau. "Will Mr. Willems be all right?"

"It will take a while. He might need surgery. Even without surgery, he'll be bedbound."

Joseph made a face. "That's too bad. But folks in town will help him out." Pa would probably send Joseph to help, too. The tradition of loving their neighbors. He knew it well. It's how they ended up with Gil eleven years ago.

Joseph pushed off from the bureau. "Now that I know you're all right, I need to feed and water the animals."

Gil bounded up. "Before you go, I need to tell you that I'll be moving into Mr. Willems's house. I'll take care of things for him and do his mail routes."

Joseph gaped at Gil. "When did you talk to the minister and deacons?" The church leaders always made the decisions when someone in the church was sick or injured.

"I didn't. Onkel Bernard and I figured it out."

Joseph snorted. "Well, for someone who's been gone so long, you've sure managed to weasel your way back in again." He stared at the hay in Gil's hair. Hay from the barn attached to Ava Flaming's house. "Go ahead and move into Mr. Willems's house. Go ahead and make his deliveries for him." He pointed at Gil. "But there's one place you aren't going to weasel your way back in again, and that's in Ava's affections."

Gil frowned. "What are you saying?" Then his eyebrows shot high. "Are you . . . and Ava . . . in courtship?"

Not yet. But Joseph would eventually win her heart. "Stay away from her, Gil." He slammed the door behind him.

Chapter Eight

Ava

AS ALWAYS HAPPENED WHEN A CATASTROPHE AS-
sailed someone in the community, word concerning Mr. Willems's accident spread quickly. By midmorning, everyone in
town knew he'd fallen down the back stairs of the bank building and was with Dr. Graves in Aiken. The minister's wife,
Rosa Ediger, sent her children door to door with an invitation
for all women to meet at the church at three that afternoon to
discuss ways to minister to Mr. Willems in his hour of need.

Ordinarily, Mama napped between two and four, but today
she refused to lie down in case she overslept and missed the
meeting. Ava hitched the gentlest of their horses, Pansy, to
Papa's carriage and drove Mama to the church. Several wagons
and horses already surrounded the building. It heartened Ava
to see such a turnout. After all, Roald Willems was a bachelor.
He didn't have a family to support, and she'd worried that
people might think a single man would be self-sufficient.

"Ach, so many wagons," Mama said in a happy voice, as if
speaking Ava's thoughts.

Ava drew the horse to a stop and set the brake. "I'll walk you
in, Mama, then wait out here."

"What? Nä, you come in, too."

Ava fiddled with the reins. "I'm not sure I should. I have

more pies to bake for Dirks Café. Besides, all the other women are wives and mothers, and I . . ." She swallowed. It hurt too much to say the words aloud.

Mama shook Ava's wrist. "You are as much a part of the community of women as anyone else."

Ava didn't feel as if she was. How could she be, without a husband and children of her own? When other women her age gathered to talk, they bragged—or complained—about their husbands and compared stories about their babies. If she had a husband and children, she would never complain about them. But would she ever have the chance to brag? A tiny hope fluttered in the center of her chest. If God answered Mama's prayer to erase the love Ava still carried for Gil, she would finally be able to accept Joseph's attentions. She deliberately counted his attributes. Joseph was handsome. Hardworking. A churchgoer. Yes, he was a good man.

He just wasn't Gil.

"Come in, Ava," Mama said again.

Ava sighed. Mama had skipped her afternoon rest. She might grow weary and need help coming down the porch steps when the meeting ended. Ava would do her daughterly duty and go in with Mama.

They entered the building, and Mama pointed to the back pew, where Dorcas Baty sat alone. Mama gestured Ava in first, and the two of them sat. They'd barely had a chance to get settled when the preacher's wife stepped onto the dais and briskly clapped her hands.

The women's chatter ended, and all turned their attention to the front.

Mrs. Ediger smiled at the group. "Thank you, each of you, for coming. I apologize for the very short notice, but not knowing when Mr. Willems will be released from the doctor's care, I felt it wise for us to have a plan in place. According to Bernard Flaming, Mr. Willems will be unable to work or care for himself for a significant length of time." She raised up on tiptoes and searched the room. "Is Maria Flaming here?"

Mama raised her hand. "I am here, Rosa."

"Oh, Maria, how good of you to come, especially since you bear your own health burden." The woman held out her hands in a gesture of invitation. "Since your Bernard witnessed the fall and took poor Mr. Willems to the doctor at Aiken, you probably know more than any of us about the situation. Is there anything else of value you can share?"

Mama stood and braced her hand on Ava's shoulder. "Bernard has asked Gil Baty to take over Mr. Willems's postal delivery routes until he is able to work again, and Gil readily agreed."

A soft murmur swept through the room, heads bobbing in apparent approval.

"I believe," Mama went on, "Gil also intends to reside with Mr. Willems and see to his chores."

Mrs. Baty stood. "Jo, he does. He informed us at the breakfast table this morning that he is moving into Mr. Willems's house, taking over all his chores, and doing his work." She sat and folded her arms over her chest.

Mrs. Ediger led the women in a short round of applause. "Dorcas, this speaks well of Gil and also of you and Hosea. You raised him well."

The woman bobbed her head. A blunt acknowledgment. In Ava's opinion, Mrs. Baty didn't seem honored by the compliment.

Mama was still standing. "Even though Gil has volunteered

to see to the postal routes and Mr. Willems's chores, I'm sure he wouldn't reject offers of assistance. After all, he's also committed to directing our men's band for the summer."

From the front pew, Mrs. Plett stood and faced Mama. "Will he continue to direct the band, considering that Mr. Willems's accident happened at the end of a practice? I should think the experience would make him nervous about bringing the band together again."

Ava spoke without thinking. "The accident won't change his mind. He will continue."

Mama sat, and several women craned their heads around, looking at Ava. If only she could shrink behind Mama the way she'd done when she was very small and embarrassed by attention. What she'd experienced the evening she watched Gil direct the men was personal. She didn't want to divulge the emotions that had rolled through her. Nor did she want to share the wonder she'd heard. The women would understand it themselves the first time they listened to how well the band played under Gil's leadership. Even still, the awkward silence lengthened, and Ava wished someone would say something.

Dorcas Baty gave Ava a stern frown. "How do you know he'll continue? Did he tell you so?"

Ava's conversations with Gil were none of these women's business, but she could attest to Gil's intentions without divulging private exchanges. "Gil made a commitment to Papa. They're good friends. He'll keep his word."

Several women nodded, seemingly content with her reply, and a few others exchanged sly grins. But they all faced forward again when Mrs. Plett took her seat. Mrs. Ediger invited the banker's wife, Sarah Siemens, to record the remainder of their meeting in the log she always carried when the ladies came together. Mrs. Siemens toted the leather-bound book and a pencil to the podium, opened the pages, then stood with the pencil poised. "I'm ready."

"Ladies, since Mr. Willems's job and chores will be adequately attended," Mrs. Ediger said, "shall we take it upon ourselves to make sure he and Gil Baty are fed for the duration of Mr. Willems's recovery?"

Murmurs of assent came from every corner of the room.

The minister's wife addressed Mrs. Siemens. "I'll start by taking a plate of food to Mr. Willems's house for Gil this evening."

Sarah started to write on the page, then paused and looked at Mrs. Baty. "Unless he is taking his meals with you, Dorcas."

Dorcas shook her head. "He said he was moving into Mr. Willems's house. He gathered up his things after breakfast, and we bid him farewell. He didn't even come to the house for lunch today."

The woman's tart tone stirred defensiveness within Ava. "He couldn't come to your house because he was on a mail route," she said, then clamped her lips closed. For someone who didn't feel as if she was an accepted part of the group of women, she was doing more than her fair share of talking. She ordered herself to be quiet for the remainder of the meeting.

Mrs. Baty stood and gave Ava a withering glare. "He's moved out. He's on his own now. And I have work to do at home." She left the building with her chin held high.

For several seconds, the women stared after Gil's aunt, as if confused by her attitude. Then Mrs. Ediger cleared her throat. "As I said, I'll take him supper this evening. Who would like to take a meal tomorrow?"

"I've already invited him to our place for supper tomorrow night," Mrs. Rempel said. "But you can write my name on Friday, too."

Mrs. Siemens put down the pencil and stepped away from the podium. "Ladies, please come record your names on the calendar yourself. I don't want to mix something up."

Mrs. Plett hurried to the podium and picked up the pencil. As she bent over the page, Ava swallowed a chortle. The woman meant well, but Gil would most likely go hungry the night she provided his supper. Other eager volunteers rose and formed a line behind the podium.

Mama nudged Ava. "Go write us down for Saturdays and Sundays."

Ava raised her eyebrows. "Both? Every week?"

Mama nodded. "Yes. The other women all have more to do on Saturdays, with additional chores and children underfoot. And your father enjoys Gil's company. He'll be happy to deliver the meals and spend some time visiting with him and Mr. Willems. Maybe after they eat on Saturday evenings, Gil could help him learn to play the trumpet." Tears winked in Mama's eyes.

Ava squeezed her mother's hand. "All right. I'll take all the Saturdays and Sundays on the calendar."

When it was Ava's turn at the podium, she found that the others had each taken a single weekday, leaving all of the weekends open. Even though Ava would prepare the food, she added Mama's name to the calendar rather than her own. It made her smile to see her mother's name on the page with the other women's. Much of the time, Mama's weak heart prevented her from attending quilting bees or wedding preparations or baby showers. But for this benevolent project, she was the overwhelming contributor.

As Ava started back to her seat, something occurred to her. She turned to Mrs. Ediger instead. "Ma'am, since Gil will be working for Papa for the next several weeks, perhaps I could take a copy of the calendar for Gil. Then he'll know which evenings a meal will come and which evenings he'll need to fend for himself."

Mrs. Ediger gave Ava a quick hug. "That is sound thinking, my dear. Please wait until all the women have made their choices, then I'll have Sarah make a duplicate for you." She sighed and sent her smile across the group. "So nice to see everyone come together in caring for a brother in need. Sometimes I think this is why God allows a hardship to befall a member, to give us an opportunity to look beyond ourselves." Then her brows came together, and she gave Ava a worried look. "I hope we haven't offended dear Dorcas by ministering to Gil."

Ava wouldn't call Gil's aunt *dear* after the way she behaved. Why had Mrs. Baty seemed so hostile? Shouldn't she appreciate the community's concern for Gil's well-being? Ava searched her mind for a reasonable excuse. "I'm sure she's only disappointed that so much of Gil's time will be taken since he's been away from the family for so long."

Understanding bloomed on Mrs. Ediger's dimpled face. "Ah, jo, that makes sense. Thank you for reassuring me, Ava. I feel better now."

Ava left the podium and returned to Mama, who said she was ready to go. As Ava drove the two of them back to town, she heard Mrs. Ediger's voice in her head. *I feel better now.* She was glad she'd been able to comfort the minister's wife, but a worry nibbled at her. She might not feel better again until Gil was back in New York, out of her life for good.

Chapter Nine

Joseph

JOSEPH STACKED EIGHT-FEET LONG PLANKS OF two-by-six-inch oak boards on the brick platform in the corner of Pa's workshop. Eventually the boards would be cut to size, glued and mitered, and turned into tables or chairs or cradles. Ordinarily he enjoyed inhaling the aroma of the freshly milled wood. How often in the past had he stopped to admire a swirl in the grain or touch a knot where a branch had once emerged, imagining the mighty tree that had been felled to provide for him and his family? But today he found no pleasure in his task.

His cousin had returned from New York less than a week ago, and already Gil was hailed as the town hero. When Joseph had taken his brother Herman to the barber for a haircut midmorning, Mr. Rempel refused payment—"Nä, today anyone with the name Baty gets a free haircut. You deserve it for giving my good friend Roald so much help." Neither Joseph nor Herman had done a thing for Mr. Willems. The only Baty helping Roald Willems was Gil.

On their way home, they stopped at Wallace Grocery & Sundries to purchase a tin of baking powder at Ma's request. The owner, Adolph Wallace, leaned his elbows on the counter and spent five minutes singing Gil's praises. If the tins weren't kept on a shelf behind the counter, Joseph would've grabbed one and departed, but he had no choice but to listen. "Ach," the man had finished with a sigh, "so good to know the big city didn't steal the heart from our hometown boy."

He'd been relieved when Pa sent him to pick up the lumber he'd ordered. Mr. Neufeldt never took time to chat. He was too business-minded to waste time in idle conversation. But to Joseph's chagrin, even Mr. Neufeldt had patted Joseph on the shoulder. "I was sure surprised when your cousin came by here today in the mail wagon. He said he's running Roald's routes while the poor man recovers from his bad fall. What a decent thing for him to do, especially since he isn't even related to Roald and has been away for so long. You must be proud of him."

Proud? No, not proud. Aggravated. And—admittedly—jealous. That Gil . . . always the center of attention. Joseph had loaded the lumber as fast as he could and gotten out of there. Now he slid the last few boards from the back of the wagon and added them to the pile. He swiped sweat from his brow and frowned at the neatly stacked planks. Each board was so in alignment, the stack resembled one big chunk of wood. Beautiful in its presentation. But he wouldn't get any praise from Pa for doing his work. Why applaud someone for doing what he was expected to do? Hard work was a reward in itself, Pa always said.

What had Ma said at lunchtime when Joseph explained why he hadn't given Mr. Rempel the quarter for Herman's haircut? She'd quoted a verse from Proverbs—something about pride going before a fall. Well, Mr. Willems took the fall, and then everyone's pride in Gil came to a full swell. Joseph ground his teeth. Sure, Gil was talented. Smart, too. But he wasn't the only smart, talented person in the Baty family. Joseph hadn't played his trombone since he graduated from high school, but he'd been pretty good. Maybe he should dust it off and join the men's band. Keep an eye on Gil. Keep him humble.

"Joseph?" Pa hollered across the workshop floor. "Why are you just standing there? Take the wagon back to the barn and put the horses away."

Joseph spun on his heel, but instead of going to the wagon, he strode to Pa. "My trombone is up in the attic, isn't it?"

Pa bit the tip of a finger on his leather glove and pulled his hand free. He grabbed the glove from between his teeth and nodded. "Jo. As far as I know, it's up there, waiting for Earl's arms to get long enough to play it."

Earl wouldn't need it for another year or so, then. "I've been thinking about joining the men's band. I was pretty good on the trombone, and since Mr. Willems won't be playing, there's a spot open."

Pa stood quietly, his narrowed gaze pinned on Joseph's face, as if he was waiting for Joseph to ask permission. Well, he'd wait a long time. Joseph was twenty-two already. He shouldn't have to ask. Yet he knew he wouldn't join the band if Pa said he shouldn't. Such an awkward feeling, to be a man yet still a boy.

"I suppose that would be a good thing," Pa said slowly, his intent focus never wavering. "Your cousin might appreciate having you there, seeing how most of the players are much older than the two of you."

A grin tugged at the corners of Joseph's mouth. "Jo, I thought so, too. I'll go tomorrow evening."

"Fine. Now go put the wagon and horses away. And when

you're done, go to the house and tell Earl and Herman I need them to sweep up in here."

Pa's orders sometimes made Joseph bristle, but not this time. He trotted off, grinning. The men in town would soon learn there was more than one musically talented Baty. And this one was in Falke to stay, unlike Gil, who would soon abandon them all again for New York.

Gil

GIL WORRIED THAT some men would stay away after hearing about Mr. Willems's accident. He worried they'd blame him. He worried if they did come, they would be morose and distracted. But he prepared for the practice because he'd promised to be the band leader.

Bernard came early and helped him set out music stands. Thirty-three of them, the same number they'd needed on Tuesday. He said Ava had baked gingerbread for their treat, and Gil hoped it wouldn't be wasted. But what if nobody came? Gil angled the last chair into position, then looked across the room. His podium stood at the front with his baton and the sheet music in place. All they needed now were the instrumentalists.

He paced back and forth behind the podium, glancing repeatedly at his pocket watch, his concern growing with every passing minute. And a little before six-thirty, he heard the sound of voices and footsteps on the stairs. He stopped and stared at the doorway. Men spilled in, one after another, carrying their instruments and smiling and chatting with one another. They went to their chairs and sat. When everyone was in place, only one chair remained empty. Roald's.

Gil stared at the chair. Everyone else seemed to focus on it, too, and silence fell. Gil gulped, sadness descending. Then the patter of someone running up the stairs intruded. As if choreographed, every man shifted in his chair and looked toward the doorway. Joseph burst in, carrying a trombone. He slid to a halt right inside the doorway and gaped at the men, who gaped back at him.

"Why, Joseph," Bernard boomed, "what are you doing here?"

Joseph untucked the trombone from under his arm. "I came to play, if the band'll have me."

Smiles broke on the men's faces. Several of them nodded, and others spoke words of welcome. Bernard gestured to Roald's chair. "Of course we'll have you. And there's a seat right over here."

While Joseph crossed the floor, Gil sent a genuine smile across the men. "I'm so glad to see all of you." Especially Joseph. He hadn't realized how much he needed his family's support until his cousin arrived. "I was afraid you might not want to come after what happened on Tuesday. If it's all right with you, I would like to dedicate tonight's practice to Roald Willems." His voice caught, and he cleared it with a gruff *ahem!* He sent a hopeful glance at Bernard, who leaned against the wall at the back of the room. "Would anyone like to open our practice with prayer?"

Larkin Plett waved his clarinet in the air. "You open us tonight, Gil."

Gil's pulse skipped a beat. As the band's leader, he probably should be the one to pray. He only wished he felt as capable praying aloud as he did swinging his baton. "A-all right." He bowed his head and closed his eyes. *Help me, Lord.* "Father, thank You for bringing us together here this evening. Please be with Mr. Willems and bring healing to his body." *Please, Lord.*

Please. "Strengthen us as we use the gifts You've given us, and let our music bring glory to Your name. Amen."

"Amen," several men echoed, Bernard's voice rising above the others.

Gil glanced at his friend and caught his nod of approval. "Onkel Bernard, do we have news from Dr. Graves about Mr. Willems?"

Bernard shook his head. "No telegram came today from Aiken. If I don't receive word tomorrow, I'll send an inquiry. I already sent one telegram to the doctor and asked him to let Roald know he doesn't have to worry about his house, his pets"—a few chuckles rumbled—"or his job. Everything is being tended to."

Mr. Plett raised his instrument again. "Thank you for taking care of Roald's responsibilities, Gil. I'm sure his chickens, ducks, and cats are glad to have someone feeding them." More laughter rolled.

Gil hadn't been surprised to find a whole menagerie of animals at Roald Willems's house. For as long as Gil could remember, the man had relied on creatures for companionship. Gil shrugged, grinning. "The cats, most especially. They liked the pickled herring I found in Mr. Willems's cupboard." Now guffaws blasted. How good it was to hear laughter.

He smiled and picked up his baton. "Let's start tonight's practice with 'When the Saints Go Marching In.'" The cheerful song would continue to brighten everyone's spirits.

While Gil directed, he couldn't resist frequently peeking at Joseph. After their heated exchange on Wednesday morning, he wouldn't have expected Joseph's support. Maybe Joseph wanted to make up and joining the band was his way of apologizing. If so, Gil would accept it.

As he'd done last week, he let the men play straight through, then offered suggestions for improvement. The piece included an eight-measure trombone solo near the middle. Apparently Bernard hadn't assigned a soloist, but Gil preferred a single instrument for impact. He paused with his finger on the opening notes of the solo and scanned the faces of the three trombone players.

Two of the men were older, with salt-and-pepper hair and lined faces. In comparison, Joseph looked very young and inexperienced. But Gil remembered how well Joseph had played in high school. How often had the two of them gone to the attic, where they wouldn't bother Taunte Dorcas, and played duets—Joseph on the trombone, Gil on a tarnished trumpet? Gil had practiced for hours in order to match Joseph's ability, and Gil credited their unofficial competition with his being able to play as well as he did.

"Joseph?" He blurted his cousin's name. The other two trombone players looked at Joseph and then each other. Gil hoped the older men wouldn't be offended, but Gil appreciated his cousin's presence. He wanted to thank him somehow. "Would you take the solo part when we go through this time?"

Joseph sat up straight and gave the trombone's slide a quick thrust out and in, a gesture Gil recalled from when they were boys and Joseph was readying himself to play. "Sure, Gil."

The other two trombone players glanced at each other, their foreheads creasing.

Gil sucked in a breath. Had he made a mistake? He waited for either of them to voice a complaint, but when neither spoke, he blew out the breath and lifted his baton. "All right, men. One, two . . ."

One of the other trombone players forgot and started the solo, then dropped out. But other than that, the second time through went very well. Gil reminded the flutes to watch for crescendos, then they practiced it a third time. The rendition was as close to perfect as Gil could have wanted, and he couldn't resist exclaiming, "Yes, gentlemen! Well done!"

Somewhere during the third play-through, Ava had arrived. Apparently she'd brought a little helper, because a young boy stood beside her. Gil bobbed his head in Ava's direction. "Our treat is here. Time for a break."

Gil started toward the cart, eager for a piece of gingerbread. Joseph shot past him, and an uncomfortable thought settled in Gil's mind. Had Joseph come this evening not to support Gil but to make sure he wasn't giving attention to Ava? After how badly they'd both been hurt when he went to New York and she refused to go, their courtship was long past. He should assure his cousin there was no reason to worry. Instead of lining up for a treat, he changed direction.

The boy darted into Gil's pathway and grabbed hold of his sleeve. "Mister, I gotta talk to you."

Gil sent Ava a curious look, but she was busy handing out napkins and squares of gingerbread, with Joseph's help, and she didn't seem to notice Gil. He shifted his attention to the boy. "All right. Let's go over there." The child followed him to the front of the room. Gil picked up a flute from one of the chairs and sat. "Now, what did you want to talk about?"

The boy stood in front of him, hands shoved deep in the pockets of his baggy trousers. "Joining your band."

Gil nearly barked a laugh. "What's your name, son?"

"Timmy."

"How old are you, Timmy?"

The boy straightened his skinny shoulders. "I'm nine-and-a-half-going-on-ten."

Gil remembered being that age, eager for his first double-digit birthday. "Well, Timmy, this is a men's band. You're not quite old enough to join it."

"But I have a horn. And I know how to play it."

The boy's bold declaration tickled Gil. No shrinking violet, this one. "Oh? What do you play?"

His chest puffed. "The tuba."

Someone was playing a mean prank. This child was here to shame Gil, to make him feel guilty about what happened to Roald. Gil tapped his leg with the flute. "You do, hmm? Then where is it?"

"I left it at the bottom of the stairs."

Just as Roald and his tuba had lain at the bottom of the stairs.

The boy crinkled his face. "It's a little heavy for me to carry all the way up here."

Gil stood and returned the flute to the chair. "Show me." With his hand on the boy's shoulder, he guided him to the stairs entrance and stepped onto the upper landing.

Timmy pointed to the bottom. A tuba rested there on its bell. Gil had expected to see Roald Willems's dented tuba. This one, although badly tarnished and bearing a few small dents, wasn't Roald's.

He frowned at Timmy. "Where did you get that?"

"It was my papa's. But he died. It's mine now."

Gil couldn't decide which was sadder—the fact that the boy had lost his father or that he could say so in such a glib tone. Either way, he was going to have to disappoint the child. "Well, Timmy, it's a fine horn, and I'm glad you have it. But as I said, this is a men's band, and you're too young to join it."

Timmy's crestfallen expression pierced Gil, but he steeled himself against it. "You'd better go on home now." He watched

Timmy trudge to the bottom of the staircase, slip his arm through the tuba's loop, then leave. He found no joy in sending the boy away, but what else could he do? The child didn't belong in the men's band. He turned to enter the practice room and discovered Joseph in the doorway.

His cousin shook his head, disapproval in his eyes.

Chapter Ten

Joseph

THIS EVENING WAS GOING BETTER THAN JOSEPH had hoped. The men now knew he, too, was a talented musician. The fact that Gil gave him the solo proved it. He'd had a nice chat with Ava, who'd seemed happy to find him with the other band players. And now this child had arrived and given Joseph a wonderful idea.

He gestured to the stairs and gave his cousin a rueful look. "It wasn't nice to hurt the boy's feelings, Gil. Hasn't he suffered enough?"

Gil's brows formed a V. "What do you mean?"

"That's Timmy Dirks. He's a sad story. He got left on his great-aunt's doorstep a couple years ago." Joseph tsk-tsked. "He never had a mother, because she died when he was born. Then his pa drank himself to death. Timmy got sent here to Falke. The aunt didn't want him. She said she had enough to do, running the café. But I guess she felt obligated to take him in."

Gil winced.

Joseph understood the reaction. The story, with the exception of how the parents died, could have been Gil's. He went on. "Timmy's a nice-enough kid, but he needs attention. Being in the band—maybe as its mascot or something—would be really good for him." And if Gil took the boy under his wing, so to speak, he'd have a hard time keeping up with Roald's responsibilities. Maybe he'd finally fall off his pedestal.

Gil sighed. "I wish I'd known all that when I was talking to him. Maybe I would have invited him to at least play with us tonight. Let him have one evening of being part of the band."

Joseph shrugged. "One time would only make him want more. But it's too late now. You already sent him away. Unless..." Joseph inched toward the stairs, talking over his shoulder. "I'll go after him. Toting that big horn, he can't move very fast. I'll bring him back."

Gil nodded and flicked his fingers. "Yes. Go. I'll talk to the men about letting Timmy be the band's mascot."

Joseph took the stairs two at a time and burst onto the street. As he'd suspected, Timmy hadn't gone far. He was sitting on the corner next to the tuba, as dejected as anyone Joseph had ever seen. Joseph called, "You there, Timmy."

Timmy peered around the tuba. "Are you calling me?"

"Jo. Come here. And bring that horn with you."

Timmy scowled at Joseph for a few seconds, then he pushed to his feet and scooped up the horn. He huffed to Joseph's side. "What do you want?"

"The band leader wants to talk to you again."

"He does?" The boy's face lit up. "Then let's go!"

Joseph carried the tuba up the stairs for the boy, and they entered the room together. Timmy left Joseph behind and darted to Gil. "Mister, are you going to let me join your band?"

Joseph deposited the tuba next to Gil and went to his chair. He sat and watched, enjoying his ringside seat.

Gil put his hand on the boy's shoulder. "Well, Timmy, as I told you a bit ago, you're not old enough to play in this band."

Joseph scowled. Why had Gil changed his mind? He aimed

the scowl at the band. The men must have said they didn't want a mascot. What was wrong with the lot of them?

"But," Gil was saying, "Mr. Siemens has a better idea."

"What is it?" The eagerness in Timmy's voice brought Joseph forward in his chair.

"He suggested forming a boys' band." Gil caught Joseph's eye and grinned. "There are boys' bands in nearby cities, but Falke doesn't have one yet. Maybe it's time to start one." He grinned down at the boy. "You can be the very first member. What do you think of that?"

The boy erupted with a cheer, and the men laughed.

John Siemens joined Gil beside the podium. "Now, Timmy, we don't know for sure enough boys will be interested to form a full band. I'm going to ask Reverend Ediger to mention it at service on Sunday morning. If other parents want their boys to be in it, they'll come talk to Mr. Baty."

Joseph sat back, stunned. Gil's pedestal seemed to grow another foot in height.

Mr. Siemens bent down to the boy's level. "You make sure you come to church with your Taunte on Sunday, because she needs to hear about the band. And you'll need her permission to be part of it."

Delight danced in the boy's eyes. "She'll give me permission. She's always telling me to go find something to do." He turned a hopeful look on Gil. "Could I stay and listen to you practice? I was trying to listen from outside, but it's a little hard to hear from on the street."

Gil nodded. "You can stay." He pointed to Bernard and Ava. "It looks like there's still some gingerbread on the tray. Go ask Miss Flaming if you can have a piece. When practice is over, I'll walk you home."

The boy scampered off, and Gil stepped behind the podium.

He picked up his baton. "Well, men, let's take a look at 'Come, Thou Fount.' We'll find out if we remember the dynamics from our last practice."

Joseph had a hard time focusing on the song. He kept thinking about Gil forming a boys' band. It would happen. The people of this community loved music. They'd leap at the chance to have their boys study under a New York composer, even if the New York composer was really only a local boy. It seemed just one more way for Gil to look important. His thoughts took a turn. If Gil was doing Roald's route, taking care of Roald's house and property, leading the men's band, and getting a boys' band started, he'd be pulled mighty thin, as Ma would put it.

Maybe, even though it wasn't exactly what Joseph planned, it would work out after all. One of Gil's responsibilities would surely suffer, and his halo would lose some of its shine. Best of all, if he was leading two bands while taking care of Roald, there'd be no time for him to think about courting. A girl wanted more than a few minutes a week with her fellow.

A boys' band. Joseph wished he'd thought of it himself. It was exactly what Gil needed to occupy his time until he returned to New York.

Gil

GIL DEPOSITED TIMMY and his tuba at the back door of the café, where he said he lived with his great-aunt. The woman thanked Gil for seeing him safely home, then immediately scolded Timmy for pestering the men. The harsh words continued to ring in Gil's ears, reminding him of so many criticisms he'd received from Taunte Dorcas when he was a boy. Nothing he ever did, no matter how hard he tried, had ever pleased her. His heart went out to Timmy. Although directing a boys' band would take a lot of time, he hoped the townsfolk would support the idea. Timmy needed someone—the way Gil had needed someone—to build him up.

Gratitude for the ones who'd been his encouragers swelled in his heart. He'd lost the chance to thank Mr. Goertz, but there were two other people who'd provided a safe haven for him. He checked his pocket watch. Only half past eight. He'd stop by the Flamings' house and tell Onkel Bernard and Taunte Maria what he should have said years ago. He'd thank Ava, too, for bringing the treats. He'd yet to enjoy some himself, but the men appreciated them. He would tell her so.

He picked up his pace, keeping time in his head with a brisk Sousa march, and found himself in the Flamings' front yard as the tune came to an end. A lamp glowed behind their parlor windows. They were still awake. He stepped up on the porch and reached for the doorbell's key. Before his fingers gripped it, the inside door opened and Ava stood framed behind the scrolled screen door.

"Good evening, Gil. I saw you coming. You seemed in a hurry." Wariness colored her expression and tone. "Is everything all right? Timmy . . . ?"

She'd think he was *daumlijch*—crazy—if he told her his speed was set by a tune only his ears could hear. "Timmy is home, and everything else is fine, too."

She let out a little breath of relief, and finally she smiled. "That's good."

Yes, it was good. Standing on her porch while crickets sang, with the screen door offering a proper separation yet letting him gaze at her pretty face, was very good. "I came to talk to your folks."

She pursed her lips. "They've already gone to their room for the evening."

"Ah. Well, then, I'm sorry I bothered you." Searing words from his childhood—*"You are bothering me, Gil. Go find something to do"*—roared through his mind. He involuntarily winced.

"You're not a bother, Gil."

Her kind statement chased away the painful memory. His stiff shoulders relaxed. "Thank you."

"May I give them a message?"

What he wanted to say he should say himself. Even if he couldn't thank Ava's parents this evening, he could thank her. He shouldn't go in the house, though. Not with Bernard and Maria closed in their room. Two wicker rocking chairs flanked a small round table in front of the parlor window. They were the same chairs he remembered from years ago, although their paint color had changed from white to green. He and Ava had sat in them and enjoyed many long conversations. Those memories were sweet. Reliving them might completely erase the ugly ones from his mind.

He whipped off his hat and held it against his thigh. "Could we talk for a few minutes? Out here?"

She hesitated, uncertainty pinching her expression, but then she nodded. "I suppose it's all right." She squeaked the screen door open and came out, then led him to the chairs. She settled in the more feminine of the pair, and he sat in the larger one, as they'd always done. Then she fixed him with a curious look. "What did you want to talk about?"

There were so many things he could say. How sorry he was to have left her behind. How sorry he was for Maria's poor health. How sorry he was for her responsibilities in her parents' house that prevented her from becoming the matron of her own home and family. How sorry he was for not making it big in New York. But talking about any of those things wouldn't change them. He'd only open old wounds and rub salt in them.

He placed his hat on the table and propped his elbow on the armrest, leaning slightly toward her. "I wanted to thank you for bringing baked goods to band practice."

She tilted her head slightly and stared at him, but he wasn't sure if she was puzzled, surprised, or pleased.

He cleared his throat. "It's an extra chore for you, and I appreciate the time, expense, and effort it takes to treat the men."

A soft, musical laugh left her throat. "You really came by to say that?"

He nodded.

She set her chair into gentle motion, a sweet smile curving her lips. "You're welcome, Gil, but I enjoy baking. In fact, if you're able to get a boys' band started, I'd be happy to make cookies for them, too." Teasing glinted in her eyes. "I'll even hide a couple in my pocket for you so you'll be sure and get some."

Gil blasted a laugh. "So you noticed I haven't had a treat yet?" He settled fully into his chair and pushed his feet against the porch floor, sending the chair into motion.

She nodded. "Yes. There's one piece of gingerbread left from tonight's practice. Would you like it?"

He wanted it, but if he said yes, she'd get up and go inside. He wanted her continued company more than he wanted the cake. "Thank you, but save it for your breakfast tomorrow."

She shrugged and continued rocking. The chairs' runners created soft, rhythmic creaks against the porch floorboards, their alto timbre harmonizing with the crickets' soprano. An unusual yet somehow pleasant serenade.

Sitting there rocking was nice, but if he didn't engage her in conversation, she might go in. He sought a topic that wouldn't be considered too personal. "So . . . what do you think about forming a boys' band in Falke?"

"The idea itself is good." She answered so promptly, he had the feeling she'd already been mulling it over. "Other communities—Aiken, McPherson, Canton, Windom, Moundridge, and Lindsborg—already have boys' bands. Falke is smaller than any of those towns, but I think the townsfolk will respond well to forming one here."

Although her words held affirmation, something in her tone raised a hint of uncertainty in Gil's mind. "But . . . ?"

She shot him a side-eye glance. "But I wonder if it's kind to get the boys excited about a band when it will only be for a short amount of time. After all, you'll be leaving at the end of the summer."

He wished he knew for sure if she anticipated or dreaded his upcoming leave-taking. "That is my intention, yes." He stopped his chair and frowned across the shadowy yard. "I have to keep trying, Ava. You said yourself that I'm meant to use the baton. The best place for me to learn and grow is New York City."

"Jo, that is true."

"There is a job waiting for me there. Not as a conductor, but as a teacher." He hadn't intended to divulge the offer from the school. The comfortable setting and easy conversation had loosened his tongue. Now that he'd stated it aloud, another idea trickled through his mind. "Working with the boys here in town would be good practice for the teaching position."

Now her lips pursed again. "So you would use them and then abandon them?"

He aimed his frown at her. "No."

She arched her brows.

He considered what he'd said. "But I understand why it might seem that way." He started rocking again. "I'll make it clear from the beginning that this boys' band is for the summer only. Will that keep the boys from feeling abandoned when it's time for me to go?"

"Maybe."

He'd expected her to say yes. "Maybe?"

She sighed. "Some of the boys will understand, but some of them . . . like Timmy, who needs more than a few weeks of someone paying attention to him . . . will still feel abandoned when you leave."

"Are you saying I shouldn't start it at all?"

"I'm saying you need to tread carefully. Don't let them become dependent on you." She didn't look at him while she spoke, but he suspected if he were able to peer into her eyes, he'd see a hidden hurt from when he'd let her down. "Teach them what you know about music, the way Mr. Goertz taught you, but don't build personal relationships with them. Then it will be easier for them to bid you farewell."

He'd owed her a thank-you and had delivered it. He also owed her an apology. It would be harder to express, but it should be said. He gathered his courage. "Ava, I—"

"For Timmy's sake, I truly hope there will be a boys' band. I'd hate to see that little boy's newly sprouted dream crushed. It's getting late. I should go in." She stood. "As I said, if you form the band and you'd like me to provide treats, I'm willing to do so. Good night, Gil." She hurried inside and snapped the door closed behind her.

Chapter Eleven

Ava

AVA SPENT A RESTLESS NIGHT. SITTING WITH GIL in the twilight had brought back so many wonderful memories of long conversations. Some of them laughter filled and others serious in tone or laced with tears, but all woven into her life's tapestry. Along with, it seemed, her love for Gil. Mama had promised to ask God to rid her of it. Why hadn't God answered? But then, Ava wasn't helping herself by consenting to join him on the porch. And why had she offered to bake cookies for the band he intended to start? Delivering them to practice would mean spending more time with Gil. Only snatches of time—mere minutes—but every minute with Gil was torture, knowing he would leave again. Why had he come back to Falke at all?

Her red-rimmed eyes staring back at her from her mirror in the morning as she fashioned her hair into its plump bun on the crown of her head taunted her. Mama's heart was weak, but her senses and sight were sharp. Would she notice and question Ava? If so, Ava wouldn't divulge the real reason. On Fridays, she dusted and swept the whole house. They'd been leaving their windows open more to bring in a breeze, and the breeze carried dust. She could say her eyes were bothered by stirring up the tiny particles. If she started cleaning before Mama was up, the story would be more believable.

She hurried through her morning routine and applied the feather duster to all the furniture in the parlor before she went to the kitchen to start breakfast. But her ruse wasn't necessary. Papa came into the kitchen alone.

He settled at the small table in the middle of the room and held out his empty coffee cup. "Your mother wants to walk to town later this morning, so she is spending a little extra time in bed to be fully rested for the excursion."

She and Mama usually shopped together on Saturday. Ava poured the steaming, aromatic brew into his cup. "Is there something in particular she wants that can't wait until tomorrow?"

"Pillows."

Ava placed the coffeepot on the stove and gave her father a startled look. "Did you say *pillows?*"

He slurped the coffee, then nodded. "Gil told me the pillows on Roald's bed were flat. Hardly a feather in them. I thought it was funny, so I told your mother. But she didn't see anything humorous about it. She said when Roald comes home, he'll be bedbound, and she wants the bed to be as comfortable as possible. She intends to purchase pillows. Four of them, she said. Two for his head, and two for his feet."

Ava cracked eggs into a bowl and beat them with a fork. "Well, she's thinking of the practical, which sounds like Mama. But why must it be done today? We don't even know yet when Mr. Willems will be released from the doctor's care."

"She wants to be ready. And that brings me to something else she wants to accomplish."

A change in Papa's voice made Ava pause before pouring the eggs into the skillet. She gave her father her full attention.

His sheepish expression further inspired unease, and she was almost afraid to ask, "What other practical idea has she sprouted?"

Papa fiddled with the napkin beside his plate. "She wants Roald's house given a thorough cleaning. According to Gil, Roald has given his pets—*all* of his pets—free rein of the place."

Ava's mouth fell open. "But he has chickens and ducks for pets. You're not telling me he allows chickens and ducks in his house?"

Papa nodded.

"Oh, my . . ." A picture formed in her mind's eye, and she giggled as she poured the eggs into the heated skillet. "Do you suppose we could gather up all the feathers and refill his pillowcases? It would save Mama some money at the general store."

Papa laughed long and hard. He shook his finger at Ava, his eyes twinkling. "Ach, Leefste, you are a frugal one. But I think she would rather all the feathers and dust and whatever else needs to be swept up be dumped in the rubbish bin instead."

Ava gently stirred the bubbling eggs with a wooden spoon. "Can I surmise, since you're bringing the problem to me, that Mama wants me to do the cleaning over there?"

Papa stood and rounded the table. He stopped next to Ava and put his hand on her shoulder. "Would you? Your mama has always held a tender spot for our neighbor. He was so good to carve the wooden crosses for your brothers' graves. It would ease her mind to know a clean house was waiting for Roald when he comes home. If she was up to it, she would do it herself."

Ava loved Mama too much to decline the request. Besides, Mr. Willems had always been one of Ava's favorite neighbors. She'd never understood why he hadn't married—he was such a kindhearted man, tender toward all living creatures no matter how humble. She needed to fill an order for the café—two chocolate cakes—but she'd have time after she baked them to give Mr. Willems's house a cleaning. "I'd be happy to ready Mr. Willems's house for him. I can do it today while Gil is on the mail route."

Papa made a face. "You forget, Ava, that there is no Friday mail route. Unless Gil finds someplace else to go while you work, you'll need to clean around him."

Gil

GIL FINISHED HIS simple breakfast of bread and butter, then scrubbed Roald's tabletop. He glanced around the small kitchen and grimaced. He should scrub the entire room. But while he was on the mail route yesterday, his inner ear had shared a tune with him. That's how it had been from his earliest memories—something inside his head suddenly playing a melody. Until he put the notes on paper, he wouldn't be able to focus on anything else. Tidying the whole place would have to wait.

With a clean surface on which to work, he retrieved his pen, ink, ruler, and portfolio of blank paper. He uncapped his inkpot and carefully drew staff lines until he'd filled three sheets of paper from top to bottom. While the ink dried, he paced around the table, humming the tune and directing imaginary musicians with his hands. The lone cat he'd allowed to remain in the house—a very well-fed gold-eyed calico—lazily washed her paw and watched his progress.

By his fourth circle, Gil was certain the lines were dry and ready for notes. Eagerly, he pulled out a chair, plucked up the pen, and wrote the title of the melody—"Prairie Song"—then added "By Gilbert W. Baty" underneath. He smiled. A song always seemed real as soon as it had a title. The notes in his head became more insistent.

He dipped the pen again, scraped the excess from the nib, and bent over the page.

Someone knocked on the door. The cat sat up and looked toward the noise but stayed on the folded blanket Gil had placed next to the stove for her. Gil, pen in hand, also looked without getting up. Should he answer it? The tune strained for release. Whoever was out there could come back another time. He lowered the pen to paper and made the first mark—an E.

The knock came again. "Gil? Are you here?"

Gil lay the pen on the table and darted to the door. He opened it, already apologizing. "Ava, I'm sorry, I didn't realize—"

She stood on the little stoop with a mop on her shoulder and a bucket in her hand.

Gil's gaze bounced from her face, to the mophead, to the bucket. "What is this?"

"Mama sent me to give Mr. Willems's house a thorough cleaning. I thought you should have better notice, but Papa received a telegram first thing this morning. Mr. Willems can come home this afternoon. So . . ." She shrugged, making the mop strings bounce. "This is all the notice you get. I'm here."

He stepped back and gestured her inside. "I planned to clean the house myself as soon as I finished . . . something."

She stepped into the house, then turned and faced him, twisting her closed fist around the mop handle. Even wearing a stained, full-length apron over her work dress, with a strand of hair trailing along her cheek and the strings of a mop hanging behind her head, she was too pretty for words. A blush brightened her cheeks, and she chewed the corner of her lower lip, drawing his gaze to its rosy fullness. His pulse skipped a beat, temptation to lean forward and bestow a kiss pulling hard. They shouldn't be here alone together.

He left the door open and folded his arms over his chest. "Do you know what time he'll get here?"

She put down the bucket but kept hold of the mop. "Papa has to wait until the train comes by to collect the outgoing mail and drop off the incoming, and then he needs to sort it. He won't be able to leave until at least three. That means Mr. Willems should be home by suppertime. Or a little before."

A plaintive meow came from the spot beside the stove. Ava leaned sideways a bit and peeked past Gil. A smile lit her face. She handed him the mop and hurried to the blanket. Kneeling, she scratched under the kitty's chin. A purr rumbled. "Aren't you a pretty girl? What's your name?"

Gil propped the mop in the corner and crossed to her. "I don't know if Mr. Willems has a name for her—or for any of his cats, for that matter. There are nine more of them out in his barn." With the chickens and ducks, which never should have been in the house in the first place, in his opinion. "But I've been calling her Patches."

Ava sent him a quick grin. "A perfect name for her. And unless you've been feeding her really well, I think she's going to add a few more kittens to Mr. Willems's feline family." She stood, and her eyes flitted to the table. Dismay flooded her face. "Oh. You're composing. Is this the 'something' you wanted to finish?"

Gil moved behind the table and stared at the single note on the page. "Yes. I just started it this morning." The music tugged at him, inviting him to sit and record the melody.

She waved her hands at him. "You write. I don't want to keep you from it. I'll take the cleaning items to the far side of the house. Maybe by the time I'm finished with the other rooms, you'll be done with the song and you can play it for me on your violin."

Instantly she drew back, her eyes widening and her mouth forming an *O*. Gil didn't need to ask what had brought the reaction. He was sure she was remembering a former time and another song. Heat filled his face, and he ducked his head. "Thank you, Ava. I would like to get it written while it's fresh in my mind."

"Then I'll"—she edged sideways and snatched up the bucket—"fetch some water from the well and . . . and . . ." She darted out the back door.

True to her word, she left him alone and let him work. How he was able to accomplish anything, though, knowing she was in the house, must have been a sort of miracle. When he lived at Onkel Hosea's and at his apartment in the big city, if anyone else was nearby—even in another room—he struggled to focus. Knowing they might come in and interrupt prevented him from submerging himself into the song's pool. So he'd written in his uncle's barn loft by candlelight after everyone else had gone to sleep or in a study room at the New York Public Library, with a Do Not Disturb sign taped outside the door. Yet on this Friday morning, while Ava worked elsewhere under the same roof, the song appeared on the pages.

He blew on the ink until it lost its sheen, then he collected his violin and opened the case. He'd played it regularly enough in New York, sometimes at a park where people would drop coins at his feet, that the strings were still taut and in tune. He nestled the instrument against his shoulder and secured it with his chin, positioned his fingers, and lay the bow's hair on the strings. Pinching the frog, he drew the bow along the strings, and the first pure note reverberated.

He played straight through, listening to each transition, silently editing in his mind. When he finished, he snatched up the pen, made a few changes to the score, then played it again. Tears sprang into his eyes as he extended the final note, gently pulling the bow back and forth in a smooth motion. He whispered, "Perfect," as the note faded.

"It really is."

He whirled toward Ava, who stood in the doorway between the sitting room and kitchen. He'd gotten so caught up in the music, he forgot she was there.

"I'm sorry if I startled you." She came into the kitchen, a soft smile on her face. "I heard the song, and I couldn't stay away. It's lovely, Gil. It reminded me of the wind whispering through the tips of wheat as harvest nears."

He lowered the violin, shaking his head. "You only said that because you saw what I wrote on the page."

Her puzzled expression invited explanation.

"The title I gave it—'Prairie Song.' You saw it here on the table."

She took a forward step, her gaze drifting to the sheet of music. She held a feather duster in her hands the way a bride carried a bouquet. The sight was so fetching that he had a hard time looking away. "'Prairie Song,'" she said in a singsong voice, matching a few of the notes from the opening bars of the tune. "I hadn't seen it before—I only noticed the staff lines—but it fits well. You captured the mournful yet sweet way the prairie grasses sing."

It seemed as if his heart doubled in size while she spoke the praise. He'd pined for approval from the musical elite of New York, but in that moment, he cared nothing about impressing those strangers no matter how influential they might be. It was enough—nä, it was more than enough—that Ava liked his song.

She angled her head, her brows pinching in a contemplative expression. "It's lovely as a solo piece. Will you leave it as such, or will you add other parts for an orchestra?"

Gil stared at Ava. Solo piece . . . or full orchestra score? This song would stay a solo piece. The simplicity of it was best served by a single instrument. But in that moment another idea bloomed in his head. And in his heart. There was a piece that should be rewritten with parts. A dozen stringed instruments. Flutes and oboes and a French horn. The full score came alive in his mind, almost dizzying in its intensity.

"Gil?"

He closed his eyes, sneaking into the private place in his head where music resided.

"Gil, are you all right?" She sounded worried.

He gave himself a little shake. "Yes, I'm sorry. I was thinking. I . . ." He waved the violin bow. "This will remain as is, written for the violin. But—" He clamped his lips closed. What was he doing, sharing his thoughts with her? Would he make another commitment he couldn't keep? Yes, the music was coming alive inside him, but he knew how much time it took to write it all out. Mr. Willems was returning this afternoon and would need Gil's care. He had mail routes to run and a band—maybe two bands—to direct. When would he find the time to write the glorious harmonies flowing through his mind? He couldn't tell her his plans for revising the song he'd written for her four years ago. Not until he knew for sure he'd be able to finish it. Ava deserved a promise, not a mere want-to.

With regret, he laid the violin and bow aside. "I'm done for today. Thank you for giving me the time to work." He straightened and forced a nonchalant smile. "Now, what can I do help with the housecleaning?"

Chapter Twelve

Joseph

FOR THE SECOND SUNDAY IN A ROW, JOSEPH WIT-
nessed people surrounding his cousin. Last week they welcomed him. This week they signed up their sons to join the
boys' band. To his surprise, Pa put Earl on the list.

"His arms are too short for the trombone yet. He can't reach
all the notes." Pa's booming voice carried over the excited chatter of other parents and children. "But he can play the old
trumpet you left in the attic, Gil." Earl stood beside Pa, beaming at Gil and wriggling like an excited puppy.

The protectiveness Joseph had always held toward this
brother welled up again. Earl was thirteen but barely taller
than ten-year-old Herman. Earl's stature and his clumsy gait
from turned-in toes shamed him and invited teasing from
other kids. Joining the band might build his confidence. Joseph caught himself smiling, happy for his brother. But what
was he thinking? Didn't he want the band to fail so Gil's repu-
tation would suffer? He hadn't counted on his own brother
possibly getting hurt in the process.

"Now I'm not sure what I want," he muttered under his
breath.

"Did you say something?"

Ava was standing beside him, also watching the activity at

the front corner of the church. He hoped she hadn't heard what he said, because he didn't want to explain it. "Talking to myself," he replied with a shrug. But she'd given him an opportunity to engage her in conversation, and he would seize it. "Looks like Gil will have a good-sized band to direct."

Her gaze remained on the group. Or on Gil. Joseph couldn't be sure which. "Jo, it does. I'm sure he'll do well with it."

Joseph prickled. "Of course he will. He does well with everything he tries."

She shifted her focus to him. Her brown eyes narrowed, and her lips pursed. "He works hard at all he does, Joseph."

"Except courtship. Or he wouldn't have chosen New York over you." Had he really said that? Well, maybe it was best she knew what he was thinking. "Gil will always work hard at music. Because music is Gil's whole life. Oh, he says he loves other things. Even other people. But he puts music first. He always will. We'll both be happier when we accept that he is only in town to work on his music and he won't be here for long."

"I know he's only in town for a short time." Her eyes spat, and her voice had a sharp edge. "I know he'll return to New York soon."

He'd touched a nerve. Now to bring a touch of healing. He leaned close. "He'll go, Ava." He spoke in a husky whisper. "But I will stay. I'll always stay. You can depend on me to be here for you."

She stared at him for several seconds, unmoving. Even unblinking. Then she gave a little jolt. "I know you will. I'll always stay, too, Joseph, because I'm committed to caring for my mother. I only wish—"

He waited, holding his breath, for to her finish the sentence. She didn't, so he prompted, "You only wish . . . ?"

She shook her head. "Never mind. I appreciate your friendship, Joseph. I'd better find Mama and Papa now." She turned with a swish of her skirt and hurried toward the doorway leading outside.

"Joseph!" Gil strode up the aisle, smiling and waving a pad of paper. "Look here. Twenty boys signed up for the band." He showed the list to Joseph and tapped the names with his finger. "The youngest one is Timmy, and the oldest is the preacher's son, Ralph. He's sixteen. His father said he'll be a good helper for me. I'll count on that. Twenty boys! I thought maybe twelve would be interested."

Joseph bit back a sarcastic retort. Why should Gil be surprised? Everything always fell so neatly into place for him. He'd only gotten the idea for a boys' band on Thursday evening. But already, at Sunday noon, he'd received permission to hold practices in the bank building twice a week.

"It's a good number." Joseph headed for the churchyard.

Gil stayed in step with him. "It is, and I'm glad Earl is part of it. I hoped Onkel Hosea would sign up Herman, too, but he said Taunte Dorcas thinks he's too young yet."

Joseph didn't believe it was Herman's age keeping Ma from letting him join. Pa called Ma a mother hen, always clucking and trying to keep her children under her wings. Ma would want to protect Herman from getting attached to Gil, dependent on his attention, and being distraught when he left again.

"I guess there isn't an instrument for him to play, either," Gil went on, "since he's too small for the trombone and Earl will use my old trumpet. Maybe after we get the band started, she'll change her mind and we'll find something for Herman to play."

Joseph snorted. "She won't change her mind." They reached the bottom of the stairs, and Joseph began walking backward to his folks' waiting wagon. "She's a stubborn one. Once she digs in her heels, she stays put. But have fun with the boys who did sign up. It'll be a challenge for you, but I'm sure you'll find a way to make it work." He spun and trotted the remaining distance, waving over his shoulder. "See you at Tuesday practice, Gil."

Gil

GIL CLIMBED UP onto the seat of the mail delivery wagon and unwrapped the reins from the brake handle. He gave the slim lengths of leather a gentle snap over the mare's back and encouraged, "Let's go, Blossom."

He nodded farewell to a few of the parishioners vacating the churchyard. He'd felt a little foolish that morning, using the post office's wagon for a drive to church, but no one seemed bothered by it. Maybe they realized he didn't have any other means of transportation besides his feet. He walked all over New York City, so a two-mile walk to the church and back wouldn't have taxed him. But the wagon was faster, and he needed to get back to Roald. Gil had left him propped up in his bed, a pillow supporting his cast-wrapped leg. By now the man probably needed a visit to the outhouse, and he wasn't supposed to move about without someone close at hand.

Thanks to Taunte Maria's kindness, a good lunch was waiting for him—leftover from last night's pot of stew. His mouth watered, anticipating another bowl of the tender chunks of pork, potatoes, carrots, and tomatoes in a flavorful gravy.

He marveled at the calendar Onkel Bernard had given him on Thursday morning. Every evening for the remainder of May, someone was bringing supper. Bernard said when he delivered the schedule that the women planned to provide meals for Gil and Roald until Roald was on his feet again. Well, the dinners were mostly for Roald, probably, but Gil benefited. In all honesty, he didn't mind cooking. He'd learned to prepare several simple dishes during his years in New York. But not having to cook would give him a little time for composing. And wasn't that what he'd come here to do?

As if he'd triggered a switch in his brain, the sounds of the horse's soft clops against the ground, birds calling to one another, and wind whistling through gaps in the wagon's compartment faded away and a song replaced it. "Ava's Song," the one he'd written for her as a betrothal gift. But not as he'd originally written it. Trills from a flute, resonating low tones from an oboe, and sweetly haunting runs reverberating from a violin's strings harmonized in his mind. His fingers itched with desire to record onto a staff the melody he heard.

With determination, he pushed the music to the far recesses of his mind and set his attention on his surroundings. The song had to wait. Wait until he'd seen to Roald's needs. Wait until he'd made a plan for tomorrow's first rehearsal with the boys' band. Wait until his responsibilities—the number of which was multiplying—were addressed. Yes, the song would have to wait, no matter how much it begged to be written down.

Gil reached town and followed the street that passed the Flamings' property. Without effort, a smile tugged at the corners of his lips. So many good memories were connected to their place. Ava, Ava's best friend, Joseph, and he had chased fireflies in the yard, guzzled glasses of lemonade, and chomped cookies on the porch. They played hide-and-seek in the barn and otherwise entertained themselves when they were children. Even way back then, when they divided into teams, it was always Gil and Ava against Joseph and—what was the girl's name?—Clara. After the fever swept through town, Clara's family moved to McPherson, so Ava, Joseph, and Gil became a trio. But somehow he and Ava always formed a pair against Joseph. Even then, Gil had wanted Ava for his partner.

He still did. But he shouldn't contemplate such a thought. Nothing had changed. He was still devoted to his music. She was still devoted to her parents. One of them would have to abandon their calling in order for them to be together. Sadness settled on him. But he didn't want to be sad. Not on a beautiful, sunshiny Sunday afternoon. He focused on the good response to the boys' band instead, his mood brightening.

He drove the wagon into Roald's small barn, unhitched the horse, and released her into the small fenced corral. Then he entered the house through the back door, calling Roald's name as he stepped in.

"I'm here, Gil. In the sitting room."

Gil darted through the kitchen and found Roald at the end of the settee with his injured leg on the cushioned seat. "How'd you get yourself in here?"

Roald pointed to the crutches leaning against the side table. "It feels mighty good to be out of bed."

Gil folded his arms. "Dr. Graves advised as little moving around as possible, and always with someone nearby, for the first two weeks. It hasn't even been one week yet, Mr. Willems. I think you should have stayed put."

The man made a sour face. "Ach, doctors. They're like women. They fuss too much. I'm fine here."

For the first time, Gil noticed the calico cat curled next to Roald's hip. The animal's presence probably contributed to Roald's desire to remain on the settee. "You look pretty comfortable there."

Roald nodded. "That I am. But I'll get up and come to the table when lunch is ready." He raised one eyebrow. "When will lunch be ready?"

Gil laughed. "I'll heat the stew now. But we'll eat in here—no coming to the table. And after we eat, you're going back to your bed."

Roald rolled his eyes. "You hiss more than a nervous cat. But I'll eat here if it makes you feel better."

While the pot heated, Gil selected bowls and silverware from the shelf in Roald's kitchen and answered questions about the morning's sermon, which was about the prodigal son. Gil had always liked that story—proof of a father's deep, unconditional love for his child. This morning, though, it had made him a little sad. Like the prodigal son, he'd left home and gone to a big city. Unlike the boy in the story, he hadn't engaged in carousing or wicked living. Even so, he hadn't received a loving welcome from his aunt and uncle. He was thankful for the warm reception given by members of the community. He comforted himself with their acts of kindness.

He couldn't resist sharing with Roald how many boys wanted to join the band. "Our first practice is tomorrow evening, so I need to have music ready. I hope the boys can all read notes."

"Don't worry about such a thing. They can read music."

Roald's voice held so much confidence, Gil poked his head from the doorway and gave a quizzical look.

The cat now reclined on the man's chest, and he rhythmically stroked her while he spoke. "Many of them took lessons from Mr. Goertz. Some for a little while, others for years, the way you did. They've sung from the church hymnals since they were small. Now, whether they all know how to find the right note on an instrument, I can't say for sure. But I think you'll find, as a whole, they are *sea klüak*." He tapped his temple. "Very smart."

The pan lid rattled, and Gil hurried to the stove. He hooked the lid's handle with a large fork and set it aside. The stew was bubbling around the edges. He stirred it, and a savory aroma arose. His stomach growled in response.

Laughter came from the sitting room. "I heard that. And so did old mama cat—she just dove under the settee."

Gil chuckled. "Well, let's hope she stays there while we eat. You'll need to put a bowl on her perch."

More laughter rang.

A good feeling flooded Gil—a feeling of belonging. He might not be in Falke for much longer, but he'd hang on to this feeling and enjoy it for as long as it would last.

Chapter Thirteen

Gil

AFTER ASSIGNING EACH OF THE BOYS A SEAT, GIL inwardly groaned. Why hadn't he taken the time yesterday after church and made note of more than the boys' names and ages? Had he been given fair warning that half the band would be made up of baritones, he would've prepared for it—if a director could prepare for such an unusual situation.

Three boys had come in toting drums—Ralph, the preacher's oldest boy, lugged a bass drum, and two younger boys carried snares. An adequate rhythm section, considering the band's size. But the remainder of the instruments were all brass. Eleven baritones, three trumpets, one trombone, one French horn, and Timmy's tuba. Gil scanned the sea of gold-toned instruments. This band would have a very different sound than the men's band with its mix of brass and woodwinds.

He screeched a chair to the front of the group and sat facing them, forcing a smile he didn't feel. "Welcome, boys. It's good to see you all here on time and with your instruments in hand." A wry chuckle formed in his throat, and he couldn't hold it back. "I see that a number of you play the baritone. Was there"—he coughed into his hand—"a sale on baritones at the general store?"

One of the older boys raised his hand, and Gil nodded at him. He stood, cradling his baritone against his rib cage. "Do you remember Mr. Goertz?"

How well Gil remembered the dear man. "I do."

The boy waved his hand, indicating the group as a whole. "Lots of us took lessons from him. Mr. Goertz said baritones can play treble clef or bass clef. They're good . . . good . . ." He glanced at the boy sitting next to him.

The boy popped up out of his chair like a hungry baby bird poking its head up from a nest. "Fillers." He sat again as quickly as he'd stood.

The first boy nodded. "That's it. Fillers. Mr. Goertz said baritones can fill in wherever they're needed. So they're a good instrument to learn." He sat.

Of course. Gil should have realized it himself. Baritones weren't common in an orchestra. Only four brass instruments— tuba, trumpet, trombone, and French horn—made up the horn section. But in a band, especially a small band like this one, having so many baritones could end up being a boon.

He slapped his knees and pushed to his feet. Sliding the chair out of the way, he offered a genuine smile. "Well, boys, to start our first practice, let's run some scales in the key of C, with a four-four tempo. Bass drum, please play on the one, and snares, please play eighth notes through each measure. Horn players, we'll hold each note four counts."

He held his breath. Would they understand his instructions?

They brought their instruments into position, eyes aimed at him.

"Remember, four full beats per note. We'll go slowly and with purpose—one, two, three, four." He moved his baton in beat with his words, hiding a smile at the way all pairs of eyes seemed transfixed by its silver tip. "Ready? And . . . one." Gil led them through one full scale, listening and observing. To his delight, they were attentive, and most followed the movements of his baton. A few horns were slightly out of tune—he'd fix that next—but his first introduction to their playing encouraged him. So far they were, as Roald had said, *sea klüak*.

They finished on a high C. When Gil snapped the baton, silence fell. Then the boys grinned at each other, and one of the younger baritone players snickered. The boy next to him bopped him on the arm.

Gil smiled at the boy who'd giggled. "What's your name?"

"Franky Ediger."

Ralph raised his mallet. "He's my brother."

Gil acknowledged Ralph with a nod. "Franky, I wonder if you were amused for the same reason I came close to laughing."

The youngster placed his lips against the mouthpiece and warbled out an E-sharp. Then he grinned. "We was all playing the same note, but we didn't all sound like we was playing the same note." He stuck his finger in his ear and rotated it, as if reaming something out. "It kinda hurt."

A few boys gawked at Franky, seemingly appalled, but Gil couldn't have been more delighted. "If you were able to hear the slight differences in tone, you have an ear for music, which is a wonderful gift. And you're right. Even though you were all playing the same note, some of the instruments are slightly out of tune. So we have an important job to do right now. We need to get every instrument to match the one next to it. How many of you know how to tune your own instrument?"

Nearly every hand went up.

"Good. This should go smoothly, then. I'm going to divide you into groups. We'll listen to each horn, choose the one that's most on pitch, then the others will work to match it. Baritones, you form a circle over here." He pointed to the northeast corner of the room. "Tuba and trombone, over there." He indicated the northwest corner. "Trumpets and French horn, there." He swung his hand to the southeast corner. "Now, I'll—"

One of the snare-drum players waved his hand over his head. "Mr. Baty? What about us?"

Ralph tapped the top of the boy's head with his mallet. "We don't get tuned, Roy. We wait quietly while Mr. Baty helps the others."

Gil sent Ralph an appreciative nod, then turned to the baritone players. "Since there's a whole herd of you, let's start here."

Joseph

SEVERAL WAGONS WERE already parked around the bank building when Joseph reached town. When he was Earl's age, he'd walked back and forth from Falke to his farm, but Ma told him to take the wagon and fetch Earl. Ma was a worrier by nature, and she'd always worried over Earl because of his feet. Her fussing got worse when Earl's growth slowed down, leaving him far behind his peers. She treated him younger than his age because of his size.

Joseph parked around the corner from the bank, then hopped down and meandered to the outside entrance of the bank's upper level. The door was propped open with a rock, and the sound of "Twinkle, Twinkle, Little Star" played by a number of horns escaped the solid limestone block building. He leaned against the rough blocks and listened, his head tilted. One side of his mouth tried to pull into a smile. The song was a childish choice, especially for boys, but they were playing well.

Reverend Ediger waited in his wagon right in front of the

building, the reins draped across his knee. He caught Joseph's eye. "They sound pretty good already, don't they?"

Joseph ambled to the horses and rubbed their velvet noses. "Jo, and it doesn't surprise me. Gil knows what he's doing." Had he really just complimented his cousin? He'd told the truth, though. Gil already had the men's band playing as well as they had when Mr. Goertz directed it. Why wouldn't he do just as well with the boys?

"This band will be good for our boys," the preacher said, his gaze lifting to the windows on the second floor. "Ralph especially needs something else to do while school is out for the summer. A boy his age can find mischief if he isn't kept busy."

The year Joseph turned twelve, Pa had put him to work in the woodworking shop. Gil wasn't expected to work in there, though, because he was taking music lessons with Mr. Goertz three evenings a week. Joseph asked for lessons, too, but Pa said no—"You can play my trombone on your own. Learning more about music is Gil's job, because Mr. Goertz says he will be a musician someday. You will be a craftsman, so you need to learn here." If there'd been a boys' band then, would Pa have let him join it? He stifled a snort. He wouldn't have joined it even if Pa said yes, because Gil would have been its star and he wouldn't have wanted to come in second. He'd always been first in the woodshop, though.

The song ended, and a few minutes later very discordant noises—chairs being dragged across the floor—came from upstairs. "Sounds like they're putting the room in order."

"Jo." Reverend Ediger checked his pocket watch. "Ending at half past seven, just the way Gil said they would." Feet thundered on the stairs. He shifted his focus to the doorway. "And here they come."

Boys burst from the entryway, holding tight to their instruments, jabbering and laughing. Earl was in the middle of the pack, looking happier than Joseph could ever remember seeing him. Joseph called, "Over here, Earl."

His brother spun around, then came at Joseph in his waddling gait, pressing the trumpet to his chest as if he carried a king's ransom. "Hi!"

Joseph chuckled. "Hi, yourself. Did you have a good time?"

Earl nodded so hard he bumped his chin on the trumpet. He yelped, laughed, and rubbed the spot. "I had a real good time. Guess what? My trumpet was most in tune, so the other boys had to match me. Then when Gil put us in order, he put me first. *First*, Joe. I've never been first. Not for anything."

A lump filled Joseph's throat. After only one practice, Earl was glowing. He even seemed taller. "That's real good. Ma and Pa will be proud of you."

"Pa will be. Dunno about Ma. She wasn't too sure she wanted me in the band. But Pa said I should do it. I'm sure glad he did." He yanked a rolled sheet of paper from his back pocket and shoved it at Joseph. "Gil wanted us to leave our music here, but I asked, and he said I could take this home and use it to practice. Will you help me find a safe place for it? Somewhere Herman or the twins can't bother it."

Joseph figured their seven-year-old sister, Louisa, would be the most likely one to take it. She loved to color with the wax crayons she'd found in her Christmas stocking last year. No piece of paper was safe around her. He slung his arm around Earl's shoulders and herded him toward the wagon. "You can keep it in my room. No one"—not even snoopy little Louisa—"will bother it there. And . . ." Should he offer? He'd never before invited any of his siblings into his private domain.

Earl marched alongside him, jolting from side to side. "And what, Joe?"

He looked into his brother's happy face, and the invitation spilled out. "And you can play your horn in there instead of the attic. It's brighter in my room, with so many windows, so it'll be easier to see your music, and the playing won't bother Ma if she's trying to get Menno and Simon settled down for a nap."

"Thank you!" Earl threw his arms around Joseph's torso.

The trumpet bit into Joseph's back, and he gently dislodged his brother, laughing. "Whoa there. You're going to dent either me or that horn."

Earl laughed, too, and tucked the trumpet tight to his chest again. "I don't want to hurt the trumpet."

"But it's all right to hurt me, hmm?" When had he last teased with Earl? He couldn't remember, but it felt good. It reminded him of the good-natured teasing he and Gil had bandied back and forth when they were a little younger than Earl.

Earl waggled his eyebrows, his grin impish. "I'm sure glad Gil came back to Falke. Being in this band is the best thing that's ever happened in my life." He sighed and resumed his pace.

When they reached the wagon, Joseph gave his brother a boost onto the seat, then pulled up behind him. Earl's statement about the band repeated in Joseph's mind as he drove home. He was happy for his brother and at the same time very worried about him. Gil was here, but not for long. Which meant the boys' band wouldn't last for long. Would this new-found excitement and joy go away when Gil left and the band ended?

Chapter Fourteen

Gil

THE FIRST MONDAY IN JUNE, GIL RUSHED THROUGH supper. He had to have the room set up and ready for the boys' practice by six-thirty, which meant being at the bank by six. It hadn't been a problem previously, since the wonderful ladies providing meals delivered them by four, about the time Gil returned from the mail route. He and Roald usually ate at five, after which Gil tended to important needs, then headed to the bank building.

But over the past weekend, steady rain falling both day and night turned the dirt roads into quagmires. The wagon wheels sank deep in the muck, and the horse's feet grew mud boots. Between the slower passage and taking time at each stop to scrape mud from the horse's hooves, Gil didn't return to Falke until a quarter past five. He hurried through releasing the horse from its rigging and jogged across the soggy yard to the house, calling as he entered, "Roald, I'm sorry I'm late. The rains—"

Roald was at the stove, crutches under his arms, stirring something in a pot.

Gil came to a halt. "What do you think you're doing?"

The man shrugged and gave the wooden spoon another lazy swirl. "Cooking." He chuckled. "Well, warming up what

117

Mrs. Regier brought. Rabbit stew, she said." He leaned over the pot and sniffed. "*Rikje goot,* jo?"

Gil couldn't argue that the dinner smelled good, but Roald had no business standing at the stove. He walked over and removed the spoon from the man's hand, took him by the elbow, and gently steered him to the sitting room. "I wish you'd waited. You're not supposed to be up so much yet."

Roald sank onto the settee and lifted his cast onto the cushion. "A man can't just sit all day."

The statement worried Gil. How much was Roald up when Gil was away from the house? Tomorrow would mark three weeks since Roald's fall. Every day the man was more restless, more determined to return to his normal activities. But the doctor had emphasized the importance of keeping weight off his leg until the bones had a chance to heal. It could be up to twelve weeks, Dr. Graves had said. Roald was going to do himself permanent injury if Gil didn't keep better watch.

The calico cat slinked out from behind the settee and put her front paws on Roald's knee. He lifted her up. "Besides, I know how awful the roads get after a good rain shower. I knew you'd be late coming in. You've got practice soon and need something in your belly."

"I appreciate your consideration, Roald. I really do." Gil meant it, but at the same time worry tugged at him. He crossed to the stove, still talking. "But the doctor"—not to mention half the town—"will have my hide if your leg doesn't heal properly. I'm supposed to be taking care of things, you know."

"I know, I know." A mighty sigh heaved from the man's throat. "I'm used to being out with folks. This sitting here . . . it's making me lazy and dull. I don't like it."

Gil filled bowls with stew and carried them to the sitting room. He handed one to Roald. "I'm sorry. I'm sure the days are long and lonely here by yourself. But if your leg doesn't heal, you might never be able to climb into the delivery wagon and make your rounds again. So you have to do what the doctor said and stay down."

Roald muttered something Gil didn't catch, then said, "Let's pray and eat." He bowed his head, and the men prayed silently. Gil added a plea for Roald's leg to heal properly to his gratitude for the food.

They ate in silence, then Gil rose. "Do you need to visit the outhouse before I leave?"

Roald held his bowl to the cat, who lapped the gravy from the bottom. "Nä. I'm fine. You go on before you're late."

Gil fidgeted, eager to take Roald's bowl to the dry sink. If he didn't take it there, Roald would. The cat kept licking. Gil checked his timepiece. He didn't have time to wait. "Leave your bowl and spoon on the side table in here. I'll tend to them when I get back from practice."

Roald glanced at him. "All right, Gil." He puffed his cheeks and blew out the air. "I wish I could practice my tuba. I miss playing it."

Mr. Plett at the hardware store had told Gil about a silver craftsman in McPherson who could probably repair the damaged tuba, but Gil hadn't had a free day to take the instrument there. He also didn't have the funds to pay for it yet. The money he earned on the mail route really wasn't his. The route was Roald's, so the pay was Roald's. The kind man wanted to share it, but Gil felt guilty taking it when there was a doctor bill to pay. But he couldn't think about that right now. He needed to get ready for the boys' practice.

He headed for the door. "I'll be back as close to seven-thirty as possible. Please—"

Roald waved at him. "I'll stay put. Stop worrying. Just go."

Gil bit back a chuckle and left. As he'd come to expect, Timmy Dirks was already waiting outside the staircase, his arms wrapped around his tuba. The boy's face lit up when he spotted Gil, and he trotted over to meet him on the boardwalk.

"Good evening, Mr. Baty. I came to help you set up chairs."

Gil put his hand on the boy's shoulder. "I appreciate your willingness. But I hope you aren't skipping your supper in order to help me."

"Nä. I ate some bread and lard before I came."

Gil grimaced. Bread and lard? What a thing to feed a growing boy. Especially considering his aunt ran a restaurant. She couldn't fix her nephew a decent dinner?

"Besides, Miss Flaming will bring something good." He smacked his lips. "I like her molasses cookies."

The child provided a steady stream of one-sided chatter while they brought out chairs from the storage room and set them up. He told Gil about his pet toads, his favorite places to play by the creek, and his being stuck inside while it rained. "That was awful, not being able to go to the shed."

"Do you play games in the shed?"

"I play Pa's tuba in the shed. Taunte doesn't want it in our apartment. She says it hurts her ears and it'll bother her customers." The boy rested his hands on the back of a chair and sent Gil a remorseful look. "You said we should practice every day, but I couldn't on Saturday or Sunday because of the rain. So I practiced a whole lot today." He rubbed his cheeks. "My face is kind of sore from all that puffing. But I wanted to be ready for tonight."

Gil admired the child's determination. His desire to do well reminded him of himself at that age. "You have a musician's heart, Timmy. I'm proud of your tenacity."

Timmy wrinkled his nose. "My what?"

Gil laughed. "Tenacity—your determination to do well."

"Ooooh." He nodded wisely. "Taunte says I stick to my tuba worse than a cocklebur. Is that tenacity?"

"Indeed it is." Gil hoped his irritation with Timmy's aunt didn't come through in his voice or expression. He started to give Timmy encouragement, but other boys began arriving, and Gil's attention shifted to the practice.

They started with scales, as had become their habit. Only a few horns required tuning, which proved they were practicing. Gil praised them for their diligence, then introduced a new piece—one he'd written himself. He'd hurriedly modified it for brass instruments yesterday afternoon while rain kept him inside, and he was eager to hear it played. Would the notes on the pages match what he heard in his head?

As he'd learned from conductors while playing in New York, he had them run straight through the first time, ignoring misplayed or skipped notes. Then he broke the song into smaller segments, on which they focused until they were able to play the section without mishaps. They'd only made it halfway through the song when Ava arrived. To his surprise, Joseph carried in the treats tray.

Gil dismissed the boys for their break, and they surrounded Ava and the cart. Joseph separated himself from the group and crossed to Gil.

"I'm sorry to intrude on your time with the boys, but I wanted to let you know I might not be here tomorrow evening for the men's practice." While Joseph spoke, he kept his gaze aimed at the crowd of boys. "Pa and I finished a step-back cupboard for some folks in McPherson, and I'll be delivering it tomorrow. With the roads still wet, I figure it'll take longer than usual."

Gil wished Joseph would look at him. Since the Sunday that

Reverend Ediger shared the idea of starting a boys' band, he and Joseph hadn't exchanged a word. Joseph had come to the last four practices with the men, but he always arrived last, spent the break time talking to Ava, then left as soon as practice was over. Now that Gil thought about it, it was probably Ava he was staring at. And he didn't like it at all.

"That's fine." Gil raised his voice, hoping Joe would meet his eyes. "You're right about the roads being bad. I had some trouble making the rounds today."

Joseph glanced at him. "The road to McPherson is better traveled so harder packed than some of our roads. It should be easier going for me, but just in case, I wanted you to know why I wasn't here."

"Thanks for telling me. I would have worried something was wrong if you didn't come."

Joseph sent him another quick look, this one with lowered brows.

Before Gil could question the reason for his frown, Timmy's laughter carried above the boys' chatter. Gil smiled. It was good to hear the boy enjoying himself. He wished there was a way to give Timmy more encouragement. With his days so taken up with responsibility, he didn't have time to work on his own projects or commit to time with Timmy. But maybe . . .

Joseph took one step away, but Gil grabbed his arm. "Joseph, you said you're going to McPherson, yes?"

Joseph shifted free of Gil's light hold and nodded.

"In town, or somewhere in the country?"

Joseph folded his arms. "In town. Why?"

Excitement stirred in Gil's chest. He still wasn't sure how he'd pay for the repairs, but he would have to trust God would make the funds available. Because he was sure God had given him this idea. "If I bring Roald Willems's tuba to you, could you deliver it to the silversmith in McPherson? Mr. Plett said he'd be able to repair it."

Joseph's dark brows rose. "Can he play it while he's bed-bound?"

Gil swallowed a chortle. Roald refused to be bedbound. "He needs something to do, and if he has his tuba, then . . ." Suddenly doubt niggled. Was he doing the right thing? Timmy's comment about having to play his tuba in the barn stung him anew. "Timmy Dirks could visit him each day and they could play their tubas together. I think it would be good for both of them."

Joseph shook his head slowly, his eyes wide. "Where do you come up with these ideas?"

Gil couldn't determine whether Joseph was impressed or annoyed. "I don't really know where this one came from. But I think maybe God gave it to me."

Joseph faced the group again. "People have been saying for the past two years, someone needs to take an interest in Timmy Dirks or he'll end up being a troublemaker. But nobody has done anything. Then you come back, you're not even here a full month, and you're already trying to fix things."

Gil tapped Joseph's arm and waited until his cousin looked at him. "It was your idea first, remember? You told me to let him be the mascot for the men's band because he needed attention. So you started it."

Joseph stared in silence at Gil for several seconds. Then he gave a little jolt. "Jo, well, whoever is responsible, I think it's a good idea. Timmy needs somebody looking after him, and Mr. Willems needs someone to look after."

"Especially now, since he can't get out of the house the way he wants to," Gil added. Guilt tried to take hold of him. If only he hadn't bumped Roald's tuba, the man's life wouldn't have suffered such an interruption. But Onkel Bernard once told him that all things worked for good in the life of the believer. Having a broken leg wasn't good, but a friendship between Timmy and Roald would be good for both of them. If it worked out.

Joseph hadn't said if he would take Roald's instrument to McPherson. "Will you take the tuba with you tomorrow?"

"I'll take it to the silversmith," Joseph said, "but do you know how you'll get it back?"

Gil hadn't thought that far ahead. But once again, he decided to trust. "Not yet, but I'll figure it out. I'll bring it to you this evening."

The boys were returning to their seats, and Ava was gathering up the napkins. Joseph started to edge away. "Never mind about bringing it. I'll go pick it up from Mr. Willems's place now, while you finish the practice."

An even better plan. "Thank you, Joseph."

Joseph didn't answer. He skirted the band and went to Ava, then helped her clean up the snack mess. There were lots of crumbs to sweep up but no cookies left on the tray. Gil had missed out on having one himself, but he didn't mind. He'd been given a good idea, and his cousin hadn't voiced a single word of opposition to it. He'd be completely happy if Ava didn't seem so at ease with Joseph's assistance.

Gil picked up his baton, trying not to watch Ava and Joseph. "All right, boys, let's work on the third section now, starting with the trumpets. Watch for staccatos. And, one . . ."

Chapter Fifteen

Ava

JOSEPH OFFERED TO CARRY THE EMPTY TRAY AND pile of napkins for Ava, and she gratefully accepted. They descended the stairs side by side, the sounds of the boys' instruments following them. She'd never heard the song they were playing before, but she liked it. Its tempo and cheerful melody invited one to step in time with it, perhaps even dance.

They moved from the enclosed stairway to the boardwalk, and Ava reached for the tray. "Thank you, Joseph. I appreciate your help."

Joseph held it away from her, his grin impish. "Let me give you a ride home."

Temptation teased. Ava was capable of walking the quarter-mile distance from the bank to her house. But sometimes her arms grew tired from the weight of whatever she carried with her for the snack. The tray was much lighter now that the boys had emptied it, but it was still cumbersome with the napkins piled on its top. A ride would be pleasant.

If only anyone but Joseph had offered it to her. She liked Joseph. They'd been friends a long time. But ever since Gil went away, he'd seemed to expect more from her than she wanted to give. She'd been very up-front about her feelings.

But he still sought her out at church, cornered her for conversation if he saw her in a store, or—like tonight—seized opportunities to be of service.

She'd appreciated him hopping down from the wagon where he'd sat reading and carrying the tray up the stairs for her. But accepting a ride could be interpreted differently than simple courtesy, both by Joseph and any townspeople who happened to see them sharing the wagon seat. She had no desire to stir speculation about the two of them.

"Thank you, but—"

He shook his head. "Don't refuse me, Ava. This tray is heavy to carry, I need to go by Mr. Willems's place anyway, and there is nothing wrong with a friend doing a friend a favor."

She searched his face for hidden motives. "Only a friend doing a friend a favor?"

"What else?" He offered an engaging smile. "Come on. Let me take you home. Aren't you tired of being on your feet?"

Ava refused to answer, because the reply might sound like a complaint. She'd done the family's laundry, including the sheets and towels, weeded the garden while the ground was moist, toted six loaves of home-baked bread to Miss Dirks for her customers—and listened to yet another cajoling sales pitch about purchasing the café—before baking several dozen cookies in addition to cooking dinner. Her day wasn't finished yet, either, because when she got home, she still needed to wash the supper dishes. She longed to sit and relax a bit. The sooner she got home and finished her chores, the sooner she could rest. If Joseph understood her agreement meant nothing more than her desire to get off her feet, she could accept.

"Very well. Thank you, Joseph."

He put the tray in the back of the wagon, then helped her onto the seat. As he took up the reins, he shot her a grin. "It's nice of you to provide a snack for the band members. I know it makes extra work for you."

The topic seemed safe. Impersonal. Ava relaxed her guard. "I don't mind. I'm baking for the café anyway, and it makes me happy when people enjoy the treats." Suddenly she remembered the cookies she'd wrapped in a napkin and put in her apron pocket for Gil. She groaned. "Oh, Gil . . ."

His eyebrows briefly pinched. "Do you need him for something?"

"I promised to save a treat for him." She laughed, embarrassed. "He's either busy with something else or the others swoop in and finish it all before he has a chance to partake of the snack. So I've been holding some back for him."

Joseph huffed, his scowl deepening.

His churlish reaction brought a rise of defensiveness she didn't understand. She said, "The director works as hard as the players. Doesn't he deserve some, too?"

Joseph's expression cleared, and he offered a half-hearted nod that took the edge off her ire.

She patted her apron pocket. "I forgot to give them to him tonight. But if we're stopping at Mr. Willems's house on the way, I could leave them for Gil there."

A teasing—or was it a vengeful?—smirk replaced the frown. "Mr. Willems will probably eat them before Gil gets back."

"I reserved four—two for him, two to share. Mr. Willems always enjoyed the treats I brought to the men's practice."

"You're a kind person, Ava."

The warmth in his tone and the approval shining in his eyes made heat fill her face. She looked straight ahead. "It's only cookies, Joseph."

"It's not only cookies." He gave the reins a slight pull, and the team slowed its pace. "It's everything you do. How many women your age would stay home and care for an ailing mother? I can't think of any others in town. You're always thinking of other folks instead of yourself. As much as I admire that, I can't help but wonder if you won't wake up someday and wish you'd spent a little more time taking care of yourself."

What a thoughtless thing to say. She folded her arms. "You think I'm letting myself go?"

"Nä, not the way you're thinking." He angled a grin at her. "You're always dressed nice, with your hair fixed in that perfect puff, and you smell good. Even now, when I know you've been working all day, I smell something . . . fruity and sweet on you."

The heat in her face increased to a blaze. She'd splashed a little orange-scented toilet water beneath her bodice before leaving for the bank to hide the scent of perspiration from her day of labor. She had no idea it was so strong. She scooted to the far side of the seat.

"You've always been attractive. Feminine. Even when you were ten years old, chasing fireflies with a ratty old net in your grubby hand, you still were every bit a little lady."

Ava had heard enough. "Really, Joseph, your flattery is not appealing."

His jaw dropped, as if she'd stunned him. "Flattery? You think I'm trying to flatter you? I'm only telling you the truth. I admire you. I always have."

She pointed ahead. "Here's the Willems's place. I'll walk the rest of the way from there."

He drew the wagon to a stop in front of the square, clapboard house, but he didn't get down. Turning sideways on the seat, he fixed her with a solemn look. "Ava, I'm sorry I upset you by telling you what I think. But what kind of friend would I be if I kept quiet?"

He would be the kind of friend she could trust. The kind with whom she would be at ease. She clamped her lips against the snide comments.

"You're a giving person. You give of yourself to your folks and to people in town every day."

She didn't want to listen, but the fervency in his voice drew her attention. She stared into his blue eyes, unable to turn away.

"But it isn't wrong to want something for yourself. While you're doing all this giving, why not ask yourself what you are giving up?"

Ava already knew what she was sacrificing—starting her own family—and she'd made her peace with it long ago. Hadn't she? She gripped the edge of the seat. "Help me down, please. Practice will end, and you won't be there for Earl. He might worry."

"Earl knows to wait for me, but I'll do what you ask because I don't want to further upset you." He set the brake, climbed down, then rounded the horses and assisted her from the wagon. He lifted the tray from the back and offered it to her, but he didn't let go when she took hold. "I'm going to tell you one more thing, because I'm worried about you, and I think it would be wrong for me as your friend to stay silent."

This man had no idea how to stay silent.

"These nice things you're doing for the bands are also done for Gil. I know that. Everyone knows it."

She gritted her teeth and wished she could yank the tray from him and flee.

"But please don't get the idea that they'll win him over. Think of Gil as the flu."

She blinked rapidly, then sputtered, "Th-the flu?" He must be teasing.

Joseph didn't grin. "That's right. The flu sweeps through, makes an impact, then sweeps out again. A lot of the time, it leaves heartache in its wake."

She bit the corner of her lip, battling tears. She'd never know which was worse—mourning the loss of her brothers or witnessing her parents' sorrow at their absence.

He let go of the tray and brushed his knuckles along Ava's cheek. "I don't want to see you heartbroken again, Ava. Be careful. Will you?"

She turned her back on him and stomped to Mr. Willems's front door. She put the tray on the porch floor and started to knock, but Joseph reached past her and rapped his knuckles on the doorjamb. She gave him a smoldering glare. "What are you doing?"

"Remember I said I needed to stop by here? I told Gil I'd take Mr. Willems's tuba to McPherson. To get it repaired." He winked. "You're not the only one who does nice deeds, Ava."

"Come in," Mr. Willems called from inside.

Joseph turned the knob and gestured her in. Mr. Willems was sitting sideways on his settee with the round-bellied cat curled in his lap. She told him about the cookies and put them on the dry sink as he instructed. She couldn't help noticing the dirty dishes and a pot of something that smelled savory still on the stove. She shook her head. Gil needed help keeping up with things over here. She'd talk to Mama and Papa about it. But she wouldn't offer to help. If what Joseph said was true about everyone thinking she brought cookies to the practices to please Gil, her assistance would only add fuel to the gossip fire. She would stomp that fire out.

And never, ever again would she let Joseph Baty give her a ride home, no matter how much her feet hurt.

Gil

GIL LOCKED THE door, dropped the key in his pocket, then turned to Timmy. He hid a grin. The boy still wore a few molasses cookie crumbs on his upper lip. Had he blown any into the tuba? He should teach Timmy how to clean the horn. But not tonight.

"Jo, well, are you ready to go?"

"I guess so." The boy heaved a man-sized sigh. "Mr. Baty, can I tell you something?"

Gil nodded, although he wasn't sure he should offer such an open invitation. The boy might tell him something his Taunte preferred remained private.

"I wish Friday came right after Monday."

The comment was so unexpected, Gil laughed. He sobered quickly, though, when Timmy's face clouded. Gil put his hands on his knees and peered into Timmy's eyes. "Why do you want Friday to follow Monday?"

"Because . . ." For a moment, the boy's chin quivered. "Because then I'd get to come back tomorrow for another practice." A wobbly grin appeared. "I like the band, Mr. Baty. I like the band better than anything else, ever."

Gil used his handkerchief and swished the remaining crumbs from Timmy's mouth. "Even better than Miss Flaming's cookies?"

Now the child laughed, brightening Gil's spirits. "They go together, don't they? Band practice and Miss Flaming's cookies."

They go together . . . The way he and Ava had once gone together. Gil pushed the thought aside. "I suppose they do. Now, come along. We need to get you home before it gets dark."

He took the tuba, as he'd done the previous times he walked Timmy home. Although the boy had jabbered nonstop before practice, he now seemed out of words. Gil wondered if he should ask Timmy about spending some time each day with Mr. Willems, practicing the tuba and fetching things for him. But he decided it was better to wait. To first ask Roald if he was willing to have the boy come around, and then ask Timmy's aunt if she minded. He sensed she would jump at the chance to get Timmy out from under her feet for a few hours every day, but he still needed to ask.

The short walk to Dirks Café was pleasant as dusk fell and fireflies began making their appearance in the patches of grass between buildings. After his years of being in the always-awake city where electric lights erased the appearance of stars, the gentle whisper of wind and the endless expanse of star-sprinkled sky were like a soothing balm on his soul. Even though taking this detour with Timmy meant a later return to Roald's, where chores still awaited him, he wouldn't send the boy alone. These were good minutes. Healing minutes.

They reached the café's false front, and Timmy held out his arms for the tuba. "Thanks for walking me back, Mr. Baty."

"I'll carry the tuba inside for you."

He shook his head. "No need. I have to put it in the shed before I go in."

Gil looked into the child's bereft face, and something he didn't expect to say spilled from his lips. "If you aren't doing anything tomorrow, and if your aunt says it's all right, would you like to ride the mail delivery wagon with me?"

Timmy's eyes bugged. "Ride the wagon with you? All day?"

Gil chuckled. "Well, not all day, but a good portion of it. I leave by nine o'clock every morning and get back to town around four. If your aunt approves, you can meet me at the post office before nine and ride along on the route."

Timmy bounced in place. "She'll say yes. I know she will." He started walking backward, smile bright and tuba wrapped tight in his arms. "Thanks, Mr. Baty! I'll see you tomorrow."

Gil waved goodbye, then headed for Roald's. He picked up his pace. He'd dawdled getting Timmy home, but now he needed to hurry and wash up the dishes before he went to bed.

He entered the house and found Roald on the settee, where he'd left him almost two hours ago. The man looked up and grinned. "There you are. I've got some surprises for you."

"Oh? What's that?" Gil kicked off his shoes and left them on a small rug beside the door.

Roald pointed through the wide kitchen doorway to the dry sink. "Ava Flaming brought some cookies by here. Said she saved them for us."

Warmth flooded Gil. She'd promised to save him treats, and she'd done so each week. When she left without giving him any this evening, he thought she'd gotten caught up with Joseph and forgotten. It made him happier than he could explain to know she hadn't. He went to the dry sink, flopped the napkin open, and took a bite of a cookie. "Mmm . . ." He spoke around the bite. "This is a pleasant surprise."

"There's more," Roald said.

Gil raised his eyebrows. "More cookies?"

"More surprises." Roald folded his arms, his expression smug. "Take a gander at the blanket beside the stove."

Gil popped the last of the cookie into his mouth and crossed to the stove. The calico cat lay curled on the blanket, busily licking . . . something. Gil jerked back and peeked out the doorway at Roald. "Did she have her kittens?"

Roald nodded, his grin wide. "But she's just started. There's only two so far."

An uneasy thought trickled through Gil's mind. "Have you been in here watching her?"

Roald made a face. "Now, Gil, how could I leave her alone for something like that? I was careful, used my crutches, and sat on a chair instead of the floor so I could get up again. I came back in here after the second one was born because my leg was hurting. You'll be able to keep an eye on her now, make sure she's all right while she delivers the others."

Gil hadn't planned on helping a cat deliver kittens this evening. Then Roald's statement sunk in. He looked back and forth from the cat to Roald. "How do you know there are others?"

"This isn't her first litter. She's been a mama three other times, and every time she has five. In every batch, there's always one that looks like her. But it isn't born yet. The two there already are gray tiger-striped."

Gil crouched next to the blanket and peeked at the tiny, rat-looking creatures splayed on the blanket. The mama cat kept its wary eyes on Gil and growled while she continued to bathe her babies. Gil backed away. "I don't think she wants me watching, Roald."

The man snickered. "You don't have to be so close. But I'd feel a lot better if we stayed awake until all the babies are born. Just in case."

Gil hoped there wouldn't be a "just in case" situation. He had no idea how to help a mother cat. He stood, returned to the sitting room, and sat at the other end of the settee. "How much work is it, having kittens in the house?"

Roald blasted a laugh. "None. Until they're big enough to walk around. Then they're into everything. Cats are naturally curious, and they like to explore. It will take some doing, keeping them corralled and out of mischief."

"How are you going to keep them corralled when I'm gone most of the day and you're supposed to be bedbound?"

Roald chewed his lower lip, his brow puckering. "Well . . . I'm not sure how."

Gil smiled. "It's all right, Roald. I think I have an idea. Do you know Timmy Dirks?"

Chapter Sixteen

Joseph

JOSEPH HELPED THE MAN WHO'D ORDERED THE cupboard carry the piece into the house and set it up in the corner of the kitchen. The wife followed close behind them, hands clasped at her throat, her smile broad. When they had the cupboard in place, the man stepped back, looked it up and down, and nodded.

"That is a fine piece of craftsmanship," he said. "Very fine." He opened his arm, and his wife stepped close to him. "What do you think, Edna? Do you like your gift?"

"Ohhhh . . ." The woman trilled the syllable. "It's wonderful, Hubert. Just wonderful."

The man extended his free hand to Joseph, and they exchanged a firm handshake. "Thank you, Mr. Baty. I'm very pleased with my purchase."

"Very, very pleased," the wife added.

Joseph puffed up at being called Mr. Baty, a title usually given to Pa. "You're welcome, sir. I'll get out of your way now so your wife can make use of her new cupboard." Before he left, he gave the richly stained oak one more lingering look. The man was right. From its decorative crown molding to its bun feet with hidden wheels, it was a fine piece of craftsmanship. The cupboard would hold up to this family's use and be available for another generation. Or more. Build things that will last, Pa always said.

As Joseph climbed up on the wagon seat, he glanced into the bed at Roald Willems's damaged tuba. The poor thing had taken quite a beating when it bounced down the concrete stairs. He hoped the silversmith was as good a craftsman with brass as he and Pa were with wood. He flicked the reins and aimed the horses for the main street of town.

Although the shop was only a narrow building between two large department stores, he located it fairly quickly and parked nearby. He grabbed the tuba by its dented loops and tucked it under his arm, then strode into the shop. A bell attached to the door clanged, and moments later a silver-haired man with a stained apron over his clothes emerged from the curtained opening behind the tall counter. The man's eyes went directly to the tuba.

"Is this the tuba I got a telephone call about this morning?"

Joseph didn't know anything about a telephone call, but how many people would call about a damaged tuba? It had to have been Gil. Still, he should be sure. "Did the call come from Falke?"

"It did. A fellow named Baty said it would arrive today."

Then it was Gil, probably calling from the post office. No one in town had telephones in their houses. "This is the one, then."

The man patted the counter's smooth wood top. "Set that right up here, young fellow, and let me take a look at it." He muttered to himself as he examined the horn from bell to mouthpiece, his thick gray eyebrows pinched together in concentration. When he finished, he straightened and gave Joseph a serious look. "Are you the Baty who called?"

"I am a Baty—Joseph Baty—but the one who called is Gil

Baty, the director for the men's and boys' bands in Falke. I'm his cousin."

"Well, the Baty who called asked for a written estimate for repairs. Can I send it with you?"

Joseph shrugged. "Jo. Er, yes."

The silversmith took a pencil and pad of paper from a little drawer. He scratched several lines of print on the page and pulled it free of the pad. Then, he folded the page and handed it to Joseph. "I'll need at least a week, but when I'm done, this horn will look brand new."

The shelves of the shop were filled with plates, bowls, pieces of cutlery, decorative lidded boxes, and every shape of cup imaginable. From the looks of the items, this man knew his trade. Joseph didn't doubt his promise. He slipped the note into his shirt pocket. "I will let my cousin know. Thank you, sir."

The man started to pick up the horn, then paused. "You said your cousin is the band director in Falke?"

"That's right." Should he also mention that Gil had only been the director for three weeks and would leave the position at the end of the summer? Before he decided, the man spoke again.

"He should come to the county's End of Harvest celebration on August 19." The silversmith plucked a printed flier from a tray on the corner of the counter. "It'll be quite a day. A parade, lots of good food, pony rides for kids . . . and a farmer from Galva plans to bring his gasoline-powered tractor to town for folks to take a gander at."

Joseph knew about the annual End of Harvest celebration, but he'd never attended one. Pa was always too busy working to take the family all the way to McPherson for a day of frivol- ity. He couldn't understand why the man thought Gil would be interested, but he took the flier to be polite. He glanced at it, and a single line, *Band Competition—Prizes!,* near the middle of the page caught his attention. He tapped the word *competition.* "What's this about?"

"Isn't that something? It's brand-new this year. Now, having bands play, that's nothing new. Bands have played at the End of Harvest celebrations for years already. But this year there'll be judges here from Topeka, sent by Governor Hoch himself." The man offered a solemn nod. "This is why the Falke band should come. Seems the governor's wanting to have a big hullabaloo in January to celebrate Kansas's forty-fifth birthday, and he's on the lookout for one special band to play on the capitol steps."

Joseph gaped at him. "In January? They'll freeze their fingers off."

The man laughed. "I can't argue with you there, but that's what I heard. After the bands play, the judges will give first-, second-, and third-place prizes. Cash prizes, I hear." He leaned forward slightly, his eyes sparkling. "These judges will go all over the state, to county fairs and such, and all the first-place bands will then compete to play at the capitol. The one that gets picked overall will have its expenses paid for travel to Topeka."

Joseph stared at the flier. The Falke band was good. Especially with Gil directing it. Did they stand a chance to play for the governor?

"Be sure and tell your cousin to bring his boys' band over for the competition. The more bands involved, the better."

Joseph shot the man a startled look. "Boys' band?"

"Mm-hmm. It's a competition for the state's youth—to encourage them in music, the governor said. Or so I heard."

So it was only for boys' bands. Wouldn't Earl's confidence

soar to take part in such a competition? Then a worrisome thought intruded. "Um, is there an entrance fee?"

The man shook his head. "No fee, but registration closes June 16."

Joseph sagged with relief. If there was a fee, the frugal community members might balk. For sure Ma would balk.

"Have him call or write to the county clerk." The silversmith flicked the sheet with his finger. "All the information is at the bottom of the flier."

Joseph rolled the paper into a tube and held it up the way Gil waved his baton. "I'll be sure and give this to Gil. Thanks for telling me about it."

"You're welcome. Have a good day now." The silversmith picked up the horn and disappeared behind the curtain.

Joseph returned to his wagon and headed for home. He couldn't stop thinking about the End of Harvest band competition and the possibility of the Falke boys' band taking part. They'd only gotten started. The chances of them winning were, as Pa would say, as likely as snow on the Fourth of July. But if they registered, they'd have something to work for. Gil would probably spend more time with them. Earl would like that. Joseph had never seen his brother so excited about anything before.

Then Ava's face flashed in his mind's eye. Despite Joseph's warnings, she would continue to seek Gil out. Continue to pine after him. Unless he was too busy to pay her any mind. Then she'd have to give up her futile pursuit. When Joseph gave Gil the flier, he'd encourage him to take the band to the competition. For Earl's sake, and for Timmy's, who needed all the encouragement he could get. And for Ava's sake. It was past time for her to let go of Gil.

Gil

GIL HAD BEEN surprised when Joseph showed up for the men's band practice. At break, his cousin cornered him and explained he'd left very early for McPherson so he could make it back in time for rehearsal that evening. It warmed Gil that he would make such an effort. Joseph also gave Gil the estimate from the silversmith and said he needed to talk to Gil after the practice was over. He said it was important.

Gil had a hard time keeping his focus on directing the men for the remainder of the evening. He hadn't unfolded the estimate yet, and he was worried about how much it would cost to fix the tuba. He also worried about what Joseph would tell him. After avoiding Gil, now Joseph was seeking him out. There must be a family emergency of some sort. Gil imagined all kinds of unpleasant possibilities as he fumbled through the rest of rehearsal.

When they were done, Joseph helped Gil put away the chairs. Gil waited for him to finally tell him what was so important, but he worked in silence. The tension between Gil's shoulders increased until a dull ache throbbed at the base of his skull. When he and Joseph finally walked down the stairs to the street, Gil slipped the estimate from his pocket and peeked at it.

He gasped and stopped in the small alcove at the street level. "Five dollars."

Joseph leaned forward and looked at the paper, too. He whistled through his teeth. "Whew. The silversmith said the tuba would be good as new when he was done, but that's a lot of money. You can buy a brand-new tuba for only twenty-five dollars in the latest Sears, Roebuck & Company catalog."

Gil scowled at his cousin. "If five dollars is hard to come by, where would I get twenty-five dollars?"

Joseph grinned. "Maybe you could win it."

Gil jammed the paper into his pocket. "Are you trying to get me kicked out of Falke? You know how folks around here feel about gambling. How many sermons has Reverend Ediger preached on the danger of seeking wealth through unscrupulous means?"

Joseph rolled his eyes. "I wasn't talking about gambling. Look—I wanted to talk to you about this." He pulled a flattened roll of paper from his back pocket and gave it to Gil. "Read the middle part, about the band competition."

A quick glance indicated there was very little written on the page. Joseph's obvious excitement intimated there was more involved, but Gil didn't have time to coax it all out of him. He'd left Timmy with Roald for the evening, and he needed to take the boy home—although he wondered whether his aunt would notice if the boy didn't return. She'd been awfully eager to send him with Gil that morning.

Gil gestured in the direction of Roald's house. "Timmy is at Roald's, waiting for me. If we're going to talk, we'll have to walk while we do it."

Joseph made a face, and for a moment Gil thought he would go the opposite direction. But he fell in step with Gil. "All right. Listen to what I found out when I was in McPherson."

Joseph told him about a special competition for youth bands at the End of Harvest celebration. Gil's chest fluttered in excitement when Joseph shared how judges would award cash prizes for the top three contenders.

"And the overall winning band will be invited to play for the governor at the capitol building. Think what a great opportunity it would be for the boys to participate," Joseph said in the most enthusiastic tone Gil had ever heard him use. "It wouldn't do you any harm, either. Those judges are important people, handpicked by Governor Hoch himself. If you compete, you could receive some real recognition as a conductor. Sure, it will take a lot of work to get the boys ready, but don't you think it would be worth it?"

They reached Roald's house, and Gil stopped at the end of the walkway leading to the porch. He frowned at Joseph, his thoughts racing. If he entered the boys and if they played one of his original pieces, they would surely stand out from the other bands. He could, as Joseph said, receive some beneficial recognition as both a conductor and a composer.

He looked at the flier again, and the date seemed to glare at him. He groaned. "It's coming up so quickly, Joseph. August 19 is only two and a half months away. The boys have only had a few practices. I'd have to work with them every day of the week to be ready for this kind of competition."

Joseph threw his arms wide. "So work with them every day."

"Have you forgotten? I conduct the men's band. I run a mail route every day." Except Friday, when he'd hoped to work on his new composition. Not that he'd had time for it yet. Every negative thought in his head found its way to his mouth. "I take care of Roald and his house and his pets—which are multiplying, by the way. Do you want a kitten?"

Joseph laughed and then spluttered something nonsensical.

Gil took the sound as a refusal. "Jo, well, neither do I, but I got some anyway. Five of them, to be exact. And I need to find a paying job if I'm going to get Roald's tuba back from the silversmith. Not to mention earning train fare so I can return to New York."

"Maybe the cash prize will be enough to pay for a ticket." Joseph blurted the comment.

Gil fell silent for a few minutes. The flier didn't indicate how much the prizes were, but if the governor was involved, it might be a goodly amount. But there was no guarantee the boys would win. Not with a newly formed band, with members averaging only twelve years of age. It was a fine idea, but not for this year. Not for this band. Not for Gil.

He hung his head. "I don't know, Joseph."

Joseph put his hand on Gil's shoulder. "Don't say no right away. Think about it. Tomorrow is Wednesday, and folks will be together for the weekly Bible study at church. You can bring it up as a prayer request. The preacher and some of the others might have good advice for you." He gave Gil's shoulder a little shake. "Where is that cousin of mine who never backs down from a challenge? Who always comes out on top? Did he get lost in New York?"

Gil detected a slight note of sarcasm in Joseph's queries, but they got his attention. He stood straight and met his cousin's gaze. "I'm still here. A little battered from so many defeats in the past few years, but still trying. I'll do what you said—think about it—and I'll pray about it, too." He wasn't sure he'd bring it up at the Bible meeting, though.

Joseph squeezed his shoulder and let go. "Good. But remember, you have to register by June 16 or the boys won't be included."

June 16 . . . ten days away. He gritted his teeth. "I'll remember."

Chapter Seventeen

Ava

MIDAFTERNOON ON WEDNESDAY, WHILE AVA WAS shelling peas for supper, someone knocked on the door. Papa was still at the post office and Mama was napping, so she quickly shifted the bowl from her lap and went to the door. One of the Schneider boys—Donnie, maybe?—stood on the porch.

Ava opened the screen door and smiled at him. "*Goot no meddach.* May I help you?"

"Good afternoon." The boy dug his bare toe against the porch board. "Ma sent me over. She is supposed to take a meal to Mr. Willems and Mr. Baty this evening, but the cows got out and trampled her garden, and she took to her bed with a sick headache."

"My goodness," Ava said, hoping she sounded concerned rather than amused. The situation itself wasn't funny—women's gardens kept their families fed—but the boy's somber recital had painted comical pictures in her imagination. "What of you and your brothers and sisters? Will you get supper tonight?"

"My sisters are fixing something, but Ma said she couldn't send any to Mr. Willems and Mr. Baty." He crinkled his face. "My sisters don't cook very good yet."

Ava suddenly wondered why Mrs. Schneider had sent the

boy to her house. "Did your mother say what she wanted me to do?" If he'd been sent here because people in town presumed she was Gil's caretaker, she might—

"She remembered on the calendar how your ma took all the Saturdays, but she didn't know who else took what days. So she sent me here."

Relief flooded Ava. The explanation made sense and eased her worry.

"She said if your ma could take supper to them tonight," the boy went on, "she'll trade her for Saturday."

On Wednesdays, because she and her folks went to the Bible meeting at church, she generally prepared something simple, much less elaborate than a meal meant for company. It was too late to change the menu now, but she could stretch the creamed peas, boiled potatoes, and fried ham enough to feed two more. "Please tell your mother that's fine. And I hope she feels better soon."

"Dank," he said, and darted off.

Ava closed the door and turned. Mama stood in the hallway. Their voices must have wakened her. "Did you hear?"

"That Rosella is trading nights? Jo." She yawned. "If you're cooking for two more, you'll need some help. What can I do?"

Ava let Mama shell the peas while she peeled and cut up potatoes. Mama hummed while she worked, and Ava couldn't help smiling. It was nice having company. The preparations went faster with four hands instead of two, and the food was ready before four o'clock. Ava filled two plates, covered them with inverted cake pans, and put them on her cookie tray. "I'll take these over to Roald now. Then they can eat when Gil gets back from his route."

"Make sure his stove has heat so the food stays warm." Mama's practical advice followed Ava out the door.

She reached Roald's house, and to her consternation, Gil pulled up in the delivery wagon at the same time and gave her a cheerful wave. She inwardly groaned. She'd hoped to be gone before he returned from the route. Joseph's comment about the townsfolk presuming she was doing kindnesses to gain Gil's attention rolled in the back of her mind. She didn't want to give people more fuel for gossip. Now that he'd seen her, she had no choice but to address him. But she would keep the exchange short.

He jumped down and strode across the yard to her, his hands reaching. "Here, let me take that."

She relinquished the tray. "Thank you. It's your supper." She turned toward her house.

"Hmm." His puzzled tone prompted her to reverse direction. "I thought Mrs. Schneider was on the calendar for this evening."

"She was." Ava briefly explained the conflict. "She'll come on Saturday instead."

"I see," he said. Then his expression turned mischievous. "When your father brings over supper, he stays and eats with Roald and me. Then he has a trumpet lesson. Do you want to come eat with us and then play some notes?"

Oh! His dancing eyes and twitching grin . . . so beguiling. She bit the tip of her tongue to keep from giggling. She shook her head.

"You'll get to see the kittens." His tone turned wheedling, and mischief continued to sparkle in his dark brown eyes. "The calico cat had five babies on Monday. One is pure white, and Roald said it will probably have blue eyes. Like the cat you had when you were younger."

He remembered her childhood cat? How she'd adored Princess, her snow-white kitty with the crystal blue eyes and a purr that vibrated her mattress like the train's wheels vibrated the ground. She'd cried for days when the kitty died. Papa buried her beneath a pink peony bush, and to this day, when she passed the bush, she thought about her beloved pet.

Gil waggled his eyebrows. "Come on, Ava. I know you like kittens."

Temptation tugged hard. But so many duties awaited her at home. She needed to set the table, fry more ham for Mama, Papa, and her, and then change her clothes for service. She didn't have time to peek at kittens. Besides, hadn't she told herself she needed to avoid contact with him? If someone saw her entering Roald's house with Gil, the tongues would wag.

"If you're worried about impropriety, don't be. Roald and Timmy are here. So we won't be alone."

Timmy? She grimaced. "I didn't realize Timmy was here. I only prepared two plates."

Gil shrugged. "It's fine. I'll share with him." He took a sideways step toward the house, raising one eyebrow. "Are you sure you don't want to peek at the kittens?"

She really should go home. But she heard herself say, "All right."

She couldn't be certain who was more surprised she agreed, him or herself, but the delight in Gil's expression made her happy she'd conceded. She followed him across the yard and entered the house. Roald was on the far end of the settee, Timmy at the opposite end, and a checkerboard rested on the cushion between them. The pair glanced up, greeted Ava with smiles, then returned their attention to the game.

Gil set the tray of food on the table and gestured to the box next to the stove. "There they are. Take a look."

She crossed to the box and crouched, gripping her hands against her stomach so she wouldn't reach in and frighten the mother. Gazing down at the little brood, her heart rolled over. Ach, they were so sweet—a calico, two tabbies, and two white babies, one of which had rusty tips on its ears. So tiny and helpless yet securely nestled in a heap with their mama. Desire to cradle one of the kittens beneath her chin nearly over-whelmed her. How she wanted to hold one of the babies. How she wanted to hold her own baby.

She shouldn't have come. She bolted upright and scurried away from the box, still pressing her hands against her waist. "Thank you for letting me see them. When they open their eyes, please let me know if the pure white one's eyes are blue."

"I will." Gil's forehead scrunched. "Are you all right?"

She wasn't, but she would be as soon as she was home. Away from the man on whom she'd once pinned her hopes and dreams for a family. She moved on shaky legs to the door. "Set the tray of dishes on the porch when you're finished. Papa will retrieve them later. Good evening, everyone."

"Thank you for supper," Mr. Willems called as she dashed out the door.

Ava hurried home, scolding herself the whole way. She must get her foolish heart into alignment with her head. But how, when every encounter with Gil took her backward in time? His simple mention of Princess reminded her how much they'd once shared. They'd bonded over great loss—his parents and her brothers—and grown together from best friends to devoted sweethearts. He was woven into her life's tapestry, and she couldn't pull those threads without unraveling who she was. But their relationship ended four years ago. The reasons for their separation were still in place. She had to weave a new life without him.

She paused at the base of her porch stairs and stared at the pair of chairs where she and Gil had spent so many summer evenings, sometimes talking, sometimes stargazing, sometimes lost in each other's eyes. She murmured, "That was then. Then is over." Truth. Yet her feelings for him were still trapped in "then." When would Mama's prayers finally be answered and give Ava peace?

Maybe she should find her own peace instead of waiting on God, who might never answer. She had two options for the rest of her life. She could accept Miss Dirks's offer to sell her the café or accept Joseph's attentions. If she was truthful with herself, even if she was capable of running a café, she'd rather cook and bake for her own family than for customers. Which made Joseph's bid to become her beau the preferred option. She stood very still, seeking her heart for its response. Only unsettledness nibbled at her. She released a little huff. Now was not the time for deep contemplation. She had work to do. She trudged up the steps and entered the house.

When Papa arrived a few minutes past five, Ava had supper hot and ready to serve. She and her parents sat around the little table in the kitchen and ate. Mama picked at her food so much that Papa finally asked if she was ill.

Mama offered a weary smile. "Not ill. A little tired. That's all."

"Well, then," Papa said, "you should stay home this evening and rest."

Mama sighed. "I hate to miss Bible study."

"There will be other Bible studies." Papa's tone turned firm. "I'll stay with you, and Ava can share the scriptures with us later."

Ava cringed. She hated attending service without her parents, sitting alone while families surrounded her. "I'll stay home, too."

"Nä. How would it look, the whole Flaming family not showing up? You prepare to go, Ava. I'll take care of cleaning up our dishes after I hitch the horse to the carriage for you." He rose and then bent and placed a kiss on Mama's temple. "Go lie down now." He strode out of the kitchen.

Ava changed into a fresh dress and entered the barn as Papa was returning to the house. He gave her a hug and reminded her to take care on the drive, as he always did when she set out. Still holding her to his chest, he said, "I know you'd rather not go by yourself. Why not ask Gil to ride with you? He's been taking the delivery wagon to the church, but there's no sense in that. There's plenty of room in our carriage for him."

Ava wriggled loose and gawked at her father. "If Gil and I come riding into the churchyard together, what will people think?"

"They'll think Gil needed a ride." He stepped around her and headed for the door. "Now go. Hurry, before he has his horse hitched up again. The beast has already put in a day's work. It needs rest, too."

Ava blew out a breath of irritation. She considered disobeying Papa and driving straight to the church. But the long-ingrained teaching to honor her father and mother stomped the notion. She climbed up into the carriage, hoping Gil would already be gone.

Let him be gone already.

Not really a prayer. More a command. But it was all she could muster. She drove the carriage around the barn to the street and turned toward Mr. Willems's house. Up ahead, the delivery wagon with Mr. Willems's horse lazing in its traces waited at the edge of the street. Ava sent a brief frown skyward. Why did God never listen to her?

She stopped her carriage and carefully climbed over the side, holding her skirts. As her feet met the ground, Mr. Willems's door opened and Timmy Dirks burst out, followed by Gil.

The boy raced up to her, all smiles. "Good evening, Miss Flaming. Thank you for supper. It was real good. Even the peas. I don't usually like peas, but I mixed them with the potatoes and liked them a whole lot better. Did you come back with dessert?"

Gil lightly gripped the back of the boy's neck. "Timmy, where are your manners? You don't beg for desserts." Gil made a show of looking at Ava's empty hands. "Especially when it's obvious she forgot."

Ava's face flamed. Teasing again! He'd always been able to coax her from her occasional sour moods during her teen years. She slammed the door on the memories. "I didn't forget. There are no band practices and the café is closed on Wednesdays, so I don't bake on Wednesdays." She tried to sound tart, but her traitorous voice emerged on a note of amusement. She cleared her throat. "Papa sent me to see if you'd like a ride to the church, since I'm going alone. Mama is under the weather, and Papa is staying with her."

"It's nothing serious, is it?"

His genuine concern once again stirred embers of affection in her chest. She shook her head, attempting to extinguish the spark. "She's only tired."

"That's good." Gil scratched his chin. "Going together makes sense, and taking your carriage instead of the delivery wagon will give the three of us more room. I'll need to unhitch Roald's horse first. Do you mind waiting?"

She preferred to use the time waiting as an excuse to leave

without him. "Not at all." She inwardly groaned. Her tongue seemed to have developed a mind of its own.

Gil jogged to the horse and grabbed its halter. "Come on, Blossom. Let's get you into the barn for the night."

Ava held her hand to Timmy. "Come with me, Timmy, and we'll wait for Mr. Baty in the carriage." Having the boy with them was a blessing. Although young, he could be considered a chaperone of sorts. People wouldn't presume she and Gil had been up to any kind of wooing if Timmy was with them. She'd have him sit in the front seat between them.

Gil returned more quickly than she'd expected and climbed up on the other side of the carriage. He sent her a grin. "Want me to drive?"

Ava kept hold of the reins. "Pansy's used to me. I'll drive."

"Good." He propped one foot on the front board, pushed his hat forward over his eyes, and slouched into the seat. "I'll take a little nap on the way. I hardly have time to sleep these days."

He didn't have an opportunity to sleep on the drive. Timmy talked nonstop, telling Ava about his day with Mr. Willems—about fetching his crutches, bringing him water, petting the cats . . . He described every detail of every little thing, pride shining on his face.

Generally Ava preferred listening to the sounds of the prairie when she was able to drive out of town, but she didn't have the heart to shush the child. Although she did wonder why he'd spent the day with Mr. Willems. If he ever took a breath, she would ask. He didn't give her the opportunity. He was still jabbering as she rolled onto the churchyard and gave the reins a gentle pull. "Whoa, Pansy."

Timmy sighed. "I'd better go sit with Taunte. Otherwise

she's all alone." He clambered over Gil and jumped down, then waved. "Thank you for the ride, Miss Flaming. I hope the next time I see you, you'll have cookies." He dashed off.

Gil watched him go, a fond smile on his face. "He's quite a boy."

"You're quite the saint for spending so much time with him." She covered her ears for a moment, grinning. "He can wear out one's listeners."

Gil laughed. "Yes, but it's worth it to see him so happy. I was worried at first, about spending extra time with him. Joseph told me not to let the boys get dependent on me since I'll be leaving before long. But now that Timmy and Roald have formed a friendship, I won't have to worry. Roald will be here for him after I've returned to New York."

Her tender feelings faded with the reminder that he would leave again. Why did she let herself get drawn in by him? She should have refused to offer Gil a ride to church. She should have dug in her heels and told Papa she would go by herself. Joseph was right when he warned her that being with Gil would lead to nothing but heartache. And she would not allow herself to be cast aside again.

She set the brake and wrapped the reins around it, her motions jerky. "Let's go in. We're late."

Chapter Eighteen

Joseph

AS THE CONGREGATION STOOD FOR THE OPENING hymn, Joseph caught movement out of the corner of his eye. He craned his head around. Gil and Ava, entering the church building. Together.

He pulled in a startled breath and held it. He stared at the door, waiting for Mr. and Mrs. Flaming to come in, too, but they didn't. He shifted his gaze to Ava and Gil. They took the same pew near the back, but Ava went to the middle, and Gil stayed on the end. Joseph's breath escaped. They'd arrived at the same time, but there was space enough between them for two people. Maybe they hadn't really driven out together.

He leaned down to Earl and whispered, "Let's go sit with Gil. He's by himself. Tell Ma."

Earl cupped his hand beside Ma's ear. Ma sent a quick frown at him and Joseph, but she didn't shake her head no. Joseph put his hymnbook in its tray and led Earl along the outside aisle to Gil's side of the pew. He tapped Gil's arm and pointed to the open space between him and Ava. For a moment he worried Gil would just move close to Ava, but he stepped into the aisle. Earl went in first, then Joseph followed.

As he joined his voice with the singers, he silently congratulated himself. He'd rather be the one sitting next to Ava, but having Earl between them looked better to others in church. This spot put him closer to the aisle, too, so he could get out and talk about the End of Harvest celebration if Gil didn't mention it during the prayer requests.

Joseph sang every verse of the hymns, and he followed along in his Bible while Reverend Ediger shared scriptures and expounded on each passage. But he couldn't honestly say he was paying attention. His mind was set on the end of the meeting, when the preacher would ask if there were prayer needs to bring before the body of Christ. He would wait a bit, give Gil the chance to mention the competition. After all, Gil was the boys' leader, so he should be the one to mention the opportunity. If he did, Joseph would go up with him in a show of support. If he didn't, Joseph would go up on his own.

He'd spent time that afternoon putting the words together in his head. He practiced them again silently while Reverend Ediger preached. His speech was so well thought out, so encouraging and heartfelt, he almost hoped Gil wouldn't stand so he could present it. Ava would surely be impressed. Back when she, Gil, and Joseph ran as a lopsided trio—her and Gil always siding against him—she would sometimes scold him for criticizing his cousin. She'd hear no criticism tonight. Only praises. Praises with the potential to start a series of events that would propel Gil back to New York City and keep him there.

Earl wriggled on the seat beside him, giving him a gentle bump on the arm. Unexpectedly, Joseph's chest panged. Gil's departure hopefully would help his relationship with Ava prosper, but it would hurt Earl. Ma complained that his brother had even taken to sleeping with Gil's old trumpet, he enjoyed the band so much. Would someone else take over the boys' band when Gil left? If they did well at the competition, someone from the community would surely say "Let's keep it going" and volunteer to direct it. Joseph pushed aside the worry about Earl. He'd get to keep playing the trumpet. But, oddly, the little pang in the center of his chest didn't go away.

"Let us take to heart what we have heard tonight from the Word of God." The preacher closed his Bible, the signal that study time was done. He sent his gaze across the congregation. "Before we begin our prayer time, are there new requests?"

People stood, one by one, and shared their burdens. Joseph sat poised, ready to leap up the moment Gil made a move. But Gil just sat there, hands clamped over his knees so hard his knuckles glowed white. Aggravation rolled through Joseph. What was wrong with him? Didn't he know how important this could be? He waited until the preacher said, "Jo, well, then let us—"

Joseph bolted to his feet. "There is one more request, Reverend Ediger. May I come up there? I have an important announcement that affects our boys' band."

The minister stepped away from the podium. "Come right on up, Joseph."

Gil

GIL SWIPED AT his cousin's sleeve as he stepped past him, but his quivering hand missed. He bit back a groan. If he'd arrived a little earlier, he would have had a chance to tell Joseph he wanted to wait a week to talk to the congregation about the competition. A week would have given him time to talk to the representative in McPherson, examine his schedule, find a place to carve out more time for the boys' band, and truly ruminate over whether it was the right thing to do. But there was Joseph, charging up the aisle, and soon the entire town of

Falke would be abuzz. Again. If they weren't in a church, he'd run up and tackle him.

Joseph gave a lithe leap up onto the dais and stepped behind the pulpit with as much ease as someone who spoke publicly every day of the week. Gil couldn't help but be surprised. And impressed.

"Folks, I made a delivery to McPherson yesterday, and while I was there, I found out about a unique opportunity for our boys' band. At the End of Harvest celebration, some representatives sent by Governor Hoch himself will judge boys' bands and choose first-, second-, and third-place winners." He went on to tell about a single band being selected to travel to Topeka and play for the governor at the state capitol building.

As he spoke, murmurs rumbled from various areas of the sanctuary. But what did the murmurs mean? Gil glanced across the gathered parishioners, trying to read their interest. Or lack of interest. Mennonites generally weren't competitive. Some chose not to involve themselves with governmental affairs at all and probably weren't even aware of the new governor's name. If they resisted having their boys play in a competition, the decision would be taken from his hands. He couldn't decide if he preferred having it eliminated or thrust on him.

"As you know, our boys' band is newly formed. But they have great leadership. Gil Baty is a tal—nä, I won't say talented. I will say he is a composer and conductor who is musically gifted. And every good and perfect gift comes from God."

A few people turned and peeked at Gil, and his face grew so hot he feared his hair would catch fire. As much as it pleased him to hear his cousin speak such affirmation, he wished Joseph had chosen to talk to him first about making the announcement. He didn't know what to do or where to look. So he stared at Joseph and tried to pretend his cousin was talking about someone else.

"The men who play in the men's band and any boys who are in the boys' band will tell you I'm speaking the truth."

More murmurs holding notes of approval.

Joseph went on. "If anyone can get the boys ready for such an opportunity, it's Gil. But there are conflicts." His expression serious, he listed everything Gil was doing, from delivering the mail to leading the bands to caring for Roald's pets and seeing to Roald's many needs.

Gil's head spun. He couldn't possibly get these boys ready for a competition. If he took them there, they'd fail. He'd already failed in New York. How would he hold his head up at all if the people from his church also saw him as a failure? He should stand up right now and tell everyone it was a foolish idea.

Joseph gripped the podium and leaned forward slightly, the way Reverend Ediger did when he was making an important point. "I'm asking you to pray for Gil. If the band is going to compete, he needs to register by June 16, and he needs to have the boys ready to play by August 19." He chuckled, raising his shoulders in a shrug. "That isn't a lot of time by the calendar, but I think it might be enough for someone like Gil Baty to make it happen, if he has prayer support and maybe some help with his other duties. Thank you."

Joseph left the dais and returned to his seat. He slid in next to Gil and gave him a wink as he sat. Gil's lips quirked into a tight smile he wasn't sure was meant to be a thank-you or a threat to get him later.

"Thank you for telling us about this opportunity, Joseph," Reverend Ediger said as he returned to his place behind the podium. "This is a big decision with potential consequences not only for Gil but for our boys. How would a win—or even a loss—affect them?"

The question rattled Gil. He liked the boys from the band. They were good boys, dedicated and respectful. They enjoyed playing their instruments. Would a win change them from humble to prideful? Would losing make them never want to play their horns again? There was so much to ponder and so little time to do it.

"Perhaps the parents of boys in the band would like to meet with Gil at the back of the church," the reverend went on, "and pray with him. Pray over him. It could be that God brought Gil back to Falke this summer for such a time as this."

Chapter Nineteen

Ava

ON THE DRIVE BACK TO TOWN, AVA AND GIL RE-mained silent on opposite ends of the carriage's front seat. Timmy had gone home with his aunt, and now she missed his bright chatter. Although the late evening offered its usual song of wind, birds, and insects and—from a distance—the mournful howl of a coyote, the absence of voices after hearing so many of them lifted together in song and prayer left her melancholy.

What was Gil thinking about as he sat quiet and still beside her? The heartfelt prayers that had been offered on his behalf, perhaps? They continued to roll in her mind. What a joy and blessing to witness people encouraging this hometown boy who'd left to make his mark on the music world. Joseph's glowing report of Gil's abilities had surprised and pleased her, too. Maybe he was finally growing up, sloughing off his old resentment toward Gil. She hoped so.

The entire time Joseph sang Gil's praises from the podium of the church, she'd kept her gaze forward, steadfastly refusing to look at Gil. But with the familiar words from the story of Esther, *for such a time as this,* reverberating in her heart, she'd angled her face and looked at him. And found him looking at her. She'd immediately turned her focus forward again, but his expression—filled with both wonder and uncertainty—etched itself into her memory and played even now in her mind's eye.

God had a purpose in everything. Papa, Mama, the preacher . . . they'd all told her so at different times in her life. She wanted to believe it, because believing it would take the heartbreak away from so many things that confused her. If it was true, then God must have a purpose in bringing Gil back to Falke.

A smile tugged at the corners of her lips as she remembered so many people, including Gil's uncle, leaving their seats and surrounding Gil. Joseph and Earl left and went to their mother. Ava should have gone elsewhere, too. She didn't have a boy in the band, and she didn't belong there with those who did, but her legs refused to move. Despite her desire to remain emotionally distant from Gil, she'd wanted to be part of the group who prayed for him. Part of the ones who, as Reverend Ediger said, prayed *over* him.

So she'd prayed. Silently, from her spot a few feet away from Gil. And oh, it had felt so good to truly speak to God. Her heart fluttered. Maybe that pull to stay and pray was *for such a time as this.*

They reached the edge of town. Gil suddenly patted his trouser pocket, sat forward, then pointed ahead. "Please let me off at the bank building, Ava."

Such an odd request. "What do you want there?"

"Some quiet." He angled his head and gave her a weary half smile. "I don't know why I put the key in my pocket this morning. Habit, I suppose. But having it now will allow me to go into the band room while no one else is around. It's a good place for me to pray about what I should do, jo?" He sighed. "I might be there awhile . . ."

Ava nodded slowly. She slapped the reins, guiding Pansy to

turn north. "Won't Mr. Willems worry if you don't return as expected?"

He grimaced. "I hadn't thought about that."

Without hesitating, she said, "I'll stop at his place and tell him where you are."

"Thank you, Ava."

She nodded. At the bank, she pulled Pansy's reins and set the brake, then she turned to Gil. "I hope you'll find the answer you're seeking."

Gil's brows furrowed. "Me, too. And quickly." A frown creased his face. "I've learned that God often doesn't give immediate answers, but I don't have time to spare. Not if it's His will for the boys to play in the competition." He gripped the edge of the seat, and the lines in his forehead deepened. "I sense God leading me to enter the competition, Ava. But there's so much to contemplate. What song should the boys play? How will we fit in more practice time? How can I prepare them adequately to accept a win or a loss as God's will for them? I can't stop thinking about what Reverend Ediger said. Winning is grand, but it can make one full of himself. Losing hurts and can leave one discouraged. I don't want either result."

He released a soft laugh. "And instead of telling you all this, I should be talking to God. Forgive me, Ava. You always were so easy for me to talk to."

Heat flooded her face, and she hoped the twilight shadows hid her blush. "He is even easier to talk to," she said, surprised by her words. When had she last found conversation with God easy?

This evening.

When praying for Gil.

He leaped down, then gave the armrest a pat. "Thank you

163

for the ride, Ava, and for your prayers. I appreciate them very much." He trotted to the building, inserted his key in the lock, and opened the door. He entered and shut the door behind him without another glance in her direction.

She released the brake and flicked the reins, her heart fluttering. Back when they were courting, if he'd entered a building without acknowledging her with a wave or a blown kiss, she would have harbored hurt feelings. But tonight she recognized that his lack of attention only meant he was eager to spend time with God in prayer, and she found not even a smidgen of insult in his rush to leave her. Jo, she was changing.

Lamplight glowed behind the windows of Mr. Willems's house. She parked the carriage and climbed down, then followed the walkway to his porch. She tapped on the door. Moments later, his voice called, "Come in."

She cracked the door and peeked inside. He sat on the settee, where he'd been the last time she was here. "Mr. Willems? Gil asked me to let you know he is spending some time in the band practice room at the bank. He'll be back shortly. He didn't want you to worry."

The man shifted on the cushions, grimacing. "I hope he isn't too long. I need to visit the . . . er . . . room outside, but I don't know where Timmy left my crutches." A mirthless chuckle sounded. "I'm as helpless as a turtle on its back."

"Would you like me to look for the crutches?"

He waved his hand at her. "Nä. I'll wait for Gil. Thank you, Ava."

Ava returned to the carriage and drove to the back of her house. She'd barely led Pansy into her space when Papa entered the barn.

He marched to her side of the carriage and put his hands on

his hips. "Where have you been? The service should have ended over half an hour ago."

Ava winced. She hadn't done anything wrong, but it pained her to have worried her father. "The service went long. I'll explain why." She climbed down, then paused, Mr. Willems's predicament giving her concern. "Papa, Mr. Willems needs help getting to the outhouse. Could you go over?"

Papa's frame relaxed, but his frown remained in place. "Why isn't Gil over there?"

"I'll explain that later, too. Is Mama all right?"

"Jo, she is sleeping."

"Good." She moved to the horse's neck and reached for the rigging. "Go see to Mr. Willems. I'll take care of Pansy, then join you at Mr. Willems's place and tell you both about the Bible meeting. I think it's best for him to know, too."

Papa sent her a puzzled scowl, but he exited the barn through the side door. Ava released Pansy and gave the horse fresh hay and water, then she hurried to Mr. Willems's house.

When she stepped inside, Papa was sitting at the far end of the settee, and Mr. Willems's crutches leaned against the table beside him.

The man sent Ava a smile. "Here you are again. Your father says you have news to report from the meeting."

Ava sat in a straight-backed chair across from the settee. "Not news, necessarily, but a prayer request that involves Gil and . . . well, quite a few people in Falke." She repeated everything Joseph had said about the band competition at the End of Harvest celebration in McPherson. Then she shared how the parents of the boys had prayed for Gil to seek and follow God's will concerning the boys' participation. She started to tell them what Gil said about the pull he was feeling, but she decided he'd shared it with her in confidence. She shouldn't betray his trust. She finished, "Gil wanted a quiet, solitary place to pray. That's why he's at the bank building."

Papa and Mr. Willems had listened intently. Now they exchanged a glance, smiles on their faces.

"I hope he takes them," Papa said.

Mr. Willems's head bobbed up and down in an enthusiastic nod. "Me, too."

Ava drew back, startled by their responses. "You do? Why?"

"Competition builds teamwork and character." Papa spoke with certainty.

"It'll give the boys something to work toward—something to take pride in," Mr. Willems added.

"But isn't pride a boastful thing?" Ava had heard many sermons on the danger of self-pride.

Mr. Willems shook his head. "Nä, not always. Many people of Mennonite heritage have an inborn ability in music. Remember the story of the servants who were given talents? The ones who increased their talents for the master received praise. The one who buried his talent did not hear those wonderful words, 'Well done, thou good and faithful servant.' The boys should grow their talents, let them shine for the glory of the One who gave them." He wriggled a bit deeper into the back cushion. "Whatever works we do, if we do them for the glory of God, then the pride goes to Him. This is good."

Papa leaned forward and fixed Ava with a steady look. "Were the parents in support of taking the boys?"

She considered all the prayers she'd heard. "They really didn't say yes or no. They prayed for Gil to make the right decision, and they also prayed that somehow he would have the time needed to work with the boys. Right now he's"—she cast a grimace in Mr. Willems's direction—"a bit busy."

The man blasted a laugh, proving she hadn't offended him. "He's more than a bit busy. He's overwhelmed taking care of two bands, my house, my route, my pets, and my helpless hide." He smacked the top of his plaster cast and glared at it. "If I didn't have this thing tying me down, I could do the routes and Gil could spend every day working with those boys."

Papa shifted his gaze from Ava to the wooden crutches. "Roald, are you able to get around pretty well with those things?"

"I make it all over the house and yard on my own."

Papa tapped his bearded chin. "Then what if you and I swap jobs for the summer? You stay in the post office and see to customers. I'll take the mail routes. The train trades our outgoing and incoming mail on Friday," he went on in a musing tone, "when I could be in the office since there isn't a Friday route. What do you think?"

Ava caught herself nodding. It was a reasonable solution.

A smile lit Mr. Willems's face. "Why, that would give Gil the whole day to work with the boys if he wanted to."

Happiness ignited in Ava's chest. Clearly Papa and Mr. Willems wanted Gil to take the boys to McPherson. Of course, they didn't have sons in the band. Would the parents of the band members work so hard to find a way for the boys to practice for the competition?

"I think we should tell Gil our idea when he gets back," Mr. Willems said. "It will ease his mind to know the route is cared for."

Ava wasn't part of the mail-delivery solution, but she couldn't stay quiet. "Papa, Mr. Willems, it's good of you to explore ways to relieve some of Gil's responsibilities. But I think you're getting ahead of yourselves."

They both turned frowns on her.

"We don't know yet if Gil will choose to take the boys to McPherson. We don't know how many of the parents will approve their boys going." She disliked seeing their excitement dim, but the decision didn't belong to them. It was Gil's, as prompted by God. "It's a fine idea you've come up with, and if Dr. Graves says it won't be harmful to Mr. Willems, it's good to have it ready to share with Gil."

Mr. Willems huffed. "I wish that young man would get back here so we could talk to him. Find out what he's thinking. I like the idea of our boys going to McPherson, getting to play for judges, letting people see this little town of Russian immigrants has something worthwhile happening in it." He sighed. "Lots of folks look down at us. They call us Krauts and think we're *domm*. But if the boys played in the competition, it would show people they're just as smart and talented as anyone else."

"If they do well, it could," Ava said, thinking out loud.

Mr. Willems pointed at her. "I said *would*, not *could*. They'd do well. They already know how to play, and Gil knows how to teach them to play well together. I'd wager no other boys' band in the whole state has a conductor as talented and dedicated as our Gil."

Our Gil. Was he Ava's Gil, too?

"My opinion might not count because I don't have a son in the band." Mr. Willems face pinched as if a pain gripped him. "But if anyone asks, I'll tell them I think it's the right thing to do."

Ava gentled her voice. "But first, we must let Gil listen to God's leading about what is best for him and the boys, jo?"

The man stared at her for a few seconds, working his jaw back and forth. Then he sighed. "Jo." He frowned toward the door. "I wish he'd get back here. I'd like to know what he's thinking."

As if Mr. Willems's wish could make things come true, the doorknob turned and Gil entered the house. He came to a stop just inside the door and glanced across each of their faces, surprise registering in his eyes. "Onkel Bernard, Ava . . . what are you two doing here?"

Papa stood and put his hand on Gil's shoulder. "Plotting your future. Come. Sit. Let's talk."

Chapter Twenty

Joseph

JOSEPH SET HIS BATTERED COPY OF *THE THREE Musketeers* aside, rose, and stretched. The hands on the windup clock on his bureau showed it was almost nine o'clock. No wonder his neck was stiff. He'd been slouched in his bed reading for the better part of an hour. It was time for him to turn out his lamp and crawl under the covers.

He was glad he'd changed out of his Sunday clothes into a nightshirt when he returned from the Bible meeting at church, because he was almost too tired to do it now. He stood and groaned as he pulled back the rumpled quilt. All of his muscle stiffness wasn't from reading. He'd put in a hard day in the woodshop. Tomorrow wouldn't be any easier. He and Pa were filling an order for eight matching ladder-back chairs. The intricate work—turning the legs and giving the staves a gentle curve—wearied a man, but seeing the end result made it worth it.

He flopped onto the bed, and his shoulder landed on his book. With a grunt, he picked it up and reached to place it on the bedside table. But his hand stilled midway, and he stared at the title, memories sneaking from the far recesses of his mind. Onkel Ezra and Taunte Elizabeth, Gil's parents, had given him the book for his tenth birthday. He'd always loved to read, and the action-adventure novel about a young man determined to become a musketeer had kept him awake far past bedtime on many a night.

As much as he liked d'Artagnan, the hero of the story, he was most fascinated by the friendship between Aramis, Porthos, and Athos. How many times had he and Gil acted out scenes from the story, with him taking the role of Athos and Gil, Aramis? They always bemoaned being forced to imagine Porthos. By the time Earl was big enough to take the role, both Joseph and Gil had given up such pretend games. They were too busy competing in their pursuit of Ava.

With a sigh, he sat up and laid the book next to the lamp. As he leaned in to extinguish the wick, his door creaked open and Pa stepped in.

"Oh. I saw the light on, so I thought . . . I didn't know you were ready for bed."

Joseph swung his feet to the floor, gesturing to the book. "I've been reading. I'm not sleepy yet." He was, but he wouldn't embarrass himself by admitting it. "Did you need me for something?"

"Jo . . . ach . . . nä." Pa closed the door and crossed to the bed. He sat at the foot and smoothed his hand over the worn squares in the quilt. "But I wanted to ask you something."

His father's odd demeanor raised the fine hairs on the back of Joseph's neck. Something was wrong. "What is it?"

"All that you said tonight at church . . . about Gil . . ." He lifted his head and met Joseph's gaze. "Did you mean it?"

Unexpectedly, defensiveness swelled. Joseph bit back a snort. "I did."

Pa stared directly into his eyes, and Joseph sat unmoving, staring directly back. Finally Pa looked down again and released a little chuckle. "It surprised your mother and me. I've heard good things from men in the band. And Earl"—another chuckle—"cannot speak highly enough of your cousin."

Jealousy tried to take hold of him, but Joseph tamped it back. "Jo, well, Gil does a good job directing. He knows what he's doing. And I think the competition would be a worthwhile experience for Earl. He's never going to excel at sports, not like I did, but he's good at music. He should have the chance to do what he's good at, to be part of a team."

"Not going to the competition wouldn't mean he wasn't part of a team," Pa said, peeking at Joseph from the corners of his eyes. "The band would still play here in Falke."

Joseph nodded. "I agree. But most teams don't just play together. They play against other teams. When else will he have the experience of competing against another team?"

Pa fully faced Joseph. "Son, ever since Gil moved in with us, you and he competed against each other. On the sports field. In the school band. Even in getting good grades."

Joseph broke out in a sweat. Would Pa mention their competition for Ava? Gil might have won those other contests, but Joseph intended to be the victor in winning Ava's heart.

"All of a sudden, instead of being his rival, you seem to have joined his team." Pa's eyes narrowed. "What brought the change?"

"I . . ." Joseph swallowed. "He . . ." What could he say that would make sense? He blurted, "Earl. Earl likes him so much. Admires him so much. I guess it let me see him . . . differently than when we were boys."

"I'm glad." Pa clasped Joseph's shoulder. "I'm glad." He squeezed, then let go and stood. "I might need your help convincing your mother to let Earl go to McPherson if Gil decides to take the band. She was worried about having Earl play at all, but she agreed to it since it was only two evenings a week. If he has to practice every day and take a trip all the way to McPherson . . ." He shoved his hands into his trouser pockets and hung his head. "It might be too much worry for her to bear."

"Well, she needs to do what is right for Earl instead of what is right for herself this time." Conviction came through in his voice. He used more emphasis than he would if Ma were standing next to Pa. But maybe it would inspire Pa to be firm with her.

A slow smile grew on Pa's face. "Thinking of someone else instead of ourselves is what Jesus would tell us to do, jo?" He moved to the door and opened it. "Good night, Joseph." He left.

Joseph sagged against his pillows and stared after his father. Why did he feel like Pa had just tricked him?

Gil

ON FRIDAY EVENING, Gil whistled as he walked to the bank building with Timmy's tuba under his arm. The boy, carrying Gil's portfolio of music, scampered alongside him. Gil had been whistling all day, so full of wonder at how swiftly God answered his prayer. He'd never had such a quick response before, but then, he'd never been so bold with God before.

Wednesday evening when he was in the band room praying, for the first time in his life he'd laid out a fleece. He told God if he was meant to enter the boys in the band competition, he needed hours to spend with them. If God provided the time, he would get the boys ready to go to the End of Harvest celebration. Then he returned to Roald's and discovered that while he was praying, Roald and Onkel Bernard had found another way to cover the mail routes, which gave Gil several hours each day. Roald would still pay Gil a portion of his salary. Roald told him, "You're going to be doing the household chores and seeing to my animals. That's worth something to me, so I won't accept no for an answer." Gil had seen the offer as God's providence.

Gil had insisted on finishing the week, though, and both Roald and Onkel Bernard agreed with him. But as of yesterday evening, he was done with mail routes and could put his whole focus on composing, directing, and getting the boys ready for the competition. Well, most of his focus. Roald, his house, and his animals would still require some attention. But he felt confident he could keep everything in balance.

What would the boys say when he told them he'd called the county clerk and registered them to compete in the End of Harvest band contest? He hoped their excitement would be greater than their nervousness. Too much nervousness could wreck a performance. Too much excitement could, too. But with enough practice and enough encouragement, Gil should be able to prepare them for the performance. Every band would play two songs, the man had told him—one piece while standing in front of the judges and another while marching in the parade, with each performance making up half their score.

His whistle momentarily faltered. He hadn't anticipated marching. The boys had a lot of work to do. But Gil knew what songs they'd perform. For the parade, they'd play the original piece he'd already started teaching the boys. He hadn't written it to be a marching song, but it had a peppy four-four beat and would work well for a marching band. As for the other . . . The tune leaving his puckered lips turned cheerful again. He'd stayed up half the night adding parts to the song he'd written for Ava before he left Falke.

Although Ava's song was originally composed for violin,

he'd always intended to make it an orchestral score. This newest version was only a variation, nothing an orchestra could play, but he hoped the horns would complement one another and give emotion and life to the melody. He wanted Ava to hear her song played by a band. For her to know he hadn't forgotten it. To please her, the same way her many acts of kindness since his return had pleased him.

The whistled notes faded as images from the night he played the song for Ava flashed in his mind. Ava's eyes, bright with tears, their tawny depths glowing with wonder. Ava's face, pale beneath the moonlight, lifted to him in rapt attention. Ava's hands, clasped as if in prayer, resting lightly against her lips. Ava's lips, rosy and full, responding to his kiss in full surrender.

His feet slowed and he stopped, his mind so caught up in the past he hardly realized where he was. Until Timmy nudged his elbow and said, "Mr. Baty? What's the matter? You feeling sick?"

Gil gave himself a little shake and turned his attention to the boy. "Nä, Timmy. I'm fine."

Timmy blew out a breath. "That's good. I thought for a minute there you had a bad bellyache."

Gil laughed. If tender reflections made him appear sick to his stomach, he'd better not get caught up in thought in public. Timmy headed up the sidewalk, and Gil followed. They reached the bank building, and Gil pulled the key from his pocket. Unexpectedly, his hand was trembling. He didn't think he'd be able to connect with the lock. He offered the key to Timmy. "Here. You open it for us."

The boy puffed up with pride as he unlocked the door with a deft flick of his wrist. He gave the key back to Gil with a huge smile. "All done. Let's go in!"

They set up the room, then Gil went from seat to seat, putting sheets of music on each stand. He needed to talk with the boys before they started practice, which meant their playing time would be shorter than usual. So he only laid out one piece—the marching song. Tomorrow they would practice it again, helping them commit it to memory. On Monday, Tuesday at the latest, he would introduce Ava's song to them.

Boys began arriving, most with a parent in tow, which increased Gil's nervousness. Had he made the right choice by registering for the competition? This decision was a big one and would affect each family in a variety of ways. Then he remembered his fleece and the quick response, and his nerves calmed. Yes, it was right. The parents could decide if they didn't want their sons to participate. But for those who wanted to go, he would prepare them.

Joseph arrived as Earl's escort, and Gil sent his cousin a smile across the heads of the seated players. Joseph nodded in reply, further strengthening Gil's resolve. How good to have Joseph on his side again after so many years of animosity. Gil waited until every seat was filled, then he cleared his throat, and the room fell silent.

"I appreciate all of you being here tonight. I'd like to start this evening by thanking you, parents, for entrusting your boys to me." He slowly scanned their faces while he spoke, making brief eye contact with each of them. "They are a wonderful group of boys with a great deal of talent. It is a joy to work with them. And"—his lips tugged upward into a smile he couldn't hold back—"it will be a real delight to play two songs at the End of Harvest band contest in McPherson on August 19."

A cheer rose from the group, and Joseph punched the air with his fist, which made Gil's heart roll over in happiness. He held up his palms, a bid for quiet.

"There are several things we need to settle before we can play. Since I know you're all eager to start practicing for the competition, let's get our business attended to as quickly as possible."

With parents' input and approval, Gil arranged a schedule, keeping their Monday and Friday evenings in place and adding midmorning practices on Tuesday, Wednesday, and Thursday. Instead of meeting in the upstairs bank room for the morning rehearsals, they would meet in the empty lot behind the bank. The area would be shaded, and the boys would become comfortable playing while standing. "Since one of the songs will be played in the parade, I'll teach the boys some simple march steps during our outdoor practices."

Gil paused, thinking through everything he'd said to be sure he hadn't forgotten something important, then asked if anyone had questions. He secretly hoped there weren't many. The boys were fidgeting in their chairs. They all wanted to get to work.

The town's grocer, Mr. Wallace, raised his hand. "Gil, my wife and I were talking about youth bands we've seen from other towns. They all have uniforms. Will our boys have uniforms?"

Gil's jaw went slack. Why hadn't he thought about uniforms? Of course they would want to look as professional as possible. "I . . . I hadn't really considered them, but it's a very good idea. What do the other parents think?"

He was met with various expressions, from excited to uncertain. A few parents muttered something to a neighbor, but none spoke loudly enough for the group to hear. Gil wasn't sure how to interpret the reactions.

Mr. Wallace pushed his hands into his pockets and rocked in place. "Gil, may I say something more?"

"Of course."

The man gruffly cleared his throat. "Pearl and I think the uniforms should be fashioned after hats and coats worn by band members in Russia. It will make our band stand out from the other bands and also show pride in the boys' heritage. I can purchase bolts of black cloth and skeins of gold piping, which we will provide to the boys' parents at our cost—to make the uniforms as affordable as possible. We can also order tall boots for the boys, also offered at our cost, but we'd need to do so quickly to ensure they arrive in time for the competition."

Mr. Hiebert frowned across the room at Mr. Wallace. "How much money will the uniforms cost, Adolph? We have two boys in the band—Clarence and Ray. If it's a lot of money, we might not be able to afford them."

Mr. Wallace's face twisted into a remorseful grimace. "I can't say for sure, Paul, without knowing your boys' sizes. The bigger boys' uniforms will cost a little more since they'll require more cloth. But I can tell you, by getting the materials and boots at cost, they will be much less than buying ready-made."

Another father, Mr. Schmidt, raised his hand. "Most of these boys have mothers who can sew for them. That isn't the case for my William nor Orly Thiessen. We rely on ready-made clothes from the catalog."

If they continued the discussion about uniforms, they would lose their entire practice hour. Gil made a quick decision. "Folks, I like the idea of having uniforms, and Mr. Wallace has made a very generous offer. I think it might be too soon for us to make a decision about them—we need more information concerning the cost. So, Mr. Wallace, would you be kind enough to write up estimates for the different sizes of boots and coats? Each family can think about and pray over the expense during the weekend. On Sunday, after church, please tell me your individual decisions."

Several nods approved Gil's idea. He blew out a relieved sigh. Then he gathered his courage to ask a question he dreaded. "Now that we know we are going and we have a schedule in place, are there any boys who will not participate in the competition?" He held his breath, silently praying none would refuse.

With tears streaming down his cheeks, Timmy Dirks slid out of his chair and stood beside it. And then, after several seconds, Earl stood, too.

Chapter Twenty-One

Joseph

JOSEPH SMOLDERED WITH ANGER. WHY HADN'T Pa come instead of sending Joseph tonight? He should be the one to give Gil a dressing down. What was Gil thinking, allowing the boys to participate in a marching band? Earl wouldn't be able to stay in step with the other boys. He'd become a laughingstock and lose every bit of the confidence he'd been gaining. Joseph wanted to punch Gil in the nose. He jammed his fists deep into his trouser pockets and ordered his feet to stay in place. He couldn't give his temper its way in front of these parents, but when he got Gil alone, he'd say—and do—plenty.

He leaned close to Earl and whispered, "Stay for tonight's practice, Earl. We'll talk about this later, *jo?*"

Earl gave a nod and sank back onto his chair. Joseph noticed Gil was talking quietly with Timmy, and the youngster also seated himself. Gil returned to the front of the room, thanked Mr. Wallace for writing up estimates for the uniforms and thanked the parents for coming. He didn't come right out and dismiss the adults, but his words gave a bold enough hint. The parents ambled out the door. Joseph, however, moved to the back of the room, grabbed a chair, and sat. Gil would have to lead this practice under his disapproving glare.

The boys had only played a few bars of a quick-paced piece Joseph didn't recognize when Ava entered the room with her cloth-draped tray. He leaped up and took the tray from her. She thanked him with a smile, then brought out the rolling cart from the storage room. While Gil continued directing the boys, the two of them worked together readying the treats. Being close to her, lending her a hand, took a bit of the bluster from Joseph's sails. Until he glanced at Ava's pocket and saw a bulge.

Cookies. Saved for Gil. The anger roared to life again.

Gil released the boys for their snack, and anger propelled Joseph across the room, directly to his cousin. Hands fisted at his side, he stuck his nose as close to Gil as possible without actually touching him and hissed, "Why did you register the boys to compete as a marching band? Did you forget that not every one of your members has the ability to keep up? Or do you not care that it will leave Earl out of the competition?"

Gil blinked, his eyes wide. "I . . . I didn't have a choice. The competition is two-part. One piece while marching in the parade and one played in front of the judges. Registering meant playing for both."

The answer made sense and should have cooled Joseph's ire, but it didn't. "Then you should have talked to Earl before you brought it up to the band. Given him a chance to stay home this evening so he wouldn't have to be humiliated in front of everyone. You're so full of yourself, Gil, you never think about anybody else. That song they were just playing . . . is it one of yours?"

Gil nodded.

Joseph snorted. "Of course it is. You want to show off your song in front of the judges. That's all. You don't care about these boys. You're just using them."

Gil's gaze narrowed, and the muscles in his jaw twitched. "You're the one who suggested I teach the boys some of the songs I wrote. And I wouldn't have signed up for the competition at all if it hadn't been for you telling everyone at church about it. Remember? You started this, so if you want to find someone to blame, take a look in a mirror."

The fact that Gil was right only made Joseph angrier. Why did everything concerning his cousin have to turn into a mess? Joseph growled low in his throat and held up his fist. "For two cents I'd knock you through the wall."

"If I had two cents, I'd give it to you, because I'm sick to death of trying to please you. What do you want from me, Joseph?" Gil stared hard into his face. "Will you make up your mind?"

Joseph didn't know what he wanted. He slowly lowered his hand and unclenched his fingers.

Gil pulled in a breath that strained the buttons on his jacket, then blew it out in a mighty *whoosh*. "Go home, Joseph. I'll walk Earl to your place after practice and have a talk with him." He pushed past Joseph and joined the group of boys who were enjoying their snack.

Joseph stayed put for a few minutes, bringing his rapid breathing under control, and then he stomped up behind Gil. He grabbed him by the arm and yanked him to the side. "Earl's not the only boy you need to talk to. I know why Timmy stood up. His old Taunte isn't going to spend money on a uniform for him. If he doesn't have one, he'll look like a fool standing with the rest of the band. Since this whole band was started for his sake, you'd better find a way not to leave him out."

Gil jerked his arm free. "I told you to go home. I'll talk to Earl. I'll deal with Timmy. And the next time you get an idea about how I should run my life, keep it to yourself. I'm done with you."

Ava

AVA REMOVED THE napkin-wrapped cookies from her pocket and gave them to Gil. Out of the corner of her eye, she watched Joseph storm from the room. She turned a nervous look on Gil. "Is everything all right?"

Gil aimed a glance at the doorway, where Joseph had disappeared from view. "No. No, it's not." Sadness pinched his face. "I might need to come by and talk to your father. Get his advice. Do you suppose he would mind?"

Mind? Papa would welcome Gil for any reason. "Nä. He will always care about the things that concern you." As, it seemed, would she, considering how much his unhappiness affected her. He held the cookies, but he hadn't taken a bite. Proof that something was deeply troubling him. "Is there anything I can do?"

"Thank you, but—" His frame jolted. He leaned down slightly, his penetrating gaze fixed on hers. "Maybe. Can you sew?"

Such a strange query. "Jo."

He spun and searched the group of boys. He snapped his fingers. "Timmy, come here, please."

The boy trudged to Gil's side. His eyelashes clumped in moist spikes, and red blotches decorated his cheeks. Had Timmy been crying? His forlorn countenance pierced Ava's heart. What had happened here this evening?

Gil took Timmy by the hand and Ava by the elbow. He guided both of them to the other side of the room. Then he told Ava that the boys would participate in the End of Harvest competition with two songs and Mr. Wallace had offered to provide at-cost materials for uniforms. "There are three boys who don't have mothers to sew for them. I don't know for sure the parents will decide to approve uniforms, but if they do, would you be willing to make them for William Schmidt, Orly Thiessen, and Timmy?"

Ava's heart swelled. How kind of Gil to group Timmy with the other boys. Even though his situation was different—his Taunte surely had the ability but most certainly lacked the desire to sew a uniform—Gil ascertained he wouldn't feel singled out. "Jo, if the families need a seamstress, I'll help." Even if she couldn't sew for her own children, at least these boys could be blessed by the work of her hands. It was better than nothing.

Gil flashed a grateful smile, then placed his hands on his knees, putting himself at Timmy's level. "Timmy, you heard Miss Flaming. She can sew your uniform, so you don't need to worry about not having one made. But fabric costs money, and someone will need to pay for it. Since you'll be the one wearing the uniform, I think you should pay for it."

The child's eyes widened. "I don't have any money, Mr. Baty."

Gil grabbed Timmy's skinny wrists and held up his arms. "But you have these. And a determined spirit. Which means you can work for the materials if you want the uniform badly enough. The question is, are you willing?"

Timmy nodded until his bangs flopped. "Jo. I am willing."

Gil let go of Timmy's wrists and stood upright. "I knew you would be. You're a good-hearted, hardworking boy. I'm proud of you."

The boy sniffled and rubbed his eyes with his fists. When he lowered his hands, he wore a bright smile. "Thank you, Mr. Baty."

Gil pointed to the cart. "Go have another cookie before break is over. You'll need the energy to work hard during the rest of our time together." He winked, and Timmy darted off. He sighed and faced Ava. "Thank you so much. That alleviated one worry."

"One worry . . ." She crinkled her brow. "So you still have another?"

"At least one, if not more, but I trust your father will be able to help me."

She wanted to help him, too. It hurt her to see the sorrow in his dark brown eyes. "If there's anything else I can do, too, please ask."

A soft smile curved his lips. "Thank you, Ava. You're a good friend."

A good friend. Kind words, spoken in a tender voice. So why did they hurt?

"There is something." He began moving slowly toward the podium, and she trailed along beside him. "I usually walk Timmy home, but tonight I need to talk to Earl. Would you mind walking Timmy home in my stead so he doesn't feel forgotten? When I'm done talking to Earl, I'd like to come by your house and talk to your father. That is, if he doesn't think it's too late."

"I'll tell him you need to talk to him. I'm sure he won't mind waiting for you."

"We should probably meet at Roald's house. I'll come tap on your door when I'm done dropping off Earl."

"That sounds fine, Gil."

He clapped his hands, and the boys all turned to him.

"Break is over. We've lost quite a lot of playing time tonight, so I expect you to work twice as hard as usual these remaining minutes to make up for it. Back to our seats now."

The boys thundered past Ava. Gil touched her sleeve and spoke above the noise of their feet and the screeching chair legs. "Thank you, Ava. And if you'd like to be part of the meeting with your father, you're more than welcome to join us."

Chapter Twenty-Two

Gil

ONKEL BERNARD ANSWERED GIL'S KNOCK, AND Gil said, "Thank you for talking to me tonight."

The man chuckled and flung his arm across Gil's shoulders. He herded him off the porch and across the yard toward Roald's house as he spoke. "It's no trouble, Gil. Ava told me you seemed unsettled. She also shared what you discussed with parents at the practice. Two songs to perform at the End of Harvest celebration, hmm? And the boys might have uniforms? This band is gaining importance."

Gil cringed, recalling Joseph's words about him using the boys to further his own career. Was his cousin correct? But then, would God have responded to him so quickly if the competition was only for him?

Suddenly Gil realized Ava wasn't with them. He glanced over his shoulder. "I thought Ava might come since I talked to her about sewing some of the uniforms."

Bernard sighed. "Maria began running a slight fever today. Ava thought it best to stay with her mama."

Worry stabbed through Gil. "Will Taunte Maria be all right? The fever won't—"

Bernard patted Gil's shoulder. "Maria gets summer colds. It's not unusual for her. But it does wear her out more than it might someone else, so Ava is smart to stay with her. To make sure Maria rests. She doesn't like being coddled and will try to do too much if we aren't watchful." Bernard stepped up on Roald's porch. "If there's something we talk about that Ava needs to know, I will tell her later."

There was much Ava needed to know. But Gil wouldn't deliver his heartfelt messages through someone else, not even someone he trusted as much as Onkel Bernard. Some things a man needed to say directly to the woman he loved. If he ever got the chance. And the nerve.

Gil opened the door and gestured Bernard inside. Gil looked toward the settee, where he expected to find Roald, but the man wasn't there. Concerned, Gil hurried toward the hallway, talking over his shoulder. "Go ahead and sit down, Onkel Bernard. I want to check on Roald, and I'll be right back."

Roald's bedroom door was closed. Gil put his ear up to it, and he picked up the distinct sounds of snoring. At breakfast that morning, Roald had complained about the kittens' mewling keeping him awake last night. He must have decided to turn in early. Gil wouldn't disturb him. He tiptoed back to the sitting room and sat facing the settee, where Bernard waited.

"Roald is sleeping. So I guess I'll talk to him tomorrow about ways Timmy could work off the cost of material for a band uniform." Leaning forward, Gil propped his elbows on his knees and linked his hands. "Onkel Bernard, Ava told you the band would do two songs at the competition. What I didn't tell her is that one of them must be performed in the parade, while marching."

Bernard nodded. "That does not surprise me. The celebration has always had a parade. It makes sense they would have the bands participate."

"I have one member in my band who might have trouble marching."

Bernard arched one eyebrow. "Are you speaking of your cousin Earl?"

"I am." Gil's conversation with Earl hadn't gone well. Earl seemed resigned to dropping out because he would, as he'd put it, make the entire band look bad. Gil sighed. "I have no choice about being in the parade. If we participate, we have to do both performances. I could ask the county clerk if every member of the band has to be part of both songs."

"I suppose that would be a good compromise, if they allow it." Bernard's tone indicated his true opinion. He didn't like the idea.

Neither did Gil. "In the song the boys are learning, the trumpets play the melody. There are only three trumpet players in the whole band. I need all three of them to make the song as strong as it can be."

Bernard sat a little straighter. "Did you tell Earl this? That he is needed?"

"I did."

"And he is still reluctant?"

Gil nodded. "But I think he could do it. Tonight, he and I walked the half mile from town to his home. He stumbled a time or two, but he kept up with me, step for step. He doesn't think he can do it, though, and I don't know how to convince him." He cringed, recalling Joseph's accusations. "Or how to convince the rest of the family. Joseph said very plainly that Earl wouldn't be able to march."

Bernard slowly shook his head, his expression sad. "Jo, your Taunte Dorcas has always protected him. This isn't a terrible thing. She loves him, and she doesn't want to see him hurt.

But too much protection has convinced him he has a handicap much bigger than it really is." He shrugged, exaggerating the gesture. "So his toes point in. So he's a little *ojeschekjt*."

Gil chuckled. The Low German word for *clumsy* always amused him.

Bernard grinned. "But the boy's feet and legs are strong. With practice, I think he could do just as well as the other boys. If he marches in the parade, it could be very good for him—and good for his mother, too, to realize he is capable. Maria and I will pray for Earl, that he will try and he will gain courage in the effort."

"Thank you, Onkel Bernard." Gil tapped his thumbs together. "There's something else. Something... more personal." He glanced at his hands, then settled his gaze on Bernard's attentive face. "Am I being selfish by directing the boys' band? By putting the boys in the competition?"

The older man's eyebrows dipped inward. "I have never thought of you as a selfish person. What makes you ask this?"

Gil gathered his thoughts. "Maybe it was selfish of me to go to New York. I left behind my only remaining family, and I left the ones who could have become my family." He'd never forget Ava's tears the night he told her he was going to New York City nor the deep loneliness that plagued him those first months, so far away from everything familiar. "And for what? All this time, I've been chasing a dream I'm starting to think I was never meant to catch."

"Why?"

The simple question wasn't so simple to answer. "The others who play in or conduct orchestras scoff at my compositions. They poke fun at me, call me a Kansas farmer's son, and they make it sound like a curse. They"—he gulped—"laugh."

"Nonsense." Bernard's stern response didn't surprise Gil.

He surmised the man would be defensive. "Stop acting like Earl."

Gil drew back in surprise. "What do you mean?"

"You're using something as an excuse for not being able to do something else. What difference does it make if you're from Kansas, born to a farmer? Show me the law that says a Kansas farmer's son can't be musically gifted."

Bernard was missing the point. "There is no such law," Gil said, "but there is an attitude. I don't know how to get past it, except to write a composition so lovely and impressive that they can't deny my ability."

"If they hold that attitude, no composition you write will change their minds." Bernard's tone lost its bite, but it didn't matter. His words discouraged Gil. "But if they keep you from trying, I will be very disappointed in you. Just as you'll be disappointed in Earl if he doesn't at least try to march with the band."

Gil flopped back and slouched in the chair, letting his arms hang limp. "I'm just so very weary of failing, Onkel Bernard."

For several minutes, the man remained silent, staring across the room into Gil's eyes. Then a grin twitched on the corners of his mouth. "Have you ever considered, my boy, that the ones who ridicule you are envious of you?"

Gil snorted.

Bernard shook his finger at him. "It's possible. In Russia, Maria's father was a well-known and well-respected violinist. Because of my family's friendship with hers, I attended many musical performances in which he played. I heard much good music. I saw impressive conducting. So I know good music and direction when I hear and see it." Bernard pointed at Gil again, but this time Gil didn't feel reprimanded. "Gil, you have a gift. Even Ava knows it. Do you know what she told her mother? She said she heard the soul of the music when you directed the men."

Gil's face heated. He looked aside. "I know. She told me, too." He would carry her words of affirmation in his heart for the rest of his life.

"Then you shouldn't doubt you have the ability."

Gil faced Bernard again, throwing his arms wide. "But what am I supposed to do with it? I've been told now by two different people that I'm only using these boys to better myself."

"Who told you these things?"

Gil should have kept his mouth shut. He didn't want to share the sources and sound like a gossip, but neither did he want to be disrespectful and refuse to answer. He lowered his head. "Ava and Joseph."

"Ach, Joseph." Bernard nearly spat the name. "He is like those men in New York, jealous and foolish. He has always been this way toward you. So take what he says with a grain of salt. Ava, though . . . why would she say such a thing?"

Gil explained the conversation when Ava asked if he intended to use and then abandon the boys. "Maybe she's right. Maybe they're both right. Maybe I am selfish and unfair. Maybe I shouldn't spend so much time with these boys this summer when I know I'll be leaving again."

Bernard's eyes narrowed to slits. "You know for sure you are leaving again?"

"If I'm to ever be taken seriously in the music world, then I need to be in New York City." Gil's throat hurt, as if every word was sandpaper dragged across his tonsils.

"Well, then, let me ask you another question." Bernard maintained an even tone, no hint of recrimination or disapproval, but Gil's flesh prickled with apprehension. "If the boys win first place in McPherson, they must later compete against the first-place winners from other counties, jo?"

"Jo."

"Will you stay and direct them in that competition, too? And if they win it, will you go with them to Topeka?"

Gil didn't know when the competition between first-place bands would take place. The school year would start after Labor Day. If he was going to take the teaching position at the private school, he had to notify them by the end of August. "Those are a lot of ifs, Onkel Bernard."

"Of this I am aware. But the boys play well. The fact that they're so young will make them stand out, which might win the judges' approval. Those ifs are not impossibilities. So tell me, what will you do if they win it all?"

Gil swallowed. "I . . . I'm not sure."

Bernard's expression relaxed. "Then you have something more to pray about."

Gil gave a thoughtful nod. It seemed he needed to lay out another fleece.

Chapter Twenty-Three

Ava

"IT SEEMS AS IF CHURCH IS NO LONGER ABOUT worship. It's all about Gil. Gil and his bands."

Surely Ava hadn't heard correctly. She turned her astounded look on Joseph. "What did you say?"

He folded his arms and scowled across the churchyard to where Gil stood in the middle of a small gathering, a notebook and pencil in hand. "I only said what a lot of people are thinking. How many Sundays have folks been delayed going home to their dinners because Gil needs to talk to them about the boys' band? 'Remember the sabbath day, to keep it holy.'" He quoted the fourth commandment, then flapped his hand in Gil's direction. "Is that holy?"

Ava pursed her lips. She now regretted walking over to talk with Joseph. She'd felt bad for him when she spotted him standing all alone while groups milled under the mild summer sun. How many times had she been by herself in a crowd of people, wishing someone would come speak to her? So while Papa chatted with some other townsfolk, she'd engaged Joseph in idle chitchat. Which had now become not idle at all.

"Joseph, shame on you. Gil isn't dishonoring the Sabbath day. He's talking to folks when they're together, being a good steward of his and others' time."

Joseph's expression turned as sour as if he'd eaten something unpleasant. "I don't understand how you, of all people, can defend him."

After pondering her options, had she really considered marrying Joseph instead of running a café? Not that she was ready to do either. But at that moment, being a spinster café owner seemed the wiser choice. "What do you mean me 'of all people'?" Her question snapped out.

"After what he did to you, courting you and then leaving you. The way he's now courting the boys with all his music talk. He'll draw them in, get them excited. Then he'll leave them, and they'll feel as betrayed and heartsick as you did."

Ava's mouth dropped open. Had he already forgotten last Wednesday, when he'd encouraged people to send their boys with Gil to the competition in McPherson? Now he was condemning him—for the very thing he'd been in favor of only a few days ago. "Joseph, you're impossible."

To her surprise, he laughed. "So you've told me before. Many times. Usually when Gil and I were bumping heads." The humor in his blue eyes faded. "You took his side back then, too. But I thought by now, given how he chose a career in New York over a life with you, you'd be done with him. I guess I was wrong." He searched her face, a hint of pleading now glimmering in his eyes. "Am I wrong?"

Ava wasn't sure how to answer. Her heart tugged her toward Gil, old feelings always simmering beneath the surface. Yet nothing had changed. As Joseph said, Gil would leave again. Pining after him was a foolish waste of time. Even so, she couldn't seem to stay away from him. Either Papa or circumstances drove them together. When would God answer Mama's prayer and let her find freedom?

She blew out a little breath of aggravation. She would think twice before engaging Joseph in conversation again. "I think you're looking for reasons to disdain Gil, the way you did all through our growing up. Why can't you realize that my being friends with him isn't an offense toward you?"

"Why can't you realize my disdain toward him is my way of protecting you?" Fervency tinged his tone and pulsated from his tense frame. "Jo, I thought the competition in McPherson would be a good experience for the boys' band. I even thought it might put little Falke on the map. We're no longer known as the falcon capital of Kansas, thanks to hunters and trappers who nearly obliterated the poor bird our town was named after. But I wish now I'd never mentioned the End of Harvest celebration, because it's become less about the boys and more about Gil making a name for himself. So he can put it on his résumé and impress the bigwigs of New York." His voice turned hard. "I think we should cancel before these parents invest in uniforms that will be worn for one performance and then stuck in the closet to rot. You said Gil was being a good steward? Well, not in this case. The uniforms will be a waste. The entire thing will be a waste."

Ava examined the boys waiting for their folks. They were smiling, eager, as excited as puppies exploring the yard for the first time. She shook her head. "It won't be a waste, Joseph. Even if they only perform in one competition, for the rest of their lives they will carry the memories of working together, of making something beautiful and sharing it with an audience." Just as she would carry memories, both sweet and bitter, of Gil forever. To her chagrin, tears distorted her vision. She blinked and turned aside.

Joseph lightly gripped her chin between his thumb and finger and lifted her face to him. "You have memories, too, Ava. Memories with Gil. I see them swimming in your eyes. But do they make you smile in remembrance, or do they haunt you? Be honest. If not with me, then with yourself. Don't you truly wish, deep down, that he hadn't returned to Falke?"

"Ava?" Papa's voice carried from behind her.

Ava stepped free of Joseph's hold. "Coming, Papa." She lifted the hem of her skirt and nearly jogged to her father. She grabbed his sturdy arm and held tight.

He looked down at her with concern. "Are you all right? What were you doing over there with Joseph Baty?"

"Nothing. Only talking." She sent a quick glance over her shoulder. Joseph remained where she'd left him, his stern gaze aimed in Gil's direction. "I don't understand him at all, Papa. One minute he acts as if he's Gil's biggest supporter, and the next he's criticizing everything Gil does. I can't keep up with him."

"Then don't try."

Papa's blunt reply made Ava laugh. "That sounded like Mama's practicality."

He patted her hand. "Your mama is a smart lady. And we've left her alone far too long. Come, let's go home." He escorted her to their carriage, talking as they went. "Did I remember to tell you that I invited Gil and Roald over for lunch?"

He hadn't, but the invitation didn't worry her. The pork roast and vegetables she'd put in the oven before they left would easily feed extras. "That's fine." She nearly rolled her eyes at herself. How quickly she'd changed her tune about Gil sitting across the dining room table from her.

"Roald wanted the chance to try a little distance with his crutches before he walks to the post office tomorrow for his first day as substitute clerk," Papa said. "Coming to our house will be a good practice for him."

Ava smiled, remembering Papa's pride at having found a

way of giving Gil time to work with the boys' band every day. "Are you and Mr. Willems nervous about trading duties?"

Papa helped her into the carriage and then climbed in. "Nä. Roald is a smart man. After our talk yesterday, I feel confident he'll do fine." Papa snapped the reins, and the horse jerked the conveyance into motion. "He says he's not worried about me, either, since Miss Dirks agreed to let Timmy ride along on the days he isn't attending band practice. The boy will hop down and make the actual deliveries when he's with me. All I have to do is drive the wagon—Timmy will do the real work."

Ava grinned up at him. "And earn his new band uniform, jo?"

Papa chuckled. "That is the idea. I'm glad the parents approved the uniforms today. The boys will look as good as they sound." He sighed, a contented smile on his square face. "Timmy is a good boy. Being with Gil and Roald has done him wonders. It's too bad this band won't last beyond the summer. I think it has already been a real benefit to Timmy as well as the other boys in town."

Ava worried her lower lip between her teeth. "Papa, about the band . . ." She aimed a sideways glance at him. "Joseph thinks it would have been better if the band was never started since Gil will only be here for the summer. What do you think?"

"I think Joseph is a jealous boy trapped in a man's body and needs to grow up all the way."

Ava burst out laughing. "Papa!"

He grinned at her. "You asked me what I thought."

"I meant about the band."

"Ah." Papa looked forward, expertly guiding the horse on the winding roadway. "I think the band is a good thing, no matter how long it lasts. New experiences are always good for growing."

"That's what I think, too." She folded her hands in her lap.

"I do worry, though, how the boys will feel when it comes to an end."

"And I worry how you will feel when it comes to an end, because it means telling Gil goodbye again. Unless"—he flicked a side-eye glance at her—"you've decided you cannot tell him goodbye again."

Ava's chest went tight. "Papa . . ."

He transferred both reins to one hand and placed his thick, warm palm over her hands. "I'm sorry, my Leefste. I know it is a tender subject, but it must be said. You never truly let Gil go. If you had, you would have accepted the affections of another man by now. Yet you reject your potential suitor." He chuckled and returned his hand to the reins. "Now, I don't mind that you reject Joseph Baty. I'm sure he has the capacity to be a good man. He is, after all, related to Gil. But he's far too immature and temperamental to be a good husband to you."

Ava covered her searing cheeks with her palms. "Papa, please, I don't want to talk about this." Especially not when very soon she and Gil would sit down at the dining room table together. How could she behave normally around him with Papa's words ringing in her ears? She smacked her hands downward. "My rejection of another suitor has nothing to do with Gil and everything to do with you and Mama. With her so sick, I can't leave you. Who would do the cooking and cleaning? You need me."

Papa released a little *humph.* "We could hire a girl to do those things. We love you, and we appreciate your goodness to us, but we do not need you as our housekeeper." He tugged the reins, and Pansy obediently pulled their carriage into the barn. He set the brake, shifted sideways in the seat, and looked into Ava's eyes. "I think, though, you need us to fill the emptiness you feel inside."

Why was he being so cruel? Ava folded her arms and scowled at her father. "That isn't fair, Papa."

"Nä? But you don't tell me it isn't true, so maybe I know what I'm talking about."

Ava hung her head. A tear rolled down her cheek and plopped onto her flowered skirt.

Papa sighed. "I'm sorry, Leefste. I didn't mean to upset you. I only want you to think. Your heavenly Father has a good plan for your life. I don't want you to hide from it out of a false sense of loyalty to your mama and me or out of fear of the unknown. I want you to seek Him and follow Him, wherever He may lead you."

Ava scooted to the edge of the seat and slid to the ground. She grabbed her skirts and shook them free of the travel dust. "If Gil and Mr. Willems are coming for lunch, I need to set the table." She hurried off before Papa could pierce her further.

WHILE PAPA AND their guests visited and partook of the roasted pork, potatoes, carrots, and biscuits Ava had prepared for lunch, she picked at her food. She rolled over in her mind Papa's comments about a hired worker being able to replace her. How awful to find out how little Papa needed her. But Papa wasn't sick. Mama was. So Mama's opinion was the one that counted most.

For dessert, Ava brought out dishes of *Plüma Mooss*. Papa was particularly fond of the chilled fruit compote. Had she known how much he would upset her on the drive home, she would have made his least favorite dessert—rhubarb pie—instead. As she placed his dish in front of him, he curled his fingers around her upper arm and delivered a gentle squeeze.

Tears threatened. She knew what he intended by the gesture—that he was sorry. She also knew she would accept his wordless apology because, despite how much his words had stabbed her tender soul, his intentions were loving. She offered him a quick smile, then turned her attention to their guests.

"Gentlemen, please feel free to stay and visit as long as you like. If you will excuse me, I'm going to take some lunch to Mama."

Mr. Willems spooned a mushy prune from his bowl and held it up as if making a toast. "Thank you for the good lunch, Miss Flaming. Please tell your mama she is in my prayers."

Such a kind man. Ava nodded. "I will. Thank you." She took one step toward the kitchen.

"Ava?" Gil's voice brought her to a halt.

Papa's earlier comment echoed through her mind. *I think, though, you need us to fill the emptiness you feel inside.* She didn't dare look into Gil's face for fear he'd read what she was thinking. *Is Gil meant to be the one who fills my emptiness?* She said, "Jo?"

"If you have time later this afternoon, I'd like to talk to you about the uniforms."

The impersonal topic almost stung. "Of course. Perhaps around three?"

"That sounds fine. Thank you."

"You're welcome." She darted into the kitchen and closed the swinging door behind her. With the men's companionable conversation rumbling from the other side of the wall, she filled a small plate for Mama and took it to her parents' room. She cracked the door without knocking in case Mama was asleep, but she saw Mama sitting up in the bed. She went on in. "I brought your lunch."

"Oh, thank you." Mama shifted a little higher against the

pillows. "I awoke a few minutes ago. I think the smell of the roasted vegetables brought me out of my sleep."

Ava draped a napkin over Mama's lap and placed the plate on top of it. "Well, I hope that means your appetite is improving. You need to eat to regain your strength."

"I'm hungrier than I've been in days." Mama picked up the fork from the edge of the plate, her gaze roving over the food. "I'm not sure I'll be able to eat it all, though. You gave me so much."

"If you clean your plate, I'll bring you some *Plüma Mooss.*"

Laughter trickled from Mama's throat, and then she coughed.

Ava snatched a rumpled handkerchief from the bedside table, pressed it into her mother's hand, then lifted the plate out of the way. She stood helplessly by while Mama coughed into the lacy square of cotton for several seconds.

Finally Mama sat back against the pillows and released a heavy sigh. She aimed a teasing wink at Ava. "You sounded so much like me, promising a treat to Rupert when he was small to convince him to eat his vegetables. Ach, but as much as I enjoyed the memory, please don't make me laugh again."

Ava put the plate on Mama's lap once more and laid the handkerchief aside. "I won't. I promise."

While Mama ate, Ava paced the room. She sensed her mother's gaze following her, but she didn't peek to confirm it until Mama cleared her throat. Ava instinctively turned.

"You are as restless as a caged lion," Mama said, her tone teasing. "Am I eating too slowly?"

The questions plaguing her begged answers. Ava crossed to the edge of Mama's bed and blurted, "Mama, do you need me?"

Chapter Twenty-Four

Ava

MAMA'S BROWS FURROWED. "RIGHT NOW, TO HELP me eat?"

Ava sat on the edge of the mattress. "Not necessarily right now, but always. To help with the housework and gardening. To do the cooking. To take care of you when you're sick. Do you . . . need me?"

Mama set the plate on the bedside table. "Why are you asking me this?"

"Papa said I'm not needed here. He said I'm only using him and you to fill a void in my life." Repeating the statement stabbed anew. If Mama confirmed it, she might not be able to bear the pain. But she had to know. "Do you think I'm taking care of you out of selfishness? Or do you understand why I've chosen to stay?"

"Ach, such a question . . ." Sympathy glowed in Mama's pale hazel eyes. She slowly shook her head. "I think you misunderstood your papa's intentions. Of course I know why you've stayed. You're a dear, dedicated daughter. You honor us with your faithful devotion to us."

Ava nearly sagged in relief. "I'm so glad you don't think I'm selfish. That I'm using you to"—she chose Papa's words—"fill the emptiness I feel inside."

"We could never be enough to do that." Mama's wise smile comforted Ava. "Only our Lord and Savior, Jesus Christ, can fill all the aching, empty holes in our hearts. And only seeking and following His will can complete us."

Ava lifted her gaze to the window, to the seemingly endless stretch of prairie. "I thought I'd found His will for me, staying here and taking care of you. But lately . . ." Her vision clouded, and she blinked to clear it.

"Lately, it hasn't seemed to be enough?"

Mama's gentle query jolted Ava. She gaped at her mother. "How did you know?"

Her mother smiled and tapped her temple with her finger. "A mother knows."

Ava returned her focus to the prairie.

"Ava, do you remember the Bible story about Naomi and Ruth?"

Now Ava frowned at Mama. Was her fever rising? The change in subject didn't make sense. "Of course I do." When she was a child, it had been one of Ava's favorites. The loving relationship between mother-in-law and daughter-in-law had reminded her of the closeness she felt with Mama.

"When I married your papa, the minister read Ruth 1:16 as part of the ceremony." She closed her eyes. "'Intreat me not to leave thee, or to return from following after thee: for whither thou goest, I will go . . .'" She opened her eyes, and a single tear trailed down her cheek. "A year later, when your papa told me his decision to leave Russia for America, it was this scripture that gave me the courage to say goodbye to all that was familiar and go with him to a new land. And I have never regretted honoring its promise.

"For you see, the commitment wasn't only between Naomi

and Ruth. It was a commitment to God the Father, for them to go where He led. I knew our Father had prompted your papa to make a new home in America. When we obey God's will, we find joy, even when the pathway is difficult." She took Ava's hand between hers. "If God the Father is prompting you to go to New York with Gil, I believe you will have more joy than regret."

Ava gasped. "Why do you think I want to go to New York with Gil?"

Mama gave Ava her "a mother knows" look.

Heat rose in Ava's cheeks. "That opportunity is gone. Neither Gil nor I are the same people we were when he asked me to go with him four years ago."

Mama's soft chortle contradicted Ava's claim. "Oh, I believe there's more of the old you inside than you're willing to admit."

Was Mama right? If she was right about Ava, could the same also be true for Gil? Her pulse galloped into erratic double beats. But what difference would it make? She couldn't leave her mother. Not while she was sick.

"Even if Gil asked me again, I can't go to New York, Mama."

"Why not?"

Ava huffed. "If I go, what will become of you?"

"If you stay, what will become of me?"

Ava drew back, confused. "What do you mean?"

Mama gave Ava's hand a little shake. "Leefste, you being here will not change one minute of the time God has ordained for me. He alone knows the number of our days. Whether you are here in Falke, in New York, or even across the sea, you cannot add one hour to what is already written in God's book for my life."

Ava buried her face in the curve of her mother's neck. "But it frightens me to think of leaving you. Of never seeing you again."

Mama wriggled her shoulder and Ava sat up. She cupped Ava's cheeks and peered fervently into Ava's eyes. "You will see me again, Ava. Just as I will one day see Anton and Rupert and my Mutta and Foda. We will all be together for eternity. You believe this, don't you?"

A sob caught in Ava's throat. "I do, Mama. I believe. But even so . . ." She swallowed hard and swished her fingers under her eyes. "It hurts to think of telling you goodbye."

Mama's hands slipped from Ava's face. She linked her fingers and rested her steepled hands at her throat. "Do you remember when you asked me to pray that God would remove your love for Gil from your heart?"

Ava remembered. "Yes, ma'am."

"I've honored your request, but I added a . . . stipulation."

Ava tilted her head. "You gave God a stipulation?" That didn't seem like something her practical, faithful mother would do.

Mama nodded. "When I pray, I ask, 'Erase Ava's love for Gil unless it is Your will that she hold it and act upon it.'"

Chills broke out across every inch of Ava's frame. She stared at Mama's pale face.

A smile ignited Mama's eyes. "Leefste, if the love has not left you, it's because it was planted deep in your heart by the One who knows what is best for you. Gil is meant for you, and you are meant for him. Can you not see it?" She reached for Ava and caught hold of her hands. Her grip was amazingly strong, insistent in its pressure. "You must be obedient to God's will, Ava. If you are not, you will never find joy. You will always have a hole in your heart. Please don't make me bear the burden of holding you back from fulfilling God's will for you."

Ava kissed the backs of Mama's hands. "I need to be alone for a little while, Mama. To think." Longing for a sense of closeness to God wrapped around her and propelled her to rise. "And to pray."

Mama nodded. "I will pray, too. For as long as I am able to stay awake." She chuckled softly. "You go. Come tell me later what God whispers to you."

Gil

GIL STEPPED UP on the Flamings' porch and went to the familiar rocking chair. He sat and ran his palms up and down the painted armrests. Smooth as silk. Someone must have given them a thorough sanding before applying fresh paint. He must have been too nervous to notice when he sat here with Ava the last time. He searched for evidence of the *Gil + Ava* he'd carved on the left arm with his birthday pocketknife when he was thirteen, but none remained. A smile tugged as he recalled how the action earned his one and only serious scolding from Taunte Maria. Then Taunte Dorcas took away the coveted knife. After only a day, Taunte Maria welcomed him back into her good graces. He never got the knife back.

When he thought about his growing up in this town, he held more good memories of being with the Flamings than he did of his uncle and aunt or even his parents. Not that his parents weren't loving people. He'd lost them when he was so young that memories from his earliest years had grown fuzzy over time. But *this* family, not of blood but so dear to his heart, were part of his life's melody. The thought warmed him.

The screen door squeaked, and Ava came outside. He greeted her with his smile, but then he got a close look at her face. Concern smote him. He stood. "Is Taunte Maria all right?"

Ava paused halfway across the porch floor. "Jo, she is resting."

His legs went weak, and he sank back onto the rocking chair's sturdy seat. "I'm so glad." But Ava's eyes were red-rimmed and puffy. Something had made her cry. If not worry about Taunte Maria, then what? If he was still the eighteen-year-old Gil who'd courted seventeen-year-old Ava, he would take her in his arms, ask what had upset her, and assure her he'd do his best to help. But the twenty-two-year-old Gil did nothing. Because the twenty-one-year-old Ava was no longer his sweetheart.

His chest constricted.

She settled into the smaller chair and pushed with her toes, gently rocking back and forth. "Papa said the parents of the band members have decided they want the boys to have uniforms."

She spoke so nonchalantly, Gil wondered if he misinterpreted the evidence on her face. He set his chair into motion, matching his beat with hers. "Jo, they thought it would make a better presentation for the judges. They all liked Mrs. Wallace's idea of fashioning Russian-style uniforms. She made a sketch." He pulled the drawing from his pocket, unfolded it, and gave it to her. "It's eye-catching, isn't it?"

Ava examined it, the rocking chair continuing its steady movements. "I like the mandarin collar. The braiding and embroidery should stand out nicely against the coat's black fabric."

"They'll be gold," Gil said.

She sent him a puzzled look. "The coats?"

"Nä." He pointed to the picture. "The braiding, embroidery, and the buttons . . . they'll be gold."

"Ah. Jo, very nice." She traced her finger down the page. "This is a good length, too, just past the knee."

"The boys will wear plain black trousers tucked into their boots. Since all the boys already have a black pair of church pants, they won't need another pair for the uniforms. This will save the families some money."

How strange to sit here with Ava the way he used to but so stiff and formal, the way he never was. He rocked his chair a little harder, no longer staying in rhythm with hers. "But there is a problem we hadn't thought about. I hope you'll be able to help with it."

"What's that?"

She didn't look up from the drawing. He wished she would. "Constructing the basic coat and sewing on the buttons is something all the mothers are willing to do. But positioning the embroidery and braiding so the uniforms match one another needs to be done by a single seamstress. Mrs. Schenk and Mrs. Plett offered to sew coats for my three boys who don't have a mother, but none of the women wanted to tackle decorating all twenty coats. So . . . I wondered . . ."

Finally she lifted her attention to him. "You want me to do the decorative work on the coats?"

"Would you consider it? You were always handy with needlework. I still have the pillow you stitched for me my last Christmas in Falke." He'd taken it with him to New York and used it as a decoration on his bed in his apartment. Right now, it was in his suitcase, where it was safe from Roald's cats. Their claws could loosen the threads. "Do you remember it?"

An odd expression flitted across her face. "Jo, I embroidered a falcon on it. After you left, I hoped it would be a reminder of the little town you left behind."

His heart fluttered. "It was. It also reminded me of"—should he say it?—"the girl I left behind."

Her chair stopped abruptly. She lay the drawing on the table between them and then curled her fingers around the chair's armrests, her focus aimed straight ahead. "I'm sorry, Gil."

He stared at her profile. Her chin quivered. Regret smote him. He'd asked too much of her. She'd been willing to sew three jackets, but embroidering twenty of them was a much bigger task. He bounced his fist on his armrest, aggravated with himself for taking advantage of her kind heart. "Please forgive me, Ava. You already do so much. I'll find someone else to—"

She abruptly faced him. "I'm not talking about the uniforms. Of course I'll decorate the uniforms for the boys. I'll help in whatever way I can."

Gil searched his mind for some other reason she would apologize. He found none. "Then for what are you sorry?"

"For . . ." She swallowed and blinked rapidly. Pink flooded her cheeks. "For staying behind."

He gaped at her, mouth ajar, too stunned to speak.

"I love Mama and Papa. I don't regret these past years with them. But I stayed with them for the wrong reasons. Papa, and then Mama, and finally God helped me see it. I stayed out of fear of being away from them. Of losing them, the way I'd already lost Anton and Rupert. And I feared them losing me—of it being too much for them to bear after burying their sons. I thought I was doing what God wanted me to do, but I never asked Him. He and I . . ." She glanced down, then met his gaze again. "We haven't been on very good terms for quite a while."

Gil cringed. "I understand. I've been a little upset with Him myself for a while."

She nodded, as if she grasped all the hidden meaning behind his simple statement. "For the first time in a long time, I talked to Him. And I listened. There are still a lot of things that don't make sense to me. Why did my brothers have to die? Why is Mama still so sick? Why does Joseph—"

Gil's ears perked up. What about Joseph?

The pink in her cheeks deepened to rosy red. "But I'm not afraid anymore. I'm ready to obey God and go 'whither thou goest,' wherever He might lead."

All thoughts of Joseph disappeared. A single line played through Gil's head, floating on a delicate melody both familiar and brand new. He bolted upright, grabbed Ava's hands, and pulled her from the rocker. He smiled at her, battling the urge to wrap her in his arms and kiss her breathless. "Thank you, Ava."

She tilted her head. "Thank you for what?"

So many things. But he couldn't speak of all of them. Not yet. He needed more than words to encapsulate the emotion swelling in his heart. "Thank you for being willing to embroider the uniforms. Thank you for telling me you're no longer afraid."

As if his arms developed a will of their own, he drew her into an embrace. But only for a moment. Then he loosened his hold, resting his hands lightly on her waist. "I am going to deliver an edict, and I don't want a word of argument."

Her palms against his lapels, she laughed. "What is it?"

"Since you're taking the responsibility of stitching the trims onto the uniforms, you are hereby relieved of cookie duty."

Her fists shifted to her hips, dislodging his hands, and her mouth opened in a little huff.

He quickly closed it with a gentle push under her chin, shaking his head. "No. I mean it. Getting the uniforms done will take up enough of your time. I'll ask the mothers of the players to take turns providing a treat. I think it's only fair."

She affected a mild pout but didn't argue.

He thanked her with a smile. "I'll have the boys tell their mothers to bring the jackets to you as they finish them. I know they'll be beautiful when you've applied your handiwork." He winked and tucked a loose strand of her hair behind her ear. "But not nearly as beautiful as you."

Her cheeks flooded with pink. She took a backward step and lowered her head. "Gil . . ."

"Good day, Ava. Thank you for . . ." He gulped. "For everything." He leaped off the porch and raced for Roald's house, the image of her blushing face lingering in his memory.

Chapter Twenty-Five

Gil

GIL AWOKE ON JULY FOURTH WITH A STOMACH-ache. Today the entire town would gather to celebrate the nation's birthday. This morning the boys' band would play their marching song, providing a good practice for the competition in McPherson. He was undeniably excited. And admittedly terrified.

He headed for the kitchen, careful not to step on the kittens who leaped at his nightshirt's hem as he went. The month-old creatures could no longer be contained and, in Gil's opinion, should be relegated to the barn. But they weren't his pets, so it wasn't his decision. One tiger-striped kitten hooked its claws and hung from the shirt.

Gil plucked it loose, grunting when its claws snagged the fabric. He held it up by its nape and shook his finger at its striped, whiskered face. "You're a menace." The kitten batted at his fingertip, and Gil couldn't hold back a laugh. "And you're also pretty cute." He put the kitten on the floor, and it darted after its siblings, its little tail puffed up.

He stoked the stove, then went through the process of making a pot of coffee. While he performed the mindless task, his thoughts drifted to the day's activities. He'd let Roald talk him into signing up for the arm-wrestling and horseshoe-throwing contests. He didn't expect to do well at either, and the way his stomach felt, he might not make it to the celebration at all. He glared at the speckled pot, willing the water to boil. Surely coffee would help. According to Roald, coffee cured whatever ailed a man.

The thump of Roald's crutches signaled his approach. He rounded the corner, and his gaze went to the pot. He huffed. "I'm too late. I should've reminded you last night not to bother with brewing any beans. Or fixing breakfast, either. Ladies always have coffee and sweets set up outside the post office for folks."

Of course. Why hadn't Gil remembered the tradition from previous Fourth of July gatherings?

"Everyone comes early," Roald went on, "so they can choose a good spot to watch the parade."

Gil's stomach flipped again.

Roald plopped into one of the chairs. One white kitten and the mama-cat look-alike scampered past. He scooped the little calico into his lap. "I bet the boys are excited about leading the parade. Usually the men's band does that."

Gil peeked into the pot. Not boiling yet. "The boys feel honored." So did he. He'd expected the parade marshal to put the boys at the end. "And a little nervous."

"You, too, I imagine."

Gil gulped. "Jo."

The kitten wriggled, and Roald set it on the floor. "Will the boys get to wear their uniforms today? Lots of folks are eager to see how they look."

"Not all the coats are ready yet." Maybe it was true a watched pot never boiled. Gil sat across from Roald and toyed with an empty coffee cup. "But if folks are curious what they look like, they can go to the booth for quilts, samplers, and other stitched crafts. Ava provided one for display."

As always, thoughts of Ava sent a flood of warmth through his center. The weeks since their talk on the porch had been wonderful, better than when Gil was growing up and they saw each other every day. Maybe because they were a little older and wiser. Maybe because, as the poet waxed, absence had made their hearts grow fonder. Maybe because they'd both been listening more intently to the Father's voice. Probably all three. He treasured every meal at her family's table, every talk on the porch, every captured moment when their paths crossed on the street or in the churchyard.

A phrase sang sweetly through the back of his mind. *Whither thou goest, I make you this promise . . .* He'd finished his rewrite of Ava's song. The boys would play the new version at the competition in McPherson for the judges and listening audience. But the most important revising—the lyrics he'd penned to express his deepest feelings—were for her only. When he knew whether the boys would compete against the other winning bands, which would give him God's response to the fleece he'd laid out, he would play his violin and sing it to her. Just for her.

Roald's chair legs scraped the floor as he stood. He reached for his crutches. "I'm going to get dressed. If we hurry, we should be able to snag some of Mrs. Schenk's apple fritters. If we wait, all that will be left is Mrs. Plett's coffee cake."

Gil sprang from his chair. He yanked the pot—which still hadn't come to a boil—from the stove. "I'm right behind you, Roald."

Joseph

JOSEPH ADJUSTED EARL'S collar, then centered his string tie under his chin. He stepped back and examined his brother from his neatly combed head to the turned-in toes of his freshly polished boots. "You look very sharp, Earl."

Earl's face glowed. "Thank you. Ma was too busy getting Menno and Simon dressed to help me." He smoothed his hands down the front of Joseph's hand-me-down Sunday suit. "I wish we had our uniforms, though."

The uniforms were still a sore spot with Joseph. The money and time spent on all those decorated coats could have been used elsewhere. "Jo, well, the band won't sound any better just because you have uniforms on. People come to hear bands, not see them."

Earl's face fell.

Joseph inwardly kicked himself. He reached out and ruffled his fingers through Earl's blond hair, making the thick tufts stand up like dried prairie grass. "But I'm sure you'll be handsome in your uniform when it's finally done."

Earl grinned and smoothed his hair into place. "Thank you, Joseph." He pulled in a breath that poked out his chest, then blew it out through pursed lips. "I hope I don't forget any notes. There's a lot to remember, especially when we're marching. I start worrying about my feet and I"—he aimed a sheepish grimace at Joseph—"almost forget to play my horn."

Protectiveness welled up. Joseph put his hand on Earl's shoulder. "You don't have to march if you don't want to. It's your choice, Earl. You know that, right?"

Earl nodded slowly. "I know. And I want to. The band needs my trumpet. Gil said so. He's depending on me. The band's depending on me." He gulped and blinked several times. "Nobody's ever counted on me before. I don't want to let them down. I don't want to let *me* down. Do you understand?"

Suddenly Earl seemed less a little boy. A lump filled Joseph's throat. He nodded. "I understand."

A crooked smile creased Earl's face. "Thanks, Joseph."

"Come on. Let's help Ma get the little ones into the wagon so we can leave for town." Joseph cupped his hand around the back of his brother's neck and herded him out the door of the summer kitchen.

Joseph wished he could stay behind. There was work to do in the shop. But Pa said no, they were all going to the community celebration. Joseph snorted under his breath. What did he care about pie-eating contests and parades and women exclaiming over each other's stitched pillowcases? He clenched his jaw. He dreaded watching the parade. Dreaded watching Earl waddle while the other boys marched. Would people point and snicker under their breath?

His hands automatically curled into fists. If they did, Gil would pay the price.

Ava

"WELL, DON'T YOU look pretty as a picture."

Ava stopped in the middle of the parlor and twirled a circle for Papa, showing off the flare of her full green muslin skirt. She supposed she shouldn't have spent time sewing a new dress when she had so many uniforms to embroider, but she'd worn the same spring dresses for the past five years. She was due a new outfit, Mama had said, and Ava decided not to argue.

She touched the lacy collar of the trim-fitting ivory blouse and beamed at Papa. "Is it too fancy for a town parade and party?"

"It's perfect." Papa took hold of her shoulders and delivered a kiss on her forehead. He pulled out his timepiece and peeked at it. "It's almost half past eight. If your mama doesn't hurry, we'll—"

Mama entered the parlor, attired in one of her nicest dresses with her hair twisted in a knot high on her crown and a cameo pinned at her throat. She looked like the vibrant mother Ava remembered from when her brothers were still alive. Ava dashed across the floor and wrapped Mama in a hug. "Oh, you're so lovely!"

Mama laughed and patted Ava's back. "Jo, well, I am dressed. I can't say I'll last all day, but I refuse to miss the parade."

Papa slid his watch into his vest pocket and held out both elbows. "Then let's go." Mama took his left and Ava took his right.

They walked three abreast until they reached Schenk's Gristmill. Wagons cluttered the side street, forcing them to follow a maze-like path to Main Street. Ava moved behind her parents, and Papa curled his arm around Mama's waist. They stepped free of the parked wagons into a teeming mass of people on the boardwalks.

Mama sighed. "We should have come sooner."

Papa paused for a moment, scanning the area. Then he pointed ahead. "There's Roald. He's waving to me. He must have reserved a space for us in front of the post office. Let's join him."

Ava touched Papa's arm. "You two go ahead. I'll catch up to you. I want to find Gil and wish him luck. He's been nervous about the boys' performance today." How it warmed her to be trusted with his thoughts and worries and aspirations. Before he'd left for New York, his plans had always scared her. But this new openness between them endeared him to her even more.

"All right," Papa said. "Tell him we are praying for his success."

Ava kissed Papa and Mama goodbye, then darted across the street. She worked her way to the corner and down toward the livery, where the parade would start. The boys' band was already lined up in the street with Gil in the midst of them. Ava stopped and observed, a smile growing on her face.

Gil moved slowly from boy to boy, pausing to brush dust from Timmy's knees, smooth Fred's cowlick, and whisper something in Orly's ear. Amazing how she knew all the boys' names now when she never had before. The familiarity made her feel more a part of things. She wanted to rush over to them, but she waited, watching, marveling at how tall and handsome and confident Gil appeared. He made it all the way to the last band member—Ralph Ediger, who balanced the bass drum against his belly—and clapped the youth on the shoulder. Then Gil turned, and his gaze met hers.

He smiled and trotted to the sidewalk. She held out her hands, and he gripped them. His palms were clammy. "Ava . . ." He leaned forward and placed a kiss on her temple. "I'm so glad you're here. I've never been so nervous."

She laughed softly, shaking her head. "Save your nervousness for the McPherson competition. Today is for fun, to show the town what the boys have learned."

His face puckered. "That's exactly why I'm nervous. I don't know those judges in McPherson. If we mess up in front of them, who cares? We'll never see them again. But if we fail today, we'll disappoint so many people. The boys, their parents, the men's band that gave up its spot as lead in the parade, and—"

She put her fingers on his lips. "Gil, Gil, hush. Don't you know by now these people love you?" As did she. "Even if the boys run into each other and play more sour notes than sweet, their affection for you won't change." Nor would hers. "Relax. Smile. Let the boys see the belief you have in them." She tipped her head and raised her brows, giving him a teasing smirk. "You do believe in them, don't you?"

He released a self-deprecating chuckle. "Of course I do. You're right. All this worry is for *nuscht*." He glanced over his shoulder, and his face went pale. "Oh. There's Mayor Lohrenz. It must be time to start."

She squeezed his hands. "Then I'll go." She backed away, giving him her brightest smile. "I'll be with Mama and Papa in front of the post office, waving as you go by."

He lifted his hand in farewell. "I'll be with the band, not waving at anyone." He grabbed his raised hand and pulled it against his chest. They both laughed, and she scampered off.

As she reached the corner, the opening notes of the song Gil had taught the boys blared out. She broke into an unladylike run and made it to her parents before the band turned from the side street onto Main Street. The crowd clapped and cheered as the formation of boys, with Gil marching at their side, came up the street.

Ava bounced in beat with the music, peeking over the boys' bobbing heads and gleaming instruments in the hope of catching Gil's eye. He never looked left nor right but kept his focus straight ahead, his spine erect, and his feet moving in perfect synchronization with the music. She waited until Ralph's bass drum passed, then she worked her way through the crowd. The parade would circle the block and end where they'd started. She wanted to be there when Gil arrived.

Suddenly the music came to a discordant stop, and a series of gasps rose from the sidelines. From where she was standing, Ava couldn't see what had happened. People were craning their necks, looking toward the front of the parade. Ava wriggled her way to the street and cupped her hand over her eyes. She added her gasp. One of the boys lay facedown in the dirt, Gil on one knee beside him.

Then Dorcas Baty and Joseph dashed to the boy, and Ava instantly knew who had fallen.

Chapter Twenty-Six

Joseph

JOSEPH SENT A GLANCE ACROSS THE GAPING WIT-
nesses. No one outwardly laughed, but he saw some smirks.
Heard their mutters. "Oh, poor Earl," someone said with a series of *tsk-tsk-tsk*, and fury rose in his chest. He'd known this
would happen. Joseph grabbed Gil by the upper arm and
yanked him to his feet. He pulled Gil close and growled, "You
and me need to have a little talk."

Gil tried to squirm loose. "Not now. I need to see to Earl and
my boys."

Joseph pointed to Ma who was helping Earl sit up. "She's
seeing to *her* boy." Then he flung his arm, indicating the parents who were retrieving their sons from the group. "They're
seeing to *their* boys. Come on." He dragged Gil off the street
and behind the false-front café. Once out of sight of the crowd,
he slammed Gil against the building's lap siding and jammed
his fist up under his cousin's nose. "Didn't I tell you Earl
couldn't march? And you made him do it anyway. Put him
right in front, where everyone would be sure to see him fall."

Gil knocked Joseph's arm aside. "I didn't make Earl do anything he didn't want to do. And I put him in the middle front
where it would be less likely for him to trip over someone's
heel."

"Jo, well, he tripped anyway, didn't he?" Joseph injected as much sarcasm as possible into his snarling comment.

Gil shook his head. "He did not trip. He told me he stepped on something—a rock or something—and twisted his ankle. It could have happened to anyone."

But it hadn't happened to anyone. It had happened to Earl. With a growl, Joseph drew back his fist and then plowed it into Gil's jaw. The impact jarred him, and he stumbled sideways a step. Gil dove at him, and the two of them hit the ground hard. They rolled, and Joseph ended up on top. He sat on Gil's stomach, used his knees to pin Gil's shoulders to the ground, and leaned over him.

"You." Joseph spat the word. "You're always so perfect. Always obedient. Always cooperative. Always doing everything right." He slapped Gil on the face, right cheek and then left, as he recited the list of traits as if they were insults. "Did you ever stop to think how it makes everyone else feel? Do you know how hard it is to never measure up to your great and perfect cousin? I had to put up with it, but I won't let Earl get stuck in your shadow. I'll—"

Gil arched his back, throwing Joseph off balance. He scrambled to regain his position, but Gil flipped on his side and rolled free. Joseph bounded to his feet at the same time as Gil and raised both fists, circling his cousin like a boxer in a ring.

Gil turned in place, keeping Joseph in his sight and holding his arms wide. "Perfect? Is that how you see me?" He barked a laugh. "Maybe I did try to be perfect when we were boys. I had to be." He danced left when Joseph danced right. "Parents love their children even when they do wrong. But I wasn't born into your family. I was forced on all of you when my parents died." His face contorted. "Don't you think I knew I was in the way? Onkel Hosea said it when he brought me to Taunte Dorcas—he said, 'We have to take him. He's my brother's son. What choice do we have?' "

For a moment Joseph glimpsed hurt in Gil's eyes and sympathy tried to rise. Then he pictured Earl flopping facedown in the dirt in front of the whole town. He sneered, "Jo, we had no choice. But you had a choice. You didn't have to put those boys in front of everyone. You didn't have to make Earl—"

"I didn't make Earl march!" Gil shouted the denial. "I can't make anyone do anything! If I could, I'd make Taunte Dorcas love me! I'd make the elite of New York applaud my works!"

"And you'd make Ava go to New York with you, too, wouldn't you?" Joseph hollered even louder than Gil. "Because that's what this band is all about, isn't it? Winning favor. Winning the judges' favor. Winning Ava's favor. Winning—" He couldn't think of anything else to say. So he lunged at Gil and slammed both palms against his chest.

Gil fell backward. His hands shot out behind him, and he landed on them. A cry of pain left his throat, and he curled up like a roly-poly bug, cradling his right wrist to his chest.

Joseph put his fists on his hips. "Oh, nä, you're not going to get out of this fight that easy. Get up. Get up!" When he didn't move, Joseph reached to jerk him up. But someone grabbed his sleeve and pulled him aside.

Pa glowered at Joseph. "What are you doing?"

Joseph pointed at Gil. "Giving him what he deserves for humiliating Earl. For humiliating our whole family." He took a step toward Gil.

Pa stuck out his arm, blocking Joseph's path. "You're done here. Go to your mother."

"But—"

"Go!"

When Pa used that tone, Joseph usually did as he was told. But not today. "Nä, I won't. This fight between us has been coming on for a long time. We will finish it."

Gil moaned and sat up. He still held his right arm against his chest. "You did finish it. I admit defeat."

Pa crouched next to Gil. "You're hurt?"

"I did something to my wrist when I fell."

Joseph huffed. "Serves you right after making Earl fall."

Pa bolted upright and cuffed Joseph on the side of the head. "Enough, I told you! Your mother and brothers and sisters are already in the wagon. Go get it and bring it here."

Joseph's ears rang from Pa's clop. "What for?"

"Your cousin is hurt. He needs the doctor. We'll take him to Aiken."

"Nä, Onkel Hosea." Gil got to his feet. "The doctor costs money."

"We're going to take Earl anyway. He cut his chin on the trumpet. Dorcas thinks it needs stitches. And I want the doctor to look at his ankle." Pa turned to Joseph, and his glower darkened. "He twisted it when he stepped on a rock. It wasn't Gil's fault." He leaned closer. "Go get that wagon right now, Joseph, and when we've finished in Aiken, you, me, and Gil are going to have a talk in the woodshop."

Gil

THE HOUR WAS approaching suppertime when Onkel Hosea drove his team onto the yard. He drew the horses to a stop near the house, set the brake, then helped Taunte Dorcas to the ground. He moved to the rear of the wagon and lifted the tailgate aside. "Adelheid, help your mama put a meal on the table. Louisa and Herman, keep Menno and Simon out from under their feet. I'll carry Earl to the house."

The youngsters clambered out and followed their mother toward the back door.

Onkel Hosea turned a soft look on Earl. "Are you hurting much?"

Earl ran his finger over the bloodstained strip of gauze on his chin. "Not too bad, Pa."

"You're a brave boy. Scoot over here and I'll get you out."

Joseph lurched up. "Here, Earl, I'll help you."

"Nä." Onkel Hosea barked the word. "You see to the horses. Make sure they get fed and watered."

Joseph leaped from the wagon, his mouth set in a tight scowl.

Onkel Hosea held his arms to Earl. "Come on now. You can do it."

With his bandaged foot in the air, Earl pushed with his hands and pulled with one heel. He reached the end of the bed, and Onkel Hosea scooped him up. "See there? You made it just fine."

"Thank you, Pa."

Onkel Hosea's gaze shifted to Gil. First to his splint and sling, then his face. "Can you get out on your own?"

"Jo, sir." He shifted to the tail of the bed.

"Goot. As soon as I have Earl settled, I will meet you in the woodshop." He paused, then snapped, "Joseph?"

Joseph looked over his shoulder. "Jo?"

"You, too. When you're done with the horses, go wait with your cousin." He strode off with Earl cradled in his arms.

Gil slid out of the wagon and waited until Joseph turned it around before crossing the yard to the woodshop. He wanted to be thankful. Neither he nor Earl had broken any bones. Only sprains, the doctor had said, but it would take time for the ligaments to heal. He couldn't stop feeling guilty for Earl's injury.

He'd told Joseph the truth—he hadn't *made* Earl march. But he'd told Earl how important it was to have his trumpet in the band. He'd left the decision to Earl, but maybe the boy had felt pressured. If Onkel Hosea blamed Gil, he would accept the responsibility. Would Joseph accept responsibility for the harm done to Gil's wrist? He couldn't wiggle his fingers without great pain. How would he hold a baton?

Gil took a seat on a stack of cut lumber. Joseph came in and stood against the wall near the door, far from Gil. When Onkel Hosea entered a few minutes later, he snapped his fingers at his son and pointed to the stack of lumber. Joseph grunted under his breath, but he trudged across the sawdust-covered floor and perched next to Gil.

Onkel Hosea grabbed a nail keg and dragged it close. He sat and fixed Gil and Joseph with a stern frown. The sight brought back memories from childhood. When they were boys, being called to the woodshop meant punishment. They were too old for a strapping, but Gil's worst reprimand had always been suffering his aunt's or uncle's disapproval. He suffered it now.

Onkel Hosea clamped his hands over his knees. "Joseph, Gil, there is something I want to tell you. Something that should have been told long before now, but Dorcas swore me to secrecy. The pain . . . She thought if we didn't speak of it, it would go away. But it hasn't. It festers inside of her, and it has spilled over onto—" He made a horrible face, as if he smelled something rotten. "By telling the secret, I hope the wound will finally heal and relationships can be restored." He took a deep breath, held it for a few seconds, then whooshed it out. "Joseph, you were not our firstborn child. Less than a year before you were born, we had a son."

Joseph exchanged a shocked look with Gil, then glared at his father. "You had a son before me?"

"Jo. He came much too soon." Hosea hung his head. "He was tiny. So very tiny, he fit in my hand." He held out his palm and stared at it, as if seeing the child resting there.

Gil stared, too, trying to imagine a baby nestled in that broad, calloused hand.

Joseph spluttered a few nonsensical noises, then blurted, "What is his name?"

"We didn't give him a name. Or a church burial."

"Then where is he?" Joseph grated out the question, his teeth clenched.

"I buried him on our property. There's no stone to mark his resting spot, but I dug up a maple sapling from the creek and planted it near him."

Chills broke out over Gil's body. The single tree in the middle of an open expanse rose like a beacon on the prairie. He and Joseph had reenacted scenes from *The Three Musketeers* around that tree. They'd sat in its shade, rested or whittled, and watched a robin's nest take shape in its branches. If he'd known his infant cousin lay at its roots, would he have spent so much time there?

"I've watched the tree grow tall and strong in place of my son," Onkel Hosea said in a somber voice.

Joseph growled and pressed the heels of his hands to his temples. Gil put his arm around his cousin, a meager attempt to comfort him, but Joseph arched away from him and glared at his father. "Why did you never tell me? Do you think I'm a weakling or a child to be cosseted? I should have been told."

Hosea sat up and gave Joseph a stern look. "I'm telling you now. And I already said your mother refused to let me speak of him."

Joseph stood and paced back and forth, his fists clenched. "Ma was wrong. She should have named him. She should have buried him at the cemetery where we could pay our respects. She should have—"

Hosea leaped up, grabbed a handful of Joseph's shirtfront, and shook him. "Stop acting like a spoiled child. What makes you think you're the only person with feelings that matter? A woman carries a baby in her womb, beneath her heart. She feels its movements and watches her body grow to accommodate it. It's a part of her in a way that we will never understand." He released Joseph with a shove, and Joseph stumbled back a few feet before regaining his balance. Hosea pointed at him. "Losing her baby was losing part of herself. We can't comprehend that kind of pain, and we won't judge her response to it."

Joseph sat on the wood again, his chin quivering.

Hosea turned to Gil. "She never let you close. But it isn't your fault. You were born the same month our son should have been delivered. Even though Joseph was already nestled in her womb, you were a constant reminder of the boy we weren't able to raise. She felt it was . . . disloyal . . . to love you. That loving you would somehow replace him in her heart." Tears winked in the corners of his eyes. "I saw it, and I didn't like it, but I did nothing to change it. I am sorry for the part I played in making you feel like an outsider in what should have been your home.

"And, Joseph . . ." He shifted his focus to his son. "Do you remember when you were boys? You and Gil were nearly inseparable. Dorcas resisted having Gil here, so I let you go to your Onkel Ezra's place as often as you asked. I'd grown up with a brother only a year older than me, and I wanted you to have a close and brotherly relationship with your cousin. You had it. Until Ezra and Elizabeth died and Gil came to live with us." Hosea sat on the barrel again, rested his elbows on his widespread knees, and looked at Joseph. "Son, I've watched you absorb your mother's attitude toward Gil. I don't approve of the way she treated him, but I understand it. With you? I don't understand. Help me understand."

Joseph flicked a frown at Gil, then faced his father. "I thought I was the oldest child, and then he came and was the oldest. And he did everything—everything!—better than me. I . . ." He dropped his chin. "I was jealous."

"And resentful," Hosea said.

Joseph sat as still as a stone for several seconds. Then he nodded. "Jo."

"Well, now it stops."

Joseph lifted his head so quickly, his neck popped.

The stern expression on Hosea's face, although he aimed it at Joseph, held Gil captive. "Gil is my only brother's only child. He's been a good son to me and a good brother to you. He will only be in Falke a few more weeks, and during those weeks we are going to treat him the way he should have been treated all along—as a beloved member of our family."

Joseph swallowed. "What about Ma?"

"I am going to talk to your mother. I know nothing will ever fully remove the pain of losing her first child, but it's time she stop using Gil as her scapegoat for it." He stood and shifted his attention to Gil. "Son—" His voice broke. He pressed his fist against his lips for a few seconds, then cleared his throat. "Son, I know I am not your father, just as I know you are not a replacement for the boy we lost. But I want you to know . . . I love you. I am proud of you. And your Mutta and Foda would be, too." He put out his hand. "Will you forgive me?"

Gil rose. "I will." He couldn't offer an official handshake with his right hand in the sling, but he stepped close and pulled his Onkel into an embrace.

Onkel Hosea wrapped his arms around Gil and held tight. His injured wrist, trapped between the two of them, throbbed, but he didn't mind. They hugged for a long time, and when his uncle finally loosened his hold, he put his hands on Gil's shoulders and looked him square in the face. "I cannot guarantee your Taunte will change in how she views you. She's carried this hurt for over twenty years. It will be hard for her to let it go. But I ask you to forgive her anyway. Will you forgive her?"

Gil's lips wobbled into a smile. "I already have."

Chapter Twenty-Seven

Ava

AVA SAT ON THE PORCH WITH A JACKET DRAPED across her lap, watching for Gil. After the unfortunate end to the parade, she'd gone to the quilts and needlework booth where one of the finished uniforms was on display. She presumed Gil would look for her there. But he never came. Each time she spotted one of the boys from the band, she'd called him over and asked if he'd seen Gil. But she received the same response every time—"Nä, Miss Flaming, I haven't. I don't know where he is."

Wilhelmina Plett finally came to the booth and breathlessly informed Ava and the other women that Hosea and Dorcas had taken Earl to Dr. Graves in Aiken. Although it concerned her that Earl had injured himself badly enough to need the doctor, she was relieved to have her mystery solved. Just after the accident, she'd caught a glimpse of Joseph and Gil running toward the alley behind the café. They'd probably gone for the wagon, and Gil likely rode along to the doctor.

But his departure stole her enjoyment of the Fourth of July celebration, so when Mama wanted to go home and rest, Ava went with her. While Mama napped, Ava sat on the porch and finished the embroidery on another jacket. Now dusk had fallen. She couldn't see well enough to stitch, but she stayed put and waited. Because surely Gil would come to her when he got back from Aiken.

Mama poked her head out the front door. "Aren't you ready to come in?"

"Not yet, Mama."

Her mother crossed to Ava and gave her an awkward, one-armed hug. "Ach, I'm sorry your day was ruined."

"Not as much as Gil's was." Ava's heart hurt for Gil. He'd blame himself for Earl's fall. She sighed. "I feel bad for Earl, but I'm mostly worried about Gil. I hope this won't make him drop out of the competition in McPherson."

Mama moved to Papa's rocker and sat. "If an accident can make him give up, then he will likely never accomplish anything of value. Life isn't perfect. Sometimes we trip over our own two feet. What matters is, do we just lie there or do we get up again?"

Ava smiled. "That's very practical thinking, Mama."

"Jo, well, it's also true." She pulled her shawl more snugly around her shoulders. "If I know Gil, he won't give up. And he won't let Earl give up, either. I only hope Earl's parents won't stand in the way. This can be a good growing experience for him if they don't allow this fall to cripple him. In here." She tapped her forehead.

The sound of approaching footsteps captured Ava's attention. She set the jacket aside and dashed to the railing. "Gil? Is that you?" He moved free of the shadows, and joy burst through her. He was back! Then she spotted the pale cloth sling against his dark suit. She sucked in a gasp and raced to the stairs. "Oh, you're hurt! What happened?"

He trudged up the steps, his left hand reaching toward her.

She took hold of it and drew him near. He tipped his cheek briefly against her hair. "It's nothing much. Just a sprain."

Mama cleared her throat. "Good evening, Gil."

Gil gave a little start, his gaze zipping to Mama. He stepped away from Ava. "Oh, Taunte Maria, I didn't see you there."

"And now you have. How is Earl?"

Gil told them about Earl's sprained ankle and stitched chin. "Taunte Dorcas is worried he'll forever have a scar on his face, but Earl told me secretly he wants one. He thinks it will make him look tough."

Mama laughed. "Ach, so like a boy." She stood. "Now that you are safely back, I think I'll go in." She moved toward the door, sending a soft smile across both of them. "Ava is afraid you'll give up because Earl got hurt today. But I told her you have more *Entschlotenheit* than that."

Gil hung his head and released a soft laugh. "Taunte Maria, you have more determination than anyone I know. We all pale in comparison to you."

Mama grinned, then she closed herself in the house.

Ava guided Gil to the rockers, and they sat. "How did you get hurt today?"

"It's not important. What is important is its effect." He glared at his limp fingers sticking out from the white fabric sling. "How will I direct the band? How will I do the chores at Roald's place? And how will I play my violin? I need my right hand." He sent her a frustrated frown. "Ava, the competition in McPherson is a little over six weeks away. I've focused mostly on the marching piece so the boys could perform today for the town. We still have another song to learn, and the doctor said it will take at least six weeks for my wrist to heal. If I can't direct, then how will the boys be ready to compete?"

He rested his head against the rocker's back and blew out a breath. "The whole walk over here, I talked to God about my fleece. I wonder if my hurt hand is His answer."

"What do you mean?"

He shifted his head and looked into her eyes. "Remember I told you if the boys win in McPherson, they'll compete against all the first-place winners across the state?" At her nod, he continued. "Well, I asked God to let the boys win the competition in McPherson if I'm meant to stay here longer."

Her heart began thudding like Ralph Ediger's bass drum.

"If they can't compete, they can't win. Maybe my hurt wrist is God's way of saying He wants me in New York."

Ava frowned. "Gil, how did you injure your wrist?"

His expression turned sheepish. "Do you really want to know?"

"Jo, I do."

"Joseph knocked me down."

Ava's mouth fell open. "He . . . he knocked you down? Why?"

"He was angry about . . . well, about a lot of things. But when he pushed me, it was in retaliation for Earl taking that tumble in the middle of the street."

Ava huffed. "Earl's fall was not your fault."

"Jo, well, Joseph saw it differently." He fingered his jaw. "It's too dark to tell, but I have a bruise from his fist, too. That won't take long to heal, but my wrist . . ."

Ava reached across the little table and placed her hand over his. "I think it's too soon to give up. How can you know if the boys will win if you don't take them? They're so excited about the contest. They have these uniforms to wear. I think they should go. I don't think you can know for sure about the fleece unless you actually compete in McPherson."

He turned his hand upside down and linked fingers with her. A soft smile lifted the corners of his lips. "Will you come to the practices and wave my baton for me?"

She laughed. "Ach, can you imagine what kind of music I would make?"

He gave her hand a tender squeeze. "I know what kind of music you make. You play my heartstrings and fill my soul with song."

A flutter filled her chest. He'd told her the same thing when he asked her to be his sweetheart more than five years ago. The words had filled her with joy then, and they affected her the same way this evening. Happy tears swam in her eyes. "Oh, Gil . . ."

He sighed, and his thumb stroked hers—up and down, up and down in a gentle rhythm. "You're right about the boys. They're excited about the uniforms, and they've worked so hard. They need the chance to compete with the other bands. It wouldn't be fair to take it away from them now. But we'd better pray hard for Earl's foot and my wrist to heal faster than Dr. Graves predicted."

"Let's do that right now."

They bowed their heads.

Gil

ON THE MORNING following what he'd dubbed the Fourth of July catastrophe, Gil arrived a little before ten at the lot behind the bank building to prepare for the boys' practice. To his surprise, the entire band—except for Earl—was already seated on the grass in a tight circle, instruments in their laps.

Ralph, the self-proclaimed spokesman of the group, bounded up and hurried across the ground to him. "Mr. Baty, we're all wondering about the End of Harvest competition. Will we get to participate since Earl got hurt?" His gaze fixed on Gil's sling. "And you're hurt, too? What happened?"

Gil put his good arm around the boy's shoulders and turned him toward the group. "Go ahead and sit with the band, Ralph, and let's talk about the competition." Gil wished he could sit in the grass with the boys, but getting down and then up again was too hard with only one hand. So he stood in front of them and assumed a casual pose, left hand pushed into his trouser pocket.

He started by praising the boys for their performance yesterday. Even though the song had come to an unexpected, abrupt end, they deserved accolades for a well-executed rendition of the song. He told them to give each other pats on the back, which they did with grins and a few chortles. The next part of what he needed to say wouldn't be easy.

"About the McPherson contest . . ."

Every pair of eyes fixed on his face and every pair of lips pressed tight. Every set of shoulders tensed, including Gil's.

He cleared his throat. "As you know, the competition involves playing two songs. I planned to spend one day a week reviewing the marching piece and the other four days working on the piece we'll play standing in front of the judges." He bounced his injured arm against his belly. "I'm sure you noticed my sling."

Heads bobbed, and two of the baritone players whispered to each other.

Gil hoped the rumor mill hadn't caught wind of his and Joseph's fight. What a poor example he'd set by engaging in a wrestling match with his cousin. Not that he'd had much choice. "I sprained my wrist. I'm not able to grip anything with my fingers, which is going to make it hard for me to direct. But

I'm going to do my best, just as I trust you'll do your best to learn the song."

A cheer rose from the group. Gil let them whoop for several seconds, then he held up his left hand. "There's one more thing we need to discuss." The boys quieted. Gil said in a somber tone, "Earl."

Leo Friesen jammed his hand in the air. "Mr. Baty, me and Jack have been talking. We need Earl. There's all those baritones, but just the three of us trumpets. We know he fell and made the band look bad, but we don't think it was all his fault. We don't want him kicked out."

"That's right." Jack folded his arms and jutted his chin. "If he isn't allowed to play, I won't play."

"Or me," someone else called out, and several others chimed, "Me, either."

Gil gawked at the group. Did they really think he would drop Earl from the band because he'd taken a fall? "Wait a minute, boys. I have no intention of cutting Earl from the band. It's true he fell, but as Leo said, it wasn't his fault. He stepped on a rock. It could have happened to anyone. His fall was an accident, and he shouldn't be punished for an accident. I want him to stay in the band, too."

Jack's sullen expression relaxed, and the boys seemed to breathe a collective sigh of relief.

Gil bounced a genuine smile across every perspiration-dotted face in the group. "I'm proud of you boys for defending your friend. When I talk to Earl's parents, I'll tell them what you said. I know it will make Earl feel good to know how you want him to be part of the band."

Leo tilted his head. "What were you going to tell us about Earl?"

"He turned his ankle pretty badly. The doctor doesn't want

him to walk on it for at least six weeks. That means he won't be able to march with us. But as Leo already pointed out, we need his trumpet for the song to sound its best. So I want each of you to think hard about how we can include Earl in the competition."

The boys started chattering with one another, but Gil needed the remainder of their time together focused on the new song. He waved his left hand over his head. "Whoa, boys. Listen, please." They quieted down and gave him their attention again. "You all do some thinking and share your ideas when we come back tomorrow. Hopefully by then we'll have a plan for how to include Earl. For now, let's go up to the practice room. We have a new song to learn."

Chapter Twenty-Eight

Gil

GIL STRUGGLED THROUGH PRACTICE. HE HAD TO focus on keeping his directing hand still, which made it hard to give the boys' playing sufficient attention. When he stopped concentrating on his hand, it lifted by reflex, and pain instantly reminded him of his mistake. He was relieved when they reached the end of the hour and he could send everyone home.

As usual, Timmy stayed behind and helped Gil put the chairs and stands away. It took longer since Gil could only lift with one hand. He suffered under the scrutiny of Timmy's pitying glances until they were finished. Finally, Gil tucked Timmy's tuba under his arm, and they headed down the stairs. Timmy led, walking sideways and keeping his gaze pinned on Gil.

At the bottom, the boy didn't reach for his horn. "Mr. Baty, can I stay with you today?"

Gil chuckled. "Timmy, I appreciate your concern, but I only have a hurt wrist. I'm not helpless." Although when he'd tried to fix breakfast, he'd felt pretty helpless. His left hand wasn't as coordinated as he'd like.

"I know." The boy sighed. "But Mr. Willems is at the post office. He doesn't need me in there. Mr. Flaming's already gone on the mail route. So now I don't have anything to do."

"Won't your Taunte expect you to come home?"

He shook his head. "She said I should shoo. She's not feeling very good and said I gave her a headache."

"Well . . ." Gil adjusted his hold on the tuba. "I planned to walk to my Onkel's place and check on Earl. I suppose you could go with me."

The boy's face lit. "Thank you, Mr. Baty! Maybe I'll get to play with Herman for a little while. I wish he'd join the band. Him and me sit by each other in school. We're good friends."

Taunte Dorcas might see Timmy—and Gil, for that matter—as an intrusion to her day. He'd forgiven his aunt, but had she yet forgiven him for being born when her baby should have been? Not knowing what kind of reception he'd receive, he wasn't sure he should take Timmy. But it was too late. He'd already issued the invitation, and he couldn't disappoint the boy now. "Let's leave your tuba at the post office with Mr. Willems," Gil said. "Then we'll go."

Mr. Willems agreed to keep the instrument, even teased he might play a few notes on it, then Gil and Timmy headed for the Batys' house. As he walked, Gil's thoughts drifted to the McPherson silversmith's shop. The call stating Roald's tuba was ready for pickup had come a couple of weeks ago already, but he didn't yet have enough money to pay the bill. The silversmith agreed to hold the tuba until the end of August, but then, he said, he would put it up for sale in lieu of payment. If the boys did well in the contest, would the prize money be enough to cover the expense?

When they reached his uncle's place, Gil went straight to the woodshop. But neither Onkel Hosea nor Joseph were there. He scratched his head and scanned the yard. None of the children were playing. Had the family left for the day? He pulled out his timepiece and checked it. Then he groaned. Of course.

Taunte Dorcas put lunch on the table promptly at noon every day. They were all inside eating.

Gil herded Timmy to the house and gave the back porch door a couple of taps with his knuckles. A few seconds later, Onkel Hosea appeared on the other side. His face registering surprise, he pushed the door open.

"Gil, why are you knocking? This is still your home. You should come on in."

Gil appreciated his uncle's kindness, but after his time away, he wouldn't barge into the house unannounced. He gestured to Timmy. "I have a friend with me. I wanted to check on Earl, and Timmy hoped to play with Herman."

Onkel Hosea braced the door with his hand and shifted aside. "Earl is in his room and the rest of us are eating. Come in and join us."

Timmy bounced after Onkel Hosea without a moment's pause. Gil followed more slowly. Onkel Hosea had invited them, but Taunte Dorcas prepared the meals. She might not have enough for him and Timmy.

They entered the dining room, and Onkel Hosea gestured to Gil and Timmy. "See who showed up at our back door in need of a good lunch?"

Everybody sitting at the table looked up. Herman broke into a broad grin, and the girls waved at Gil. Joseph seemed to focus on Gil's sling.

Taunte Dorcas's gaze met Gil's, then quickly lowered. "G-Gil. *Goodendach.*"

"Good afternoon," Gil said. "I'm sorry I interrupted your lunch. I wanted to check on Earl. I should have paid more attention to the time."

"Nä, nä . . ." Taunte Dorcas stood and eased around the

table, her face downcast. "There are enough sandwiches and pickled beets for two more. I'll get plates." She slipped around the corner.

Onkel Hosea pointed to the table. "Timmy, you take Earl's usual place there beside Herman. And, Gil, grab that chair—" He winced. "Ach, what am I thinking? You can't lift it from its hooks with only one hand. I'll get it and put it next to Joseph. Wasn't that always your spot?"

Gil swallowed. "Jo. It was."

As Timmy slid into the empty seat with a bright smile, Joseph rose. "I'll get the chair for him, Pa."

Onkel Hosea offered a quick nod and sat down.

Joseph unhooked the chair from the pegs on the wall and placed it at the end of the long table, next to his own chair. He sent a side-eye look at Gil and patted the ladder back. "Here you are. Better sit so Ma knows where to put your lunch." He returned to his spot and picked up his sandwich as if he'd never been interrupted.

Gil sat, careful not to bump his arm.

Taunte Dorcas carried in two plates, each holding a ham sandwich, a pile of cubed purple beets, and a fork. She put one in front of Timmy, then reached across the table with the second. "Joseph, give this to your cousin."

Joseph did so. "Will you need me to feed you those beets? You never could do much with your left hand." A hint of teasing colored his tone—an apology his pride prevented him from uttering.

Gil gave him a grin, his means of accepting it. "Nä. You'd probably stick them in my ear instead of my mouth."

Adelheid giggled, and Herman and Timmy exchanged snickers. Onkel Hosea gave him and Joseph a meaningful look

Gil remembered well from his childhood. It said both *very funny* and *enough silliness*. And it made him feel more at home than he could explain.

He picked up his fork and made a clumsy stab at a beet chunk. "I wanted to tell Earl what the boys said about him at practice this morning." Taunte Dorcas and Joseph stopped eating and looked at him. "The other trumpet players, Leo and Jack, said they needed him." He managed to skewer the beet. "And the entire band said they would all quit if Earl didn't come back." He popped the beet in his mouth and chewed, letting his gaze move from his aunt, to his uncle, to his cousin.

Onkel Hosea looked at Taunte Dorcas and nodded. "That's nice, isn't it? That they miss Earl so much?"

Taunte Dorcas dropped her attention to her plate. "Jo, it is, but . . ." She whisked a frown at Onkel Hosea. "He can't go back. Not while he's hurt."

"But," Timmy piped up, "we're all thinking of ways for him to be able to march with us in McPherson. Orly Thiessen told Charles Wallace that Earl could ride in a goat cart and play his horn while we march."

Gil nearly choked on the beet. "He did? When?"

Timmy's bright gaze shifted to Gil. "When you were helping Alfred tune his trombone."

Taunte Dorcas shook her head. "A goat cart? Goats are unpredictable. They need a firm hand to guide them. If Earl was playing his trumpet, he couldn't control the cart at the same time. It might take off with him in it. He could be hurt even worse than he was yesterday." She shook her head again, the movement adamant. "Nä, don't you even consider such a thing, Gil."

Despite his aunt's reaction, Gil couldn't help but contemplate the idea. Would it work? His eagerness to include Earl overrode any hesitance about addressing his aunt. "If I assigned someone to lead the goat, would you let Earl ride in the cart and play with the band?"

Onkel Hosea cleared his throat. "I think we should let him try it, Dorcas. Being in the band has been very special to Earl. He's so glum about falling. He thinks he let everyone down. This would make him feel a lot better, don't you think?"

Taunte Dorcas bit her lower lip, uncertainty lining her brow.

Onkel Hosea put his elbows on the table and leaned forward, his expression pleading. "If Gil finds someone trustworthy to guide the cart, will you let Earl ride in it?"

Gil stared at his aunt, his heart pounding in hope. Her approval meant so much to him. Her refusal would crush him.

Finally she sighed. "I suppose I would let him try. Only if you find someone who knows how to control the goat."

Timmy let out a whoop. Everyone jolted and gaped at him. He grinned. "I know who can do it."

Gil swallowed a chortle. The boy looked so sure of himself. But he'd never gone up against Taunte Dorcas. Depending on whom he suggested, he might suffer a mighty defeat in a few seconds. Gil asked, "Who do you think should do it, Timmy?"

Timmy flipped his hand in Herman's direction. "Him."

ORLY THIESSEN'S FATHER delivered the goat and cart to the Batys so Herman could practice with it as often as needed to win Taunte Dorcas's trust.

The first few times the band rehearsed with Earl riding in the cart, Joseph walked alongside, keeping a close eye on his brothers. Gil coached the boys to modify their stride or even march in place for a couple of beats if the goat's pace didn't remain consistent. There were a few mishaps, and at times he wondered if the idea would really work, but by the third practice the boys and the goat were working well together. During the cookie breaks, he and Joseph engaged in conversation. Though still more stilted than Gil would prefer, at least the deepest animosity seemed to have disappeared. For this, Gil was grateful. It gave him hope that he and his cousin might one day return to the close friendship they'd shared when they were younger.

The last Monday in July, as the boys gathered for their morning practice, the goat clopped up the street with Herman in the lead. He drew the cart to a stop next to Gil and beamed up at him. "Ma said we should go in by ourselves instead of keeping Joseph from work. So here we are!" His pride was unmistakable, and Gil thrilled at the silent message it sent. Finally, Taunte Dorcas had chosen to trust. Not only Herman and the goat, but Gil, as well.

If only the practice on Ava's song could bring such success. He couldn't hold the baton tightly enough to control it. The boys followed the signals he made with his left hand for crescendos or decrescendos, increasing or decreasing the volume in response to his motions, but he needed his right hand to direct the tempo. Though the song was written for moderato—a standard tempo—there were phrases that begged to slow into a graceful adagio or quicken the listeners' pulse by speeding into allegretto. And his left hand refused to deliver those instructions.

Every night, he prayed for regained strength in his injured hand. But every day, pain in his fingers forced him to relinquish his hold on the baton. He couldn't possibly win the contest if he couldn't direct the boys to play the song the way it was intended to be heard. And he *needed* to win. For the prize money. For affirmation of his calling. For confirmation of where he was to go next. The fleece he'd placed before the Lord was always in the back of his mind.

The women of the community continued delivering evening meals, which Gil appreciated more than ever. Especially given his inability to do little more than stir cornmeal mush with his clumsy left hand. Between Roald's dependence on his crutches and Gil's weak wrist, the housework also suffered until Ava took it upon herself to come over on Saturday mornings and help.

He resisted at first. He felt guilty relying on her so heavily. But she'd pointed at him with her feather duster and confessed, "All this helping I do for people . . . for a long time it's been my way of nurturing someone. Of being motherly. And, selfishly, making myself feel as if I matter. God revealed this to me, and even though it wasn't a pretty thing to see, I'm glad I realized it. Because now, when I offer to help, I'm offering to use an ability He gave me for His glory instead of doing it to make me feel better about myself."

As much as it still bothered him not to be able to see to the cleaning himself, he appreciated her company. Their conversations. Their friendship blossoming again. Sometimes he felt as if the four-year separation had only been a bad dream. He couldn't wait until he was able to grip his violin bow. He prayed the words he'd written for her song would express what she meant to him. He prayed she would receive them as his commitment to her.

The first Saturday in August, when Onkel Bernard brought dinner and his trumpet for another lesson, both Ava and

Taunte Maria came with him. Taunte Maria carried a cake, and Ava held a stack of dishes, napkins, and cutlery. Gil watched them parade past him, his mouth hanging open.

As they laid the items on Roald's table, he scooped up the kitten batting at his pant leg and followed. "What is all this?"

"A celebration," Taunte Maria said.

Gil searched his mind. Had he missed an important date? "What are we celebrating?"

Ava sent a shy smile in his direction. "All the missed birthdays from the past four years." She crossed to him and stroked the kitten's chin. "Don't you remember coming to our house for dinner on your birthday?"

How could he forget? Taunte Dorcas didn't bother with birthday parties. She always said they were too much work, but now he wondered if they were a painful reminder of the birthdays she never got to celebrate with her firstborn. Despite his aunt's attitude, he'd never felt neglected because Ava's parents had celebrated the day and made him feel as if he was part of their family. "Of course I do."

"Jo, well," Onkel Bernard said as he plinked forks next to each of the plates, "we decided we needed to do something to make up for the ones we missed. And since you likely won't be here when your next one comes around, the cake will have to suffice for that one, too."

If the boys won in McPherson, most likely he *would* be in town for his twenty-third birthday in September. Should he tell them what he was thinking? Before he had the chance, Roald came in the back door, leaning heavily on his crutches. He stopped and gaped at the activity happening in his kitchen.

"What is all this?"

Gil laughed. "Roald, we've been living together too long if we say the same things." He repeated what Ava had told him, then added, "Since this is a missed-birthdays celebration, I guess we can say yours are included, too."

The man grinned. "That sounds fine to me." He frowned at the kitten Gil held. "There you are, you blue-eyed rascal. I rounded up your mama and brother and sisters and herded them to the barn. No easy task, I can tell you, even for someone with two good legs! But you hid too well." He looked at Gil. "Do you want to carry him out with the others?"

Ava took the fuzzy cat from Gil. "I was hoping you might let me have this one, Mr. Willems. He reminds me so much of a kitty I had when I was a girl. Her name was Princess, so I'd call this one Prince. I'll give him a good home."

Roald gazed longingly at the kitten. "Well, I've grown fairly attached to him. And he's still kind of small to be taken from his mother. But since you live right close, and I'd probably see him from time to time, I suppose it's all right. If you'll let him do a little more growing before you take him for good."

She beamed. "Thank you, Mr. Willems."

Then his brows formed a sharp *V*. "But will you be here to take care of a kitten? You and Gil will recite vows before too long. Then you'll head off to New York with him. You wouldn't cart that little cat all the way to New York, would you?"

Gil covered his eyes with his hand and swallowed a groan. Roald had just, as it were, let the cat out of the bag.

Chapter Twenty-Nine

Ava

MAMA RELEASED A STARTLED GASP. PAPA MADE A gargling sound, as if he swallowed a chuckle. Gil slowly slid his hand from his face and gave Ava the most embarrassed look she'd ever seen. She had no idea how to interpret it. So she stood in silence and waited for him to say something.

But he didn't.

Roald released a gruff *ahem!* that broke the silence. "Did I say something wrong? The way you two have been getting along, I assumed . . ." He looked from Gil to Ava to Gil again, a sheepish grimace creasing his face. "Maybe I misread things."

Gil slowly shook his head. "Nä, Roald, you didn't misread things."

Ava's pulse scampered into double beats. She cradled the kitten beneath her chin and held her breath, anticipating what Gil would say next.

"But you're getting ahead of me. Of my plans." He ran his fingers up and down the edge of his sling, a habit he'd recently acquired. "I love Ava, and I would like nothing more than to ask her to marry me. But I wanted to get Onkel Bernard's and Taunte Maria's blessings first. And I wanted to"— he swallowed—"finish something before I asked."

Papa rounded the table and put his hand on Gil's shoulder. "Son, Maria and I have loved you since you were a little boy. You had our blessing before. You still do. But I think, right now, we better put that subject aside and pretend it was never mentioned."

Ava's breath eased out in a disbelieving huff. What a ridiculous suggestion. How on earth would she forget Mr. Willems's ill-timed comments? Or Gil's response to them?

"This way," Papa continued, "you can ask her in the way you planned, and it will still be a surprise, jo?" He patted Gil's shoulder and then gestured to the table. "Come now. Let's sit and eat before Ava's good chicken and noodle casserole grows cold."

Ava put the kitten on the settee, where it curled in a ball, then she sat at the small table next to Gil. Papa, Mama, and Mr. Willems chatted as they ate, but neither she nor Gil contributed to the conversation. She couldn't be certain why he was so quiet, unless he needed his full attention to eat. His left hand wasn't nearly as adept as his right in wielding a fork. She was quiet because she couldn't escape her thoughts.

She shouldn't be upset with Mr. Willems for blurting out what he said. He hadn't done it out of spite or meanness. What mattered was Gil had proclaimed his love for her out loud, with three witnesses present. Papa had given his blessing. Eventually Gil would ask her again, and this time she would accept. But she couldn't deny feeling as if she'd been cheated of something precious.

She dipped her fork into the noodles and accidentally brushed Gil's arm. He peeked at her out of the corner of his eye, and she peeked back. A sweet, shy grin lifted one side of his mouth, and his dimple winked.

He leaned over and whispered directly into her ear. "After I give your father his trumpet lesson, I would like a few minutes of your time."

Delightful shivers danced across her scalp. Her lips quivered into an answering grin, and she offered a quick nod. Then she averted her gaze before their flirtation captured Mr. Willems's notice.

They finished the casserole, and Mama cut slices of cake for everyone. Gil dropped icing down the front of his sling, creating a chocolate smear. When he bemoaned the mess, Mr. Willems teased, "Just turn the sling inside out. No one will know," and they all shared a round of laughter. After enjoying dessert and coffee, Mr. Willems, Papa, and Gil went to the sitting room for Papa's lesson. While Papa blew the notes for "Bringing in the Sheaves" loudly enough to alert the entire town, Ava and Mama washed the dishes and made a neat stack on the kitchen table.

Finally, Mama said, "Bernard? It's growing late. We have church in the morning. We should go."

Papa reluctantly lowered the horn. "You're right. Roald, thank you for letting us use your house for our party."

"If you bring cake, you can have a party here every night," he said, and more laughter rolled.

Mama picked up the clean dishes, then turned to Ava. "Are you coming?"

She glanced at Gil.

He stepped forward. "Onkel Bernard, I'll walk Ava home in a few minutes. After we take Prince to his mama in the barn."

Papa nodded. "All right. Not too late, though, jo?" Mama and Papa exchanged a smile before they left through the front door.

Gil glanced around. "Now, where is that kitten?"

Ava pointed to the spot she'd put him. "He was here just a bit ago. Papa's trumpet playing must have frightened him into hiding."

Mr. Willems harrumphed. "He's a sly one. He could be under or behind anything by now."

Ava waited while Gil searched the sitting room, then headed up the hallway. A few seconds later, she heard his short burst of laughter. He returned with Prince tucked inside his sling. "The little stinker was waiting to ambush me. He leaped out from behind a door and snagged my pants." He handed her the kitten. "Are you sure you'll be able to put up with something so ornery?"

She fluttered her eyelashes at him. "I put up with you, don't I?"

He laughed, then gestured to the back door. "Shall we go out that way? It's closer to the barn."

And out of sight of any passersby should he decide to kiss her. She fully expected a kiss under the stars. After all, what was a marriage proposal without a kiss? With Prince tucked against her shoulder, she headed for the back door. Just as they reached it, someone pounded on Mr. Willems's front door.

"Mr. Willems! Mr. Baty!" The frantic cry carried over the thumps.

Gil jolted. "That's Timmy." He jogged to the door and swung it wide.

Timmy rushed through the opening and collapsed against Gil, sobbing.

Mr. Willems grabbed his crutches and hobbled over. "Timmy, what's the matter, boy?"

The child lifted his tearstained face to the man. "My Taunte. She fell down in the kitchen and went to sleep on the floor. I can't wake her up."

Ava's heart leaped into her throat. "I'll get Papa to hitch the horse to the carriage." She darted out. Not until she reached her house did she realize she was still carrying Prince, but it was too late to take him back now. She scrambled up the porch stairs and inside. "Papa! Papa!"

Papa came from the parlor. "What's the matter?"

She repeated what Timmy had said. "It doesn't sound good. Please hurry."

Papa gave her a quick kiss on the temple. "Stay with your mama. I'll be back as soon as I can." He ran up the hallway and left through the connecting door.

Ava found Mama in the parlor, sitting in her favorite chair with her Bible open in her lap. When Ava told her about Timmy's unexpected arrival, Mama set her Book aside and immediately began to pray. Ava couldn't find words, so she simply paced the room while petting the kitten, begging, *Please, please,* and trusted the Lord to understand.

By the time the mantle clock chimed nine, Mama was drooping in her chair. Ava convinced her to go to bed, chiding, "Staying awake won't change the outcome."

Mama offered a weary smile. "I seem to recall a wise woman giving similar advice to you not long ago."

"Jo, and she was smart enough to take it to heart."

Mama looked at Prince sleeping in the curve of Ava's arm. "If that one is staying the night, he needs to go to the barn."

Ava ran her fingers down the kitten's silky spine. She found comfort in his warm presence, and she hated to give him up. But Mr. Willems's query about whether she'd take a cat all the way to New York made her ponder the wisdom of growing attached to the little creature. "While you ready yourself for bed, I'll return him to his mama."

"A wise choice."

Ava crossed the wide, grassy patch separating their house from Mr. Willems's place. Although the evening was warm, she experienced a shiver as she walked through deep shadows beneath a star-sprinkled sky. She couldn't help thinking about Timmy running across town all by himself without even a kitten providing company. What a brave boy. And now, if what she suspected was true, a very alone boy. Her heart ached for him.

She located the mama cat and other kittens in a box lined with an old, mouse-chewed blanket and placed Prince with them. Then she hurried home and continued her pacing. Had the hands on the clock ever moved so slowly? Finally, at a little before eleven, Papa scuffed through the door.

Ava ran to him. "Was she . . ."

Papa nodded. "She was." He opened his arms, and she stepped into his embrace. Then he escorted her to the parlor. He sat in his chair, and Ava took Mama's.

"How is Timmy?" she asked.

"Inconsolable." Anguish tinged Papa's expression and tone. "The Edigers offered to let him stay the night with them, but he wanted to be with Mr. Willems. Gil and I made a pallet at the foot of Roald's bed. Roald said he's welcome to remain with him until the End of Harvest celebration."

"And after the celebration? Then what?"

Papa hung his head. "If someone doesn't take him in, he'll likely go the orphans' asylum in Topeka."

Ava gasped. "Oh, Papa, no! He'll wither and die there."

Papa sank deeper into his chair and hung his head. "It gives me no pleasure to think of taking him there. But the boy doesn't have any other family. This is why the asylums exist, to provide a place for children like Timmy."

Ava wouldn't argue. Not tonight, with Papa so exhausted

and heartsore. But if they tried to take Timmy to Topeka, she would argue with every bit of breath she possessed.

"Miss Dirks is laid out in her bed, and she is at peace." Papa struggled to his feet. "After we alerted Reverend Ediger, we went by the Batys'. Hosea and Joseph will ready a casket, and we'll have a service as soon as it's done, probably Tuesday morning. For now, there's nothing left to do but turn in. I'm sure the situation will be addressed in tomorrow's service." As he passed her, he patted her hands. "I'm sorry, my Leefste. This isn't the way I hoped this evening would end for you."

Nor the way she'd hoped. But her worries seemed petty in light of Timmy's great loss. She rose and slipped her hand through Papa's elbow. "Don't worry about me, Papa. There's time for Gil and me to talk."

But as she closed herself in her room, she couldn't help looking ahead. In only two more weeks the boys' band would compete at the End of Harvest celebration. The outcome would determine whether Gil accepted the teaching position in New York or not. Only two weeks. Was it enough time?

Gil

WHATEVER SERMON REVEREND Ediger had planned for that sunny Sunday morning in August was pushed aside to tend to one of their own. Gil remembered similar meetings after the fever swept through Falke. During the weeks of the illness's rampage, so many families were devastated—parents left without children and children left without parents. He'd been one of the lucky orphans, with a family member willing to take him in. But there was no one left for Timmy.

Roald had stayed home from the service with the distraught boy. Gil almost stayed, too, after missing a ride with the Flamings. But Roald asked Gil to speak on his behalf concerning Timmy, and Gil agreed to go. In Gil's mind, the two should remain together. Roald needed a family as much as Timmy did, but Roald insisted he couldn't be responsible for the boy forever.

"I'll keep him here until the competition. Then, if nobody offers to give him a home, I'll take him to the orphans' asylum myself. They'll find a good family for him," he'd told Gil with tears swimming in his eyes. "A boy should have a mother and a father. He never knew his mother, then lost his pa at such a young age. He should have a chance to have two parents."

Gil understood the man's reasoning and applauded him for wanting to do what was best for Timmy. But at the same time he wondered whether anyone would care about Timmy as much as Roald already did.

Reverend Ediger stepped down from the podium and stood in front of the congregation. "As we all know, Miss Dirks was guardian to her great-nephew, Timmy, who is now without a family member to look after him. Since there's no guardian to make plans for him, we, as his church family, must decide what's best for him."

Gil stood. Ava and her parents sat across the aisle. He sent them a brief look he hoped conveyed his need for prayer support, then pulled in a fortifying breath. "Reverend Ediger, I'm sure everyone here knows that Timmy and Roald Willems have established a friendship."

The man nodded. "Jo, he's been a good help to Roald during his time of need."

"He has." Gil glanced at Ava and took courage from her steadfast attention. "Last night, when Timmy couldn't wake his aunt, he came to Roald's place because he knew he'd find assistance there. Roald would like to keep Timmy with him at least until the End of Harvest competition is done. The boy has worked hard along with others in the band, and especially after what he's lost, he deserves something to look forward to. Roald is also willing"—his heart pounded so hard, he marveled he could take a breath—"to help transport Timmy to the orphans' asylum in Topeka. But he hopes it won't be necessary to take him there."

A few people murmured, and someone behind Gil said, "Doesn't Roald want to provide a home for Timmy?"

Gil looked over his shoulder and recognized the speaker as the town's barber, Mr. Rempel. "Roald believes that Timmy would benefit from a home with both a mother and father present. As much as he likes Timmy, he worries he won't be able to meet all of the boy's needs." Gil sat, glancing across the aisle as he did. To his surprise, Ava was glowering at him.

She shot to her feet. "Reverend Ediger, may I speak?"

"Anyone is welcome to share right now, Miss Flaming. Please go ahead."

She half turned, addressing everyone in the congregation. "Timmy Dirks is a wounded little boy who's lost the last person in this world who bears a blood relationship with him. Right now he is deeply grieved and very frightened. I'm grateful he had a good friend to run to, but Timmy needs more than a good friend. He needs a family. Will he find that at an orphans' asylum, where he'll compete with dozens of children for attention and affection? At his age, is it likely a set of parents will choose him? New parents want babies, not nine-year-olds. If he goes there, he'll languish. The boy is too bright, too personable to be sent to such a fate."

She snatched her Bible from the pew and ruffled pages. She held the Book open and read, "'Pure religion and undefiled before God and the Father is this, to visit the fatherless and widows in their affliction . . . '" She closed the Bible and pressed it to her bodice. "So it says in James 1:27. Can we call ourselves religious and ignore this child's needs? I think not." She sat, laid her Bible in her lap, and stared straight ahead.

Gil's heart pounded. On one hand, Ava was only doing what Ava did—taking care of other people. But on the other hand, the fervor in her voice and fire in her eyes expressed a deep concern for Timmy. She wasn't only *taking care*—she genuinely cared. And it stirred determination within him. "She's right," he heard himself say.

Reverend Ediger turned to him, a puzzled frown marring his face. "Did you say something, Gil?"

He nodded and pulled himself upright again. "I did. I said Ava is right. We're Timmy's church family. Although I mentioned the orphans' asylum, I actually don't think sending him to Topeka is the best thing to do. I think he needs to stay here in Falke, where he's known and where he feels secure. He needs to be with a family who will love him and train him up in the nurture and admonition of the Lord."

Mr. Siemens turned around from the front pew. "Wouldn't it be too hard for Roald to have the boy here in town but not living with him?"

Gil ran his fingers up and down the edge of the sling. "It might be hard, because he does care a great deal about Timmy. But he told me what he wants most is for Timmy to go to a good family. A family with a mother and a father." He sat again.

Reverend Ediger sent a serious look across the congregation. "I commend Miss Flaming for speaking words of wisdom from the Book that is meant to guide us in life. We should always seek God's will. I also must admonish that taking a child into one's home is a large responsibility. Thus, it is not a decision to be taken lightly. I think it best, as Gil suggested, to let Timmy remain with Roald Willems until the competition. This will give us—all of us—time to pray and seek our hearts for God's guidance. We will address the issue of Timmy's permanent home the Sunday after the competition."

He returned to the podium. "For now, open your hymnbooks to 'O God, Our Help in Ages Past.' Let's praise our Father in song."

Chapter Thirty

Gil

AFTER THE MINISTER RELEASED THE CONGREGA-
tion with prayer, Gil stepped across the aisle to Ava. "Thank
you for sharing the scripture from James. What you said will
make people pray, and God will open someone's heart to taking Timmy into their family. I believe it."

"I believe it, too." She didn't sound confident, though. "Gil,
did you come in the mail delivery wagon?"

"Jo, I didn't have another way to get here. I'd hoped to catch
a ride in your family's carriage, but when I knocked on your
door, no one answered. You'd gone without me." He grinned
as he spoke so she'd know he wasn't upset.

"I'm sorry. We presumed you'd stay with Timmy."

Her unsmiling countenance concerned him. "Ava, is something wrong?"

She glanced around, then cupped her hand beneath his
elbow in lieu of taking his arm. "Let's find Mama and Papa. I'd
like to ask their permission to ride home with you. Is . . ." Her
brow pinched. "Is that all right?"

Time alone with Ava was a gift. "Jo, I would enjoy that."

Onkel Bernard and Taunte Maria were already in the carriage, waiting. Gil stood to the side while Ava spoke with them.

At Bernard's nod, Gil's heart sputtered. They truly trusted him with their daughter, and he determined to never betray their trust.

He assisted Ava onto the delivery wagon's narrow seat, then awkwardly pulled himself up on the opposite side and unwrapped the reins.

She observed him, eyebrows low. "How did you hitch the team one-handed?"

"I did it three-handed."

Her fine brows shot high.

"Roald helped. You can imagine how long it took, with him leaning on his crutches and me fumbling around with my left hand. That's why I was a few minutes late to service. But don't worry. The wagon will stay attached to the horse."

"I'm not worried."

But she was clearly worried about something. Timmy? Or something more? He flicked the reins, and Roald's old mare obediently pulled them from the churchyard. They fell in with the line of buggies and wagons carrying families home. Home, where meals waited in stoves and tables were set with the dishes reserved for special occasions and Sundays. Oddly, the thought made Gil homesick. When would he finally have a house, a wife, and children with whom to gather around the table?

He cleared his throat. "Was there something you wanted to talk about?"

"Jo, there is." She stared straight ahead, as if afraid to look at him. "Gil, what you told Papa at Roald's yesterday, about l-loving me—did you mean it?"

His hand tightened on the reins. Oh, to have two good hands right now so he could put one around her and draw her close. "Jo, I meant it. I've always meant it. I . . . I feel as if I've loved you forever, Ava."

"And last night, when we planned to go to the barn, did you intend to ask me to be your wife?"

How he wanted to ask Ava to be his bride—his wife, his love, his life—but would it be fair when he wasn't even sure where they would live? "I wanted to talk about it, jo. To tell you why I hadn't asked you yet."

She swallowed. "Tell me now."

He examined her profile, wishing she would turn her face toward him. "There's so much uncertainty yet. Where would we live? What would I do to support you? I cleared tables and washed dishes at a small café to pay my bills in New York while I peddled my music and auditioned to conduct or play in orchestras. My job paid enough for me to cover food and half the rent on an apartment, but I wouldn't want to return to a setup like that with a wife."

She gave him a quick peek with her eyes without turning her head. "What about the teaching job you told me about? Wouldn't it support you and a . . . a wife?"

He made a face, turning his attention to the road. "It's a small school, Ava. The only reason I considered taking the position is it would still allow me time for musical pursuits outside the classroom. Would the salary be enough to pay for a house, for us to afford children? Nä, it wouldn't." He sighed, glancing at her sweet profile. "I know I am to work with the boys' band. I know I am meant to take them to the competition. God made that very clear to me. But what I'm to do when the contest is over? I don't know. I won't know until we've played and I find out whether we've won or lost. Because the outcome will either require me to stay in Kansas longer, where I will have to find a full-time job when Roald is on his feet again, or send me back to New York to the same situation I had before . . . barely getting by while hoping to finally sell my compositions."

He took a deep breath. "I want nothing more than to ask for your hand. I even have a special way I plan to do it."

She finally fully looked at him, her face tipped at a curious angle. "You do? What?"

He shook his head. "Ach, nä, you'll have to wait."

"Until when?"

"Until my hand lets me hold the violin bow."

Her expression changed from curious to confused. "What?"

He smiled at her. "You must trust me with this."

She stared at him for several seconds, as if her penetrating gaze could read beneath the surface and uncover his intention. Then she sighed. "I love you, Gil. It's taken me a long time to admit that my love for you isn't going away. I believe God planted it within me. I don't want you to go to New York again without me. But I can't go to New York with you if we aren't wed."

Gil gulped. Was she proposing to him?

"I'm Mama and Papa's only remaining child. They never got to see Anton or Rupert court and marry. I want them to have the pleasure of seeing their daughter wed. I don't need a fancy wedding. I don't need a new dress or even a big party afterward. All I need, Gil, is"—she slightly leaned toward him—"you promising your love to me."

The words he'd written for Ava's song whispered in the back of his heart. He longed to sing them to her and deliver the promise she requested. But the time wasn't yet ripe. He had to wait.

Town waited just ahead. A town with houses with windows and pairs of eyes to peek out and see them. He pulled the reins and guided the horse off the road into the thick grass, set the brake, and turned sideways in the narrow seat. He placed his hand over hers. "You already have my love, Ava. Given the circumstances and how little time we have to plan, I'm glad you'll be happy with a simple ceremony. Since you likely won't get all the fancy things other brides anticipate, it's all the more important that I give you a special proposal. And I can't do that until—"

She sighed. "Your hand heals and you can play your violin."

He smiled. "Jo."

She sighed again, but a hint of teasing glittered in her eyes. "I suppose this is what I deserve for falling in love with a musician."

"So you forgive me?"

She tapped her chin with her fingertip, eyes rolled upward as if in deep contemplation.

He laughed and pulled her into a hug with his good arm. His wrist got caught between them, causing him pain, but it was worth it to hold her even for a few seconds. He kissed her temple. "I do love you, Ava Flaming. I have ever since you were a freckle-faced tomboy."

She smiled up at him, beguiling in her sweet innocence. "I only pretended to be a tomboy so I could be with you."

He gazed into her adoring upturned face. Ach, the overwhelming temptation to kiss her rosy lips. But they weren't officially betrothed. The kiss, too, must wait. He forced himself to shift forward on the seat and take up the reins. "Your folks are probably wondering what kept us. We should go."

She cupped her hand over his arm. "You will ask me to marry you, won't you, Gil?"

Did he glimpse uncertainty in her light brown eyes? "I will. I promise."

Her hand slipped away, and she settled into the seat, facing ahead. "Please hurry."

Please hurry home, or please hurry and ask for her hand? Most likely, she meant the latter. As he urged the horse back onto the road, he sent a glance to the crystal blue sky beyond the clouds where he'd always envisioned God residing. He hoped God had heard Ava's sweet entreaty and would respond by bringing healing to his wrist. He longed to ask her as much as she longed to be asked.

Hurry, Father. Please hurry.

Joseph

JOSEPH SANDED THE edges of the pine box, ascertaining no slivers would pierce the hands of those assigned to carry it. Of all the things he and Pa built in the woodshop, coffins were his least favorite. On a practical level, they could probably sustain a good living making them. After all, death was a certainty for everyone. But such a depressing task, preparing a person's final resting place. He wished Miss Dirks had family who would buy a coffin from the undertaker in McPherson so he and Pa could focus on tables and chairs and cradles, the furnishings of living.

Pa lined up staves on the work surface, his brow puckered in concentration. He must have found them pleasing, because when he finished his examination, he placed them in a crate next to the work bench. If one hadn't matched or had showed a slight split, it would go in the kindling box. Then, at least, the wood wasn't wasted. But Joseph hated throwing a finished product into the cookstove.

His father strode across the floor and ran his finger along the opposite side of the long narrow lid. "This is looking good,

Joseph," he said in his solemn voice. Pa always used a solemn voice when they built a coffin.

When Joseph was a boy, he'd found a bit of humor in Pa's serious countenance over a box. But now, he understood. It seemed disrespectful to be playful or even apathetic when preparing a burial box. "Dank. It should be done in time for tomorrow's service." When the casket would be placed in the ground and covered with dirt. "You know, Pa, I used to think it foolish to spend so much time on something that would be buried. Now I think . . . this is the last gift we can give a person. It should be the nicest it can be."

Pa sent Joseph a smile of approval. "That is a good thought. It's a man's thought. I'm proud of you."

So seldom had he heard those kinds of words from his father. They washed over him like one of Ma's healing balms, and his nose burned—a sign of tears gathering. He sniffed and leaned over the lid, applying the sanding block to the wood. "I'm glad you let Herman take the goat cart into town and spend the day with Timmy. Since Gil canceled practices today and tomorrow, Timmy needs distraction."

"Timmy needs more than distraction. He needs a family to take him in." Pa's solemn tone returned. "Every night when I say my bedtime prayers, I ask God to let me live long enough to see all my children grown and on their own. To think of Menno and Simon, Louisa, Herman, and Earl left without your mother and me is a frightening thing."

Joseph glanced up. "What about Adelheid and me? Don't you worry about leaving us?"

Pa selected a sanding block from the tool table and set to work on the opposite side of the casket. "You and Adelheid are old enough to take care of yourselves. I wouldn't willingly leave you, even now, but I wouldn't worry the way I would over the younger ones." He aimed a speculative look at Joseph. "If something happened to your ma and me, would you stay here, take care of your youngest sister and your brothers, make sure they were raised right?"

Joseph stopped and stared at his father. "Why are you asking me this? Are you sick? Is Ma sick?"

Pa shook his head. "Nä, we're fine. Older, but fine." He paused and fixed Joseph with a serious frown. "Miss Dirks's unexpected death and Timmy being left without someone to take care of him make me think of my own mortality. My own children's fates. I had the same thoughts when my brother and his wife died. We'd agreed to be responsible for each other's families should death come. I didn't expect to need to, though."

"But you didn't hesitate to take in Gil."

Furrows formed across Pa's brow. "He is my brother's son. Of course I didn't hesitate. But . . ." He went back to work. "It wasn't easy. Not for any of us. Taking in someone else's child, even when you know it's right, makes changes. As Reverend Ediger said, it isn't a decision to take lightly."

He fell silent, focused on swishing the sanding block against the wood. Joseph waited, but when Pa didn't speak again, Joseph also turned his attention to work. But something in his father's face, in his voice, made him wonder if Pa had wanted to ask him more than he'd said aloud.

Chapter Thirty-One

Ava

AVA TOOK MAMA'S ARM AND LED HER AWAY FROM the graveside, relieved to leave the mound of fresh-turned, fragrant soil and the gaping hole where men had lowered Miss Dirks's pine coffin. They wove between the many rock headstones scattered through the plot of grass behind the church. As they passed the two bearing the names of Ava's brothers, Mama stumbled.

Ava gripped tighter, keeping her mother upright, then she slipped her arm around Mama's waist. She whispered, "Almost to church."

"Nä," Mama rasped, "take me to the carriage."

"You don't want to go to the dinner inside?"

"Nä. I am too . . ."

"Weary?" Ava provided.

Mama nodded, but Ava suspected that *emotionally wrought* would have been a better description.

Mama sighed. "Please have your father catch a ride to town with Gil. I need to go home."

"All right, Mama. I'll tell him after you're in the carriage."

As Ava helped her mother onto the seat, she wondered how much of her mother's exhaustion was due to reliving the days

Anton's and Rupert's caskets were placed in the ground. Ava had hardly taken a full breath since her family arrived at the church this morning for Miss Dirks's funeral. Now, with the burial complete, Ava could breathe again. But her chest still ached. For Timmy. For Mama and Papa. Even for herself. She believed what the Bible said, that death for the believer was merely a glorious new beginning that would last for eternity. But death for the ones left behind gave a different kind of beginning—a beginning of mourning without a true end despite the hope of being reunited one day.

She patted her mother's hand. "I'll go tell Papa you want to go home, and then I'll be right back."

As she made her way across the short-cropped grass, her gaze roved across the small, somber group remaining near the graveside. Mr. Willems held Timmy's hand, Gil on Timmy's other side with his arm around the boy's narrow shoulder. Reverend Ediger stood at the foot of the hole, the pages of his open Bible rustling in the mild breeze, watching Papa and two other men transfer shovelfuls of dirt from the mound onto the coffin. Such a picture of finality. She knew the image would sear itself into her heart.

She shouldn't interrupt Papa in his mournful task, so she went to Gil, carefully avoiding looking into the hole. "Mama needs to go home and rest." She whispered, unwilling to break the reverence of the setting. "Can Papa ride back with you and Mr. Willems when the dinner is over?"

"Jo." Gil also whispered, his dark brown eyes sending a silent message of heartache. "Does this mean you plan to stay with your mother and not come to the church?"

Ava glanced back at Mama, who sat slumped in the seat, her head low. "I think it best."

Gil couldn't touch her without removing his hand from

Timmy, but his tender expression was like a gentle brush of his fingers on her cheek. "I'll see you later."

She offered a sad smile, then hurried to Mama. They were silent on the ride home, and Mama retired to her bedroom after informing Ava she wasn't hungry. Ava changed from her dark dress into something cheerier, then fixed herself a simple lunch she didn't eat. While she waited for Papa and Gil, she stitched gold braiding onto the front of one of the jackets—the one Mrs. Plett had sewn for Timmy.

A picture of Timmy clinging tight to Mr. Willems's hand at the graveside flooded Ava's mind. The boy had become very attached to Mr. Willems, and the man clearly cared about the boy. She understood Mr. Willems's feelings about Timmy going to a home with both a mother and father, but she couldn't help wondering if taking the child away from his good friend would do more harm than good, given what he'd already lost. She intended to speak to Gil about it. Perhaps Gil could convince Mr. Willems to raise Timmy after all.

She bit the thread that secured the braiding from the shoulder to the waist. As it snapped, she heard the connecting door from the barn open. She laid the jacket and needle aside and crossed to the hallway. Papa was coming in, followed by Gil and Timmy.

Papa briefly embraced her and delivered a kiss on her forehead. "Is your mother resting?"

Ava nodded. "She hasn't stirred since we got back."

"Let her sleep as long as she wants." Papa's eyes seemed haunted, no doubt plagued by the same thoughts that had troubled Mama at the cemetery. "I need to deliver the mail." He held his hand to Timmy who stood looking bereft and uncertain beside Gil. "Timmy, I could use your help. Would you come with me on the route?"

Timmy glanced up, and Gil put his hand on Timmy's head. "I think you should go. Then Mr. Flaming won't be alone." He leaned down and whispered, "He's feeling sad, too. You'll be a comfort to him."

Timmy squared his skinny shoulders. "Jo, Mr. Flaming. I will go." He took hold of Papa's hand, and the two walked out together.

Ava waited until her father had latched the door behind him, then she turned to Gil. "You're so good with him, Gil."

Gil slid his fingers along his sling's edge. "Jo, well, he reminds me a little of myself when I lost my folks, how he needs someone to pay attention to him and make him feel wanted. He's a good boy. I don't want him to feel unloved."

She touched his sleeve. "He is loved. And so are you."

His tender smile thanked her.

She returned to Mama's parlor chair, and Gil followed. He sat in Papa's chair, leaned back, and sighed. "We missed our marching practice this week. But since Herman brings Earl to town every day with the goat cart, we'll be able to march tomorrow. Then I'll ask the boys if they can come an hour early on Thursday and Friday for some extra rehearsing on our"—he flicked a wary glance at her—"other song."

Ava picked up the gold embroidery thread, snipped a length, and threaded the needle. "What are the boys playing for their second song?"

"One of my compositions." Gil seemed fascinated by the line of connected loops alongside the braid trim. "You're doing an excellent job with the embellishments, Ava. But then, I knew you would. Has it been difficult for you to get them all done in such a short amount of time?"

She frowned slightly. "No more difficult than it's been for you, fitting in so many practices."

"Ach . . ." He flapped his good hand as if shooing a fly. "It's not so hard. But I still worry about how it will go. A conductor's left hand is meant for dynamics and the right for tempo. Without both, the heart of the music suffers. Right now, the song is only half what it could be. I need to hold my baton in order to give the song the life it deserves."

Ava paused and frowned at Gil, something niggling in the back of her mind. "Gil, are you unable to move your arm at all?"

He slipped his arm from its sling and then bent it at the elbow, raising his hand high. "My arm isn't the problem. My wrist and fingers are what's tricky." He curled his fingers, grimacing. "It's getting better, but it still hurts too much to keep my hand clasped around something small."

"Like a baton," she said.

"Jo."

She laughed.

He scowled at her. "Ava, I don't see what's funny. I've been praying and praying for my wrist to fully heal so I can hold the baton. But—"

"I'm not laughing at your injury. I'm laughing at you."

His scowl deepened.

She set the jacket aside and rose. He still held his arm upright like a flag, and she gently cupped his hand between her palms. "Gil, stop and think for a moment. Where does the music originate? Does it grow from within your heart, or does it grow from something you hold in your hand?"

He stared at her, his eyebrows dipped low. Then his expression cleared, wonder replacing the irritation.

She smiled and nodded. "The gift is within you. The baton is merely a tool for showing it. I understand why you want to hold the baton. It's the conductor's instrument, and your baton was given to you by someone you hold dear. But, Gil, you don't need the baton to direct the boys. Your hand put the notes on the page. It can bring the notes to life."

He bent his fingers slightly, pressing them to her hand. "You're right, Ava. I don't know what I was thinking." Resolve filled his eyes. "Tomorrow, we march. Then Thursday, I will teach the boys the heart of the song."

Gil

BY NINE O'CLOCK Thursday morning, all twenty boys were in their seats, ready for practice. Well, almost ready. A few were still chortling about Earl's ungainly way of ascending the stairs. Since he couldn't put weight on his twisted ankle, he came up on his bottom, lifting himself with his hands and good foot one step at a time. It took him a while, but it worked, and he didn't seem to mind the teasing, presumably understanding that no malice underscored it.

Gil went to the front of the room and whisked the sling over his head. The boys fell silent when he tossed the cloth onto the nearest windowsill.

Ernie Schenk sat forward in his chair, eyes round behind his spectacles. "Mr. Baty, is your hand all better?"

Gil chuckled. "Not quite, Ernie, but my head is finally healed."

The boys glanced at one another, frowns marring their brows.

"Boys, I made a terrible mistake." He slipped his baton from inside his jacket and held it up between the fingers of his left hand. "I've been giving too much power to this piece of ebony and not enough to God, who is the true Giver of gifts. But today, it changes." He returned the baton to his pocket and raised his right hand. "I might not be able to move my fingers or wrist well yet, but I can move my arm. I'm going to trust Ralph"—the boy straightened, pride squaring his jaw—"and the other drummers to keep their eyes on the movement of my hand. The rest of you, watch my motions but also listen to the drummers' beat. Stay with the tempo they set. And, as you play, listen to what your horns produce. Listen for the heartbeat of the song." He smiled. "I believe that by the end of practice today, you will be able to hear the soul of the music."

Joseph

WAS HE SEEING what he thought he was seeing? Joseph moved to the front window of the general store to get a better look. Sure enough, Ava was pushing a wheelbarrow up the boardwalk. He called to Mr. Wallace, "I'll be right back for that order," then darted out the door and intercepted her.

He grinned. "What are you doing?"

A blush stained her cheeks. "I'm sure I look ridiculous, but how else could I transport all of them at once?" She gestured to four neat stacks of folded black jackets riding in the deep tray.

He touched a gold button on one of the uniforms. "So you're done, huh? They look real good." They did. Professional. The boys would look sharp in them. "When I saw you coming with that wheelbarrow, I thought you were delivering a whole passel of pies and cakes to the café. That maybe you'd decided to take it over for Miss Dirks, after all."

She gaped at him. "How did you know Miss Dirks wanted me to take over the café? I never told you."

He chuckled. "Ava, you know how people talk. There are no secrets in Falke."

"I suppose that's true."

Would she take over the café now? The townsfolk, especially the unmarried men, needed a place to get a good meal. Ava was smart and a good cook. She'd probably be a good businesswoman. Strangely, the thought of her operating the café didn't irritate him the way it once had. Why was that?

She wiped perspiration from her brow. "I need to get to the bank building before the practice ends so I can send these uniforms home with the boys today, so please excuse me." She reached for the wheelbarrow handles.

He stepped in front of her and took hold. "Allow me. I don't have anything else to do until Mr. Wallace finishes filling Ma's grocery order."

She wrung her hands, her expression worried. "You're taller than me. You might spill them out."

He rolled his eyes. "Then steady the top of the stacks and let's go before Gil sends the boys home."

She pursed her lips, but she braced her hands on the front two stacks and waddled along beside him. As they neared the building, notes from the song the boys were playing floated from the open windows. He tilted his head, straining to recognize the tune. Lilting and sweet, definitely attention-grabbing, but unfamiliar to him. He glanced at Ava, prepared to ask if she knew what it was, but her face had gone white.

He abruptly stopped. "Ava, are you all right?"

She pressed both palms to her bodice and stared up at the second-story windows. "That's . . . That's . . ." Her mouth flopped open and closed like a catfish gasping for air.

Was she going to swoon? Joseph grabbed her elbow. "That's what?"

"My song." The words grated like sandpaper on wood. She

turned a wide-eyed look on him. "The boys . . . they're playing my song."

Joseph shook his head. "I'm sorry, Ava. I don't understand. Did you write the song?"

She huffed and jerked her elbow free of his hold. "Of course not. Gil wrote it. He wrote it for me. He wrote it for me to tell me—" She closed her eyes. "It was my betrothal gift. He said it was *our* song. Special. Personal. Intimate . . ." She opened her eyes and tears spilled. "Why would he teach the boys our special song, Joseph?"

"Maybe because he knows it will impress the judges." Joseph said the first thing that popped into his mind. Once it was stated, he realized how unkind it sounded. Hadn't he told himself he was going to stop being resentful of Gil? But he couldn't take it back, so he scrambled for a reason that might make her feel better. "Maybe he didn't have time to write something new for the competition, so he dug it out and used it because he forgot why he wrote it."

The pain reflected in her light brown eyes told him he'd said the wrong thing again. Fresh tears rolled down her pale cheeks. "I have to go home." She took a stumbling backward step. "P-please see that the boys get their jackets." She turned and ran.

Chapter Thirty-Two

Gil

GIL INSTRUCTED THE BOYS TO LEAVE THE STANDS in place. The men's band would put them away after their evening practice. Then he and Earl led the pack down the stairs, Earl sliding down on his bottom beside him. They reached the street level, and he gave his young cousin his crutches. "There you are, safe and sound. I'll see you tomorrow." The sound of a clearing throat caught his attention, and he glanced up and found Joseph in the doorway of the small entryway. "What are you doing here? I thought Herman was bringing in the goat cart for Earl."

"Change of plans," Joseph said. He flipped his hand toward a wheelbarrow holding the finished jackets. "Look what's here. I kept watch over them until you got done."

The boys crowded around the wheelbarrow, jabbering excitedly.

Gil glanced up and down the street. "Where's Ava?"

Joseph shifted his attention to Earl. "Ma said Timmy should come out and spend the afternoon with Herman." Timmy whooped, and Joseph grinned at him. "The wagon's in front of the mercantile. You two go wait for me there. I'll bring your jackets."

Timmy took off. Earl gave the jackets a longing look, but he hitched his way up the boardwalk.

Joseph leaned close to Gil. "Ava got upset when she heard what you were playing."

Gil groaned. He waved his good hand at the boys. "All right, quiet down, please. Ralph, where are you?"

The youth pushed to the front of the group.

"Each jacket has a tag pinned inside with the name of the owner. Would you distribute them, please? I need to talk to Joseph."

"Sure, Mr. Baty."

Gil sent a firm frown across the group. "Now be careful with these. Take them straight home, no playing with them on the way. We want you to look your best for the competition."

"Jo, Mr. Baty," they chorused.

Gil escorted Joseph several feet away from the boys. "What did Ava say?"

Joseph shoved his hands into his pockets. "She wondered why you taught the boys a song that was supposed to be personal, between the two of you." He angled his head, his brows dipping. "Did you forget it was her song?"

"Of course not." How could he forget something so special? "But I hadn't intended for her to hear the boys play it. Not yet." Remorse struck hard. Another surprise spoiled.

Joseph gaped at him. "In a town this small, I can't believe you thought you could keep something like that from her."

Gil thought he'd put together a good plan by keeping Ava busy stitching and excusing her of snack duty for the boys. But his plans didn't seem to work so well. He hung his head. "I better go talk to her."

"You might want to stop at the general merchandise store

for some boxed chocolates before you go. She's going to need some sweetening up."

Gil didn't have money to squander on a box of chocolates. His explanation would have to do. "Thank you for watching the coats."

Ralph sauntered over with Earl's and Timmy's coats and gave them to Joseph. Then he turned to Gil. "Mr. Baty, there isn't a uniform for Herman."

Gil couldn't make sense of Ralph's comment. "Herman isn't in the band."

"He doesn't play an instrument, but he leads the goat cart with Earl in it." Ralph scratched his head, making his red-brown hair stand up. "Won't it look funny if he doesn't have a coat, too?"

Joseph patted the jackets draped over his arm. "Before Ma sewed a new one for Earl, she considered remaking one of my old coats. I'll ask her about doing it for Herman instead."

Ralph nodded and hurried off.

Gil sighed. "Thank you for talking to Taunte Dorcas about another coat. I should have thought of it myself."

Joseph winked at Gil, reminding him of the way they used to tease with each other. "You have bigger things to worry about. Good luck."

Gil waved goodbye, then scuffed to the empty wheelbarrow. He'd put the sling back on after practice because his wrist was aching. Now he glared at the thick cloth. How would he push the wheelbarrow one-handed? He grabbed hold of a handle and lunged the wheelbarrow forward. It turned itself in a circle on the boardwalk.

"Are you practicing for the circus, Gil?" The teasing comment came from inside the barber's shop.

Gil shot a tight grin at Mr. Rempel and his customer. "Nä, I have enough to do without joining a circus."

The men laughed, and Gil wrestled the wheelbarrow into the right direction. After a few moments of contemplation, he grasped one handle close to where it met the barrow's tray and pushed with his knees. The conveyance rolled straight. The tactic was ungainly but effective, and he managed to push it all the way to Ava's barn and put it away.

Then he knocked on the connecting door. Taunte Maria answered. By the expression on her face, he knew Ava had told her mother what she'd overheard. "May I come in?"

She moved aside and gestured him into the house. "Ava and I were just sitting down for our lunch. Are you hungry?"

He wasn't. The worry that he'd upset Ava had chased away his appetite. "Thank you, but I only came to talk to Ava. Will she speak to me?"

Taunte Maria gave an uncertain shrug and led him up the hallway to the kitchen. As he entered, Ava was settling into one of the chairs at the little table in the center of the room.

She glanced up, spotted Gil, and shot to her feet. She scuttled behind the chair and gripped its stamped back, glaring at him. "How could you share that song with the band? Does it mean nothing to you?"

Taunte Maria clicked her tongue on her teeth. "Ava, Ava, is that any way to speak to a guest?"

Ava sent a brief glower in her mother's direction. "He is not a guest right now. He is an unwelcome intruder." She jerked her scowl to him. "Joseph tried to tell me the only thing that mattered to you was music. That you would stop at nothing to become successful. I didn't believe him, though. Not until this morning when I heard . . . when I heard . . ." She pressed her fist to her mouth for a moment. "You told me that was our song, Gil. But now it's the band's song. The competition's song. The song you're laying out before strangers as part of your fleece."

The tears swimming in her eyes pained Gil worse than Joseph's fist to his jaw had. He longed to take her in his arms and assure her his intentions were honorable. He took a hesitant step forward, but she raised her hand in the air, palm outward, and he automatically froze in place.

"You told me a win or loss at the competition will determine what you do next with your life. I presumed I would be part of your 'next,' but I never dreamed you would take something so precious to me and selfishly use it." The tears spilled down her face, and she swished them away with both palms. Her chin quivered, but she held her head high. "I should have listened to Joseph. He was right. Music will always come first." She darted through the opening to the dining room, and moments later the front door slammed.

Gil started after her, but Taunte Maria caught his sleeve. "Let her go, Gil."

He flapped his hand in the direction of the door. "But she doesn't understand. I need to tell her—"

"She isn't ready to listen." Ava's mother offered a soft smile. "She is hurting right now. And she is *stoakoppijch*, like her Mutta."

Gil almost chuckled. "You aren't stubborn, Taunte Maria."

"Ach, jo, I am, and I am proving it by making you stay here right now." She gave his arm a gentle pat. "I'm sure you have a reason for choosing to teach the boys the song you wrote for Ava, but until she has calmed enough to release her anger, she won't hear anything you say. Let her be for now." She pulled out the chair Ava had vacated. "Sit and have lunch with me. Wait for Ava to return on her own."

Gil swallowed. "And if she doesn't?"

"Then we'll pray together for this rift to find a quick resolution." A frown pinched her brow. "And you might consider finding a different song for the boys to play at the competition."

Gil sank onto the chair's seat, his spirits lagging. The competition was only nine days away. Was there time to learn a different song?

GIL REMAINED AT the Flamings' house until almost two o'clock, waiting for Ava to return. But when Taunte Maria confessed she needed to rest, he left. He wished Onkel Bernard was at the post office instead of on a mail route. He needed someone to talk to. Someone who wasn't, as Taunte Maria had said, *stoakoppijch* and would listen to reason. He walked to the post office thinking he might talk to Roald, but customers were in the little building, so he went on past. He found himself leaving town and following the dirt road to Onkel Hosea and Taunte Dorcas's place.

Louisa, Timmy, and Herman were chasing each other around the yard. They dashed up to him, gave him a quick greeting, then ran off again, laughing and squealing. He watched them for a few minutes, remembering the days he and Joseph played such chasing games in the yard. The memories seemed a lifetime ago.

With a sigh, he trudged to the woodshop and stepped inside. He glanced around. He didn't see Onkel Hosea, but Joseph was in the back corner, assembling what looked like the spindled back for a chair. A sudden resolve filled him. Maybe it was good he'd come and found Joseph alone. He needed to talk to him about what he'd said to Ava. He strode across the floor and stepped to the opposite side of the worktable, directly in Joseph's line of vision.

His cousin glanced up, and surprise registered on his face. "Gil. Did you find Ava? Was she still upset?"

"I found her. And, *jo*, she was still upset. So upset she wouldn't talk to me." Then he snorted. "Well, I suppose she talked. I should say she wouldn't listen to me."

Joseph laid the small brush over the pot of glue. "I'm not surprised. I hadn't seen her so mad since the time we put the frog in her lunch pail at school."

Gil would not be distracted by funny stories from their childhood. "She said you told her I didn't care about anything except music. Did you really say that to her?"

Joseph's face contorted into a grimace. "*Jo*, I did." Then he shook his head. "But it was a long time ago, when I was angry at you. It was a *domm* thing to say. I'm sorry for it now."

If he hadn't apologized, Gil would be able to stay angry. But Joseph rarely apologized. It proved his remorse. Gil hung his head and picked at a bit of chipped wood on the corner of the worktable. "I'm sorry, too. Because now she might not listen when I tell her why I wanted the boys to play that song."

"Why did you teach it to them?"

The reason was also personal, between Gil and Ava. He searched his mind for a truthful yet cautious answer. "I . . . wanted to surprise her with a different variation of the one I'd played on my violin."

A mirthless chuckle rumbled. "Well, you surprised her, for sure."

Gil released a soft snort. "*Jo*, I suppose I did."

Joseph rounded the table and stopped near Gil. "Gil, I am sorry I told Ava you didn't care about anything else as much as music. I know you care about her. The hurt in your eyes tells me how much it bothers you to have her angry at you."

Gil slowly nodded. "It does. But it must make you happy to know she listened to what you said, remembered it, and believes it. When I got back to Falke, you told me to stay away from Ava. Now she's staying away from me. So you're getting what you wanted." He waited for Joseph's ire to flare, for him to even punch Gil again.

His cousin looked aside, his jaw muscles tense. "Jo, there was a time Ava was what I wanted. But I realize now why I wanted her so much." He shifted his eyes and met Gil's gaze. "Because you had her. Winning her affection was just another competition between us." He fully faced Gil. "I don't love her. Not like you do. And if you think it would help, I will talk to her again. Tell her I was wrong in what I said."

His willingness touched Gil deeply, but he shook his head. "Thank you, but nä. This is between Ava and me. If she won't listen and believe me, then maybe"—pain stabbed his heart— "she isn't as committed to me as she said. If that's true, it's best for me to know."

Chapter Thirty-Three

Ava

AVA HID IN MR. WILLEMS'S BARN WITH THE MAMA cat and kittens until midafternoon. With the café closed, she didn't have any baking to do, but other chores awaited her. She couldn't ignore them forever. She sneaked back into the house, relieved to discover Gil had gone and Mama was sleeping. She performed her duties by rote, surprised how well she functioned when her heart was surely broken.

Mama awakened a little after four and came to the kitchen. She seemed surprised to find Ava at the ironing board. "Shouldn't you be baking?"

Ava frowned. "Why? The café is closed. I don't have orders to fill." Maybe she should open it herself. It would keep her too busy to think about how much her heart ached. If loving someone caused this much pain, she would be better off never marrying. The thought created a bitter taste on her tongue.

Mama still gaped at her. "Ava, the men have band practice this evening. I realize the boys' mothers have been taking snacks to the youth band, but the men will expect you to bring their treat."

"Jo, well, I'm not taking them one." Ava applied the iron to Papa's shirt. "They can do without until Papa is directing them again."

Mama stomped across the floor and yanked the iron from Ava's hand. "I will iron. You bake."

Ava stared at her normally patient mother.

Mama nudged Ava aside. "You heard me. You won't be hurting Gil a bit by not sending a treat, but the men will be disappointed." She sent Ava a brief glower. "Don't be petty."

Chastened, Ava mixed the batter for gingerbread cakes and readied the oven. After supper, Ava placed the cooled cakes and stack of napkins on the platter and held it out to Papa. "Here. Take this with you."

Papa sent a startled look from the tray to Ava's face. "You aren't bringing it?"

"Not tonight."

"Are you not feeling well?"

Ava set her lips in a tight line and refused to answer.

Papa glanced at Mama, who shrugged, and he took the tray. "Very well. Thank you. The men will enjoy this."

When Ava finished cleaning the kitchen, she told her mother she intended to spend the evening in her room, reading.

Mama raised one brow. "Don't you mean sulking?"

"I've spent every evening for the past several weeks stitching the boys' jackets." Defensiveness and no small amount of irritation exposed itself with her tone. "Now that they're done, am I not allowed some time to relax?"

"Jo, you're allowed." Mama spoke as sharply as Ava had. She flicked her fingers at her. "So go. Read your Bible while you're in there. I suggest 1 Corinthians 13. You need the reminder."

Stung by her mother's apparent lack of sympathy, Ava went to her room. She bypassed her nightstand where her Bible lay and chose a novel from the few books on the scrolled shelf hanging on the wall. But the story failed to capture her attention. She laid it aside and stared out the window at the distant prairie. Its emptiness reflected the aching emptiness she felt inside.

She rose from her chair and paced the small space, remembering the pain of the first weeks after Gil left for New York. How long had it taken her to accept he was gone? Months, at least. And now she would experience that agony yet again. How foolish she'd been to allow him into her life a second time. Hadn't he and Joseph both told her that he wouldn't stay? And she'd offered him her heart anyway.

She stopped and glared at her Bible, directing her anger not at the Book but at its Author. "I asked You to remove this love for Gil from my heart, and instead You let it flourish. Why must You be so cruel?"

Charity suffereth long, and is kind . . . Doth not behave itself unseemly, seeketh not her own . . .

She covered her ears, a ridiculous attempt to silence the voice in her head reciting familiar words from the chapter Mama had suggested. But it wouldn't hush.

Charity never faileth . . .

She sat on the edge of her bed and put her face in her hands. She whispered, "Nä, God, You are wrong. Sometimes it does . . ."

OVER THE NEXT week, Gil knocked at the front door two or three times a day. If Mama was sleeping, Ava pretended she didn't hear. But if Mama was awake, Mama answered the door and shared a few quiet words with him, and then he went away. Although Mama didn't do any more scolding, Ava felt her mother's disapproval.

On the Friday before the competition in McPherson, Gil returned for a third time that day. Ava finally stomped to the door and flung it wide to find Gil standing there. His sling was gone, and he held his hat against his front with his right hand. For a moment, delight rose within her that he was able to securely grasp the hat brim. Apparently his wrist had healed in time for the End of Harvest celebration, as they'd prayed it would. But then she deliberately squashed the fleeting joy.

"When will you give up?" she said in her sharpest voice.

"Not ever," he said, his voice raspy and his unblinking eyes pinned on her face. "I love you too much to give up."

The sweetness of his words flowed over her, and she inwardly strained to accept them, believe them, cherish them. But the hurt of him using their song to determine his future returned. She drew herself as tall as she could. "What are the boys playing tomorrow?"

His attention didn't waver. "The marching song they played at the Fourth of July . . . and the one I call 'Ava's Song.'"

She closed her eyes for a moment, struggling against a wave of bitter anguish. When she opened them, he was holding out a folded piece of paper. She glared at it. "What's this?"

"Take it, please."

She crossed her arms.

"Please, Ava?"

Why must he be so appealing? And so obstinate. She shook her head and tightened her arms across her aching chest. "Gil, I don't understand how you can have the boys play that song for strangers. You wrote it as a gift to me. That's what you said when you played it for me and then asked me to marry you."

"It is your gift, Ava. I—"

"You took back your proposal." She spoke loudly, drowning out his voice. "It took years, but I came to understand. To accept that going to New York was right for you. But then you came back, and I fell in love with you all over again, and I thought you fell in love with me."

"I did!" He still held the paper, and he crushed it in his hand. "I never stopped loving you, Ava."

"But you love music more! You want success more than you want to please me!" The hurt in his eyes nearly undid her. She glared at the crumpled note in his hand. "Nothing written on that paper will convince me otherwise. Playing that song at the competition means it belongs to the judges whose decision will determine whether you stay or go. It's not mine anymore."

He hung his head, then stood silent and motionless before her. She waited for him to speak, to defend himself, and when he didn't, she started to close the door.

"Are you coming to the End of Harvest celebration?"

The quiet question froze her in place. The townsfolk had arranged several wagons to transport people to McPherson to support the Falke boys' band. Mama and Papa intended to take their own carriage, which would provide a more comfortable ride for Mama and Mr. Willems. Although they hadn't expressly said so, she knew her parents expected her to go. She intended to conveniently suffer a headache.

"I don't believe so."

He slipped the paper into her apron pocket. "I hope you'll change your mind. If you do, bring that with you, but don't look at it until the band plays in front of the judges." A *V* briefly marred his brow. "If you don't come, please burn it. And I'll never bother you again." He put his hat on his head and strode off the porch.

Ava stared after him, the small bulge in her pocket seeming to burn like a hot coal. She gingerly reached in, pinched it between her fingers, and held it out the way she'd hold a snake.

Temptation to unfold it pulled hard, but fear of what she'd find on the page overcame curiosity. She placed it on the little table beside the door and returned to her chores, her heart heavy.

Gil

GIL SCUFFED UP the boardwalk, his chest aching so badly he marveled he could draw a breath. He had many reasons to be joyful. The boys had grown so much as musicians, and he believed they had a real chance at taking first place in the competition despite their young ages and lack of experience. He was able to grip his baton tightly enough to direct the band, even though his wrist still throbbed afterward. He and Joseph had mended their differences, and his cousin had even confided that if Gil returned to New York he might want to come, too, to look for work there, try living in the big city for a change. It would be good to have family with him. Especially since it seemed Ava was no longer interested in going with him.

Whither thou goest . . .

The words he'd penned haunted him now. Apparently she hadn't meant what she'd said that night on the porch when the lyrics for the song he'd written seemed to descend from heaven and fill his heart. If she hadn't been truthful, then the words were meaningless. But she should still know she'd inspired them. That they were true for him. That they'd always be true.

"You there, Gil!"

The call took him back to the day he'd arrived in Falke. He'd almost ignored it, wanting to avoid Ava's family. He might be happier today if he'd been able to do so. He turned and stepped into the post office, forcing his lips into a smile. "*Goodendach,* Onkel Bernard."

"I thought you'd be resting after your long practice." The man sorted through mail scattered all across the counter from the morning's delivery. "Are the boys excited for tomorrow's activities?"

"Jo, they're very excited. And very ready." Gil's chest went tight. "I'm proud of them. Every one of them. They've worked hard, and they deserve to win tomorrow. But I've told them no matter what the judges say, they are winners already because they have given their best in preparing for this competition."

Bernard nodded, his eyes glowing with approval. "Much of their preparation is due to your good leadership, Gil. I'm proud of what you've accomplished with them. You should be proud of yourself, too."

Gil hung his head. "I want to be, Onkel Bernard. But I made such a mess of things with Ava, I'm only . . . sad."

Bernard rounded the counter and took hold of Gil by the shoulders, the way he'd done dozens of times when giving Gil fatherly advice. "Listen to me. You have no reason to blame yourself for what happened between you and Ava. Your motivations were pure. That she misunderstood and refuses to let you explain is not your fault."

"But—"

"Nä!" He gave Gil a little shake. "You are only responsible for your own actions. You cannot control what anyone else does, only the way you respond to their choices. Ava made her choice. You have chosen to respond with kindness. You've done all you can do . . . except pray God's will over the situation. Are you praying for God's will?"

Gil nodded. He stepped free of Bernard's light hold and leaned on the counter. "I am, and I was prompted to do something . . . risky." He absently flicked through envelopes as he spoke. "I already told you I wrote words to go with Ava's song." He'd shared the secret, along with the reason for teaching the boys the song, with Bernard the evening Ava overheard the band practicing. He needed someone to understand why he hadn't kept the song between just him and Ava.

"Jo, I remember."

"Well, I wrote the lyrics out on a piece of paper and gave it to Ava a little bit ago. I told her to bring it to the competition tomorrow and look at it when the boys played. I also said if she didn't come, she should burn the page. It won't matter anymore if she doesn't come."

Bernard returned to his post and began sorting again, shaking his head. "That daughter of mine rarely shows it, but she has a stubborn side that is hard to penetrate when she chooses to use it. Maria and I are praying for her to come to her senses." He glanced up. "I'm still her papa. I can make her go to the competition, whether she wants to go or not."

Gil didn't want to create friction between father and daughter. "Thank you, Onkel Bernard, but I think it's better if Ava makes this decision on her own. If she comes, it will tell me she still cares. At least a little. And maybe after she hears the song, she'll understand and will be able to set aside her anger."

Bernard picked up an envelope and examined it, his bushy eyebrows low. "What school did you say asked you to come teach music to its students?"

"The Clineburg Academy for Juvenile Boys. Why?"

"You have a letter from them."

"I do?" Gil took the envelope and frowned at his name written in slanting script. "How strange. When I ended my interview, I told the school's dean that I would be in Falke for the summer and would notify them of my decision by the end of

August. I wonder why they've written to me." He slid his thumb beneath the flap and peeled it open, then removed a single sheet of typewritten paper. He read the short missive, aware of Bernard's curious gaze pinned on him. He finished and returned it to the envelope.

"What do they say?"

If anyone else had asked, Gil might not have answered. But he didn't keep secrets from Onkel Bernard. "Another small, private school closed, and most of the boys are transferring to Clineburg. The increased enrollment has brought more revenue, so they reconsidered the salary offer. They raised it by seventy-five dollars for the year."

Bernard's eyebrows shot upward. "That is a very fine offer."

Gil chuckled. "It would be a very fine offer in Kansas. Expenses are higher in New York. Still . . ." He tapped the edge of the envelope on the counter. "If I was careful, I could adequately support myself with it."

"This is good news then, jo?"

Bernard looked so hopeful, Gil smiled and said, "Jo, it is." He wouldn't divulge the uneasiness creeping through his thoughts. He'd laid out a fleece and trusted God to answer at tomorrow's competition. Was this salary improvement a sign that he would be sent back to New York?

Chapter Thirty-Four

Ava

NEITHER MAMA NOR PAPA BELIEVED HER STORY about having a headache and insisted she come to the celebration. After all, they wheedled, she'd done so much work on the boys' uniforms, she should see how they looked. So Ava gave in.

She had to admit as the boys marched past, with the exception of Herman guiding the goat cart at the very front of the band, the boys appeared as professional as any of the other bands. She tried hard not to look at Gil, but her traitorous eyes sought him out anyway. And regret smote her. How handsome and respectable he appeared in his dark suit, but why hadn't they decorated a jacket for him, too? The next time the boys performed, he should have one. But then she pushed the thought aside. He might never lead the boys after today. A uniform would be a waste of time and money.

The parade lasted more than an hour, and by the end of it Ava's head pounded for real. So many people. So much noise and dust and activity. She longed for a quiet place to slip away. Papa found a small grassy spot in the shade of a towering cottonwood and left her and Mama there while he bought lunch for them. While they waited for his return, Joseph, Earl, and Herman passed by, still using the goat cart. Mama called them over.

Joseph left his brothers with the cart at the edge of the street and ambled to them, a relaxed smile on his face. "*Goodendach,* ladies. Are you having a good time?"

Mama folded back the brim of her bonnet and beamed up at him. "We are. I was so happy to see Earl participating. What a clever idea, using the goat cart."

Joseph nodded. "Some of the boys in the band thought of it. I was surprised when Ma approved it, but I think she knew how much being in the parade meant to Earl. And Herman has had so much fun, he's begging Ma and Pa to let him try playing my trombone in the band."

Ava gave a start. "Has someone volunteered to direct the boys' band after Gil leaves?"

Joseph shrugged. "You'd have to ask Gil about that." He shifted from foot to foot. "It's nice to see you ladies, but I should go. Pa sent us to get good seats for when the bands play in front of the judges. I'm sure the front row will fill quickly." He took a step toward the street, then turned back. "If you'd like, I'll save some spots for you. You'll want to see and hear everything well, too."

Ava started to refuse, but Mama spoke first.

"That would be very kind of you, Joseph. Thank you."

He tipped his hat. "I'll see you a little later then."

Ava touched her mother's arm. "Mama, we don't have a child in the band. We should leave the front row for parents."

Mama sighed. "You're right. I was only thinking how hard it would be for me to climb up in the stands. A selfish thought. When we go, we'll have Joseph free up those seats for someone else."

Imagining Mama having to climb rickety stairs changed Ava's mind. "Nä, you take the seat on the front row. Papa and I can stand to the side instead."

Mama nodded. "That is a good compromise."

Papa returned with a brown sack. He sat, opened the sack, and pulled out some kind of long, plump sausages in buns and three bottles of Dr Pepper. He grinned as he handed them the odd sandwiches. "The vendor selling these said they were featured last year at the World's Fair in St. Louis. So I thought we should try them."

Mama examined hers from several angles. "Ach, Bernard, maybe we should have brought something from home. This looks inedible."

Papa took a big bite of his. He waggled his eyebrows and said, "Mmmm. Try it. It's good."

It was surprisingly tasty, especially when washed down with the warm, sweet, fizzy pop. Ava enjoyed every bit of her lunch, and by the time she finished, her head no longer ached. Such a blessing.

Papa gathered up their empty bottles and put them in the sack. Then he stood and held his hand to Mama. "The second part of the competition will start soon. Let's go to the arena and find the Batys." He helped Mama to her feet, then gave Ava the same assistance. As he released her hand, he suddenly patted his pocket. "Oh! I found something you will need when we get there." He slipped his hand into his pocket and removed the folded piece of paper Gil had given her. He pressed it into her hand.

Ava automatically gripped the page. For reasons she couldn't understand, her heart fluttered. "W-where . . . ?"

"I found it lying on the entry table and was concerned it would be misplaced." Papa briefly cupped her cheek. "Come. It's time for us to cheer for our band and their leader."

Gil

THE BOYS STOOD in a straight line, instruments in hand, eyes glued on Gil's face. He kept an encouraging smile fixed on his lips, but underneath, his heart was banging worse than the clapper in the church bell alerting the surrounding countryside to a prairie fire—positively raucous. Three other bands had already played, all performing well-known songs, and he would judge their execution as excellent. The fourth group finished to rousing applause, whistles, and cheers. This competition was tougher than Gil had imagined, but he wasn't nervous for the boys. He had full confidence in them. He was nervous about one person in the audience.

Thanks to Earl telling him, he knew Ava had come. How he wanted her to hear the soul of this song. How he wanted her to realize it was him unashamedly laying his soul bare in front of witnesses. Would she set aside her resentment and open her heart to listen?

"Next," the announcer hollered, "is the Falke Boys' Band under the direction of Mr. Gilbert Baty."

Despite the hot summer sun beating down on him, Gil broke out in chills from head to toe. With Earl's trumpet under his arm, he escorted Earl to the middle of the performance area where the wooden stool he'd requested waited. He traded the trumpet for the boy's crutches, then nodded to Roy Hiebert, the first boy in line. Roy began lightly tapping his snare drum. The boys marched out in time with the beat, heads high, instruments held erect, and formed three rows. The drums were at the rear, baritones in the middle, and the lone trombone, three trumpets, and Timmy with his tuba in front. A few chortles sounded when Timmy marched out. Gil understood. The small child with the big instrument looked comical. But no one could deny the determination etched into the little boy's face.

Gil moved to the director's stand, laid the crutches on the ground beside him, and faced the audience. His gaze landed on his aunt and uncle, then slid to Maria Flaming. Her bright smile bolstered him. He scanned the crowd, seeking Bernard and Ava, but he didn't spot them. Had they left? Disappointed, he forced himself to focus on the performance.

He cleared his throat. "We will play 'Ava's Song,' also titled 'Whither Thou Goest,' by Gilbert W. Baty."

A few murmurs rolled through the crowd, and the three judges seated at a long table in front looked at paperwork and then at one another in surprise.

Gil quickly turned to the boys, removed his baton from his pocket, and ran his finger from the handle to the silver tip. In those few seconds, he remembered Mr. Goertz's smile and certain words, *"You have a God-given gift, Gil."* He closed his eyes for a moment, committing the performance to God's glory. Then he tapped the baton on the stand.

The boys jerked their shoulders back. Every eye stared at him. He abruptly lifted both hands, and the drummers positioned their sticks while the horn players raised their mouthpieces to their lips. Then Gil signaled the downbeat, and the song began.

Ava

IN THE SHADE of Papa's bulky form, Ava unfolded the piece of paper Gil had given her and began to read. The tune Gil had played on his violin four years ago, now broader with its harmonies added, swelled around her, a familiar yet new song. She suddenly realized the words on the page paired with notes in the melody. The combination was so lovely, so heart stirring, she could hardly contain the emotions rising up inside her.

I remember back when we played in the yard,
When we were both young and carefree.
The sunlight wove ribbons of gold through your hair,
And your smile was joy I could see.
Though but a boy, I knew even then
There'd never be another for me.
You were my heart, my light and my joy,
And my soul longed only for thee.

She dared a quick peek at Papa, who stood gazing down at her with love shining in his eyes. He gave a gentle nod toward the paper, and she continued to read.

After all these years together
You're still my forever.
'Til the day I die, I will be true.
And whither thou goest,
I make you this promise—
My heart ever belongs to you.

Tears distorted her vision. She impatiently swept them away, unwilling to miss a single word.

Life took a turn that brought heartache and pain,
But God turned our tears into song.
He made beauty from ashes, what a wonderful God,
And nurtured our love through His own.
Now as a man, I know even more
There'll never be another for me.
You are my heart, my light and my joy,
And my soul longs only for thee.

Suddenly the music rose in both tempo and volume, filling her senses with wonder and joy.

Whither thou goest, no matter how far,
You'll never walk alone.
What God brought together never will part.
My heart is forever your home.

She lifted her attention from the paper to Gil's erect frame, to his hands in their graceful motions. The chorus repeated itself in her mind as the glorious combination of notes carried her to a plane of emotional connection where she, Gil, and the music became one.

After all these years together
You're still my forever.
'Til the day I die, I will be true.
And whither thou goest,
I make you this promise—

She found herself singing the final line with the band. "'My heart ever belongs to you.'"

Gil held his hands high for several counts, then gave a quick swish of the baton. The song came to an end. A hush fell, an almost reverent intake of collective breaths, and then applause erupted. Gil stepped away from the podium and swept his hand toward the boys. They bowed in perfect unison. All across the audience people were rising to their feet, still applauding. Then Ralph Ediger took one forward step and gestured to Gil, who took a bow. The applause intensified, and someone yelled, "Encore! Encore!"

Tears rained down Ava's face as she gloried in the recognition of Gil's incredible talent. What if she'd stayed home today? Oh, what pleasure she would have denied herself. Forever she would remember the details of this performance, from the bright sunlight glinting off the instruments, to the scent of popcorn and sausage wafting on the warm breeze, to the tautness of Gil's jacket across his back, to—above all else—the indescribable feelings that pulsed through every fiber of her being.

He'd moved her. Oh, how he'd moved her. What an incredible gift he possessed.

The boys were leaving in rows. Ava tugged Papa's coat sleeve. "I want to follow the band, Papa, and tell Gil how wonderfully they did."

"Go then. Hurry, before they are swallowed up by the crowd." Papa gave her a gentle push in their direction.

Ava scurried after them, gripping the words to her song. Many of the parents had also left their seats and swarmed after the band. Ava lost sight of Gil in the throng, and she stood on tiptoe, searching. She finally spotted his wavy cap of dark, thick hair, and she waved the sheet of paper over her head, calling, "Gil! Gil!"

He spun, and his eyes found hers. A smile lit his face, and he started in her direction. But an older man she'd never seen before stepped into Gil's pathway. Gil stopped, his uncertain gaze shifting back and forth between them. Then his eyes widened, and he turned his full attention on the man.

Ava lowered her arm to her side. She waited, watching for Gil and the stranger to part ways, but the man put his arm across Gil's shoulders and led him in the opposite direction. Gil sent a quick, frantic look over his shoulder at her, and then he disappeared into the crowd.

Chapter Thirty-Five

Gil

AT A LITTLE BEFORE FOUR O'CLOCK, AS THE BAND-leaders had been instructed, Gil gathered up the boys and they formed a small cluster near the edge of the performance arena. The judges' decisions would be announced soon, and he would know whether or not his boys would advance to the next level of the competition. The boys wanted to win. He saw it in their hopeful expressions, in their tense frames, and in their singular focus. In truth, he wanted to win, too. But not for himself anymore. For them. They deserved it.

The announcer took a sheet of paper from one of the judges and moved to the podium. He lifted a megaphone to his lips, and his voice blared out. "The judges have made their final choices. Leaders, if your town name is called, the director and two band members should move to the performance circle."

Gil had already selected the two boys to represent the Falke band—the eldest and youngest members. He beckoned with his finger, and Ralph and Timmy scurried to his side. He put his hands on their shoulders and held his breath.

"Lindsborg!" the man bellowed.

The Lindsborg director and two boys swaggered to the circle while the audience clapped.

"Marquette!"

303

More cheers as another director and a pair of uniformed youth took their place in the circle.

"Falke!"

Gil's breath whooshed out and Ralph and Timmy gasped. The three of them joined the others awaiting the final verdict.

"Before we announce the first-, second-, and third-place bands," the man called, "please give a round of applause for all of our participants. It has been a wonderful competition."

Gil and his boys clapped along with the audience. Then the announcer waved his hand in the air, and the crowd quieted.

He put the megaphone to his mouth. "In third place, receiving a prize award of three dollars, is the Marquette band under the leadership of Lanny Scholes."

While more applause rang, the director and boys received handshakes and an envelope from the judges. When they'd rejoined their band, the announcer lifted the megaphone again.

"In second place, receiving a prize award of seven dollars, is the Falke band under the leadership of Gilbert Baty."

Gil's heart momentarily sank. But Timmy leaped in the air, and Ralph released a whoop. Ralph swept Timmy off the ground and hugged him. Out of the corner of Gil's eye, he caught sight of his entire band jumping and pounding each other on the back. Joy exploded through him. Their delight in second place was as sweet to Gil as a first-place victory.

He crossed to the table, shook hands with each judge, and accepted the prize envelope. Then he trotted to his boys, who surrounded him, jabbering in excitement. He herded them to their waiting parents, who received them with hugs and congratulations. Fathers slapped Gil on the back, and mothers thanked him for the time he'd spent with their boys. Onkel Hosea came, too, and grabbed Gil in a mighty hug.

"I'm proud of you, Gil. You put Falke on the map today."

Gil's heart swelled. He squeezed his uncle and said, "Thank you, Onkel Hosea. That means a lot to me."

His uncle released him and flicked the envelope in Gil's hand. "I guess this is your ticket money for New York, jo?"

Gil smiled and shook his head. "This will pay for Mr. Willems's tuba and"—he raised his voice so the boys would hear him—"buy cotton candy for all the members of Falke's band."

More whoops and hollers filled the air. Gil peeled two dollar bills from the stack in the envelope and gave them to Ralph. "See that everyone receives their treat."

"Jo, Mr. Baty." Ralph waved the money. "Come on, boys! Let's go!" The group, accompanied by several of the parents, hurried off with Ralph in the lead.

His responsibilities done, Gil wanted to find Ava. He turned to his uncle. "Did you see where the Flamings went?"

"Jo, *Mumkje* Flaming wasn't feeling well. They left after the performance."

Gil's elation faded. "Ava left?"

Onkel Hosea nodded. "And Roald, too." He slung his arm across Gil's shoulders. "But that doesn't mean your celebration must end. I have a nickel in my pocket. You should have some cotton candy, too. Let's find your boys."

Gil had no desire for cotton candy, for there was a concern he needed to address. He pointed to the emptying stands. "Could we sit over there for a minute instead? There's something I need to ask you."

THE BOYS ALL wanted to ride back to Falke in the same wagon. It was a tight fit, but they made it work. They even put the little goat in with them, which created much merriment. Gil followed in the wagon that held all the instruments, and the whole way to Falke he listened to the boys' happy chatter. Happiness filled him, too. How good to know the band would continue even though he wouldn't be leading it anymore. Onkel Hosea agreed it was too important to be only a one-summer activity, and he promised to speak to the other parents. Together, they would find a way for the boys to continue to play together. He even added, "I think we'll let Herman join, too."

The moon was halfway up the dusky gray sky when their parade of wagons rolled onto Falke's main street. People climbed out of the wagons' beds, calling farewells to one another and congratulations to Gil. His heart felt so full, he wondered if it would burst from his chest. He'd grown up around these people, had always felt as if he belonged with them, but it seemed that on this day he was more a part of them than ever before. He pondered the feeling, and he realized it was because of the music. Making music together connected people, gave them a common ground.

Returning their goodbyes, he retrieved Roald's tuba from the back of the wagon and shook off the bits of hay used to cushion the instrument. The horn indeed looked brand-new after its time with the silversmith. As he walked to Roald's house with a tuba under each arm and Timmy skipping along beside him, he wondered why he had never felt connected with other musicians in New York. Maybe because they were too busy competing with one other, the way he and Joseph had battled each other over the years. He liked it much better when everyone contributed their strengths and pooled their talents and made something bigger and better than each could do on their own.

He carried the tubas into the house and enjoyed Roald's happy reunion with his instrument. Timmy asked if they could play a duet, and Roald said, "Not tonight, son. It's too late. You need to take a bath and then go to bed." The boy fussed a bit, as he always did when told to apply a washcloth, but he yawned mid-argument and sheepishly admitted he was tired. So was Gil, but before he turned in, he wanted to see Ava. To ask if she'd been pleased with the variation of her song. To find out if her attempt to reach him after the performance meant she'd forgiven him. To tell her the wonderful thing that had happened as a result of playing her song for the judges.

He put water on to heat for Timmy's bath, then walked the short distance from Roald's to the Flamings'. To his disappointment, no lights glowed behind the windows. Not even behind the one clear at the back, which was Ava's room. His talk with her would have to wait until tomorrow after church. With a sigh, he returned to Roald's.

ON SUNDAY MORNING, Roald got himself up and dressed for the drive to church. He hadn't attended services since he hurt his leg, but he told Gil during their simple breakfast, "If I could ride as far as McPherson with my cast, I can ride to church. It's time." Then he lowered his voice and added, "I want to be there for the discussion about Timmy."

Gil understood his desire to go, so even though it took some doing to get Roald up on the seat of the delivery wagon, they made it happen. Those who had attended yesterday's End of Harvest celebration were still chattering about it before church began. Gil received several questions about what he would do next, and he gave vague responses. Before he talked to anyone else about his plans, he needed to share them with Ava. She was the only one who would be affected by them.

He didn't have a chance for a word with her before the ser-

vice, though. She and her parents arrived just as the congregation rose for the opening hymn. He tried to catch her eye as
they sang, but she kept her gaze on the hymnbook. Then he
realized Taunte Dorcas was observing him. He aimed his attention to the front and kept it there.

The reverend delivered a brief sermon based on Psalm 28:7.
Gil underlined the words in his Bible with his finger as the
minister read aloud. "The LORD is my strength and my shield;
my heart trusted in him, and I am helped: therefore my heart
greatly rejoiceth; and with my song will I praise him." Such a
fitting scripture considering everything that had happened
since May. So many mishaps—Roald's accident, Gil's hurt
wrist, the death of Timmy's aunt, his disagreement with Ava—
yet the Lord saw him through every calamity, and he'd been
able to share the song of his heart. He had a reason to rejoice,
too. The glory for his rejoicing went to the One who'd given
him the ability.

At the end of the message, Reverend Ediger offered a prayer
of praise for God's hand of direction in the lives of everyone in
the congregation. Then he requested God's will concerning
the important issue they would soon discuss. After his "amen,"
he turned to his wife, who was seated on the front row in her
usual spot with their sons.

"Rosa, please take the children to the side yard and keep
them entertained while we have our church meeting."

Parents sent their children out the door with Mrs. Ediger
and her boys. Roald sent Timmy. As soon as only adults remained, Reverend Ediger sent a slow look across the room. "I
asked you to pray and search your hearts concerning what
should be done with Timmy Dirks. Would anyone like to share
what God has spoken to you?"

Roald grabbed the pew in front of him and pulled himself upright. "Reverend?" Every face angled in his direction. He sent a quick glance at several people, then shook his head. "I know what you're thinking. That I've stood up to say I want to keep Timmy myself." He blinked rapidly. "I do want to keep him. I've grown to love the boy. But sometimes you have to love someone enough to do what's best for them, and living with a set-in-his-ways bachelor who cooks beans for most of his meals isn't what's best for a boy like Timmy. He needs to be with a good family.

"So I stood up to say whoever takes him is in for a treat. He's a smart boy, a good-hearted boy, and he'll bring a lot of love and laughter to someone who pays him the kind of attention he needs. I also want to say . . ." He sniffed hard, rubbed his eyes with his fist, and lifted his chin. "Whoever takes him in needs to be pretty special, too." He plopped back down.

Gil gave Roald his handkerchief, and the man noisily blew his nose.

"Are we good enough?"

The woman's voice was so soft, Gil almost thought he imagined it. Frowning, he searched the room, and his pulse gave a leap when he realized who was standing.

Taunte Dorcas slowly left her pew and came up the aisle. She stopped beside Gil and Roald. "Mr. Willems, you said you wanted Timmy to go to a good family. I need to ask Gil, are your Onkel and I good enough?"

Gil, still stunned by her unexpected response to Roald's plea, couldn't find words.

"I know how important Timmy is to you," she went on, speaking in a near whisper. "Taking him in and raising him won't change anything about the way I . . . I raised you . . ."

Tears trailed down her cheeks. "But maybe you'd feel more kindly toward me if I love him the way I should have loved you."

Gil swallowed. He'd not received the best from his aunt, but he'd seen her give her best. She was a protective mother who read to her children from the Bible every night and taught them right from wrong. Despite everything, he appreciated her giving him a home when he needed one. He rose and put his hand on his aunt's shoulder. "Taunte Dorcas, I know you did your best. And I love you for it. Timmy would be blessed to live with you and Onkel Hosea."

A smile—the most heartfelt one she'd ever bestowed on him—ignited her moist eyes. She turned to the minister. "Reverend Ediger, Hosea and I would like it very much if Timmy came to our place to live."

Onkel Hosea stood up. "Jo, we would."

Light applause broke out through the room, and a few people offered words of thanks or support to the couple.

Reverend Ediger beamed at Taunte Dorcas. "Thank you for opening your heart to Timmy. I'll come to your place later today to talk more." He raised his arms, inviting everyone to stand. "Let us end our time together with prayer."

After the minister released the congregation, Gil quickly made his way to the Flamings. Taunte Maria greeted him first, then added, "I'm so grateful to your Onkel and Taunte."

Bernard wasn't smiling, though. He put his hand on Gil's shoulder. "Are you sure you are all right with Timmy going to live with Hosea and Dorcas? I wondered"—he flicked a quick peek at Ava—"if you might decide to raise him yourself."

Gil glanced at Ava, too. He hoped she would approve what he said next. "I'm very fond of Timmy. But I'd rather be like an older brother, the way I am with Earl and Herman, than his pa.

And I think it's better for him to grow up in a house with siblings near his age."

Bernard's hand tightened on Gil's shoulder for a moment and then dropped away. "I understand."

Maria smiled up at Gil. "It is such a relief to know a happy ending awaits our dear little Timmy."

"Jo. A happy ending awaits Timmy." Gil shifted his attention to Ava, who peeked at him from the corners of her eyes. "But what about us?"

Bernard took Maria's hand and placed it in the bend of his elbow. "My dear *Frü*, let's go home and put dinner on the table. Ava and Gil can eat when they get there . . . after they walk home from church." He ushered her out.

Gil watched them go, a smile tugging at the corners of his lips, then he turned to Ava. "Roald will need my help getting into his wagon, but he's capable of driving. I like the idea of us walking to town together. If you're willing to go with me."

She lifted her face. A shy smile ignited her eyes. "I'm willing."

He held out his elbow, and she took hold. "Then let's go."

Chapter Thirty-Six

Ava

AVA WAITED WHILE GIL ASSISTED ROALD INTO HIS wagon. The two men exchanged a few words, then Gil called Timmy over. He swung the boy up onto the seat, the child's giggles spilling forth. Finally, he turned to her.

At the tenderness in his expression, her heart rolled over in her chest. She didn't deserve his kindness after the way she'd rebuffed him. She'd asked God's forgiveness, but she still needed to ask for Gil's. She suspected he would offer as much grace as God had, but at the same time she wondered what the future held for the two of them. The band had lost, which gave the answer to Gil's fleece—he would return to New York. But would he take her with him?

He strode across the grounds toward her, lifting his hand in farewell to others departing the churchyard. He finally reached her, and he offered his arm. "Are you ready?"

Her frame suddenly began to tremble, and she took hold of his elbow with both hands. "Jo, but first I must tell you—"

He put his finger on her lips. "Nä, Ava, don't apologize. I've had some time to think about it, and I should have talked to you about using your song for the competition. Even though I meant it to be a pleasant surprise, I understand why you were

312

hurt. From now on, I will only play 'Ava's Song' for you, and the words will always be only for your ears."

His dear face blurred behind her tears. She blinked and cleared her vision. "I don't deserve the beautiful things you wrote in your song, Gil."

"What do any of us deserve when we consider how often we stumble and disappoint the One who created us to do good works in His name? But He forgives. We can do no less." He leaned forward and kissed her forehead. "No more speaking of the past. We must look ahead, jo?"

She blew out a dainty breath, bringing her quivering limbs under control. "Jo. And . . . what awaits ahead, Gil?"

He gently urged her into motion, and they strolled up the road toward town. "Well, the boys won't continue in the competition since they didn't win."

She sent a quick glance at his profile. Seeing no disappointment in his face encouraged her. "So this means you'll take the teaching position in New York?"

He squeezed her arm against his ribs. "I could. I received a letter from the school. They increased the part-time salary by an additional seventy-five dollars. This means I would be paid almost thirty-five dollars a month."

Ava gasped. "Gil! That is a very good salary!"

"Jo, it is. And only three dollars more than what the president of McPherson College offered me to start a new band program at the college."

What had he said? She came to a halt, trying to process his comment. Like tiny puzzle pieces falling into place, a picture formed in her mind, and her mouth fell open. "The man who approached you after the boys played our song . . . is he the college president?"

Gil nodded, his lips twitching into a shy grin. "President Frantz asked about my experience as a conductor and if I'd written any other compositions. I told him I had a broad portfolio and had worked in New York. He was impressed with my credentials and what he witnessed at the contest." Then he crinkled his face. "Because I don't have my teaching certificate, he couldn't offer a higher salary, but"—his expression brightened again—"he said I could take courses for gratis while I build the band program and earn my degree. When I have my certificate, my salary will go up."

"So you're going to live in McPherson, not in New York City?"

Gil slipped his arm free of her grasp, then took her hands. He peered down at her, his eyes shaded by the brim of his hat the way they had been the day he strode from behind the barn three months ago. But today, from her vantage point, she received a full view of the wonder glowing in his deep brown eyes. "When I offered my fleece, I told God that I would receive a loss as my instruction to return to New York and continue working to make a name for myself there. Your encouragement, when you told me I had a gift, also seemed to point me to New York. Then the letter from the school added to my belief that I'm supposed to go there. But . . ."

Ava tipped her head. "Gil, if your hesitance has to do with me, I made my peace with leaving Mama and Papa. I'll go with you."

"'Whither thou goest,' you will go?"

The tender question seemed to dance on the breeze and tease the corners of her heart. She nodded. "I will."

He wrapped her in a breath-stealing hug. "Your willingness to go with me, wherever I go, delights me, Ava. How I love you."

She nestled her cheek against his chest, his heartbeat thrumming in her ear. "I love you, too, Gil." She felt him brush a kiss on the top of her head, and then he released her.

"I know I can teach. My time with the boys has proven that to me. Yet, despite this confirmation and so many fingers seeming to point me to New York, there was still an . . . unsettled feeling . . . deep in my soul. These past days when I wasn't allowed your company"—

She hung her head, sorrow at contributing to his heartache striking her anew.

—"I spent many hours in prayer, begging God for direction." He paused, then took her hands again. "Look at me, Ava."

Hesitantly, she lifted her face and found him gazing fervently at her. "I asked, and He answered. These past months in Falke have shown me where I truly belong. I'm not a big-city boy. Having my name renowned by strangers doesn't mean what it once did. Being known and loved by people who I love . . . that's what God wants for me. It's what I want for me, too. God gave me gifts, and I'm meant to use them here, in Kansas, where I'm near my family, where I can build a life with the one He chose for me when I was still a boy . . . with you."

"Oh, Gil." She melted against him, relishing the feel of his strong arms encircling her. "We will live in McPherson, then?"

"*Jo*, but first, I must ask . . ." Once again he gently released her and cupped her face in his hands. "Ava Maria Flaming, would you do me the honor of becoming my wife?"

Joy exploded through her, almost dizzying in its effect. Such a simple proposal, nothing like the one he'd given four years ago after playing her song on his violin. But somehow, here on the open prairie with wind tousling her hair and birds singing a sweet chorus from nearby brush, it was perfect.

She searched for a fitting response for this glorious moment in time, and a lilting melody floated from the center of her heart. She placed her hands over his and smiled through tears as she sang, "'What God brought together never will part, my heart is forever your home.'"

His eyes shone with love and joy. He tipped her face to him and placed a tender, sweet kiss on her lips. Then he took her hand, mischief dancing in his dark eyes. "Do you remember trying to outrun me when we were little?"

A giggle escaped, dozens of happy childhood memories filling her mind. "I remember you always slowed down a little and let me pass you."

He raised her hand and delivered a kiss on her knuckles. "Jo, well, today I want to run hand in hand all the way to Falke to tell your folks our news. And then, my precious Ava, we will remain side by side for the remainder of our earthly journey." He braced himself like a runner at the mark, grinning at her. "Are you ready?"

"Jo!" She took off, yanking him into motion beside her. With their combined laughter filling the air, together they raced hand in hand across the rolling prairie toward home.

Letter from the Author

Dear reader,

Thank you for visiting Falke with me and becoming acquainted with its residents. Although the town and characters are fictitious, they were built around pieces of my heritage.

In 1872, my mother's Mennonite grandparents, Bernard and Maria Klaassen, came from a Molotschna Colony in Russia to America and brought with them their Plautdietsch (Low German) language, a dialect similar to, but unique from, German. The Plautdietsch words in this story were taken from *Kjenn Jie Noch Plautdiesch? A Mennonite Low German Dictionary* by Herman Rempel. Because every village had their own variations of the dialect, it is a challenge to ascertain every word is 100 percent correct, but my best efforts for accuracy were made.

My grandparents also brought a deep love and appreciation for music, which seems to permeate the heart of Mennonite history, and of course a strong, sustaining faith in Jesus Christ. I am so grateful to descend from such faithful saints, and I pray my children and grandchildren—many of whom are musically gifted—will carry that faith into future generations and use their gifts for God's glory.

Thank you again for spending time with Ava, Gil, Joseph, Timmy, and the other residents of Falke. I appreciate my readers!

May God bless you muchly as you journey with Him!
Kim Vogel Sawyer

Readers Guide

1. Gil left Falke in pursuit of a dream inspired by his God-given abilities, but success eluded him. Why do you think he wasn't able to take his place among the musical elite? Does God measure success differently than people do? In what way(s)?

2. Ava chose to remain in Falke with her parents instead of marrying Gil and going to New York with him. Do you understand her reasoning? Have you ever sacrificed something in order to meet another's needs?

3. Joseph accused Gil of trying to be perfect to make himself look good. What was the underlying reason Gil strove for perfection? Have you ever felt unloved? Research Scripture passages that offer assurance of how much you are loved by your Creator.

4. Ava felt as if God did the opposite of what she asked in her prayers. Have you ever felt God wasn't listening to you? Have you seen Him answer in ways you didn't request or expect? Recall a time when His answer was what you needed even though you wanted something different.

5. Bernard and Gil developed a father-son relationship. Do you suppose this would have happened if Bernard's sons had

lived? How did the relationship benefit Gil? How did it benefit Bernard?

6. Maria and Bernard lost their sons to fever; Dorcas lost her first child. These losses still impacted them years later. Is it possible to heal from the loss of a child? How can we support and comfort parents who mourn the loss of a child?

7. Gil reflected that making music together connected people. Have you found this to be true with music or another art form? Why do you think working together to create something beautiful binds us with others?

8. Women business owners aren't uncommon today, but it was unusual in 1905. How would becoming the owner of the café have changed Ava's life? Do you think she would have found satisfaction in running a business in 1905? Would the satisfaction differ if the year was 2022? Why or why not?

9. After Bernard suggests Ava is helping her parents as a means of filling the emptiness she feels, Maria tells Ava, "Only our Lord and Savior, Jesus Christ, can fill all the aching, empty holes in our hearts. And only seeking and following His will can complete us." Do you have any aching, empty holes in your life? Have you asked Jesus to be your filler? If not, will you seek Him today?

Acknowledgments

I always thank family first, so thank you, Dad, Don, my girls, and my granddarlings. You are my joys and motivations for everything I do. I also must thank my brother, Brad, for the help with the musical descriptions. It's great to have an actual composer/conductor in the family! And extra props to my daughter, Kristian, for providing the lyrics to "Ava's Song." It made the song so much more meaningful.

Mom, I still miss you so much, even though I'm grateful you're no longer hurting and are completely joyful with the Savior you loved and served so faithfully. Your Mennonite heritage and much of your wisdom found its way into this story. Your legacy lingers. I suspect it always will.

I've been blessed with some great brainstorming partners. Thank you, Connie, for plot bouncing with me. Your what-ifs always get the creative wheels turning.

I'm ever grateful for the prayers sent up on my behalf by my Sunday school ladies and Lit & Latte Book Club ladies. You all are very special to me.

Thanks to the Inman Historical Museum in Inman, Kansas, for posting the article on Facebook about the youngest youth band in the state. The photos and information planted the story seed, and I had great fun seeing it sprout. (Truly, if you want to visit a wonderful museum, hie thee to Inman!)

I appreciate the people who help make my books the best they can be. Becky and the entire publication team at Water-

Brook, thank you for your partnership. I'm fortunate to work with such talented, dedicated folks.

Finally, and most importantly, thank You, God, for letting me live out my childhood dream of being an author. I pray the stories always share Your truths and encourage readers in their walks with You. May any praise or glory be reflected to You.

About the Author

Kim Vogel Sawyer is a highly acclaimed, bestselling author with more than 1.5 million books in print in seven different languages. Her titles have earned numerous accolades, including the ACFW Carol Award, the Inspirational Readers' Choice Award, and the Gayle Wilson Award of Excellence. Kim lives in central Kansas with her retired military husband, Don, where she continues to write gentle stories of hope. She enjoys spending time with her three daughters and grandchildren.

An Essential Historical Fiction Collection by Bestselling Author
Kim Vogel Sawyer

Find more titles at kimvogelsawyer.com